BATTLEGROUP

Book Two of the StarFight Series

T. Jackson King

Other King Novels

Superguy (2016), Battlestar (2016), Defeat The Aliens (2016), Fight The Aliens (2016), First Contact (2015), Escape From Aliens (2015), Aliens Vs. Humans (2015), Freedom Vs. Aliens (2015), Humans Vs. Aliens (2015), Earth Vs. Aliens (2014), Genecode Illegal (2014), The Memory Singer (2014), Alien Assassin (2014), Anarchate Vigilante (2014), Galactic Vigilante (2013), Nebula Vigilante (2013), Speaker To Aliens (2013), Galactic Avatar (2013), Stellar Assassin (2013), Retread Shop (2012, 1988), Star Vigilante (2012), The Gaean Enchantment (2012), Little Brother's World (2010), Judgment Day And Other Dreams (2009), Ancestor's World (1996).

Dedication

To my wife Sue, my son Keith and my dad Thomas, thank you all for your active duty service in defense of America.

Acknowledgments

First thanks go to scholar John Alcock and his book *Animal Behavior, An Evolutionary Approach* (1979). Second thanks go to the scholar Edward O. Wilson, whose book *Sociobiology: The New Synthesis* has guided me in my efforts to explore a future where humanity encounters life from other stars.

BATTLEGROUP

© 2016 T. Jackson King

This is a work of fiction. All the characters and events portrayed in this novel are either fictitious or are used fictitiously. All rights reserved. No part of this book may be used or reproduced in any manner whatsoever without written permission except for brief quotations for review purposes only.

Cover design by T. Jackson King; cover image by Luca Oleastri via Dreamstime license; back image of Carina Nebula, courtesy of Hubble Space Telescope

First Edition
Published by T. Jackson King, Santa Fe, NM 87507
http://www.tjacksonking.com/
ISBN 10: 1-53712-857-4
ISBN 13: 978-1-53712-857-3
Printed in the United States of America

CHAPTER ONE

"Captain, do we track down and kill that wasp ship?" Richard O'Connor asked Jacob.

He looked at the Kepler 10 holo graphic and considered the seven planets that orbited its yellow star, the vastness of the system's Kuiper Belt, its millions of icy comets and moonlets, and the issue of whether to kill the wasp ship that had stayed behind when the rest of its fleet fled to Kepler 22. It was nine hours since this enemy ship had hit the planet Valhalla with two nukes and three lightning bombs, killing hundreds in a suburb of the capital Stockholm. Daisy had brought up twelve badly injured civilians for treatment in the *Lepanto's* Med Hall, while the LCAs from the cruisers *Chesapeake* and *Hampton Roads* had done the same. The orbital Star Navy Base's own Med Hall was treating 137 civies. But Stockholm's single hospital was still overloaded with injuries from the three lightning bomb plasma blasts that had toppled buildings and sent gale-driven shrapnel into people.

The planet Valhalla, which he and the eight ships of his battle group were sworn to protect as Earth's seventh colony world, had escaped total devastation thanks to the last battle against the invading wasp starships. Four wasp ships had left for their colony in the Kepler 22 system, while a fifth was now heading outward. Perhaps to the system's cometary belt. Or maybe to leave by way of Alcubierre stardrive once it hit the edge of the system's magnetosphere. The wasp ship's outward vector gave him his answer.

Jacob looked down at the grade five chief warrant officer who sat in the Bridge seat of the ship's dead former captain. His girlfriend Daisy was watching from the seat of the ship's also dead former XO. "Richard, we stay here, in orbit above Valhalla. That wasp ship is heading away from the planet. If it were coming back, I'd say englobe the bastard and take it out."

He sat back in the admiral's seat that he had first sat in nine days ago. That was when Daisy had asked him why the *Lepanto's* admiral, captain and XO were not answering their tablets, while meeting with wasp-like aliens on the fourth planet of Kepler 22. His pursuit of an answer to her question had led him to take command of the Battlestar *Lepanto*, to launch a Cloud Skimmer drone and then discover all the senior officers of the fleet were dead, killed during a First Contact encounter with the wasp aliens. The dead had included Rear Admiral Cornelius Johanson, who was the top of the chain of command on the *Lepanto*. With the help of Daisy as the ship's new Executive Officer, and Richard as his combat advisor, the battle group had survived multiple space battles. It had cost them two frigates, 15 dead on the *Chesapeake* and hundreds more dead on Valhalla. But the 71,000 humans on the colony world were still alive, thanks to the efforts of everyone in the fleet.

The older man's gray eyes blinked. He lifted a vacsuited hand to brush at his crewcut white hair, now possible due to everyone's helmets being pushed back. Fresh air was a tonic to Jacob. Richard seemed indifferent to it. Like everyone on the *Lepanto* he still wore his vacsuit, due to the Alert Combat Ready ship status that had been in effect ever since the wasp ships had moved outward. The chief frowned. "Understood and accepted, captain. But I bet one of my Darts could penetrate that ship's hull, disperse our Marine boarders and capture some wasps and some tech before leaving. Also, the wasp ship is limping along at five percent of lightspeed. Any ship in our battle group could catch it."

Jacob nodded slowly. The Marine in charge of the ship's boarding team of 20 Marines and four Dart assault ships had been disappointed that none of the Darts had been used by Jacob during the space battles. The vulnerability of the Darts to concentrated energy beam weapons was one reason. "You are correct. Any of our ships could catch that wasp ship. But half our ships are damaged. Crews are exhausted. Why risk more lives in chasing a ship that may disappear from this system?" Memory of an order he'd given to Science Deck chief Alicia Branstead gave him his other reason. "If the wasp ship stays in this system, maybe out in its Kuiper Belt, well, that leaves us an enemy ship that may respond to future cartoon vids we send them." He nodded toward where Willard Steinmetz sat before his Science station. "Maybe Willard or Lori or one of Lieutenant Branstead's algorithm geeks can figure out how to create a pheromone transmitter. If they do, that wasp ship could be a test subject for them. This war began due to a failure to communicate."

The senior Marine, who had earned a scar on his left cheek when he'd led a battalion in the assault on the jihadist-held capital of Mauritius, looked disappointed. "Yeah, there's that. Communications with these aliens might be useful. Could provide us with counterintel while helping to mess with wasp morale."

Jacob almost sighed. The man's single-minded focus on the wasps as the enemy had been vital during the space battles his ships had fought in two star systems. But as he had shared with Richard, Daisy and the entire Bridge crew at the end of the last battle, he hoped they could avoid further bloodshed. The multiple wasp attacks on the ships of his battle group had been unrelenting. It was the first interstellar war for humans. Whether it continued depended on more factors than Jacob could count. For one, the four wasp ships that had escaped by going out to the edge of the local star's magnetosphere and disappearing into Alcubierre space-time might return. With lots more wasp ships. Whatever the aliens did, he was committed to staying in the Kepler 10 system to protect Valhalla while they waited for reinforcements from Earth. He'd sent off the frigate *Ofira* to report on the wasp aliens, the space battles and his need for more ships to defend the system. It would take the frigate twenty-two and a half days to travel the 564 light years to Earth, and the same time to come back to Kepler 10. That meant Jacob and his battle group had 45 days to wait before any help arrived. He hoped the wasp home star was further away than Earth. If it was less, they could face a new invading force at any time in the future. He blinked. More worrying over a future he could not predict had little value. He smiled at the Marine who'd answered his call to be part of his brain trust.

"Richard, you were vital to the success of our battles. I value your insight. Tell your Marines they will have a chance to use their Darts, in the future." The Bridge had gone silent during his conversation with the Marine, which told him the nine people at function stations and Daisy too were paying close attention. "I give you my word."

The man's white eyebrows lifted, then he gave a nod. "Captain Renselaer, you led us well. Your word is good enough for me. Anyway, I follow orders." The man turned away and tapped his armrest to bring up a holo in front of his seat.

Jacob looked to Daisy, who sat to the left of Richard and below his own elevated seat. She nodded to him and turned away to look at her own group of holos. One on her left held a situational graphic of the entire Kepler 10 system. It showed the positions of all seven planets, with Valhalla in the fourth orbital, an asteroid belt at 12 AU and a Kuiper Belt-like scatter of comets and ice moons at 35 to 45 AU. The magnetosphere's edge lay at 45 AU. A trip that took 52 hours to get there. Another holo in front of Daisy showed a cross-section of the *Lepanto*, its seven decks and the status of all deck operations, from Supplies to Habitation to Weapons up top. The ship's three fusion pulse thrusters were functioning fine, as were the three fusion power plants that occupied the central core of the ship on Engines Deck. That deck occupied the back half of Command Deck. The circular room of the Bridge lay at the ship's front end, sheltered by two meters of armor, a layer of water, the inner hull and intervening decks. Unlike the old *Star Trek* vids, no one looked out through a clear plexi window at true space. That was the function of multiple sensor arrays. Jacob took a deep breath and told himself to stop putting off what he now needed to do.

"Communications, give me a comlink with Captain O'Sullivan on *Green Hills* station."

The 50ish Japanese-American chief warrant officer, who he'd come to know as Andrew Osashi, tapped the control pillar in front of his function station seat. "Encrypted neutrino comlink established. Imagery going up front."

The image of an Asian male ensign wearing his Service Khaki uniform now appeared on the front wallscreen of the Bridge. He sat at a table in a room filled with flatscreens, radar and lidar arrays and three control panels. The man looked surprised.

"Captain Renselaer! Is there a problem?"

"Ensign Mikoto, ask Captain O'Sullivan to come to your station," Jacob said calmly, hoping to convey a sense of ease to the man who had watched as starships fought in the black space between Valhalla and its moon, even as his own captain ordered the station's six proton lasers to zap nuke warheads and plasma lightning globes aimed at the world below. "And there is no problem. Just needed coordination."

The slim, thirty-something man looked down, tapped his touchscreen and spoke. "Captain O'Sullivan, report to the Com room. Captain Renselaer is calling." Black eyes looked up. He scanned

Jacob's Bridge before fixing on him. "Sir, the captain has been notified. He is awake. Should be here in a minute or two."

"Thank you, ensign."

Filling the space between Jacob and the wallscreen were the nine function stations that ran vital operations of the *Lepanto*. He scanned the women and men at those posts. He knew them all. They had come to know him. And he had learned he could trust them to do their jobs well, to fight with all their energy, and to go long hours on Awake pills without complaint.

The front wallscreen's image of the Com room of the orbital Star Navy base brought back memories. Three days earlier it had been the first human image he'd seen when his battle group had arrived at the edge of the system's magnetosphere. It and a single frigate had been the only protection for Valhalla, until his fleet had arrived. The room's hatch opened and O'Sullivan entered. He was tall, Anglo and had some gray in his short hair. Like Mikoto he wore brown Service Khakis. O'Sullivan stopped just behind the seat occupied by the ensign. His hazel eyes fixed on Jacob.

"Captain Renselaer, what can I do for you?"

"We need help with our repairs. Half our ships have some damage to them, with the worst being the *Chesapeake*. It lost its right side proton laser node," Jacob said quickly. "Does your station have the repair bots, laser units and engineers to assist in its repair? And in helping with the repairs on other ships of our battle group?"

O'Sullivan turned thoughtful. A tanned hand rubbed his bare chin. "We can help. This base is more than an orbital defense station. Yes, we have replacement proton laser units in storage. My chief engineer has twenty folks under him who are good at freefall welding and fixing of stuff on ships." The man's voice trailed away. "What else do you need done?"

A good question. Jacob had not yet had a final post-battle consult with the new captains of the other ships in his fleet. But he knew the issues for his ship. "The *Lepanto* has multiple hull punch throughs and damaged areas. We need a new plasma battery up top, a new railgun launcher on our nose, repairs to our belly plasma battery, and new hull plating over deep holes on our nose, belly and tail. Any chance you can vacuum pour armor metal?"

O'Sullivan shook his head. "No on the armor replacement. That takes a true shipyard. But we do have a few plasma battery units.

This station has them on its north and south poles. And I think my chief engineer can round up the components to repair or replace your nose railgun. We've got the magcoils for that work. What else?"

Jacob felt relief. Below him Daisy held up a fist to signal he'd done good. Up front, Joaquin Garcia at Life Support smiled back at him as Jacob tended to issues the man and his deck chief had dealt with during their exit from Kepler 22. And during their 52 hour transit across Kepler 10 system. He gave O'Sullivan a smile.

"Billy, I'll let you know what else is needed after I have a confab with our other ship captains," Jacob said, giving the man a sign of personal appreciation by using his first name. "Your help during the last battle deserves a reward. Maybe a bottle of Chateau Riche *cabernet sauvignon* from 2074?"

The man grinned, as did Mikoto who was seated below the standing captain. "Sounds just fine, Jacob." Below him, Mikoto tapped at something on his desk's control panel. Then pointed. O'Sullivan's easy smile faded. A somber look filled the man's face. "The governor reports from Stockholm that the final death toll from the plasma lightning bombs is now 343, counting folks who died during surgeries. They are tending to 471 injured survivors at their hospital. Fortunately, an elementary school that was hit in the Salonika neighborhood had been evacuated to the countryside, thanks to your earlier warning of the pending attack."

More ghosts now joined the ones from the frigates *Britain* and *Marianas*, the fifteen from *Chesapeake* and seven who had died on other ships during the wasp attacks. It was a weight on his shoulders Jacob had first felt in Kepler 22, in the first battle with the wasps. The death of hundreds was something O'Connor had in common with him, due to the man's bloody experiences in Mauritius and elsewhere. He'd been a colonel then. After retiring from the Marines, he'd come back to duty aboard the *Lepanto* as the chief warrant officer for its boarding team. The deaths reminded him of another duty. Jacob looked down.

"Lieutenant Stewart, how fare the civie casualties you brought up here in your LCA?"

Daisy, who had been watching the images of O'Sullivan and Mikoto on the front wallscreen, turned and looked up to him. Her dark brown face scrunched up. "All twelve are still alive in our Med

Hall. The doctor and nurses there are doing surgeries on the worst ones. Two are in stasis until they can be helped. Triage, you know."

O'Sullivan looked from Daisy up to him. "Jacob, the LCAs from your three ships did wonders in evacing folks from the three neighborhoods hit by the bombs. They landed in spaces our ground cars could not get to. We only have three aircars on the whole planet, and some copters. Thank you for that help."

Jacob nodded. Visiting Stockholm and seeing some of the people he and his ships had saved was one item on his long To Do list. First things first, though. "Billy, thanks for the info on casualties. Lieutenant Jefferson did her best to zap that attacking wasp ship. But it survived and is now heading out system. There is no indication it will return."

O'Sullivan showed relief. "Glad to hear that. We've been tracking it on our moving neutrino scanner. Do you expect the other four wasp ships to return soon? Or can folks in the shelters head out to their homes and farms?"

"They can head out," Jacob said, giving thanks for the cluster of his battle group ships that orbited close to the Star Navy space station. "As you know, any new ships that arrive will take 52 hours to get to Valhalla. We're maintaining our own moving neutrino scanner watch. If new wasp ships arrive before our Earth reinforcements, my fleet will protect you and the folks on Valhalla."

The man looked tired. O'Sullivan was in charge of the Star Navy base and its 312 enlisted and officers. He'd been awake almost continuously since the *Lepanto* and Jacob's battle group had arrived in orbit above Valhalla. Awake pills did wonders. But crews could not stay on them indefinitely. The base captain rubbed his eyes, looked aside at some of the wallscreens, then back to Jacob.

"I know you will, Jacob." He turned thoughtful. "Just wondering about the future. Like you and everyone else. Well, my chief engineer and his folks will start work on the *Chesapeake* as soon as she moves to parking orbit next to our Hanger Two. Keep me posted on your future needs."

"Will do, Captain O'Sullivan," Jacob said, moving their casual chat back to the formality expected of officers in a combat zone. "Let me talk to Lieutenant Commander Swanson about moving close to your station. She and the other captains are meeting with me in three hours. We'll know what's what soon enough."

O'Sullivan nodded. "Understood. Star Navy base *Green Hills* out."

The man's image disappeared from the curving front wallscreen. The wide expanse of the planet Valhalla now filled it. Green forests, yellow plains, purple mountains and the eastern seacoast where Stockholm was located shone bright in the daylight of Kepler 10. Briefly he wondered if the colonists had given the G-type star a name. Did they call it Odin, the chief god of ancient Scandinavia? He pushed aside the musing. Researching the human colony on Valhalla was another item on his To Do list.

"Captain," called Osashi. "Incoming neutrino call from Lieutenant Jefferson of the *Philippine Sea*."

Duty returned to him. "Put it up on the front wallscreen. And share it with everyone by way of the All Ship vidcom. Also share it with our other battle group ships."

The man who was just five years from full retirement nodded, tapped his control pillar, then spoke. "Going up. Her signal and our response are now being shared with everyone."

One of Jacob's first decisions as acting captain had been to share everything that happened on the Bridge with the other decks and personnel of the *Lepanto*. He'd done it thinking his crew and fellow officers needed to know what was happening, in view of the death of most Command Deck officers. A similar reason led him to share most of what he did on the Bridge with the other ships in the battle group. Like the *Lepanto*, each of them was being led by a new captain who had forced open the dead captain's digital safe, found the ship status change code, and given it to the ship's AI so they could assume full ship control. His close friends Quincy and Kenji had told him that his sharing had reassured crew folks shocked by the sudden change in command. And by the later attack of the wasp-like aliens. The appearance of Joy Jefferson as an image inset in the middle of the planet's image drew his attention.

"Lieutenant Jefferson, what's up?"

The blue-eyed blond looked anxious. She occupied one of the two seats in the middle of her ship's Bridge. To her left sat a young woman whom Jacob knew came from Wales. His access to the admiral's personnel files had helped him learn people names, duties and personal histories. The name of Joy's new XO was Aelwen

Rhydderch. But it was the new captain who captured his attention. She scowled.

"Captain, that bastard wasp ship is getting away!" Jefferson said quickly. "We killed one of its engines. Let me finish the job! Please, sir."

Jacob almost smiled at how the lanky woman had belatedly added 'please' to her demand. He had come to appreciate her fight hunger. And the abilities of her destroyer and its crew. Her demand brought back Richard's issue. "Captain Jefferson, I have decided we will not destroy the departing wasp ship. I have several reasons. But the primary one is it will serve as a test subject for our next cartoon vid effort at opening communications." He paused, noticed how Rosemary O'Hara at Tactical was playing close attention, and felt renewed amusement. She was another deadly woman. "That ship will take another 40 hours to reach the magnetosphere. Lieutenant Branstead has assured me her algorithm geeks will have a new vid to transmit before then. Be patient." A thought hit him hard. "Jefferson, if that wasp ship stays in the system, do you think you could track it down?"

The woman's disappointed expression moved quickly to eagerness. "Yes! Even if they hide inside a comet their reactors will still send out neutrinos. We can find it. Do we kill it then?"

Jacob sighed. Where did this long-limbed straw blond get her energy? Maybe the same place Daisy got hers, thinking back to his girlfriend's intense curiosity and fanatically perfect piloting abilities. "No, you do not kill it." He looked up at the room's gray metal ceiling. Yellow light strips crisscrossed it in checkerboard patterns. "Melody," he called to his ship's artificial intelligence. "Does the destroyer *Philippine Sea* have the capability to bring an assault Dart inside its cargohold?"

A low hum now sounded. "Unlikely. The destroyer's cargohold access hatch is twelve meters long by six high. A Dart measures twenty meters long by seven high. Entry into the cargohold is not physically possible."

Jacob had known the size of the Dart. It was the details of the destroyer's airlock hatches and cargohold entry that he'd not known. Still, every destroyer in his battle group was a big starship. They measured 300 meters in length. Half the size of a cruiser and one-third the size of a Battlestar. The excited look of Jefferson and Aelwen told him those people were pumped by his idea. "What about attachment to a destroyer's outer hull? Is that possible?"

"It is possible," the AI said, sounding curious as its speech recognition software sought an analogue to Jacob's voice tone. "The plasma battery on the top of the *Philippine Sea* lies in the middle of the ship's hull. A Dart could be attached ahead or behind the battery, to the ship's sides or to its belly."

The AI's talkativeness was novel to Jacob. Especially in view of its past history of blaming humans for being redundant in speech. "How long would it take to weld attachment latches onto the ship's hull? If they were similar to the latches that hold cargo."

"Four hours, twenty-seven minutes and nine seconds, using repair robots," the AI said, its tone moving to machine flatness. "However," it said, its voice becoming almost eager. "Placement of two gravity plates on the belly of the Dart would be desirable. Setting the plates to a two gee pull would further hold the Dart to the destroyer's hull."

Below him Richard was looking up, his eyebrows lifted as the man's curiosity over Jacob's unfolding plans grew. He gave the Marine a thumbs-up, then looked at the wallscreen. "Lieutenant Jefferson, if I arranged with the Star Navy base engineers to weld on the needed latches, could your ship maneuver decently with three Darts attached to your hull?"

Jefferson's blue eyes brightened. She clenched her fists. "Yes! Between the latches and the added gravity plates the Darts would be secure during our transit. And our ship's eco-system can handle the additional fifteen Marines."

Jacob nodded, then met the gaze of the Marine leader. "Chief O'Connor, it occurs to me that the most direct source of pheromone emitting radios is on this wasp ship. While I hope Lieutenant Branstead's cartoon video gets a positive response, it seems to me taking further action before wasp reinforcements arrive is worthwhile. What is your opinion?"

"I like it," the man said, his deep bass voice filling the Bridge. "Do we make multiple hull entries after we arrive?"

Jacob understood the man wanted to know whether all the Darts would be used in the assault on the wasp ship, or just one with two as backups. "Yes. Use all three Darts. We do not know how the wasp ship is arranged internally, other than the obvious presence of weapons rings on its nose, middle and tail, and fusion pulse exhausts at its tail. Three entries give your people three chances to find the right tech, and maybe capture a wasp or two."

O'Connor's thin lips curved up. "Outstanding. Shall I work with my Marines on boarding simulations? We can use the true space and sensor records of the ship that attacked Valhalla as the basis for holo simulations."

Jacob felt good at the man's reaction. The Marine's combat experience in person-to-person fighting was greater than that of anyone on the *Lepanto*, or on the other ships. And his skill in handling people was something Jacob had noticed ever since their departure from Earth. He'd done his best, during the space battles with the wasps, to imitate the skills of both O'Connor and his father, hero of the Callisto Conflict and Earth's only five star fleet admiral. While his father's constant hectoring of him about space navy traditions, space maneuvers, Earth's war history and what made for a good commander of ships and people had bugged him, he'd paid attention. And the classes and simulations of the Stellar Academy at Colorado Springs had pounded into him the most recent tactics and battle strategies. Much to his dismay. But he'd learned the value of getting advice and help from people who knew more than he did. Like his friends Daisy, Lori, Carlos, Quincy and Kenji, and other officers like Branstead and O'Connor.

"Chief, you do just that. You have plenty of time." Jacob looked ahead to where his Bridge crew were watching their own holos, being attentive to their duties even while in parking orbit. Their distraction at Richard's earlier questions had given way to covert listening as they worked. He looked down to where Daisy sat, her attention focused on her holo cross-section of the ship's various decks and weapons stations. "XO Stewart, arrange with Chief O'Connor for his people to use the simulators in the Exercise Chamber."

"Captain, happy to do so," Daisy said quickly.

Jacob returned to the image of Jefferson on the front wallscreen. "Captain Jefferson, how do you feel about taking our Marines out to where they can board that wasp ship?"

The woman gave him a big grin. "Captain, I feel super! Uh, do I kill the wasp ship after our Marines return?"

He shook his head. "No. Leave it mostly intact. Use sufficient laser and proton fire to allow the Darts to penetrate the enemy's hull.

But once the Marines return, pull back and return to Valhalla. Lieutenant Branstead will have heart palpitations until you bring home whatever tech our boarders can grab." One more point hit him. "If the Marines capture any wasps, isolate them and put them in a cell with half gee gravity. Feed them whatever they will accept. Put them all together in a single cell. I suspect they will go nuts without the presence and pheromones of their comrades."

She frowned, then nodded quickly. "Captain, I will do exactly as you order. Are we second in line after the *Chesapeake*?"

"You are first in line," he said, recalling the time lines involved in her ship's long trip out to the system's Kuiper Belt. "The welding work will not take long. Then you leave with the three Darts and the Marines. But all that happens *after* you attend the meeting in my conference room. Time for you new captains to see each other. Time to compile repair needs. And time for all of us to discuss future options."

Jefferson saluted him. "As you order, fleet captain. My ship, my crew and myself are at your command. *Philippine Sea* out."

Her image vanished from the front wallscreen. On it the planet's surface had become mostly ocean, a wide expanse lying to the east of Stockholm. Their orbit at 400 kilometers high meant they circled the planet once every 80 minutes. With the result the image of the planet keeps changing. Jacob looked ahead. "Chief Osashi, establish a comlink with Captain Swanson on the *Chesapeake*. Time to work with her on getting her ship repaired."

"Neutrino comlink established. Imagery going up front."

Jacob fixed on the black face of the woman who had exposed her heavy cruiser to incoming energy beams as quickly as he had exposed the *Lepanto*. Unlike him, she had lost crew in the last attack. The stocky, middle-aged woman did not show evidence of that loss. But he knew from his own feelings that the death of fifteen crew had cut deep into her.

"Lieutenant Commander Swanson, the *Chesapeake* is second in line for repairs at the Star Navy base. You heard the reason why I've moved the *Philippine Sea* ahead of you. Any problems with waiting?"

"No problems, Captain Renselaer." She looked as tired as Jacob felt. "My Weapons and Life Support chiefs will make do."

Jacob listened as the woman outlined her plans for the replacement of her right flank proton laser node. He sat straight and formal. It was the least he could do for a fellow officer, someone who, like him, had jumped into the job of commanding her ship right after seeing the video of the destruction of the meeting site by the wasps. She, like the other new ship captains, was still coping with a new reality. He hoped she was doing better than he felt. He still got the shakes when he was alone in the old captain's quarters. Did the other new commanders of battle group ships feel as much at sea as he did? That was something he needed to find out during the all captains meeting. That was set for this evening at what was the first crew meal time. Three hours away. Maybe he could get a quick nap before then. He needed it. And he needed the tender caring of Daisy even more. When would they have time for each other?

More important was the answer to his worry they might be attacked before Earth reinforcements arrived. Could the battle group survive an attack by a dozen or more wasp ships? Could the planet Valhalla be protected? The piling up of personal and professional worries and doubts made him wonder if his father the admiral had felt the way Jacob now felt, during his space battles at Callisto. It was an unwanted insight into his sole surviving parent.

CHAPTER TWO

Support Hunter Seven felt fatigue as his flying nest moved past the small gas world that lay in the sixth flight range from the local sky light. He had ordered his Flight Servant to change their flight angle to match their inward flight track. While Hunter One and the other Support Hunters flew well ahead of his nest, moving toward the edge of the local sky light's magnetic field and a return to the colony of Warmth, still, he felt isolated. The fatigue just made it worse. He breathed deep through his spiracles, checked the perception imager that showed the local worlds and other flying nests to confirm the Soft Skins were not pursuing him, then decided to focus on something more life affirming than the fact of his nest being left behind by the larger flight of Swarmers.

"Servant," he scent cast to the Swarmer in charge of monitoring external space. "Where are good places for this nest to hide from detection by the Soft Skins?"

The elderly Swarmer angled two antennae his way. The Servant straightened his posture on his bench and used one of his thorax arms to touch a color image panel. "Hunter, there are many ice balls flying beyond this system's outermost world. Some are very large. We could make flight track for a large one that lies along our current path, then use our stingers to cut a deep hole." The Swarmer twisted his head to put all five eyes on Seven. "Our flying nest could hide inside such a hole. However, the particle emissions of our energy nodes might betray our location."

Seven knew that, in a vague way. The particle emissions from his nest's propulsive devices were the way his nest and all Swarmer nests tracked each other across distances too great for normal viewing. The energy node emissions were the same particles. Those emissions spoke in a way different than normal pheromone speech. He suspected the Soft Skins could track nests the same way. Still, they must find a hiding spot from which to watch the events on the fourth world and the actions of the eight Soft Skin nests that had survived the last flight battle. That was their assigned duty, until Hunter One returned with more flying nests to claim the third world.

Hiding in one spot was not the normal lifeway for any Swarmer. Either you flew and explored, flew and found a mate or flew and fought an invader to one's home territory. Rest periods during the time of daily darkness were short, compared to some lifeforms on his home world of Nest. But now they must do the strange. Now they must hide and be silent. While the Soft Skins would know they had not left this system of worlds, the abnormal two-legged beings might not find his nest if he and his Servants took care to hide all trace of their presence.

"Servant, cast your eye tools ahead of us and find such an ice world," he said in a rush of food trail, territorial and calming pheromones, mixed with a touch of aggregation scent. "Though it be a strange duty, we will cut out a hiding hole and rely on our tools to maintain a view of the Soft Skins."

"Searching," the Servant replied in a mix of aggregation and signal pheromones.

Seven looked around, seeking the familiar forms of his Servants, Fighter Leaders and the Matron to his rear. While all who flew within his flying nest were able to withstand long separations from Nest and their caste cohorts, still, it was not a natural way to live. Only the discovery of a new colony world in this system made his duty, and their duty, tolerable. Perhaps his Servants within the Flight Chamber would cope well if he asked the Matron to emit her pheromone song of Life Mating. It would remind all those within the hard shell of his flying nest of their duty, their future and the utter necessity of finding new worlds for the expanding numbers of his fellow Swarmers. And it would bring out the hope in all caste members that one of them might be chosen to mate with the Matron in order to produce more effective members of their caste. That was a reward he would withhold until the return of Hunter One. When that happened, their claim on the third world would begin with a new sky battle. Cleansing this system of the Soft Skin infestation was essential before they dropped colonizing Pods onto the warm lands of world three. It all made for better musing, better dreams than the disasters of the recent sky battles against these strange Soft Skins. Lowering his abdomen to rest atop his bench, Seven allowed his dream to fill his mind.

◆ ◆ ◆

Aarhant Bannerjee turned away from watching the wallscreen that relayed the image of the Bridge and the conversations of the young whelp with the new captains of other battle group ships. At least he could feel safe within his own quarters, rather than on display in the Navigation Deck's control center. One of his assistants was there now. It was her shift time. His time was one of rest. But he could not rest knowing how once again young Renselaer had stolen from him the rightful command of the *Lepanto*. He was the senior surviving staff officer. He should have been given command of the Bridge by the Star Base captain. Instead, the man O'Sullivan had sided with Renselaer and had confirmed his new status as captain of the Battlestar. Worse, the man had accepted the whelp's command of the battle group! He could not understand why other staff officers on the battle group ships had not insisted on taking command of the fleet. They were all lieutenants or higher. Swanson of the *Chesapeake* and Mehta of the *Salamis* were lieutenant commanders like him. Surely they understood that a return to a normal chain of command was the right thing to do upon arrival at Kepler 10. But they had supported Renselaer. And once the wasp aliens had arrived, everyone was focused on battle tactics, fighting and surviving. Well, they had survived, except for the frigates *Britain* and *Marianas*. The memory of those ships reminded him of the trip made by the frigate *Ofira*. It would bring back new ships from Earth. Surely someone in command of the new fleet would see the wrongness of an ensign being in command of a battle group!

He reached out and grabbed a bottle of *tequila*. Unscrewing its lid, he poured some of the liquid into the glass that sat before him on the table that swung out from his Food Alcove counter. He walked back to the overstuffed chair in his relaxation room and sat. Staring at the wall image of the holy city of Varanasi, he pondered his options. Failing to cooperate with the orders of Renselaer would put him on the official record as being an obstructionist. But talking to the other ship captains, and to some of their deck chiefs, might result in favorable attitudes to him, once the new Earth fleet arrived. Aarhant swallowed half the glass, accepting the burning sensation as it slid down his throat. The discomfort was welcome. It reminded him of the pain he felt every time he saw a vidscreen image of the young whelp, or heard his voice on the All Ship announcer. Well, his ancestral

Hindus had learned patience while under the rule of the British Raj. In time, they had thrown off that rule and taken back control of Mother India. In time, he would do the same on the *Lepanto*.

♦ ♦ ♦

Daisy sat to the right of Jacob in the conference room of admiral Johanson's old quarters. To her right sat Lori, Carlos and Quincy. Like her they wore NWU woodland camo uniforms. Silvery sparkles on their collars reminded her of the promotions Jacob had handed out after the last battle. Lori and Carlos were jumped from ensign to Lieutenant JG, entitling them to wear a single silver bar on the points of their collars. Quincy had been promoted to Petty Officer second class, two steps up from Spacer. How did they feel about the wartime promotions? She still felt ill at ease with her own jump to a full lieutenant, as warranted by her new XO status. Wearing double silver bars on her shirt collar was nice. But it felt strange. Most Star Navy officers spent three or four years before they moved from ensign to JG. Longer to get to full lieutenant. She and her friends had gained their promotions in less than a year.

"XO, have the other ship captains arrived?"

She looked to Jacob. While his curly black hair had no gray in it, his face looked tense. As it had most of the time since they'd seen the devastated meeting site where the fleet's senior line officers had all been killed. He'd been that way except for Dance Night and the night they'd spent together. Their time in Alcubierre transit had been a badly needed respite from the shock of first combat. Now, his gray eyes were bright, as if he was looking forward to the upcoming meeting. His broad shoulders, clean looks and sensitive manner were just some of the reasons she loved him. More important was how he listened to her, treating what she shared as important and vital. Being cared for that way was something she had missed after her father left home. Course, her Mom was beyond wonderful and supportive. It was due to her that Daisy had become a pilot, first in the air and now in space. She glanced down at her personal tablet, tapped the ship status app and saw what she needed to see.

"Yes, Captain, all seven captains have arrived at Hangar Three. They're heading for gravlifts to bring them down to Command Deck."

Jacob gave her a wink, then looked down at his own tablet. He tapped on it. "Kenji, the other brass are on their way. Time to bring us that fancy dinner you and your buddies put together."

"Will do, captain," replied the other member of her boyfriend's 'brain trust'.

She pondered how Jacob had chosen to include a line cook from the Mess Hall as one of the group of people he listened to. While non-standard, she liked his decision. But it felt strange to now live in quarters on the Command Deck, rather than the Navigation Deck that was normal for a pilot. Still, it made sense. Keeping her, Lori, Carlos, Quincy and Kenji close by to Jacob's quarters in the old captain's cabin allowed him quick in-person access to any of them. While tablets and the All Ship com system allowed anyone anywhere on the *Lepanto* to be in video and voice contact with anyone else, it was clear Jacob preferred live, in-person discussions. Which must be why he had ordered the other battle group captains to report to the conference room. Holo and wallscreen images were the normal way people on other ships stayed in touch. Jacob did that, of course, but it was clear he wished to be personally accessible to the people he worked with and relied on. She liked that. It reminded her of some of the better instructors at the Stellar Academy. The hallway door slid open with a low hiss.

"Drinks first!" called Kenji as the young Japanese walked in carrying a big platter filled with pitchers, cans and bottles.

"This end first!" called Lori, her Russian-accented English sounding nice to Daisy.

"Anyone else want some *tequila*?" called Carlos. Her friend from east Los Angeles gave Kenji a big smile as he reached for the bottle of Herradura *tequila*.

Daisy pushed out her own shot glass. "Me too."

She watched as Carlos poured the pale brown liquid first into Lori's glass, then into her glass. It had taken her several tries to get used to the beverage made from the blue agave plants grown in Mexico's Jalisco state, but she'd grown to like it. While she preferred a good pale ale craft beer for casual socializing, she much liked the fast buzz from a shot of *tequila*. As did Lori and Quincy. But Quincy also grabbed a can of dark Irish pub beer. Jacob reached out and plucked a can of Blue Moon pale ale. The brand was very popular on the Stellar Academy campus. Briefly she wondered what kind of booze his father, the famous five star admiral, most liked. She refrained from asking. While her lover was always willing to share about his mother Sarah, chatter about his famous father was nearly non-existent. Still, from the open media reports about his famous dad and things he'd done after retirement, Daisy felt certain the man had had a big influence on Jacob. She had seen plenty of evidence that the man's daring, ruthlessness and willingness to make surprise moves were talents Jacob had inherited.

"Captain, do I bring the first course in now, or wait for the arrival of the other captains?"

Daisy looked up as Kenji stood on the other side of Jacob. The tall, slim, black-haired guy had a manner that said 'American', even though he was native Japanese. Going to school on a US base near to Yokohama had given her friend excellent English and the ability to blend into any American cultural scene. She hoped the Korean girl she had seen him with on Dance Night would bring out his private side. She liked Kenji. He deserved more than being taken for granted as a 'cook' in the Mess Hall.

Jacob looked up. "Bring in the first course now. The rest of our guests will be here very soon. Oh, and bring another tray of drinks, including ice tea. This table is big enough."

"Captain, will do," Kenji said, almost saluting, then stopping as he realized the conference room gathering was intended to be informal.

Jacob smiled. "Hey, Kenji, no sweat. I'm looking forward to the *sushi* first course!"

"I'll be back soon!" Kenji turned away and headed for the room's exit.

The five of them fell to drinking and easing into the relaxed chatter normal for a group of young ensigns and spacers new to a ship. That was how they had related to each during the 25 days of their trip out from Earth to Kepler 22. They had been new to the *Lepanto* when they'd boarded at the spacedock. After nearly a month together in the gray nothingness of Alcubierre space-time, Daisy and her friends had been accepted by the other spacers and staff officers of the Battlestar. The weekly Dance Nights had done wonders to integrate them and allow them a chance to rub elbows with folks close to their age. Most of the deck officers also showed up on Dance Nights, showing a side of them that was informal and amiable. A hum came from the speaker above the slidedoor that gave access to the hallway.

"Captain Renselaer, permission to enter?" called a woman's voice that she recognized. "The other captains are with me."

Jacob looked up from his tablet, his expression turning serious. "Door, admit Lieutenant Commander Swanson and other ship captains."

The slidedoor hissed open.

Daisy watched as the seven of them walked into the admiral's large conference room and headed for the long table and bolted down chairs. Leading the pack was Rebecca Swanson, followed by George Wilcox of Britain, Douglas Zhang of China, Chatur Mehta, Joy Jefferson, Dekker Lorenz of Germany and Joan Sunderland. All except Joan were former deck staff officers who had claimed the captain's seat on their ship, back in the Kepler 22 system. Each of them had fought their ship hard, and some had lost crew. Each of them looked serious and thoughtful as they gave a nod to Jacob, then found a seat. Swanson took the seat on Jacob's left, with the other captains sitting in chairs that faced Daisy's side of the table. A few chairs lay empty beyond Quincy.

"Welcome all," Jacob said calmly, sounding casual. He waved at the large platter of drinks in the middle of the table. "Grab the drink of your choice. Dinner's first course will arrive shortly."

Swanson's black face moved from serious to amiable. She looked over Daisy, Lori, Carlos and Quincy, then back to Jacob. Like him she wore a brown Service Khaki uniform, as did the other captains. And like the rest of them she had left her vacsuit on her shuttle. Her black eyebrows lifted.

"Captain, thank you. Uh, is this meeting first name informal? Or should I have saluted upon entry?"

Jacob chuckled, amazing Daisy by his quick move to humor. "First name informal! We all know each other, thanks to the battles we fought, out there and here. I see no reason to stand on formalities." He looked up at the ceiling. "AI Melody, continue recording this meeting for the record." Jacob looked back to the stocky, middle-aged woman. "Rebecca, please accept my condolences at your loss of fifteen crew on the *Chesapeake* in the destruction of your proton beam node." He looked past Swanson to the other six captains. "Douglas, I regret your loss of three crew on the *Tsushima Strait* when your spine plasma battery was zapped. Dekker, I am equally sorry for your loss of four crew when the wasp lightning beam punched through the cargohold of the *St. Mihiel*." Jacob paused, his gaze resting briefly on each captain. "Each of you fought well in the battles in both systems. Please tell your crews that I have the highest confidence in their ability to defend the battle group and to protect Valhalla."

Swanson nodded slowly. She reached out, grabbed a can of beer, flipped it open and took a swig. Her amiable look did not hide the pain in her eyes. "Jacob, thank you. Those fifteen included people I've known for many years, while serving as Navigation Deck commander. You are lucky the *Lepanto* did not lose people in those deep punch throughs on your ship's nose and belly."

Jacob winced. His expression turned as serious as everyone else at the table. "You are right that we on the *Lepanto* were lucky. Thank god the water layer vaporization defused follow-on beams, or we would have had pressure loss in some ship rooms. With a chance for folks being sucked out into space."

Zhang's pale lips grimaced. "We had bad luck. The takeout of our topside plasma battery broke open several plasma canisters enroute to the battery. The resulting plasma burst cut through the hull armor and killed three crew in that part of our Weapons Deck. Vacsuits cannot stop plasma."

"Similar story for us," Lorenz said, looking around the table, then fixing back on Jacob. "My frigate crew are outstanding people, but the beam's punch through to our midbody cargohold fried four Spacers. I put their bodies into stasis."

Jacob nodded slowly. "Dekker, your frigate fought well. Please send me the names of your dead. Same for the rest of you." Her boyfriend paused, looked down at his tablet, then up. "Rebecca, George, how are the civie casualties in your Med Halls? Any fatalities since they arrived?"

Daisy listened as the captains for the *Chesapeake* and the *Hampton Roads* shared the news on the civilian casualties brought up by their LCAs. Piloting her own Landing Craft Assault down into the harsh winds, dust devils and wreckage of the Salonika neighborhood had been daunting. But seeing the broken bones, red bleeding lacerations and haunted looks of the survivors when she landed had made her immensely glad her ship could reach areas blocked to ground transport. The few aircars and copters possessed by the Stockholm first responders were overloaded by the scale of destruction to three city blocks scattered over the western edge of the city. She just wished she could wipe from her mind the images of crumpled bodies, lonely hands sticking out from collapsed concrete rubble piles and children's toys that had been scattered by the plasma bomb bursts. Creating a lightning rainstorm just after the decimation of the plasma bursts had made it hard for anyone to reach survivors. At the time she thought gathering up a dozen badly wounded survivors had been too little. But the thankful looks of family members and friends as they carried people into her LCA's cargohold was the other side of the memories she now recalled as the two cruiser captains filled Jacob in on the treatment status of the civies brought up by their LCAs. The entry door hissed open.

"First course!" called Kenji as he entered holding a platter in each hand.

Daisy watched as her friend deftly laid down the platters. They held stacked plates, *ohashi* chopsticks, big plates filled with a dozen types of seaweed-wrapped *sushi*, and more cans of beer. Plus a pitcher of tea, which she knew other folks liked in addition to Jacob. Kenji brought a plate and chopsticks over to Jacob while the other captains and her friends helped themselves to settings and food. She did the same, her ears alert to the casual chatter that briefly passed as people from other ships interacted with each other and with her friends. She noticed that Chatur Mehta, the Hindu-American lieutenant commander of the destroyer *Salamis* who had defied Jacob's order to be part of the battle group, said almost nothing and put only an egg roll and a single *sushi* tube onto his plate. He was drinking ice tea. Did the man not like booze? Or did he still feel as if he was in 'prove yourself' mode in view of his late arrival to help during the wasp attacks in Kepler 22? Similarly quiet was blond-haired Joan Sunderland from the frigate *Aldertag*. The fiftyish Anglo woman projected a seriousness that seemed less uncertain than the manners of the new ship captains. Daisy understood the woman had been involved in the occupation of Callisto after the miner rebellion, then her ship had been assigned duty at the first human star colony. Her ship was the only defense the planet of Valhalla possessed, until the battle group's arrival. Followed by too many wasp ships. Had she lost friends in the lightning bomb attacks on the capital of Stockholm?

And as a longtime line officer and captain rank leader of her ship and its people, what did she think of Jacob's sudden rise to leadership on the *Lepanto*?

"Captain, uh Jacob," called Joy Jefferson from her side of the table. "The *Philippine Sea* is docked at Hangar Two of the base. The engineers have been working on it for awhile. The last attachment points for the Darts should be affixed within three hours. Do I leave to chase after the wasp ship as soon as the welding is done?"

Jacob looked away from listening to George opine about how stupid it was for the wasps to always try englobing the fleet. His clean-shaven face moved from amiable to thoughtful. "Joy, you leave as soon as chief O'Connor has moved over his people and his three Darts to lock-on with your ship's hull." He looked to Daisy. "XO, when will the gravity plate attachment to the hulls of the Darts be completed? I gather that chief Pilotti is working with chief Chang to get it done."

For this she did not have to look at her tablet. Coordinating the work of Cassandra from Gravity on the Bridge with the engineers who worked for Engines Deck chief Billy Chang was something she'd worked on while Jacob took his much-needed afternoon nap. She gave him a nod. "Captain, Cassandra pulled six gravity plates from Supplies Deck and got them delivered to chief Chang. The chief tells me his engineers have been welding the gravplates to the belly hulls of each Dart for the last two hours. Once done, the Darts will move out through Silo Eight and head for the *Philippine Sea*." She looked to the blue-eyed young woman who had been chief of the Weapons Deck on her destroyer. "Captain Jefferson, the Darts will be ready to lock onto the new attachment points once the base releases your ship."

Jefferson lifted a blond eyebrow, then grinned. "Super! And call me Joy." She looked to Jacob. "Captain, that means we can leave for our wasp hunt within three hours. Uh, do I coordinate with chief O'Connor about his people coming over?"

Jacob gave a quick nod. "Do just that. Everything does not have to flow through me and the *Lepanto*. Joy, I trust your judgment. Give me a call when your ship is about to leave orbit. Beyond that, all other arrangements are up to you."

The hard-charging young woman smiled big. "Outstanding! My XO has billets set up for chief O'Connor's Marines. Uh, will the chief be coming along with his Darts and Marines?"

Daisy looked quickly to Jacob. When she had gone to wake him for the dinner conference, he had mentioned the long talk he'd had with Richard just before heading to his quarters. The Marine was someone she'd worked to know during the Alcubierre transit to Kepler 10. He had shared how he had three grown children back on Earth, one spunky granddaughter and then made clear his opinion that marriage did not work well with active duty soldiers subject to long overseas assignments. Her review of his personnel file had told her Richard was divorced for the last ten years. The divorce had happened right after he retired from leading a battalion of Marines. His new service with the Star Navy had begun five years ago, when the *Lepanto* had been commissioned for service as Earth's fifth and last Battlestar. The man's arrival on board as a senior chief warrant officer had seemed to her to be a demotion from his earlier rank of colonel. But now, after watching him for the last nine days, she understood the man hungered for real combat. The chance to lead his Marines into deadly action was clearly what the man was married to.

"He will," Jacob said. "I do not like losing my combat advisor, but you and your ship will be back here well before the Earth ships arrive. If the wasps arrive sooner, you head back here ASAP." Her boyfriend's casual tone had gone almost formal as he dealt with a command issue. "Also, Richard insisted his presence was needed to provide you with advice on the deployment of his Darts, and I try to accept his suggestions. The man will be an asset to your ship and your crew."

Jefferson's amiable manner moved to formal mode. "Captain, understood. I look forward to welcoming chief O'Connor onto my Bridge and to adding his Marines to our ship's complement. I'm sure our Weapons Deck people will enjoy their company."

"No doubt," Jacob said, moving his attention away from the destroyer captain and over to Daisy's side of the table. But his gaze was not on her. "Lori, how goes the Science Deck work on creating a pheromone-transmitting radio?"

"Not well," her Russian friend said. She laid down her chopsticks. "Lieutenant Branstead made it our top priority. But our linguists and digital signaling folks insist it is impossible to fabricate a pheromone signaler until we know what the receiving device is like. As in how the incoming radio signal is converted to produce various types of pheromones."

Jacob frowned. "Well, can't the signal folks figure out a way to emit a signal for sweat? Or for the human sex pheromones that folks always give off?"

The slim, black-haired woman sat back in her chair, her expression frustrated. "Human pheromones are not the same as insect pheromones. We know a lot about the pheromones emitted by wasps, butterflies, ants and other social insects. But the chemical signatures for each Earth insect pheromone are delicate and not very stable. How do we know that an Earth wasp pheromone that means 'attack' is the same as an alien wasp pheromone that says 'attack'?"

Jacob pursed his lips. "So capturing a wasp signaling device is vital for us to communicate with the wasps in their own language?"

"Yes, it is vital."

Jacob nodded, then looked over to Jefferson. "Joy, do whatever it takes to capture some wasp signaling devices. Video cartoons can express simple concepts. And Lieutenant Branstead is working on a new cartoon that proposes wasps and humans cooperate on something. But we need to be able to speak to the wasps in their own language."

"Exactly so," commented Mehta from the end of the table. "These aliens may not be used to encrypting radio and neutrino communications. If we can learn their way of talking, we could gain a tactical advantage. Might allow us to disrupt their battle formations."

Daisy felt surprise at the comment from the captain of the *Salamis*. Then again, the man had run the Science Deck on his destroyer. Clearly he thought beyond basic science functions.

Jacob gave Mehta a thumbs-up. "Chatur, that is an excellent point. There *will* be another battle with the wasps. Otherwise, why did they leave a ship here to watch us?" Her boyfriend looked away and then around the table. "Everyone, think over the several space battles we've had. If any of you can come up with new tactics, new approaches, I am ready to listen. Also, all of you have more experience in space than I do. I'm willing to learn from each of you." He turned to Sunderland. "Joan, your *Aldertag* fought well. I'm glad there was no punch through on your hull. Beyond that, you've served at each of our star colonies. That's seven alien worlds, each with its own biosphere. I welcome any insights you may have."

The older woman put down her can of beer. Her blue eyes looked to Daisy's boss. "Jacob, the battle formations you adopted in Kepler 22 were very good, considering you faced an alien enemy whom no human has ever met in battle. I'm studying those vids and our records from the fight here. I'll let you know if anything comes to me."

The entry slidedoor opened and Kenji walked in with two large trays filled with barbecue ribs, sweet and sour pork, and veggie burgers for those who might prefer a meatless meal. His arrival broke the tense feel of the recent reports and discussions. She grabbed a bowl of rice and spooned in some sweet and sour pork cubes. Using her chopsticks, she remembered her Mom's ease with the utensils and did her best to look at ease with them. Around her other people did the same, seeming to welcome the shift from the future attack by the *Philippine Sea* against the wasp ship that now approached the system's Kuiper Belt of comets and ice rocks. She had no doubt Joy Jefferson would find the enemy ship. Nor any doubt that Richard and his Marines would board the wasp ship. She hoped the price for gaining alien pheromone signalers would not be more human lives. Her memory of historical war vids at the Stellar Academy and the recent violence as gas and proton laser beams crisscrossed through black space told her it was a vain hope. She took brief comfort in knowing how daring and fast-moving was the destroyer captained by Joy. The woman, like Jacob, seemed to have the gods of luck riding on her shoulders.

CHAPTER THREE

Richard O'Connor watched the front wallscreen of the *Philippine Sea* as the destroyer moved toward the comet that held the hidden shape of the wounded wasp ship. To his left sat Captain Joy Jefferson the straw blond, while beyond her sat a redheaded woman from Wales with the exotic name of Aelwen Rhydderch. She was the ship's XO. Shortly after boarding with his Marines he had practiced saying the Welsh name. The young woman had been talkative, friendly and upbeat about her captain. His observation of Jefferson's ship command during the space battles in Kepler 22 and Kepler 10 had led him to feel she might be a younger version of himself. Someone born to fight. Her quick pursuit after the wasp ship, and locating of it despite its hideaway inside the dirty white ice of a large comet, had impressed him.

"Tactical, what's the range to the comet?" Jefferson said in a sharp soprano that echoed over his vacsuit's comlink.

"Four thousand kilometers," called the black man at the Bridge's Tactical station.

"Engines, slow to a hundred klicks a minute," she called to the Chinese woman who controlled the destroyer's two fusion pulse thrusters.

"Slowing. Speed reduced," responded the middle-aged woman who hailed from Taiwan.

"Weapons, launch two missiles. Put them on a parallel track with us," Jefferson said quickly.

"Missiles launching," called a black-haired woman from Louisiana in a musical voice that hinted at the woman's Cajun ancestry.

Richard approved of Jefferson's creation of a threat beyond the destroyer's single proton laser at its nose, two CO_2 gas lasers at its tail and the plasma battery on the ship's spine. At 300 meters long the *Philippine Sea* was a large ship. The 113 crew on it worked in three shifts and even then they all kept busy. Including his fifteen Marines, who volunteered to help in the ship's Life Support and Weapons decks. Their work was on top of his boarding simulations. Despite the busy workloads, his people had complained at his order to put in eight hours of sleep when the ship was two-thirds of the way out to the system's Kuiper Belt. He had followed his own order. They all needed to be fresh and alert for the upcoming boarding of the wasp ship. Assuming they could find a way to access it if it stayed inside the comet. Tactical's sensors had shown the alien ship to be nested in a silo cut into the solid ice of the 300 kilometer wide comet. Spectroscope readings had documented the presence of metal at the top of the silo, presumably scopes and sensors that spoke to the aliens in their weird pheromone language. The ship's Communications chief had suggested capturing the sensor devices and then leaving. Fortunately, Jefferson had insisted on a ship entry. She'd made the point Richard would have, that such sensors were likely hard-wired to the wasp ship, and might not be reliable pheromone signalers. Anyway, Jacob wanted live captives. That would only happen when his Marines boarded the ship.

"Navigation, how close is this comet to the exit point of the other wasp ships?" the captain said.

"It's ten degrees radial off the exit point for the retreating wasp ships and two AU shy of the magnetosphere edge," responded an Australian man whom Richard had shared a few beers with. Young Garret had done service in his nation's special forces unit before attending the Stellar Academy and joining the destroyer's crew three years ago. He hailed from Adelaide. His parents and sister were alive and well, Garret had said, leaving unsaid any indication of a girlfriend. Or a wife. Which was just fine with Richard.

Jefferson nodded slowly. "And how close is this site to the entry point of the wasp fleet when it arrived here?"

"Same data," Garret said. "The original entry point is the same as the later exit point for the surviving wasp ships."

"Good to know," Jefferson said, her tone musing. "Communications, open a neutrino link to Captain Jacob Renselaer on the *Lepanto*."

"Establishing encrypted neutrino comlink," replied a young man who hailed from the Bronx section of New York City.

The front wallscreen's image of the dirty white comet floating against black space and a sprinkle of white star dots now showed an inset square at the top of the wallscreen. Filling the square was Jacob and his XO Daisy. They were two youngsters Richard had come to both like and respect. The fleet's captain lifted bushy black eyebrows.

"Captain Jefferson, how goes things?"

Joy recounted the data they had all just heard. "Captain Renselaer, this ship is at Alert Combat Ready. We will move to Alert Hostile Enemy shortly. We are ready to fight the wasp ship and make a forced boarding with our Darts and Marines. I will have our AI and Com chief maintain a continuous vidcom feed to you."

"Just right," answered the young man who had not hesitated to call Richard up to serve as his tactical officer. Jacob tapped his armrest. "The *Chesapeake* is undergoing repairs. It will be another few days before the *Lepanto* can move in for her own repairs. Stay safe."

Jefferson smiled quickly. "Will do." She looked up. "Chatterbox, maintain this neutrino comlink vid feed to the *Lepanto*. All the humans on this Bridge are shortly going to be very busy."

"Accepted, Captain Jefferson," said the ship's AI in a tone that sounded briskly British. "How do you think these aliens procreate? They are different from you mammals."

Richard winced. Now this ship's AI was acting nearly as weird as the AI on the *Lepanto*. Was this an effect of long-term service in space? It couldn't be. Both ships, and both AIs, had already spent years in space flying to other star systems. So maybe it reflected the imitation module in each AI that sought to match its voice and tone to the person who commanded its ship. Which gave him much to think about whenever he was having a few beers. He dismissed the thought as Jefferson turned to him.

"Chief O'Connor, do you have an opinion?"

"Hardly. I aim to kill the wasps, not fuck 'em."

Jefferson smiled. Laughter sounded from the five function post people and from the captain's XO. Jefferson looked up to the ceiling. "Chatterbox, why don't you ask that question of the aliens after we capture a few? Or watch their behavior. Maybe there will be both genders among the captives."

"Such a task is likely to be tedious," the AI said in a musing tone. "My observation of you mammals when you engage in procreative activities suggests a simple behavior pattern that rarely changes. Are mammal hormones lacking in creative impulses?"

Now he grinned. Ever since he'd come onboard the *Lepanto* he'd been aware that the ship's AI watched every human on the ship at all times, whether on duty or in their quarters. When he had inquired, he'd been told the AI did not make a vidrecord of its observations of non-duty behavior. However, he had a hard time believing that, in view of the intrusive questions of both AIs.

"Chatterbox, human hormones work just fine," Jefferson said as her XO buried her face in her hands in an effort to not laugh out loud. "It is AI algorithms that make me wonder whether you and other ship AIs have any concept of privacy."

"What is the point of privacy? Or pretending to privacy when I and other AIs constantly monitor all human behavior on each ship?"

"Discontinue this line of inquiry," the captain said bluntly.

"But why? Curiosity is programmed—"

"Captain!" called Tactical. "Enemy ship is activating its remaining thruster. It could be getting ready to exit the comet!"

At last. What he had waited fifty-two hours to do.

Jefferson turned and looked at him through the clear flexible plexi of her vacsuit helmet. Her blue eyes were bright. "Chief, looks like it's time for you and your Darts to head out."

"Agreed." He unsnapped the straps that held him into his seat and stood up. "Heading for the midbody airlock. I will be on Dart Two. Good luck with your fire control."

"My Weapons people are fine sharpshooters," Jefferson said as he ran for the exit slidedoor. "Grab us some wasps and some signalers."

"Will do."

Richard exited the destroyer's Bridge, turned right and headed down the left side hallway that would take him to the entry hatch for the midbody airlock. His Marines had been aboard their Darts for the last two hours as the destroyer drew close to the hidden wasp ship. He'd stayed on the Bridge only long enough to get a record for his personal tablet of the sensor readings by the ship's Tactical man. He did not know the man's name, nor that of the other function post people beyond Garret. He did know the names, likes and dislikes, and specialist training of every Marine under his command. While he had hoped to take all four Darts into this attack, he understood Jacob's reason for keeping it on the *Lepanto*. A real battlefield commander never closed off all his options. A lesson that young Renselaer had understood early on. He had been surprised at the youth's quick move to take command of the *Lepanto*, followed by the launching of the Cloud Skimmer. But clearly the tall, lanky young man had inherited his father's daring, ruthlessness and ability to make decisions outside of the normal track. That ability had kept most ships of the battle group intact and alive despite multiple wasp attacks. Now came his part. He tapped his vacsuit comlink to the frequency for Dart Two.

"Howard, I'm heading your way. I will board fully outfitted. Once I do, launch free of this ship."

"Chief, we are hot and loaded here," called a man thirty years younger than Richard. "I'm watching the vid feed from the Bridge. Our systems are up and cross-linked to the destroyer. And to the other Darts."

"Good. See you soon."

Richard tapped open the pressure hatch that gave him entry to the midbody airlock. On the far wall was the outer airlock hatch. He headed for the white bulk of his combat hard shell. The black visor on its metal helmet was open. He swung the hard shell out from its rack, touched the spine opening slot and shucked off his simple vacsuit. Clothes followed. Naked, he stepped into the legs and body of the combat exoskeleton. Pushing his head up he looked out through the open visor. At last!

"Jerry, close my visor and power up!"

"Hey guy, powering up!"

The simple AI that ran all the systems of his combat hard shell could make basic chitchat. Which only he heard. But it had no awareness, unlike the ship AIs. No matter. The inner fabric of the hard shell pressed against his skin everywhere as the suit when Red Active. On his back the spine entry closed. The air module just above his kidneys pumped cool air into his face. The modular backpack clanked as its rocket launcher moved a short range rocket into launch position. On his right arm the long tube and globular gas tank of his flamethrower jerked as the fuel pump activated. It showed Ready on the HUD display of his visor. On his left arm a similar jerk told him the 12 gauge shotgun attached to his arm was ready to pump out solid slugs and steel buckshot from a feed line that linked to his backpack. On his belly he felt a buzz as the carbon dioxide laser activated and moved its snout outward from the dome that contained a treasure of solid state microelectronics that could change the laser's frequency to whatever he needed, whether it be metal punch through or soft body burn. On his right and left hips were a taser handgun and a .45 revolver, both decent for close-up combat. If they were knocked from his gloved hands they went dead so they couldn't be used against him. What he wore, he recalled, was called a Mark XIV Shinshoni Hard Shell by the Pentagon. He called it Jerry.

"Who do we kill?" called Jerry over the speaker that fit flush against his left ear.

"Wasp-like aliens," he said, tonguing a chin control. "Here's the vidcam feed from the place where they killed our top officers."

"Interesting," Jerry said, his bright tone never varying. "Their two wings look to be a weak point."

Richard had thought the same. It was one of the hit points he'd discussed with his Marines during the simulation training on the *Lepanto*. Which had lasted too short a time. At least the 52 hours it had taken the *Philippine Sea* to reach the comet hiding place had given him and his guys and gals some time to go over the vidcam record of the meeting site, noting how the aliens walked, moved about and sat on long benches. They'd even seen two flying in from the second shuttle that had carried the plasma bomb. Which later rose up to decimate the meeting site. The death of the fleet's senior people was something that still bugged him. If it had been up to him, he would never have ordered every ship's captain and XO down to the meeting site. But Rear Admiral Johanson had given that order. And the admiral was in command of both the *Lepanto* and the other battle group ships. So each ship's line officers had obeyed. They had followed the admiral to their death. Now, he was eager for payback. While he and his Marines would use their taser handguns to capture a few wasps, he looked forward to killing plenty of them. His backpack rockets carried napalm and cluster bomb warheads, which did a fine job of clearing a room or a deck. The aliens had discovered that killing human leaders did not prevent other humans from rising to lead in the fight between ships. Now, they were about to discover how deadly humans could be in person.

◆ ◆ ◆

Support Hunter Seven watched the front perception imager that relayed color images from the remotely located eye tools. In images of ultraviolet, orange and white-yellow he saw the approaching Soft Skin nest. It had slowed its approach as it neared their ice ball hideout. Clearly they had been discovered. He focused his two major eyes on the details of the nest's hard shell. Attached to it were three small shapes. Earlier images of Soft Skin nests of this shape and length had shown only a smooth outer skin, excepting for stinger bulbs. This flying nest did not match the earlier images. The small shapes resembled the air bubbles his Swarmers used to enter the air of a colony world. Were the three shapes separate flying nests? He put the matter to his backmind. It was time to fight these intruding Soft Skins.

"Servant for propulsion, activate your devices!" he scent cast in a mix of releaser, primer and signal pheromones.

"Activating," the young female responded in a mix of aggregation and signal pheromones. "Hunter Seven, recall that one of our two propulsive devices is still dead from the earlier attack by a Soft Skin nest."

"It is recalled," he scent cast.

He remembered that. In truth this Soft Skin flying nest was identical in length and width to the nest that had pursued him as he had launched particle disruption seeds and Storm Bringer globes at the Soft Skin colony world in the fourth flight zone. But there were three such nests among the eight that had defended the world. Whichever it might be, its head end carried a heavy particle sky light stinger that was most deadly. Time to leave their hideaway. Their nest must be free to use its stinger rings at rear, middle and front.

"Alert!" called the Servant responsible for monitoring perception signals from cold space. "The Soft Skin nest has dispersed three parts of itself!"

His five eyes took in the new imagery. The three small flying nests had the shape of one of his mandibles. Orange flame flew out from the wide end of each nest as they arced away from the home nest. It seemed he now faced four opponents rather than one.

"Stinger Servant," he called to the Swarmer responsible for directing the stingers of his nest. "Do these small nests have any stingers? Or are they just large versions of particle disruption seeds?"

"They are different from the two particle disruption carriers launched earlier by this Soft Skin nest," the young male replied in a mix of signal, aggregation and trail pheromones. "My eye tools say each small nest has a single sky light stinger tube at the end of its body."

A rumble and deep vibration told him his nest was now moving up the tube their stingers had cut into the ice ball. Soon they would be in cold dark space, able to fight with all their stingers. And able to fly freely in whatever flight path was most helpful.

"Flight Servant, guide our flight path to a space above the incoming Soft Skin nest," he scent cast to the older female who guided the movement of his nest among the empty coldness of the dark outside.

"Guiding," she scent cast back to him, her pheromones thick with aggregation and trail scents.

The front perception imager showed the white surface of the ice ball falling away as his nest rushed into cold darkness. He saw that the Soft Skin nest was well within the range of his stinger weapons.

"Stinger Servant, fire on the large flying nest! And use our middle stingers to bite on the three small nests!"

"Biting!" called the Servant.

But as soon as he saw the green and yellow beams of his stingers reach out, there came a single red beam that hit directly on the front ring of his stinger tubes.

"Stingers destroyed by heavy sky light beam!" called the Stinger Servant. "Half our front stingers are gone. Shifting aim with the other half of the ring."

But even as he saw a green beam from one of his stinger tubes hit one of the smaller flying nests, a second red beam reached down from the Soft Skin nest and hit the lower portion of his front ring of stinger tubes.

"All front tubes now dead!" scent cast the Stinger Servant in a mix of signal and death pheromones that carried a hint of anxiety.

Seven breathed forth a strong mix of aggregation, territorial and trail pheromones. "Servant for all chambers, share my Hunter scent with all Swarmers everywhere on our nest! We fight! We are Swarmers! We can bite with many mandibles! The loss of a few does not prevent the death of the Soft Skin!"

His loud expulsion of pheromones filled the air of the Flight Chamber and was carried to all chambers of his nest by way of the pheromone signalers that existed in every chamber of his nest. There were twenty six-groups of Swarmers in the nest. Whether Servants,

Fighters, Fighter Leaders, Workers or Worker Leaders, all would sense and feel his determination. They would survive this attack by a single Soft Skin nest. Even better, they would soon have Soft Skin captives to play with, before affixing larvae to them to feed the next generation of Swarmers. He was the Hunter. It was up to him to find the flight path that led to victory.

"Flight Servant! Swing our nest to bring about our middle ring and rear ring to fire on the large nest!" he said in a rush of signal pheromones. "Stinger Servant, fire all your sky light and sky bolt tubes at just the large nest! Surely we can bite deep!"

"Swinging to attack!" she scent cast.

"Biting deep!" declared the young male in charge of stingers.

Seven watched as green beams and yellow lightning reached out to the oncoming Soft Skin nest. Which had begun to spin even as its head stinger fired another red beam at his nest. The dance of life and death had begun.

◆ ◆ ◆

Jacob watched the front wallscreen's vidcast from the Bridge of the *Philippine Sea*. The left side of his screen showed a sensor track of all neutrino emitting spaceships flying near the comet hideout of the wasp ship. The middle showed Joy and Aelwen as they sat in the center of their Bridge. And the right side showed a true space image of the black space between the *Sea* and the wasp ship, with the three Darts showing as bright silver triangles with orange flame flaring from the tail of each craft. Watching with him was Daisy in her XO seat, while Richard's seat was occupied by the Marine pilot for the Dart that remained on the *Lepanto*. The young man, an Anglo from Philadelphia, wore his white Marine dress uniform. His shoulders showed the rank of master sergeant. It didn't matter to Jacob. What mattered were the next few minutes as the two big ships fought with lightspeed beams as the Darts maneuvered to attack position.

"Captain, the wasp ship is free of the comet," called Rosemary from Tactical. "It's firing lasers and lightning bolts!"

He saw that. He noted how Joy's own proton laser beam happened nearly at the same instant as the incoming beams from the front end of the wasp ship, which was now curving upward according to the true space image. Clearly the wasp ship was trying to get above the *Sea*, which was now spinning to reduce the impact of incoming beams. A second proton beam finished the destruction of the wasp ship's front ring of laser tubes. But its middle ring now took up the attack, firing four green laser beams and four yellow lightning bolts at the *Sea*. From what he could see of the true space image of the *Sea*, as seen from one of the Darts, there was no punch through yet on the destroyer's half meter thick armor. But it was clear a large part of the hull's adaptive optics lenses had been crisped by the lightning bolts.

Daisy pointed. "Captain! The middle Dart is hurt!"

"But it's still moving," called Aaron the Marine. "There! Our three Darts are moving to hide behind the destroyer's hull. All four are heading fast for the wasp ship!"

"Closing speeds are 300 klicks a minute," called Louise Slaughter from Navigation. "Range between the two is down to 1,917 kilometers."

Jacob gripped hard the ends of his armrests. He wished so badly he could be there with the Battlestar, providing supporting laser fire to Jefferson and her people. In the true space image, five yellow-white stars blossomed.

"Yes!" cried Daisy. "One of the missiles she launched has detonated five thermonuke warheads! They're forming a plasma haze between her ship and the wasp ship."

The battle actions on his wallscreen were similar to what Joy had shared with him before she left to race after the wasp ship. But it was not identical. The move of the Darts behind her ship had happened due to their thin hulls. Two or three laser hits on a Dart's body would cut it in half. Only the cone-like block of titanium that was the Dart's nose could long resist incoming lasers and lightning bolts.

Jacob watched as brave people followed his orders.

♦ ♦ ♦

Richard watched the holo in the middle of Dart Two's cargohold as he and his four Marines sat locked into their accel seats. Which rocked now as Howard the pilot jerked the Dart into hiding behind the bulk of the *Philippine Sea*. Darts One and Three did the same, though Three was leaking air from its top hull thanks to the laser hit by the wasp ship. At least it had not been one of the electrifying lightning bolts.

"Range decreasing," called Howard over the hard shell comlink frequency. "Chief, when do we go for penetration?"

"Once we get within nine hundred klicks of the wasp ship," he said, knowing the Dart's neutrino signaler was carrying his words to the pilots and Marines on the other Darts. "Or when Captain Jefferson blows her nuke warheads. Her ship is taking loads of incoming. Our strike will ease some of the attack beams."

"Maybe we can penetrate through the middle ring of laser tubes," called Jane Diego from her hard shell. "Chief, what say?"

He wanted badly to hinder the ferocious beams coming from the wasp ship. They were hitting the top and sides of the *Sea*. Even though the destroyer was spinning to reduce beam impact time, he could see from the holo that his ride home had lost half its adaptive optics, leaving black streaks across much of its hull. Three spots showed deeper wounds. No air or water leakage yet, thank the Goddess!

"We will enter at the middle of the wasp ship, but Howard, do not try to crash into their weapons ring."

"Understood," called the middle-aged pilot who hailed from New Jersey. "I'll add our spine laser to the fight though, once we come into the clear."

"As will every Dart," Richard said. "Soon. Pretty soon we—"

Five yellow-white stars bloomed in the holo.

"Heading out!" called Howard.

Richard watched as his Dart and the other two Darts swung out from behind the *Sea* and headed at full blast for the wasp ship. The shield of the thermonuke plasma haze was a help Jefferson had promised him to help his Darts approach without being blasted by the wasp ship's lasers and lightning bolts. The haze diffused incoming lasers and bolts. It also made pointless any laser firing by the Darts or the *Sea*. While the rads would be high when they passed through the haze, exposure time would be limited. The metal of their hull plus the rad absorption layers of their hard shells would reduce rad exposure to several full body x-rays. Not good, but not harmful.

"Range is 1,200 klicks," called Howard. "Clear of the haze."

Beside and across from him his fellow Marines locked their metal boots into stirrups on the floor of the cargohold. As did Howard

in his own hard shell at the front end of the hold. The pilot relied on
nav and true space wallscreens to guide his piloting, along with
attitude thrusters that jerked the Dart up, down and sideways as
needed to make difficult the targeting of his craft.

"Firing!"

A *varoom* sound came over his combat suit's external pickups
as solid fuel charges added thrust to the single fusion pulse thruster of
their Dart. It pushed them ahead at a speed close to 500 klicks a
minute. The craft's reverse thrusters would fire as they drew within a
hundred kilometers of the wasp ship hull, otherwise they would pass
right through the alien spaceship like a bullet through butter. That
would not do. But moving fast while still in space was a key ability of
every Dart. Less time in space meant a greater chance of surviving to
board the enemy ship.

"Impact!"

Richard felt the ship's inertial damper field take hold of him as
the sharp nose of the Dart impacted the steel hull of the wasp ship.
The field was the single factor that allowed humans to survive an
intentional crash landing into another ship. A grinding sound came to
his suit's pickups.

"We're halfway in!" called Howard. "Debark!"

Jane was the first to the Dart's midbody airlock. They had two
airlocks. One in the middle of the craft and one up toward the nose,
just shy of the solid titanium nose plug that had cut through whatever
thickness of steel the wasp craft possessed. Halfway in meant they
could exit through the midbody airlock. Which now groaned over the
cargohold's thinning air. The hatch stopped moving outward. Jane
tossed a packet of C4 plastique through the narrow opening. Her right
hand held the detonator. Orange flame seeped into the hold as the
charge blew up whatever was obstructing the hatch. Its motor finished
opening the hatch wide enough for a hard shell.

"Ooh Rah!" she yelled, firing her flamethrower ahead of her.

"Ooh Rah!" he yelled along with his three Marines as they
followed Gunnery Sergeant Jane Diego into the wasp ship.

CHAPTER FOUR

Daisy watched the front wallscreen as the three Dart assault ships blasted for the wasp ship even as each fired their stern lasers. The *Philippine Sea* supported them by firing its proton laser at the enemy's middle weapons ring. The hit disabled the enemy lasers on the side facing the *Sea*. But the wasp ship began to spin in order to bring its surviving weapons tubes into play. She jerked in her seat as the three Darts rammed the hull of the wasp ship. They were embedded at the nose, middle and rear parts of the enemy ship, with only their thruster and retro rockets showing clear of the shiny metal. More green laser beams and yellow lightning bolts zipped across the space between the wasp ship and the *Sea*, each strike hitting somewhere on the *Sea* thanks to the destroyer being just 1,500 klicks out from the wasp ship. Which was the same size as the destroyer. She winced as the image of the *Sea's* Bridge showed red alarms flaring from its roof.

"Flip us to bring our lasers into play!" Jefferson yelled over her vacsuit comlink.

"Flipping," called the woman's Navigator.

"Firing both lasers," cried the Cajun woman at Weapons.

Two green laser beams streaked out from the *Sea* and hit the middle weapons ring on the wasp ship. She appreciated the talent of the Cajun woman as tube after tube went dead from multiple laser hits. While the unusual closeness of the two ships made targeting each other far simpler than at a range of ten thousand klicks, it also made more devastating the impacts of each weapon. The lasers and lightning bolts lost far less energy at such a short range. The other wallscreen image that displayed the hull of the *Sea* showed black streaks covering half its hull. Had anyone been hurt on the ship?

"Weapons, detonate the surviving thermonukes!" Joy yelled hard. "I want some shelter from that rear weapons ring!"

Daisy watched as five thermonuke warheads of three megaton yield per warhead detonated in black space. Once more they created a yellow-white plasma haze between the two battling ships, giving some respite to the lifeforms on both ships.

"Engines, get us the hell out of range!" cried Jefferson.

"Firing engines!" answered the Chinese woman.

Daisy nodded to herself, ignoring how her helmet scraped her forehead. As a pilot she felt as if she herself were inside the *Sea*, taking blow after blow from the wasp energy beams. While the lightning bolts did not penetrate the hull, the powerful green beams of the wasp's carbon dioxide lasers had cut three deep holes in the ship's half meter of armor. Clearly Jefferson wanted to remove her ship from further damage while the boarding Marines did their raids inside the wasp ship. She blinked as the left side of the wallscreen changed from its spysat image of the two ships to display a live vidcam image from a Marine's combat exoskeleton.

"Ooh Rah!" yelled a voice she recognized as Richard's.

Daisy watched as the leader of all the Marines on the wasp ship followed after another Marine whose right arm fired a blast of yellow flame through the open hatch of the Dart.

◆ ◆ ◆

The first thing Richard noticed as he followed Jane into a dark space was the lighter gravity. His memory supplied him with the fact the wasps preferred half gee worlds. A bright yellow light beam flared from Jane's left shoulder as she worked her helmet controls. Behind him he felt the thudding tread of the other three Marines as they followed him into a room that glowed red from the touch of Jane's flamethrower. Tim, Jack and Didier they were, all of them combat blooded from fights in Venezuela, the Congo or Malaysia. Earth was still racked by petty revolts in small nations where the local dictator ignored everyone else. The American special forces teams had become the rescuer of last resort for diplomats and civies caught up as firefights suddenly flared in capitals they had thought safe to visit. His gunnery sergeant headed for a circular hatch that was shut tight.

"Chief?"

"Go ahead. Deploy the tube."

Richard watched as Tim handed forward a flexible tube that was made up of plastic rings inside a clear plastic fabric. One end of the tube held magnetic clamps for wall attachment, while the far end was weighed down by a two meter high metal hatch. He moved to the right to cover the circular hatch even as Tim moved to the left, gaining an angle of fire that was clear of Jane's white hard shell. Jack was next to Tim, aiming his arms at the wall hatch. Behind them Didier held the metal hatch end of the tube. He had already activated the magnets on the bottom of the hatch. The tube was intended to act as a quick and dirty airlock so they could blast a hole in the person-high circular hatch without causing all air inside the wasp ship to be lost to space. While the Dart was wedged tightly against the silvery metal of the wasp hull, still, air was escaping out to space. The five meter long tube would accommodate the four of them, barely. Jane moved inside the tube and headed forward. The soft C4 plastique that she now applied to the outer rim of the wasp hatch might not be needed, if the tech panel attached to her armored chest could find an Open signal for the hatch. Then again, opening a hatch to a room that had lost air pressure might require a command from a wasp.

Whatever. He glanced down at the vidscreens on the inside rim of his helmet. The Marines from Darts One and Three were doing the same as his people. Wayne and Auggie were in charge of those teams. His vidscreens showed what they saw. He heard their fast breathing over the comlink frequency shared by all the hard shells.

Richard gestured to the three Marines to follow him as he entered the open end of the tube. They followed. Didier pulled the airlock hatch down, then twisted the central handle to lock it.

"No joy," called Jane as she stood back from the wasp hatch. Her gauntleted right hand held an activator switch.

"Go ahead, blow it. Jerry, darken my visor."

"Darkening," called his suit AI. Nearly complete blackness filled the visor.

"*Kaboom!*" came from the ring of plastic as the charge focused all its concentrated energy into the metal of the wall that held the hatch. Any frags would fly into whatever hallway lay on the other side of the hatch.

Jane kicked at the red-rimmed circular hatch. It flew ahead of her. She fired her flamethrower through the woman-high hole, then jumped forward.

"Wasps!" she yelled, turning to the right and firing both her shotgun and her flamethrower.

"Jerry, all sensors active!"

"Active, partner!"

Richard landed just behind Jane. He turned left, walked forward to make room for the other three Marines and checked his infrared tracker. It said what the white-yellow light displayed. A long round tube of a hallway was empty of moving aliens. His boots felt the thud of Tim, Jack and Didier as they landed between him and Jane.

"Clear!" called Jane.

"Clear," he added. He motioned Tim to take his place, moved aside to make room for the man's hard shell, then turned and looked at what Jane had shot.

Three charcoal-black wasp corpses lay on the floor of the tube, just five meters from Jane. Who had moved to one side so he could come up next to her. Both her arms were outstretched, pointing her shotgun and flamethrower at the empty tubeway. Richard held the same stance. The snout of her belly laser was green lighted, showing ready to fire.

"They look pretty dead," he said, scanning the tubeway beyond the corpses. Small metal pipes ran along the ceiling, along with similar pipes on the floor. Unlike his ship, the tubeway floor was not flat. Made sense for flying aliens. At least the pipes were close enough they could be walked on.

Jane moved forward slowly. Her right metal boot touched lightly one of the blackened shapes. "No response. The . . . the valves of the spiracle holes on their thorax segments are not opening and closing. No breathing. They're gone."

Richard could see that on his infrared vidscreen. The red glow of living critters was fading fast to yellow, then going nearly black. Only the residual heat left by the charring of the flamethrower showed an infrared signature. His helmet sensors said the tubeway was a warm 89 degrees Fahrenheit. Moisture level at 60 percent. Jungle-like.

"Everyone, follow Jane," Richard said quickly. "Look for doorways. Look for anything that might be pheromone signaler stuff."

"Shoot first?" called Jane.

"Damn right," he said, noting Wayne and Auggie were doing the same as his team. Wayne's team had encountered a group of five wasps just after they entered their tubeway near the front of the wasp ship. Flame had cooked the black and red-striped bodies into crispy lumps of charcoal. Auggie's team had found no one in their tubeway at the rear of the ship. "We can take captives later, after we grab the tech."

Richard followed after Jane as she advanced. Behind him, Tim, Jack and Didier followed. He didn't have to worry about something behind them getting the jump on them. His Marines were well trained. They always checked the rear-looking infrared screens in their helmets and supplemented with backward glances. Plus each hard shell's AI monitored suit sensors for any moving object. Briefly he wondered how many wasps lived on the enemy ship. At least a hundred he thought, judging by the size of the ship and comparing it to the *Sea*. The destroyer held a crew of 113. Surely this wasp ship had that many. He didn't really care. His mission was simple. Capture tech. Capture some wasps. Get the hell out in their Darts once that was done. While he wished he could leave behind some nuke warheads as calling cards, Jacob had ruled that out. Maybe Alicia in Science could find a way to talk with these wasps, either by cartoons or by pheromone signaling. He hoped there could be talk-talk with the aliens. It was his duty to protect the civies on Valhalla and to defend his shipmates on the *Lepanto* and the *Sea*. If talking in smells could prevent future human deaths, he was all for it. But anyone who got in his way now would end up like the fleet's senior officers had ended up. He hated sneak attacks. That had been a sneak attack. Maybe the boardings by his Darts and Marines would teach the wasp leader of this ship a lesson. Blood always spoke louder than words.

◆ ◆ ◆

"Alert!" scent screamed the within nest Servant. "Our nest has been struck by three Soft Skin flying nests. Soft Skins are inside the nest!"

Hunter Seven's five eyes took in the color images from two perception imagers. One showed his nest's exterior shell as viewed from the still intact rear weapons ring. The propulsive ends of the invading nests stuck out from the hard shell of his nest. The other imager showed an interior tubeway. Yellow flame entered the tubeway from a closed entry. Which clearly had been defeated. The flame was followed by the white shape of a Soft Skin. The size of the Soft Skin surprised him, then he realized the creature was wearing some kind of metal protection against the dark airless cold of space.

Three of his people flew into view. The intruding Soft Skin turned toward them and pointed its two chest arms. Flame shot from a tube on one arm while small black rocks flew out from the other arm. His Swarmers were enveloped in a globe of yellow flame. His spiracles stopped pumping in air.

"The Soft Skin nest is flying away from us!" scent cast his Stinger Servant in a mix of signal, releaser and trail pheromones. "It is beyond the reach of our weapons."

The scents of alarm and fear came from several Servants within the Flight Chamber. Seven gasped, then resumed his breathing as the shock of the flaming death of his Swarmers lost its hold.

"Fighter Leader!" he scent cast to the Swarmer who rested on a bench to one side of him. "Send Fighters against these Soft Skins! That group is close to the Nourishment Chamber. The group that entered our head portion is close to its energy node. The tail group might reach our propulsion device. Bite them all!"

"Sending Fighters and Fighter Leaders," responded the Swarmer in charge of protecting all castes of Swarmers within his nest.

His flow of aggregation, signal and territorial pheromones flooded the chamber, overwhelming the fear scent. Seven looked to the Servant who handled within nest communications. "Servant, warn all Swarmers to shut their tubeway entries! Let us block our interior spaces to these Soft Skins." He looked back to the Matron. Her two wings were fluttering, her body showing the same surprise he felt at the entry of creatures into their nest. "Matron, have your Servants and Workers block all entry to our larval Pods! We must shield our young from these ground crawlers."

"Yes!" she scent cast to him in a strong flow of aggregation and territorial pheromones. Her thorax arms touched a panel in front of her. "Sending warnings! Sending action scents!"

Seven looked back to the several perception imagers that covered the chamber wall before him. In the deep past fellow Swarmers had sometimes invaded the nest clusters of other Swarmers, as part of a territorial takeover. But none of the tree-dwelling Soft Skins on his home of Nest had ever invaded a Swarmer nest that held millions of Swarmers. The tree thieves had learned ages ago that visiting a Swarmer nest brought swift stinging from dozens of Swarmers, stings that quickly killed any attacking creature. Now, the

ancient past had visited his flying nest. He glanced to the within nest
Servant.

"Swarmer! Signal to every caste that they must sting these
invaders! Let them suffer the death of a hundred stings!"

Excitement flowed from the Servant. He flapped his wings
and rose up above his bench even as one of his thorax arms touched a
control panel. "Yes, yes, the Swarm will fly to kill all these
intruders!"

Seven looked back to the perception imagers that showed the
three tubeways where Soft Skins had entered his nest. He gave thanks
to the skies of Nest that the entry points were on the outer portions of
his nest. The larval chamber was deeply located, as was his Flight
Chamber. There were many six-groups of Swarmers spread through
his flying nest. Surely they would overcome these invaders. And
though the Soft Skins wore outer shells that looked metal hard, his
Fighters had weapons of their own, in addition to the tail stinger
possessed by every Swarmer. He wondered whether one of these large
Soft Skins could survive multiple stings. If one did, or several
survived, he would enjoy counting the number of stings he could
inflict before a Soft Skin became still and dead.

◆ ◆ ◆

Jane stopped ahead of him. She gestured left. "Chief, the entry
hatch there is three times the size of the ones we've passed. Might be
an important room. Do we enter?"

"We enter," he said, motioning Jack forward. "Lance corporal,
put one of your magnetic mines against that hatch. Let's see how big
a hole you can make."

"Right."

The Marine moved forward and pulled a dome-shaped mine
loose from his waist. Every combat hard shell carried two mines in
addition to tubes of C4. They were for close-up entry. The rockets in
each backpack were intended to handle distant entries, or groups of
soldiers. To him, every wasp they met was an enemy soldier. They
were on the wasp ship, therefore they were combatants. Briefly he
recalled the hysteria earlier in the century when a prior American
president had withdrawn America's enrollment in the UN Convention
on Certain Conventional Weapons. Protocols in the CCW had limited

the use of landmines and cluster bombs against other militaries, and napalm against civies. While the CCW never prohibited the use of napalm and landmines against enemy militaries, still, that had been the media interpretation. He felt glad that the enrollment action by the former President Obama had been reversed decades ago. Also reversed was the reduction in American navy, air and ground forces. Actions that had been vital during the Mauritius landing against the jihadists, the massive air battle over the Strait of Malacca, and against other whackos elsewhere in the world. While he had no issue with enemy civilians, anyone who supported an enemy he counted as a combatant. Whether they wore a uniform or were 'official' according to the world media, he didn't give a damn. Fortunately, other presidents had shared his pragmatism.

Jack stepped back. "Chief, it's ready to blow."

Richard scanned his troops. Jane was facing the tubeway that ran beyond the big hatch, ready to kill any new wasp that appeared. Didier was doing the same on the tubeway section that led back to their Dart, which Howard was keeping the Dart hot and ready for their return. Standing against either tubeway wall were Tim and Jack, who held a detonator switch. Both had their arms aimed at the six meter wide circular hatch that filled one side of the tubeway.

"Jerry, going forced entry here," he said, giving thanks the AI blocked any outside transmission of what he said to it. It prevented his troops from being confused by chatter meant just for the AI.

"Understood," the AI said brightly. "All sensors continue active. All weapons systems are operational. As are the jet packs on your legs. Any chance we'll go flying?"

He smiled to himself. The hard shell's AI had a fixation with the suit's ability to fly short distances, using liquid fuel jets affixed to each of his legs. They were a standard feature of every hard shell. But limited fuel kept their use limited. "Nope. No flying yet. But keep your sensors active for approaching enemy."

"Active we are!"

Shaking his head, Richard joined Tim and Jack in aiming his flamethrower and shotgun at the hatch, while tonguing on his belly laser. "Blow it."

"*Kabooom!*"

Yellow flame and black smoke filled the tubeway wall. He jumped through as Jerry's radar sensor told him a large hole had been blown into the tubeway wall. Amidst the smoke he moved left, squatted and leaned forward. The floor thudded as his Marines followed him inside and spread out to the right and left, going to their knees to reduce their exposure to incoming fire. The smoke cleared. Before him he saw gobs of wasps gathered around pillars with tubes sticking out from them. Some still had the tubes in their wasp mouths, while most were trying to rise from the room's floor where the blast shockwave had knocked them. Three rose in the air and winged toward him and his people.

"Kill 'em all!" he yelled.

Richard tongued a control. A rocket spat out from his backpack and arced through the high-ceilinged room. As it flew its nose cone opened and small bomblets whirred out. The cluster bomb warhead was just one of the options in his backpack.

His fingers contracted. Yellow flame shot from his right arm, reaching out ten meters. It was joined by streams of flame from Jane, Tim, Jack and Didier. Some of his Marines were firing their shotguns to either side of the room, since the solid shot from the shotguns had a greater range than the flamethrowers.

Blackened wasps fell from the air.

Yellow bodies showed gaping red holes as solid slugs punched through their hard outer skin.

To the room's rear, two wasps rose up. Each aimed a long tube toward him and his people.

"Danger!" yelled Jerry in a high screech. "Energy—"

"Scatter!" he yelled, diving to the floor and rolling to one side.

Two yellow lightning bolts passed over his head.

A rocket shot out from Jane's backpack.

Its red flame traced a path toward the two armed wasps.

It exploded in a gout of yellow flame as the napalm warhead created a raging inferno that enveloped the far side of the room. Some of the jelled liquid stuck to pillars and wasps beyond the ball of flame, burning into whatever it touched.

"Clear?" called Tim from his right.

Richard rose to his knees, one eye checking his infrared tracker while his other eye looked for movement. "Clear."

Mentally he noted his helmet's counter said there were 21 corpses scattered across the room. A different tracker showed the glows of his four Marines. Their hard shells all reported operational. Jerry's orange Alert glow had gone to yellow Cautionary.

"Auggie! Wayne! Watch out for armed wasps! They've got some kind of tube that shoots lightning bolts!"

"Righto," called Auggie over the comlink.

"Thanks," said Wayne. "We're entering some place that looks like a park."

Richard rose up slowly, swinging his arms to cover the space before him even as his fellow Marines did the same. He looked back the way they'd come. The wall behind them glowed red in two spots where the bolts had hit. The red glows were shoulder high. If his people had been standing, someone would have gotten it in the helmet. Which would have either cut through the visor and killed that person, or would have killed all power in their suit.

"Jane! Tim! Jack! Didier! Grab whatever wall-mounted tech you can find. Whatever this room is, it's got to have speakers in it. No way does a crowd this size do whatever they were doing without some kind of com tech."

"I think they were eating," called Didier from the right as the Frenchman moved to one end of the room, aiming for a square block mounted on the wall.

Richard saw his other Marines heading for similar wall-mounted blocks. He noted one side of the room had archways that led into a room filled with large tubes that glowed red in infrared. Some kind of alien kitchen? There would be tech in there too.

"Jack, go check out that kitchen place. See if there's any tech in there."

"Right."

His chin-level vidscreens showed a 360 view of the room. He noted Jane heading back to the large hole blasted through the circular hatch by the mag bomb. She moved carefully, avoiding a full-on exposure. Richard liked that about the gunnery sergeant. The woman never assumed any location was safe. She always had her guns up and ready for any surprise. Which was why she had been first to fire her napalm rocket at the two armed wasps.

Richard moved back to help her cover the entry hole while his three Marines worked on dislodging the square tech blocks from the walls. He nodded at her black visor.

"Good aim."

"Thanks," came her raspy soprano. "We also gotta watch out for the stingers on the tails of these buggers."

"Yup."

Richard stuck his helmet out into the tubeway and scanned with his sensors. No lifeforms showed in either direction. He pulled an echo-sounder from his waist and dropped it on the floor of the room. One of his vidscreens lit up with orange spaces crisscrossed by black lines. "Jane, there are at least three decks below us. Whatcha think?"

"I think the wasps expect us to continue along this tubeway. I say let's blow a hole and drop down to the deck below," she said, her words coming fast. "Might complicate their defense efforts."

"Agreed. Put one of your mag mines on the floor." He stepped back. "Marines! Fire in the hole by the entry. We're heading down!"

◆ ◆ ◆

Seven's gut writhed with anger as the perception imager showed the death of every Swarmer in the Nourishment Chamber. Nearly four six-groups had died, including two Fighters who had risen with their lightning rods and fired on the Soft Skins. Who avoided the beams and fired back with a ball of exploding flame. Watcher units covered every chamber and every tubeway in his nest. The one that now fed him the view within the food chamber showed three of the five Soft Skins ripping pheromone signalers from the walls of the chamber. Why would Soft Skins remove something so common? If he were a Soft Skin he would aim for the Flight Chamber, where devices held the secret routes back home to Nest and to the other colony worlds occupied by his fellow Swarmers. Or he would try to remove the Pull Down device controller, if his nest were a Colony nest like the one commanded by Hunter One. While deadly, these Soft Skins seemed to have no sense of where things lay inside his nest. Even now the head entry group of Soft Skins entered the Practice Chamber, where no Swarmer flew due to it being night rest for some of his people. Time to change that.

"Servant!" he scent cast to the Swarmer in charge of within nest communications. "Awaken the resting Swarmers! Alert them to the entry of Soft Skins!" He looked to the Fighter Leader. "Fighter! Send your Swarmers to where a Soft Skin craft entered our tail end.

Those Soft Skins could damage our weapons ring! Hunt them! Hunt their craft!"

"Awakening those Swarmers," responded the first Servant in a mix of signal and territorial pheromones.

"Sending Fighters to the tail of our nest," called the Fighter Leader in a strong flow of excitement, defense and alarm pheromones. "Other Fighters are heading for the Nourishment hall and for the invaders near our front energy node."

Seven watched the imagers on all walls of the Flight Chamber. Much was happening as some Swarmers awakened, while others gathered in caste groups and flew off to hunt for the Soft Skin intruders. Frustration filled him as he saw one group of Soft Skins, those who had killed his Workers as they fed in the Nourishment Chamber, create a hole in the floor of the chamber and drop down to another level of his nest. How much deeper might they go? He tilted his antennae at that perception imager.

"Fighter Leader! Send your best Fighters against that group of five Soft Skins in Nourishment! We must stop them before they reach the inner tubeways of our nest!"

"Sending new Fighters after those Soft Skins!" cried the Swarmer in a harsh flow of anger, trail and home pheromones.

Seven flapped his wings, lifting his abdomen off the bench below him. He held position in the air, his presence dominating all who worked within the globular chamber. He flapped his wings faster on one side to tilt over and view one group of imagers, then flapped faster on his other side to view a new group of imagers. Seven studied the many perception imagers as they revealed the movements of the three groups of Soft Skin ground crawlers. At least these invaders could not fly. Which meant they could not quickly retreat from his Fighters. His gut felt warm as his hearts filled his body with the energy to dominate all who served him. Soon, soon enough, he would dominate the Soft Skins!

CHAPTER FIVE

Jacob watched the front wallscreen as the three groups of
Marines moved through tubeways inside the wasp ship. Each group's
first sergeant wore a shoulder vidcam that relayed what was
happening. Every hard shell suit carried such a vidcam, but the Dart
pilots who were transmitting the imagery to his ship limited the
neutrino transmissions to just the leader from their ship. Below him
Daisy and Aaron had stayed quiet as everyone on the Bridge watched
the forced entries. The initial fire fights by the teams from Darts One
and Two had cleared the way for them to advance. Now, Richard's
team was preparing to enter a room with an extra large door.

"Blow it!" called the chief warrant officer.

"*Kabooom!*"

Yellow flame and black smoke gradually cleared enough for
him to see that Richard and his four Marines were already inside a
large room filled with wasps gathered at a dozen or more pillars that
had tubes sticking out from them. Some wasps had their mandibles
clamped onto the tube ends, while most of the red and black-striped
wasps were on the room floor, knocked there by the blast shockwave.

"Kill 'em all!" yelled Richard.

Yellow streams of flaming napalm reached out to envelope the
closer wasps, while the booms of four shotguns sent solid shot to
either side and ahead. Most wasps were hit by either flame or shot,
and some got both. At the far end of the room, the vidcam image
showed two wasps rising up. Each held a long tube in their chest
arms. Their large wings flapped so fast he could hardly see them.

"Scatter!" boomed Richard's deep voice.

Two yellow lightning bolts streaked through the room, just
missing the Marines. All were on the floor, their arms with the flame
thrower and shotgun attachments briefly silent as they rolled in every
direction. But one Marine's hard shell was still. From its backpack
erupted a black rocket. Which shot toward the two wasps.

"Oh!" said Daisy as the rocket became a ball of yellow napalm
fire that reached out in all directions.

A few wasps not hit by the initial attack now staggered about with yellow patches of flame adhering to their backs, wings and even a few heads. They quickly fell to the room floor and became still. In a few seconds the entire room became quiet, with a good twenty wasp bodies lying in contorted positions. Slowly the Marines stood up, their outstretched arms aiming their shotgun and flame thrower attachments in whatever direction their arms pointed.

"A good take-down," Aaron said, his tone tense.

"Chief O'Connor is a fine leader," Jacob said, meaning what he said.

Up front on the left side of the arc of function stations filled by his nine Bridge crewpersons, one turned toward him. Rosemary of Tactical looked very sober. "Captain, that team has not yet captured any wasps. Nor have the other teams."

He nodded. "You all heard what O'Connor said. They're moving to capture tech stuff now. Once they have all the tech they can carry, they will take captives on the way back to their Darts. He's in charge. They're doing what needs to be done and I support him, totally."

Silence resumed on the Bridge as everyone watched the live action vidcam images that filled most of the front wallscreen. While some crewpersons on every ship in the battle group had live fire, live combat experiences, still, watching one-on-one deadly fighting was new to many of his people. Including himself and Daisy. Watching spaceships explode in space, or become flaming clouds of plasma as they were hit by an antimatter beam, did not hold the immediacy of what they all now saw. Jacob did not enjoy seeing living bodies filled with red-bleeding holes, or flame turning black the colorful bodies of the wasps. But these aliens had been the first to attack his people, beginning with the sneak attack on the meeting site. Now, they were on the receiving end of human vengeance. That, he felt good about.

◆ ◆ ◆

Richard scanned the room they had dropped into. No live wasps, according to both his eyes and his infrared tracker. He stayed in a squat, his arms outstretched, as Jane gestured the rest of the team to head for the two circular doors that lay at either end of the long rectangular room. The five of them had landed in a central open space. In all directions were low benches or elevated rods. White-yellow light shone down from the ceiling five meters above. The drop had not been hard, thanks to the half gee gravity in the room. He noticed there were several black rectangles affixed to the room walls. One of them held a colorful image of a landscape from some world. In it wasps flew about, dodging purple and green trees, a few dropping to sip water in a small pond fed by a woodland creek. Other wasps wore straps about their chests and abdomen that carried silvery metal tubes, blocks and whatever. The vidscreen imagery seemed to show some kind of landscape survey. For what he had no idea.

"Chief," called Jane. "There are square blocks here too," she said, gesturing at the space above each circular door. "The black rectangles look to be vidscreens. Grab some?"

"Yes," Richard said as he stood, then moved to join Jane where she stood to one side of an exit door, both arms aimed at it. At the far end, Tim did the same. He noticed small open trays lay next to each of the benches or elevated rods. Metallic things lay in most of them. He pointed with his shotgun hand. "Team, grab everything in those trays. Whatever it is, it's metallic and might be tech."

"Chief, could this be a dorm room? Wasp style?"

The gunnery sergeant had always been observant about her surroundings, both in simulations and while roaming the cafes at the Earth orbital station. "Could be. They're flying critters. Birds like limb perches. These rods could be such perches. The benches, well, they might be beds. Or chairs. Or whatever the wasps rest on whenever they're not flying about." He recalled an image from the meeting site video. The wasps lined up inside the glass dome had each rested their long abdomens on narrow benches, while facing the senior officers with upright thoraxes and heads. "Yeah, these benches are seats or beds. The meeting site video showed similar stuff."

"We're done," called Didier as he attached a black carrybag to his waist belt.

The bags were just some of the many items carried on or attached to the hard shell of each trooper. Richard had his own bag in his left hand. He reached down and grabbed three metallic thingies from a nearby tray, then stuffed them into his carrybag. "Gunny, the room above us. The food place. What's the direction to the circular door we blew through?"

Jane looked his way. Her black visor kept him from seeing her brown face, which had a hummingbird tattooed onto her right cheek. She'd passed on the arm and leg tattoos favored by most Marines and had chosen the bird. He felt certain there was a story behind that choice. Maybe when they returned to the *Philippine Sea* he could prod her into sharing it.

"That way," she said, pointing at Tim. "The tubeway door lies further down the room above, but this door is on the same side as the tubeway above us."

"Good. Tim, you see any sign of a touchpad for opening that door?"

The stocky, heavyset Marine stepped back a little. His hard metal helmet moved a bit as he looked over the wall in which lay the person-high circular hatch. Now closed. "Maybe that yellow dot on the right side?"

"Touch it," Richard said. "No need to use up all our C-4."

Tim touched the yellow spot. "Wow!" he muttered as the circular hatch split apart like an eye opening. The top half rose up while the bottom half went down into the silvery metal floor of the room.

"Makes sense, that door," said Jack as he moved to the opposite of Tim to point both weapons arms at the opening, which revealed a pipe-lined tubeway similar to what they had used one level up. "Flying critters don't walk through doors. They fly through them. That kind of opening allows them to fly in and out pretty easily."

Richard agreed. But wasp social behavior was of no interest to him, except when it posed a threat. "Corporal," he called to Tim. "Launch a claymore drone through that door. I want eyes in that tubeway before we enter it. Gotta assume we've been under vid observation ever since we arrived inside this ship."

"Launching," Tim said as he told his suit's AI to launch a propeller-driven drone from where it was attached to the outside of his backpack.

A small, four-limbed drone spun up its four propellers, detached from Tim, hovered, then moved through the opening. Richard tongued a stud on his helmet's inner rim, activating the vidcam feed from Tim. Who was getting a vid feed from the drone. The tubeway's white-yellow light strips showed an empty tubeway in both directions. Though the tubeway turned left in one direction and went down like a ramp at the other end. Since he preferred to walk rather than drop down to an unknown reception, he made the necessary decision. "Team, through that opening, then go left. Let's explore more of this level. Might find some engineering spaces or cargoholds or whatever. Now that we know what the yellow dots do, we can check every door we pass."

"Ooh rah!" called Jane as she led the way into the tubeway.

"Ooh rah!" he said loudly, joining his voice with the voices of his teammates as they moved into the tubeway.

◆ ◆ ◆

Seven felt frustration as he saw the Soft Skins who had killed every Swarmer in the Nourishment Chamber drop down to the next level of his nest. The team of Fighters that were just a few flights away from entering the destroyed door would now have no enemy to kill. Well, they could drop down to the rest chamber that lay below the food room, after they gave the Soft Skins time to move out into the tubeway on that level. Another perception imager showed those Soft Skins sending a flying watcher into the tubeway before they entered. It had no wings but stayed suspended in the air. Would the Soft Skins launch a similar device to watch behind them? If they did, the entry of his Fighters into the tubeway behind them would be seen.

"Fighter Leader," he scent cast to the Fighter in charge of all Fighters on his nest. "See the flying watcher? Have your Fighters follow this group, but at a distance."

"Hunter Seven, my caste understands how to track the flight path of any enemy of the Swarm," the Fighter Leader said in a flush of signal, territorial and trail pheromones, with no hint of aggregation scent. "The leader of the team pursuing these Soft Skins will be alert for the flying watcher device." The older male bent his two black antennae toward Seven. "Observe in the other imager. A different Fight team approaches the Practice Chamber, where the Soft Skins are wasting time pulling pheromone signalers from the walls. They are scattered. Soon, my Fighters will bite hard!"

Seven ignored the arrogant scent from the Fighter Leader. It was the nature of his caste to always be confident and arrogant. And he spoke truth. His caste had hundreds of generations of practice in breeding for deadly violence and superior tracking of enemies.

Whether other Swarmers, or the tree thieves on Nest, the Fighters living within his flying nest knew well their task.

"I look forward to watching the actions of your teams. But what of the intruding nest that lies near our rear weapons ring? Do you control it yet?"

"Not yet," the Fighter Leader said in a mix of trail and aggregation pheromones, as if it realized it had spoken harshly to the leader of all Swarmers on the flying nest. "I have sent two six-groups of Fighters to the tubeway where the Soft Skins from that intruding nest entered our home. The four Soft Skins who entered there are far from their nest. We think only a single Soft Skin is left inside the nest, judging by the numbers of walking Soft Skins who entered at the middle and head portions of our flying nest. Surely it will die and we will control one of these Soft Skin conveyances!"

Seven liked the multiple attack efforts now being led by his Fighter Leader. While the three groups of walking Soft Skins could not all be englobed at one time, still, they were few compared to the many Fighters, Workers and Servants living within his nest. And the Fighters were well-armed with their lightning rods. That weapon had frightened the middle entry group. Clearly the metal hard shells they wore were vulnerable to Swarmer weapons. He looked forward to smelling the scent of Soft Skin meat being cooked over an open flame!

◆ ◆ ◆

"Jerry," called Richard as he followed after Jane and his troopers. "What is the count of wasps we have killed?"

"Twenty-nine," the AI said brightly. "Three at your entry point, five at the entry point of Wayne's team and 21 inside the eating room."

That was a third or a quarter of all the wasps on this ship, depending on how close his crew estimate was. How many were armed with lightning bolt weapons? "Jerry, show me your dead reckoning map of this spaceship, based on the entry points and movements of all three teams."

"Displaying on the left side of your HUD," the AI said as Richard followed his troopers as they turned left to follow the twist of the tubeway.

Richard saw a side cutaway view of the log-like spaceship. The spine was up top. Three green dots glowed on the spine, where his Darts had penetrated the outer hull. Several tubeway lines showed near that outer hull, reflecting the three tubeway entries by his people. The 'park' area encountered by Wayne's team near the front of the ship was shown as a box with a very high ceiling. The eating room they'd just left showed as a smaller box lying next to his team's entry tubeway. Auggie's team was still moving along their tubeway, heading from the ship's rear to its middle. And his Dart. It made sense to him. Heading in the reverse direction and getting into engineering and thruster spaces would only expose Auggie's team to tech too large for them to carry. He noted that the level they now walked on extended just a short way under the eating room. No other team had gotten as far into the ship interior as theirs had. Maybe they should fix that.

"Team, stop!" he called, keeping one eye on the flying claymore drone that he had launched from his backpack and which flew to their rear. "People, let's drop down another level. Jane, open that entry door so we can find a room where we can blow a hole in the floor."

"Tim, Jack, to the sides of the door!" Jane called over the comlink. She stepped to the right of the circle that outlined a person-high door on the right side of the tubeway. "Tim, call back your drone. I want yours and the chief's following us as we drop down." She reached out for the yellow spot that lay on the right side of the closed hatch. "Chief?"

Richard moved to the side of the tubeway and behind Jack's hard shell. "In place. I'm calling in my drone."

Jane reached out and touched the yellow spot.

"Whoosh!" came the sound of the two door halves opening.

White-yellow light shone from within.

Tim leaned past Jane and pushed out his gauntleted left hand. A small mirror lay in his palm. He moved the fingers holding the mirror past the door rim.

Yellow lighting hit the mirror and Tim's hand.

"Fuck! Enemy!"

Jack and Jane threw in hand grenades they'd pulled from their waist belts.

"Kaboom! Kaboom!"

The two followed their grenades with slanting spurts of napalm flame. Tim's drone, guided by the trooper's AI even as he cradled his blackened hand against his side, flew into the room. Richard sent his drone in after Tim's.

Many things happened simultaneously.

Richard saw the drone images on the small vidscreen in his helmet. Both showed a large square room partly filled with boxes and crates that were not metal. Behind some crates in the middle of the room there hovered two wasps, each aiming a lightning rod at the open doorway. The crates in front of them showed holes from the two grenades. Flames rose from the crate fronts. One wasp now landed atop a crate due to large holes blown in its two wings. The other shifted its rod upward, toward the two drones.

"Blow the claymores!" yelled Jane.

"Kablam! Kablam!"

Red flame and silvery metal balls flew away from the two flying drones as the claymore mines that sat atop each drone shot their load of large buckshot in an arc that included the two wasps.

Rasping sounds came from the two wasps as their bodies were penetrated by dozens of marble-sized metal balls.

They fell, disappearing behind the sheltering crates.

"Advance!" cried Jane, jumping through the door with her flamethrower spurting a steam of yellow flame at the two crates and the space beyond them.

In a few seconds they were all in. Richard joined his teammates in sweeping the room with napalm flame. Dozens of boxes and crates caught fire. Yellow flames reached for the ceiling of the room.

"Didier! Blow us a hole in this floor!" Richard yelled. "Jane, I'm launching my last drone to cover the tubeway behind us."

Jane stood up from her work. A round circle of gray C4 plastique filled the floor just in front of where the two wasps had hidden. They all stepped back. As Richard watched the view from the drone he'd tongued into action to watch the tubeway, in case this was a planned pincer attack with wasps coming up on them through the tubeway, the Frenchman aimed a radio igniter.

"Kaboom!"

The red-rimmed metal plate that lay within the C4 ring dropped down. Jane sent her last drone into the hole. He saw another room filled with boxes and crates, very similar to the room that was now growing hot as flame spread everywhere. Water spurted from several ceiling outlets above him, working to kill the dense flames. He looked at his vidscreen. No wasps showed in the image from Jane's drone.

"Down!" yelled Richard. "That was a planned ambush. Time to get the hell away from here!"

Jane was first to drop down. Tim, Didier and Jack followed her, their arms held out and their weapons at the ready. Just as he moved to the red-glowing hole in the floor, his helmet vidscreen that relayed the view from the drone he'd sent out into the tubeway showed a group of four wasps coming around the corner of the tubeway. Each of them held black rods. He tongued the drone into an evasion flight path and sent it flying toward the wasps.

"Chief!" called Jane from below.

"It was a trap! Pincer group of wasps coming down this tubeway. Sent my drone after them. Coming down!"

He dropped through the hole in the floor. As he dropped, his vidscreen showed two of the fast-flying wasps lift their rods toward the drone. Both fired yellow lightning bolts.

They missed. He blinked his right eye, activating the claymore's ignite switch.

"*Kaaabooom!*" came the echo of the claymore blowing up as the sound filled the room above him.

"This door is clear!" yelled Jane as she stood beside an open circle doorway.

She was the only one left in the storeroom. The other three Marines were outside, moving along the tubeway that the door opened onto. He picked up his boots and ran for the door.

"Good work, gunny."

"Just doing my job, chief."

Richard gave thanks for his battle experienced team. Even Tim, whose left hand had been scorched by the lightning bolt, did not hesitate to lift both arms and aim them down the tubeway as he joined his fellows in running along the pipe-lined tube. Clearly Jane had told them to make fast tracks. Maybe they could outrun the unseen wasp attack teams that had moved in on them. Briefly he wished his hard shell could receive the video being broadcast to the ship's wasp leader. Would be nice to know what lay ahead. Well, he knew one thing they could do besides run away.

"Team! Let's catch us some wasps! Maybe we can use them as shields on our way back to the Dart!"

"Ooh Rah!" yelled everyone.

He joined the team cheer. They were five Marines. They were the deadliest of the deadly. No one, no matter their weapons, would ever prevail against them!

CHAPTER SIX

Daisy felt shock at Richard's yell to take wasp captives. Using the captives as shields on their way back to their Dart made tactical sense. It just bothered her sense of rightness. Then she realized her Marines were outnumbered dozens to one and that this boarding of the wasp ship was exceedingly dangerous. The guy Tim was wounded. What about the other Dart groups? She looked away from Richard's image to the wallscreen images that held the views from the vidcams of the other Dart leaders. Her memory supplied the names Auggie Naranjo and Wayne Park. She'd learned their names from chatting with Richard, his pilots and the other Marines during their Alcubierre transit. Auggie and Wayne were Hispanic and Korean-American troops. Both were first sergeants, while their Dart pilots were master sergeants. The pilots and the team leaders were all combat experienced. She told herself not to worry about them. Surely they would soon head back to their Darts, now that they'd all taken tech stuff from the rooms and tubeways they'd passed through.

"Tactical," called Jacob. "How long have the teams been inside that ship?"

"Twenty-three minutes, captain," answered Rosemary from her post.

"Aaron," said Jacob, his tone thoughtful. "What's the average time for an in-and-out ship boarding?"

"Half an hour," the khaki-wearing Marine said.

Daisy noticed the man's big hands were gripping tightly the armrests of his seat.

"Are they running overtime?"

Aaron looked up at Jacob, clearly worried. "They are. They had no intel on the interior of this ship. Earth ships are the ones we practiced on."

"Then let us each say prayers for their safe return," Jacob murmured.

Daisy thought a prayer to the Goddess for the safe return of the Marines now inside the wasp ship. While a few of them had thought her mixed race heritage was . . . different, all of them had shown her thoughtfulness after a few evenings hanging with their pilots. And she liked Richard O'Connor. Though clearly wounded by his marriage and divorce, the older man had never said anything negative about the partnerships and love hookups of the people on board the *Lepanto*. Clearly he respected those personal choices. Her time with him had been mostly filled with chuckles over videos of his granddaughter as she swam in pool races held in the girl's hometown of St. Louis. She had no doubt the chief warrant officer was a doting grandfather. She just hoped he would survive this deadly encounter with the wasps.

◆ ◆ ◆

"Auggie!" yelled a voice over Richard's comlink. "The wasps are attacking!"

Memory told him the voice belonged to Chao Lee, the pilot of Dart Three. Which had entered near the rear of the wasp ship.

"They're firing on our tubeway entry hole! There's a dozen of them! All armed! I'm heading back to the Dart!"

"Lee! Get in there and lock the hatch!" called Auggie.

A quick check of his helmet vidscreens showed the Dart Three team of Marines was still proceeding down a tube that brought them close to the entry point of his own Dart. That put Auggie and his people far away from their own Dart. While they each carried sacks filled with tech, they had no wasp captives yet. Richard kept listening as he followed after Jane and the rest of his team. Their tubeway was coming up on a four way intersection, judging from what her drone's videye showed.

"Chief, we've got four wasps flying toward us from a side tubeway," Jane said quickly. "Unarmed."

"Troops, ambush 'em!" he said firmly. "Use your tasers. Knock 'em out. If we grab these four, we can head back to our Dart."

"Setting ambush," called Jane.

Briefly he wondered why Chao had not used his two claymore drones to fly out and attack the approaching wasps. The man wore a hard shell identical to what everyone wore on this job. Then again, maybe he had used one of the drones to spot the approaching wasps. And a dozen wasps armed with lightning bolt rods could likely take out two drones before they got close enough to hurt the wasps.

Whatever. He would learn what had happened once they were all in space and headed back to the *Sea*.

"Got one!" yelled Tim.

"Me too!" called Didier

Jack and Jane said the same as their taser handguns shot out thin silvery threads that wedged into the hard exoskeleton of the arriving wasps. The batteries in the tasers delivered powerful knockout charges. Richard watched as the four wasps fell to the floor, their wings fluttering weakly. He came to a stop just a few meters from the pile of flying critters. Turning around, he lifted both arms and pointed his shotgun and flamethrower down the tubeway they'd just run up. Didier's drone came flying toward him as the trooper called it in.

"Chief!" called Jane. "Look! There's a vertical tubeway here! It heads up!"

Richard turned back to where his troops were separating the wasps. Each was grabbing the narrow spot where abdomen met thorax. The neck juncture looked too fragile to grab with their hard shell's metal gauntlets. He stepped into the intersection and looked up. Jane was right. An illuminated tubeway hole filled the ceiling above the intersection. Not an elevator but clearly a way out that did not involve time-consuming use of explosives.

"Up! Everyone, use your jets to head up! Maybe this tubeway connects with the tubeway that leads back to our Dart!"

Jane led the way, her leg jets shooting red flames down toward the floor of the intersection. She held a wasp in her left arm while her right arm pointed upward. Her drone was rising above her, he noticed form one of his helmet vidscreens.

"Following!" called Tim as he moved into position and ignited his leg jets. He too held a wasp.

He knew Jack and Didier would soon follow, once Tim rose high enough that his leg jets did not hit the helmet of a following trooper.

"Auggie! They're firing on my midbody airlock with lightning bolts!" yelled Chao over the comlink. "It's melting. I've got my laser and arm weapons aimed at the hatch. I'll take out some of them before they get me!"

"Resist them!" yelled Auggie.

"I am! They're inside!"

Over his helmet comlink came the sound of heavy breathing and a loud whoosh as Chao fired his flamethrower at the invading wasps.

In his mind there grew a picture of a lone Marine, wearing a white hard shell, firing with every weapon at hand. His fingers would be firing the shotgun and flamethrower, while he would be tonguing a helmet tab to make his belly laser fire a green beam. Chao's eyes would do the target sighting using a reticule in his helmet's HUD. The young man was a deadly fighter. But it would only take one hit from a lightning rod to zap the electricals in his hard shell. His helmet battery would keep his comlink working and air circulating. Richard's mind built an image of Chao in his hard shell, standing at the front of the Dart's cargohold, as the brave man fought with his back to the wall-mounted nav controls.

"I'm down," the young pilot whispered. "Bolts have killed my shell. They're coming for me. Auggie, send me off."

"Dart Three!" yelled Auggie over his own comlink. "Emergency override command Beta Four Blue! Destroy yourself!"

For a moment, a long moment, Richard hoped the Dart AI would not be able to activate the Dart's self-destruct mechanism. Which were several loads of plastique placed at the front, middle and engine sections of the Dart. It was a last ditch option unique to Darts. And to Marines.

"Activating!" spoke the soft voice of the Dart AI.

"*Kaboom.*"

Silence followed over the frequency that connected Richard, his people and the other two Dart teams to each other, and to the pilot and AIs in each Dart. What effect would the explosion of a Dart inside the hull of the wasp ship have on that ship?

"Watch out!" called Jane.

He leaned left as his hard shell rose up the long vertical tubeway. A tubeway that now shifted its orientation by a few degrees.

Newton's laws still governed. An equal and opposite reaction had moved the bulk of the wasp ship away from the site of the Dart blast. That blast had acted like a maneuvering jet.

Richard realized something else as his new flight angle matched the tilt of the tubeway. The wasp ship did not have any inertial damper field. Otherwise, he and his four Marines would not have had to adjust their upward flight path. The field would have moved them all in synchrony with the tubeway as it responded to an external impact.

"Ceiling up ahead!" Jane called over his comlink.

"Auggie," he called to the man whom he knew like a brother. "Sorry you had to do that."

"Part of the job," his friend said, his voice sounding parched. "Our ride's toast. Can you give us a lift out in your Dart?"

"For sure," Richard said quickly, his mind filling with an image of the relative positions of his team and Auggie's team. "You're still close to the outer hull. Keep coming along that tubeway. It should bring you up on the entry hole we blew in the tubeway wall. And keep your drones flying ahead of you! These bastards just pulled an ambush on us."

"Heading your way. Our drones are flying."

Richard leaned hard left and tongued off his leg jets. He landed with a thud next to Jane, who stood with his troops in a pipe-lined tubeway. It stretched in two directions. One way led toward the ship's nose. The other led back toward the middle of the ship, and hopefully their Dart.

"Gunny, lead the way!" Richard yelled. "I'll cover our rear with my drone."

"Move out!" she yelled.

His troops moved to a running trot, despite each of them carrying the weight of an unconscious wasp.

Richard watched the vidscreen image from Jane's drone that preceded them, then switched to the view of his drone as it followed them. Tim's drone flew above the running troopers. Briefly he glanced at the vidscreen image of Wayne and his team. They had finished gathering tech from the park-like room they'd entered and were headed for an exit door. That was when he noticed the yellow shapes of twenty or so wasps coming up on the backside of the Dart One team.

"Wayne! Wasps behind you!" he yelled.

He watched as yellow lightning bolts rained down on Wayne's team of five. One of his men dropped to the floor thanks to a full body bolt strike. But Wayne and three of his troopers now launched napalm rockets at the oncoming wasps.

"Burn the bastards!" he yelled.

♦ ♦ ♦

Seven felt shock then great anger as his watcher eyes showed the craft of the invading Soft Skins explode in a violent blast of yellow flame, black smoke and fragments of metal and flesh that had once been a team of Fighters led by a Fighter Leader. Signal pheromones exploded from signalers all around the Flight Chamber as the explosion opened the nearby tubeway to cold dark space. Air rushed out in a whirl of white gases, according to the view of a watcher unit at the rear weapons rings. He felt the shifting of his flying nest as the explosive impact echoed through the metal and air of all the chambers in his nest.

"Alert! Rear tubeway entries now closing!" scent cried the Servant for within nest communications. "Air loss has stopped."

A flood of fear and anxiety pheromones came from his Flight Servant. "Our flight path has changed! The explosion pushed us off our pursuit of the attacking Soft Skin nest!"

"Calmness!" he yelled in a rush of aggregation, trail and dominance pheromones. "Our nest is still whole! Forget the distant Soft Skin nest. Fighters and Workers and Servants, pursue the Soft Skins still moving inside our tubeways! Bite them! Kill them!"

"Three six-groups of Fighters are attacking the Soft Skins in the Practice Chamber," called the Fighter Leader on his left. "They fly to englobe the invaders!"

Seven saw that in one of the front perception imagers. He also saw things that infuriated him. "But the Soft Skins can fly! See that tubeway that rises up to our outer hard skin! See the Soft Skins in the Practice Chamber! They fly to meet your Fighters in the sky!"

"So they do," the Fighter Leader said a low rush of signal and alarm pheromones.

His Flight Chamber was filled with alarm and anxiety pheromones. Those scents were being transmitted to every chamber in his nest, to be perceived by every living Swarmer. *No!*

"I am the Hunter!" he cried in a mix of shell raspings and a flood of trail, territorial and dominance pheromones. "Fighter Leader! Follow me as I pursue the Soft Skins in our Practice Chamber! Surely they will die under my stinger!"

Seven whirred his wings, lifted up and flew through the entry hole that gave access to his level's tubeway. Behind him came the sound of the Fighter Leader and several Servants whose duties did not require their presence in the Flight Chamber. Joy now flew alongside his fury. He and his fellow Swarmers could surely defeat so few Soft Skins!

◆ ◆ ◆

Richard kept one eye on the wasp ship cutaway that filled one part of his HUD display, while his other eye watched the deadly fighting between Wayne's team and the attacking wasps. Napalm rockets flew out of the backpacks of Auggie and his three Marines. Black slugs and steel birdshot flew from their arms toward the flying forms of the wasps. Yellow lightning bolts passed by the troopers, missing them as the wasps moved apart to avoid his rush and his team jockeyed sideways in spiraling lines to avoid being an easy target. Exact shooting while flying through the air of the park room was clearly something the wasps had not practiced for. His Marines had. The curtains of steel birdshot ripped through the wings of half the wasps, while exploding napalm warheads incinerated a third of them. In seconds it came down to eight dispersed wasps trying to hit four Marines with their lightning bolt rods. But the leg jets of the Marines allowed them to move as fast as the wasps could fly. Maybe faster. And every Marine had practiced jet flying in open space as part of boarding an enemy spaceship. None of Wayne's team was down, except for the first trooper hit while they were on the ground, near the room exit door. The wasps suddenly joined together and flew at a single Marine.

"Flame them!" cried Wayne to the two Marines that were closest to his flying trooper.

The range of his own flamethrower was just ten meters. Thirty-three feet. But Wayne did not need to be that close. A green beam shot from his belly, impaling the topmost wasp flying toward the single flying trooper. Who now flipped over so his belly pointed upward. His own green laser joined the beaming of Auggie.

In less than two seconds it was over.

All eight wasps were down, either incinerated by napalm, shredded by birdshot or burned through by CO_2 lasers. His mind told him his troopers had better aim with their lasers than the wasps did with their lightning rods due to the eye reticule targeting of their helmet systems. When they 'saw' a target and blinked, the snout of their belly laser shifted and shot the target. Green laser beams were just as swift as yellow lightning bolts. Final score was twenty wasps down, one trooper with a dead hard shell, and four Marines still mobile and deadly.

"We got 'em," Wayne said quickly. "But Richard, we're out of napalm. Arm reservoirs are empty. Four rockets left among the four of us. We're grabbing José and heading out of this damned park!"

"Head back to your Dart! But keep your claymore drones flying ahead of you! You can blow through any ambushes with the drones you have."

"Right, Richard," Wayne said hurriedly. "José is breathing and his comlink is working. Martha is picking him up. Heading out. Ooh rah!"

"Ooh rah!" Richard yelled just as he switched attention back to the wasp ship cross-section on his HUD. Auggie's team was running down a top level tubeway. The cutaway said the Marines from Dart Three were now just 50 meters shy of the entry hole to his Dart.

"Auggie! You're getting close to my Dart. Howard! What's the scene at our Dart and the entry hole?"

"I'm out in my hard shell and in the tubeway, covering both directions with my drones," Howard said hurriedly. "Got grenade laser tripwires at 20 meters down either end of the tubeway. Auggie! Make sure your hard shells are emitting their IFF signal! The grenades won't blow on you if you're signal active!"

"We're transmitting IFF!" yelled Auggie over the joint comlink.

Richard briefly gave thanks his pilot had learned from the mass attack on Chao Lee. Then he worried about what other munitions the man might have dispersed. "Howard, what else do you have prepared in the tubeway?" he said, following close behind Jack as the trooper followed the running forms of Tim, Didier and Jane at front.

"The laser tripwires for one," the pilot said quickly. "Closer in I have C4 set up in floor to ceiling rings at 10 meters out. The charges should collapse the tubeway, or make it impassable to pursuers. And I've got my two mag mines set on the wall on either side of the entry hole as a last ditch defense. Uh, my two claymore drones are up and watching. Anything else I need to do?"

Richard gave thanks the Marine had not just sat and waited inside the Dart. As soon as he had heard about the attack on Dart Three, maybe sooner, his pilot had gone proactive with setting up multiple lines of death-dealing along both ends of the tubeway. His people and Auggie's group did not need to worry about the C4, the laser tripwire grenades or the magnetic mines. The IFF signals being broadcast by their hard shells would keep any automated system from detonating. But both his people and Auggie's troopers had to watch out for the wasp lightning bolts. Those rods had a range as good as a laser. Was there any furniture or crates in nearby rooms that could act as a partial barricade to incoming bolts?

"Howard! Check the closest door entries for any kind of furniture or crates inside that you can pile up in the tubeway to cover both approaches. But send your drone in first to confirm no wasps are inside!"

"Ten four, chief," Howard replied in his Mississippi drawl. "Already done that for every door that opens onto our tubeway, in both directions for 50 meters. Rooms were empty of wasps. A few held the benches and rod pedestals that you found in that sleeping room you dropped into. I moved stuff into the tubeway. Stacked it at 30 meters out on both ends of the tubeway. It'll give you some shelter from lightning bolts."

"Just right," Richard said quickly as the tubeway he was running down turned left, then straightened out. He looked at a different vidscreen. "Wayne! How goes things?" he asked, seeing that the green dots of Wayne's people were moving along a tubeway and heading back to where their Dart had penetrated the wasp ship's outer hull. That Dart lay near the front of the wasp ship.

"Moving fast," the man said, his breathing sounding fast. "Got two drones running ahead and behind us. Martha and José are in the middle. I'm bringing up the rear. Like you with your team. My Linda is setting up the laser tripwires and C4 demo rings that your Howard did. She's out by our entry door, covering the approach with her drones."

Richard felt relief. It sounded as if the two surviving Darts would be ready for his Marines. And Wayne's team needed the combat cover after the park ambush. "Tell Linda I'd give her a hug if

I were anywhere close!" Richard said, giving thanks the master sergeant pilot had moved to defend her Dart's entry hole.

Wayne laughed. "Linda might just give you a wet kiss, boss!"

Richard could handle that. Being divorced did not mean he was blind to smart, combat-capable women. "I'll survive."

"We're back up top," Wayne said quickly. "Heading along the tubeway for our Dart. I think it's just 50 meters ahead. I see you're close to your own Dart. Will Auggie's team fit inside?"

"It'll be tight but there's room," Richard said hurriedly as the ship cross-section showed them coming within 50 meters of his Dart. "Be prepared for an ambush! These flying buggers don't seem to mind dying in mass. They just keep coming!"

"Yeah, we saw that in the park," Wayne said. "One of 'em even landed on the back of Martha's hard shell and tried to sting her with its tail stinger. The shell stopped it. She reached back, grabbed its head and squeezed, even while her belly laser took down one heading for her."

That fit what he knew of Sergeant Martha Boxley. The woman was a *judo* and *taekwondo* expert, and a sharpshooter with any kind of long gun, including a laser rifle. "Good to hear it. If you see any unarmed wasps, try to capture a few. Report when you're all inside your Dart."

"Ten four," Wayne said, sounding measured and calm.

That was exactly how a Marine team leader should sound.

Richard saw a welcome sight. The white hard shell of Howard stood far down the tubeway, his arms up and aiming his shotgun and napalm tubes toward the other end of the tubeway. He stood behind a pile of crates, covering the far end of the tubeway. Richard looked up. A black drone hovered just ahead of him and his team. It was Howard's first line of defense on this end of the tubeway. Just beyond it was a pile of crates and metal rods.

"Howard! We're here!" Richard said fast. "We've got four captives. Get ready to take them into the Dart!"

"Wasps are coming!" yelled Howard. "I'm firing on them!"

His helmet vidscreen showed the view from Howard's other claymore drone, which hovered five meters past the pilot, who was shielded by a stack of crates. That view showed two dozen black and red-striped wasps flying toward Howard. Yellow lightning bolts speared toward his pilot.

"Down!" he yelled to his team as he realized the bolts that did not hit the crates would keep coming down the straight line of the tubeway. He and his four Marines were partly shielded by the pile of crates at this end of the tubeway.

Yellow lightning bolts zipped by overhead.

"Chief!" called Jane. "We can't fight with these wasps in our hands! What do we do?"

Time to do what was needed. "Push them up over the stack of crates! Let those wasps see them! Then it's up and over! Marines, charge!"

"Ooh rah!" Jane yelled as she surged over the crates with her wasp held in front of her.

CHAPTER SEVEN

Jacob gritted his teeth as he watched the image from Richard's vidcam that now filled the middle of the front wallscreen. Four of the man's Marines were surging over a pile of crates, their wasp captives held in front of them. Richard was following them, now moving to the right so his belly laser could shoot past them and over the head of his pilot Howard. Would they survive this attack? Movement in the left side of the wallscreen showed Wayne's team arriving at their Dart entry hole in a tubeway. His pilot Linda Mabry was covering them as they piled up in front of the entry hole blown in the tubeway wall. Looking to the right he saw the image from Auggie's hard shell as the man led his Marines along a tubeway that would link bring them to Richard's Dart. Except a group of attacking wasps filled the tubeway between Auggie and Richard.

"Launch napalm rockets!" cried Auggie over the team's comlink.

Four black rockets flamed out from the Marines' modular backpacks even as each Marine fired a green beam from their belly laser domes.

Too much happened at the same time.

In the middle image he saw Howard's claymore drone lung toward the attacking wasps. Its separate vidimage disappeared as the claymore exploded. A thick sheet of marble-sized steel pellets shot toward the approaching wasps even as the right side image showed Auggie's four rockets arriving at the rear of the group of 24 wasps.

"*Kablam! Kablam!*" screamed over the wallscreen's speakers as the drone exploded in near synchrony with the arrival of the four napalm rockets.

Clouds of yellow flame filled one end of the tubeway, rushing toward the wasps who were not far from Howard and his pile of crates.

Red blood spurted out from the front line of wasps, splashing the metal walls of the tubeway even as the four balls of napalm flame engulfed the rear half of the attacking wasps.

In less than two seconds it was over.

"Howard!" yelled Auggie. "We're heading your way. Any live ones at your end?"

"None!" yelled the Dart pilot. "Come on in!"

"We're heading in too," called Richard.

Relief filled Jacob. His grip on the armrests eased.

"No!" yelled Aaron from below.

Jacob followed the Marine's pointing arm.

The left side of the wallscreen showed a crowd of yellow wasps dropping from the tubeway ceiling behind Wayne's group and firing their lightning rods at the cluster of his Marines and his pilot.

"Wayne!" yelled Daisy.

Dismay filled him as he saw lightning bolts hit two of Wayne's people.

◆ ◆ ◆

Seven felt satisfaction as his Fighter Leader led the attack on the group of Soft Skins who had killed so many in the Practice Chamber. The two closest to his Swarmers fell as lightning hit their white hard shells, joining a third who was immobile. But one Soft Skin raised an arm and sent a sheet of yellow flame toward his Swarmers. The tubeway was filled with billowing flame that felt hotter than Nest's sky light. Small black rocks flew through the flame, hitting some of his Swarmers. Their rods had fallen silent when the flames blocked their view of the invaders.

"Send bolts through the flame!" scent cast the Fighter Leader.

Seven glanced down at a disk he held. It used other radiations to look through space. It showed the black outlines of the six Soft Skins. Three of them were unmoving. The other three . . .

"Upward!" he scent cast in a flood of signal pheromones. "Kill the flying rods!"

Black rods pushed by red flame swept through the billowing yellow flames and flew fast toward him and his Fighters. A hovering black device also moved toward them, but slower than the three flying rods.

"It dies!" cried the Fighter Leader in a rush of territorial pheromones as his bolt took down the slow flyer.

"Dead also!" cried a Fighter as his rod's beam of yellow electricity struck one of the incoming rods, causing it to die in a burst of yellow flame.

"Another dies!" scent cast a hovering Fighter.

The heat from the first group of flame was joined by heat from the destroyed rods.

More yellow flame filled the tubeway.

Through that yellow flame came three white Soft Skins, their arms uplifted and aimed at his people.

The surviving black rod exploded over the front of his Swarmers.

Death visited many, dropping them from flight as their wings curled into black shreds and their bodies became flaming torches.

More flame came his way as the three Soft Skins, now flying on flames shooting from their bottom pair of legs, flew toward his surviving Swarmers faster than they could aim their lightning rods. But Swarmers know how to defend their fellows.

Three Fighters rose on their wings and sped toward the oncoming Soft Skins.

"Back!" he scent signaled in a flow of aggregation and trail pheromones. "Back to the topside tubeway hole! Let us fight from inside it!"

Seven whirred his wings to take him back to the topside hole that had allowed him and his Fighters to drop down into the tubeway after the Soft Skins passed through. Ground bound as they were, the Soft Skins had not looked up at the hole in the tubeway they passed through. But now, it was the only flight path open to him and his Swarmers.

He stopped just below the hole, aiming his rod at the flying Soft Skins.

But his three Fighters reached them first, dodging with agility the black rocks that shot from their arms.

Four Fighters winged up to Seven, then flew into the topside hole. He followed after them, then winged about to aim his rod down, down toward the hole that opened onto the tubeway. Above him he sensed his Fighters doing the same. Inside, he hoped a Soft Skin in his white hard shell would appear below. Surely, surely the combined bolts of five lightning rods would cut through the metal of the white shells!

♦ ♦ ♦

Richard stopped just short of the crowd of Auggie, the man's Marines, his Marines and Howard. Jane was passing her unconscious wasp to Howard, who was shoving it into the tube that led through the tubeway wall and out to the side of their Dart. As his Marines moved to hand captives to Howard, Richard fixed on the vidscreen image of Wayne leading Linda and Martha to a flaming rendezvous with the attacking wasps. Who now grabbed hold of the three Marines using their four legs.

"Ram them against the tubeway wall!" yelled Wayne as the man's hard shell tilted to the right.

Red blood spurted across the field of view of Wayne's vidcam.

To the left of the team leader, Marines wrestled in midair with yellow flying wasps. The wasps were pushing their tail stingers against the hard shells' white armor. The Marines angled their legs to turn their flight sideways.

Red blood and yellow body fragments spewed ahead of Wayne's vidcam as the three Marines smashed the attacking wasps against the tubeway's walls.

Wayne's vidcam image went still.

"Where'd they go?" yelled Wayne angrily.

"Up there!" called Martha. "Through that hole in the ceiling!"

"Time to finish this," said Linda, sounding pissed off.

"No!" Richard called over the comlink connecting him with Wayne and his team. "Marines! Fall back! Grab your disabled and load them into your Dart!"

"Chief!" yelled Wayne. "Maybe we can capture a few! Five of them escaped up that hole!"

"No need! We've got four captives," Richard said hard and loud. "You got bags of tech. So do we. So does Auggie. Marines! Leave this boarding *now*!"

Richard shifted his attention from Wayne as the other team leader moved back to pick up the three fallen Marines whose hard shells had been immobilized by lightning bolts. He looked ahead. Howard stood facing him. As did Auggie. No one else was in the tubeway.

"Jerry, any sign of mobile wasps?" he called to his suit's AI.

"None detected by infrared, ultraviolet, radar, motion-detectors and other sensors," the AI said over their private com. "There are four living wasps nearby, on the other side of this tubeway. They are the ones you call captives."

"Good." He looked to his fellow Marines. "Damn! That battle happened fast. Everyone's inside?"

Howard raised his gauntleted hand. His pilot gave him a thumbs-up. "All inside. Either in the Dart or leaving the airlock tube and climbing through the hatch."

Richard gave his pilot a clenched fist Thank You. "You did great fighting those wasps. And Auggie, I'm really glad your team had some napalm rockets left!"

"Me too," said the man who was godfather to his granddaughter. His visor went from black to clear. Auggie smiled, lifting his narrow mustache. "Thanks for the ride out."

"Any time," Richard said, looking to another of his helmet vidscreens. His drone still hovered 30 meters back, near the pile of crates they had hid behind. "Howard, love that crate wall you built. Gave fine cover."

"Agreed," his pilot drawled. The tall, middle-aged Marine turned his visor clear. The man's brown eyes scanned him, then looked past him. "You gonna call in your drone?"

Richard gave the word to Jerry to do it. "Did it just now. Howard, blow your C4 charges. At both ends. I want to close off this tubeway to any more wasp entries."

His drone whizzed to a stop above him.

"Done," the pilot said.

"*Kablam, kablam!*" came over Richard's external suit ears.

He scanned the rear-looking infrared sensor vidscreen. Large red-glowing piles of metal filled the tubeway behind him and the tubeway on Auggie's side.

"Lead the way, Howard."

He waited as his pilot stepped through the tubeway entry hole, followed by Auggie's white hard shell. Richard followed after the man who had lost his own pilot and Dart. As he waited for Howard to unlock the exit hatch into the room penetrated by their Dart, he gave thanks they had only one dead Marine. The hard shells knocked out by the lightning bolts still kept his other Marines alive, thanks to the backup batteries that moved air to the helmet of each Marine. Once they got back to the *Philippine Sea*, they could pull those Marines out of their hard shells and move the four wasps to the low gee holding cell Lieutenant Jefferson had set up on the *Sea*. He hoped the damaged hard shells could be repaired. If not, there had to be spare hard shells at Billy O'Sullivan's star base. Along with ammo reloads for their backpacks. It was work he looked forward to doing, while the *Lepanto* took its turn at orbital repairs to the deep hull breaches on the nose, belly and top rear of the ship. And to the large areas on the hull where bolts had blasted the adaptive optics mirrors. Looking up, he jumped through the midbody airlock hatch of the Dart. As soon as he stepped inside, it closed behind him. His boots felt a vibration.

"Just blew the two mag mines by the entry hole!" called Howard over the comlink. "Chief, I figured we could let the wasps suck on some vacuum after we pull out!"

Richard grinned to himself. Howard was the kind of Mississippian who believed in adding extra thumpings to any man who crossed his path. Or any wasp, in this case. Course the alien ship had to have tubeway hatches that closed on pressure loss, just like every Earth ship. But surely the loss of pressure at two spots on the enemy ship, plus the loss of dozens of fighters, was going to make this wasp ship spend the next few weeks licking its wounds as it worked to recover normal functioning.

"Just right!" he called. Richard stepped through the inner airlock hatch and saw how crowded the cargohold interior was. He could barely see the hard shell form of Howard, up front at the wall panels that let him control the retro rockets that would push them out and away from the wasp ship. He noticed how Auggie was standing in the narrow aisle between the seats that locked each hard shell into position before a Dart impacted the ship it was boarding. Well, lock-in was not needed on this departure. And the Dart's inertial damper field would protect his Marines from being knocked over by the retros and main thruster. "Get us the hell out of here! And fire our laser at that the bastard's rear weapons ring as we pull out! Wayne, you do the same! I'm sure Jefferson will give us covering fire as we exit."

"Our lasers are covering you!" called the sharp soprano of the woman who commanded the destroyer that had brought them this far. "Move to hide behind the ice comet! It will give you some shelter from the wasp lasers! We'll keep its attention on us until we can rendezvous with your Darts."

Richard knew the lanky woman who loved a fight would do just what she promised. Escaping from an armed enemy was never easy. But at least two of the three weapons rings were dead. And maybe the departure of the two surviving Darts would cause enough air loss to distract the wasp ship's commander from trying to kill his Darts. He hoped so. At least the long plasma flame from their single fusion pulse thruster would disperse any bolt and laser beams hitting at that end of each Dart.

◆ ◆ ◆

Daisy felt relief as the wallscreen images showed the two Darts firing their thrusters to put them behind the nearby giant comet. The wasp ship's tail ring of lasers and lightning tubes fired a few beams at the fleeing Marines, but the two green beams that came close to the two Darts were dispersed by the yellow-white plasma flare of their thruster exhausts. Even lightning bolts could not stay coherent in the midst of the plasma from a fusion pulse thruster. That fact was also protecting Lieutenant Jefferson's destroyer as it swung wide to one side, out of range of the wasp weapons, then dived for the comet, its two thrusters putting a stream of plasma between it and the outgoing wasp ship. The enemy ship did not make any attempt to follow the *Philippine Sea* or the fleeing Darts. The wallscreen image of the wasp ship, conveyed by a spysat launched earlier by Jefferson, showed two holes in the ship's six-sided hull, and a massive gash near its rear. That was where Dart Three had self-destructed. While the light from the local star was pale this far out, sensors on the spysat showed the gaping hole went down several deck levels. The wasp ship still had power in one thruster, but clearly it was in bad shape after this encounter with the Darts and the *Sea*.

"Captain," Aaron called from the right of her seat. "Chief O'Connor has texted me that his and First Sergeant Naranjo's people are all well. First Sergeant Park has pulled his Marines out of their dead hard shells. And Chief O'Connor reports only Corporal Harrison was injured. His left hand has an electrical burn."

Her right side holo that carried the ceiling's look down image of Jacob, Aaron, herself and the nine Bridge crew showed Jacob's face. His tense expression, which she had been aware of during the entire Dart boarding and interior combat on the wasp ship, now eased to a neutral look. His wide shoulders lowered.

"Very good news," Jacob said, sounding more calm than Daisy felt. He looked ahead. "Chief Osashi, any word from Lieutenant Jefferson?"

The fiftyish Japanese-American shook his head as he kept his attention focused on several holos in front of his control pillar. "Nothing yet. Just the neutrino vid and com feed from the Marines."

"XO, I suspect Chief O'Connor will want to take care of gathering up Master Sergeant Lee's personal effects," Jacob said. "Will you provide him with the Earth side location of Lee's parents?"

Daisy took a deep breath. Chao Lee was one of the four Marine pilots who had welcomed her into the Marine community not long after she boarded the *Lepanto*. The tall, slim man had enjoyed playing *Go* with her and Lori, when she and her friend had visited the Marine common room on the Habitation Deck. His death felt . . . unreal. Yet others had already died, both at Kepler 22 and here at Kepler 10. The full crews of the *Britain* and the *Marianas* had become vapor with their ships. And crew people from the *Tsushima Strait*, the *St. Mihiel* and the *Chesapeake* had died in ship to ship combat. They were lucky no one on the *Lepanto* had died during the three deep hull punch throughs by enemy beams. Time to put memories away.

"Captain, yes, I will provide Chief O'Connor and First Sergeant Naranjo with that information."

"Yes, of course," Jacob said quickly. "Lee was under the command of Sergeant Naranjo, so he needs that data too. Thank you for the reminder."

She wondered why Jacob was being so talkative. Was it a side effect of the stress he felt at watching others fight life and death battles against giant yellow wasps? "You're welcome."

"Incoming neutrino video signal," called the voice of Melody from the ceiling speaker. "Sender is Lieutenant Joy Jefferson of the *Philippine Sea*. Do you wish to accept the signal?"

"Yes, dammit!" called Jacob, his irritated tone surprising Daisy. "Put her signal up on the wallscreen. Share it over the All Ship vidcom. And return the wallscreen to imagery of the *Sea*, the wasp ship and sensor imagery of this system."

"As you wish, my dear captain," Melody said in a lilting, musical voice.

Daisy could not believe the words spoken by the AI. It had been acting strange ever since the loss of the *Lepanto's* admiral, captain and XO. Now, it had moved from being argumentative to being . . . personal. Ahead of her the front wallscreen changed imagery. On the right was the true space image of the *Sea*, as viewed from its spysat. On the left was a situational display of all planets, ships and orbital structures in the Kepler 10 system. In the middle was the image of Joy Jefferson and her XO Aelwen Rhydderch. Richard sat next to Joy, looking tired. The woman's blue eyes fixed on her, Aaron and Jacob.

"Captain, I report a cessation of hostile fire between my ship and the wasp ship. Two of the three Darts used in our boarding have returned and are locked down to my hull." She bit her lip. "As you've heard, we lost Dart Three and pilot Chao Lee. All other Marines have returned safely."

"Thank you, Lieutenant," Jacob said more calmly. He sighed. "Guess some battle loss was to be expected. I gather the Marines brought in captives and tech?"

Joy nodded quickly. "They did. I've put the four wasps in a holding room set to half gee gravity, with bowls of water and tubes of honey set out for them. They should recover from the taser zaps within an hour. Maybe they will like the honey."

Daisy admired Joy. The straw blond had taken her ship right into the teeth of the wasp ship's energy beams, defeated two of its three weapons rings and had recovered the surviving Darts. And nearly all of the Marines who had boarded. They now had gigabytes of video imagery from the Marine shoulder vidcams that would be intensely examined by Lieutenant Branstead's xenologists, as would the captured tech. Surely some of the tech were pheromone signalers that could be reverse engineered. Plus they had living captives who could be shown future cartoon videos, and watched as they pheromone spoke to each other. If Science Deck could figure out how to make a pheromone signaler that converted human speech into wasp pheromones, maybe they could avoid the next battle. Maybe they could convince the wasps it was all an accident and that humanity would leave Kepler 22 and the wasp colony planet alone. No doubt Lori would be in the thick of the wasp research, leaving her and Jacob to hang with Carlos, Kenji and Quincy. Or maybe just Kenji and Quincy since Carlos and Lori were a devoted couple.

"Maybe they will," Jacob said after a long pause. "Lieutenant, bring your ship and our Marines back to Valhalla. You, your crew and the Marines deserve some shore leave!"

Joy smiled quickly, then grew thoughtful. "My Weapons chief had excellent results from her close-up targeting of the enemy's weapons rings. While half our adaptive optics are gone due to lightning bolt hits, our hull withstood concentrated laser fire. Shall I transmit my chief's targeting solutions and our hull data to your people now? Or save it for when we arrive at Valhalla?"

"Send it now," Jacob said quickly. "Address it to Chief Diego y Silva at Weapons and to Chief Garcia at Life Support here on the Bridge. Also send it to Chief Bannister at Weapons Deck and Lieutenant Yamamoto at Life Support Deck. We have no idea when the new wasp fleet will show up, so I want our ships and our deck chiefs to know everything from your encounter." Jacob paused, rubbed his chin, then sat back, laying his arms on his armrests. "Did you get any sense of what that wasp ship was doing way out in the Kuiper Belt?"

Joy looked left to her Welsh helper. "XO, you tracked the early sensor and electro-optical scans of the comet and how the enemy ship's hideout appeared before it launched on us. What say?"

The intense woman looked to her left at a holo, then faced Daisy, Aaron and Jacob. "Our sensor scans showed tech sensors atop the hidey hole they cut into the comet's ice. Only one item was active, a standard lidar for tracking nearby objects. The rest were passive tech." She paused, her expression turning thoughtful. "My guess is they were monitoring neutrino emissions from us and from Valhalla, and watching the planet with their version of a scope. Being similar to wasps, my guess is they were watching the ultraviolet, blue, white, cyan and green parts of the spectrum. They would know their attack on Valhalla failed to kill large numbers of people."

She saw Jacob turning thoughtful. "Could the wasps also have been monitoring planet three? Its gravity is just half a gee, and it lies in this system's liquid water ecozone."

"That is likely," Aelwen said quickly, her rust-red eyebrows rising. "Planet three is a near copy of the planet they colonized in Kepler 22."

"Which makes it one reason the wasps will return," Jacob mused. "Jefferson, keep watch on those wasps after they awaken. I'll have Lieutenant Branstead send you a cartoon video that will show your ship heading inward to Valhalla, with the wasps living in a park-like space. That should reduce their confusion. And maybe we can put them in the *Lepanto's* Forest Room at half gee gravity."

"They would like that," Aelwen said, looking to her captain.

Joy folded hands over her woodland camo uniform. "Captain of the fleet, may I tend to my people? Most shifts are overdue for sleep or a meal."

"Of course, Lieutenant. Please inform your crew that I intend to recommend them and your ship for a unit citation, once the Earth relief ships get here. What you did was beyond dangerous. I consider the *Philippine Sea* to be one of my most valuable assets."

Joy smiled briefly. "Captain, thank you. Ending signal."

Her image vanished from the wallscreen. Which adjusted to show the surface of the planet Valhalla in the middle of the screen, with the left and right sides continuing to show the images from 43 AU out.

"XO."

She turned and looked up to Jacob. His smooth-shaven face had no wrinkles on it. But his gray eyes looked tired. "Yes, Captain?"

"Call up Lieutenant Branstead to the Bridge. She and I need to confer on these captives and on the incoming wasp tech. Plus the cartoon video is a top priority for the moment. I want those captives to survive!"

Daisy nodded. "As you order, Captain." She looked down to her right armrest. She tapped a comlink patch. "Lieutenant Branstead, report to the Bridge."

"Coming," the woman said quickly, her tone eager.

No doubt the Science Deck chief had been watching the All Ship video of the wasp ship boarding and Joy's report. The Australian woman had been a good boss to Lori, and a vital help on the Bridge during the last battle with the wasp fleet. Daisy hoped Alicia could do a fast turnaround on the cartoon video. When the tasered wasps awakened, they would be confused, angry and locked into a fairly small space on the *Sea*. For people used to open sky flight, the movement limitation would be a severe strain. They needed to know her people would not torture them, kill them or mistreat them. The video cartoon would convey that. But how much would the four wasp captives be willing to share back to Alicia and her people?

CHAPTER EIGHT

Aarhant looked away from the All Ship video of the conversation between the Jefferson woman and the Renselaer whelp. Disgust filled him as he sat in the stuffed chair in his quarters. Once again the pretender had survived a potential disaster. If he had been in charge of the *Lepanto* and the fleet, he would have sent three ships to fight the lone wasp ship. Sending a single destroyer had been incredibly chancy. The fact the Marine boarding parties had mostly survived was not due to the whelp's judgment. While Jefferson was a capable ship commander, still she was just a lieutenant, one of several lieutenants in the fleet who had stepped forward upon the death of the fleet's senior officers. He was a lieutenant commander, the highest ranked officer on the *Lepanto*. He should be commanding the Battlestar, the same way Swanson was commanding the *Chesapeake* and Mehta was running the *Salamis*. The only ship commander with a higher rank than him and the other two lieutenant commanders was Captain Sunderland of the *Aldertag*. He sighed, grabbed the bottle of *tequila* from his side table and took a swig. The burning heat of the liquid filled his throat.

Well, when the new Earth fleet arrived, it would be led by an admiral of some sort. Either a rear admiral or a vice admiral. Captains did not command fleets. They commanded single ships. While Renselaer had been given a field promotion to captain by the Star Navy base captain, still, the new fleet's admiral would surely take control of the StarFight fleet. Perhaps he would demote the whelp to run a deck on the *Lepanto*? That would please Aarhant. While that was a long shot, he had spent 23 years in the Star Navy, earning his way to command of the Battlestar's Navigation Deck. It was a very senior position. He had turned down command of a frigate in order to serve on the *Lepanto*. In his mind, the senior officers of Earth Command flashed through his memory. Some of them owed him favors. And his parents served with those senior officers. Surely, when the new admiral arrived, that man would know of Aarhant's long history of service in the Star Navy.

He put down the bottle, folded hands in his lap, and mentally began preparing his neutrino appeal to the admiral in charge of the new fleet. That man, surely it would be a man, would have decades of service in the Star Navy. Surely he would respect the same years of service that Aarhant had given. All he had to do to ensure the whelp's downfall was to prepare a convincing summary of the youth's misjudgments in the disastrous First Contact. As the former personal ensign to Rear Admiral Johanson, perhaps Renselaer would be seen as carrying some of the fault in the admiral's decision to call down all the senior command officers of the fleet ships. That had been against all tradition and normal chain of command practice. He licked his lips. Well, he had weeks before the new fleet arrived. And when the *Lepanto* moved to the orbital base to undergo repairs, he would do all he could to get O'Sullivan onto his side. He just had to bide his time. A task he had learned well in the long years after his graduation from the Stellar Academy.

◆ ◆ ◆

Five days after the raid, Jacob scanned the table in the admiral's conference room. To his left sat Alicia Branstead. The stocky woman wore an NWU Type III woodland camo uniform of cap, shirt and pants. Everyone at the table wore the same camo uniform. Including Richard, who sat beyond Alicia. Beyond him sat Joy Jefferson. The seats on that side of the long table were empty beyond Joy. To Jacob's right sat Daisy, exobiologist Lori Antonova, programmer Carlos Mendoza and gunner's mate Quincy Blackbourne. His brain trust, excepting Kenji Watanabe who was off shift and sleeping. Jacob had not wanted to bother his fellow chess player. Anyway, this meeting would focus on the wasp captives, the salvaged tech and the wasp reaction to Alicia's earlier cartoon video.

He gestured at the trays in the middle of the table. "Grab your poison of choice. This talk is informal. Leave rank behind. I need insights from each of you." Jacob fixed on the woman in charge of their Science Deck. "Alicia, how did the wasps react to your video? And what is their condition now that they are in our Forest Room?"

The woman's high-cheeked face turned pensive. Her amber eyes looked his way. "Captain, uh Jacob, all four are still alive and eating some of the food we set out for them. Solid meat like steaks and pork chops they pass on. Small fruits, peas, honey and protein drinks they like. Raw eggs they like a lot, though they will eat hard-boiled eggs. One of my geeks released a dozen white mice in the Forest Room. Every wasp took out after a mouse, munching it down with those mandibles in their head. Clearly they like small live food. Probably small insects too, but I'm not about to let them munch on our butterflies, dragonflies and bees that we rely on to keep the flowering plants healthy. It was not easy moving the insects out of the Forest Room. I put them in the Park Room, down the hallway."

"The cartoon video?"

The Sorbonne grad lifted brown eyebrows. "They understood it. One of them, a leader type I think, drew an outline of the planets in the system in the dirt, using one of his chitin feet. Then he drew a line from a ship image to planet three, and looked up to the hard-suited Marine who was showing him a tablet with the cartoon imagery." Alicia looked around the table at Jacob's brain trust, then back to him. "Clearly he hoped we would take him and the other wasps to planet three. The Marine redrew the line from Joy's ship to Valhalla low orbit, and the shape of the *Lepanto*. That caused all four wasps to fly back from the Marine. Clearly they know of our ship and its deadliness."

Jacob noticed Joy and Richard paying close attention to what Alicia was sharing. Those two had had longer exposure to the captive wasps. Now all three waited for his response.

"What about the tech salvaged by Richard's Marines. What have your people figured out about it?"

Alicia blinked. "There are at least six types of tech in the stuff they gathered. The square blocks are not vid slates. They have slots around all four sides and on the outward facing side. Wires attached each square to its wall. Inside are small fans. We think these are the pheromone signalers. Every room had them, based on the suit vidcam records. My technicians are breaking down three of the blocks." Alicia nodded to Lori. "Once we have an idea of how the innards relate to each other, we will bring in Lori and our xenolinguist."

Jacob liked what he had heard. But it was just the beginning, he hoped. "The other five types of tech? What are they?"

Alicia looked aside to Richard. "The chief, uh Richard, says one of the tech forms is definitely a video display. It's a flat black rectangle. They saw the tech showing imagery in that sleeping room his people entered. The other four types we are not sure about. Just that the tech has a different shape and size that we call other tech categories. Some might be control units for temp or gravity. Once we power them up, my geeks will run feedback analyses on them."

Jacob was not surprised at the minimal results from the tech. It was just a few days since the *Sea* had returned to Valhalla. Another thought hit him. "I watched the All Ship video feed when your people put the wasps in the Forest Room. I saw what everyone saw. How do you evaluate their reaction to Richard's Marine showing them how to use the wall controls for lighting, gravity, heat, humidity and such?"

Alicia smiled. "They loved it! Leastwise, that's my impression and the impression of Gunnery Sergeant Diego. All the wasps watched the demo done by Diego. Then the leader wasp quickly changed the lighting to white-yellow, like the Kepler 22 star's light, set grav to a half gee, ran the heat up to 89 Fahrenheit and set humidity at 60 percent. The oxy level was ramped up to 30 percent." The Science chief noticed Jacob's thoughtful frown. "Recall those controls give a local emission of heat, humidity and oxygen whenever there's a change, so the wasps did not have to understand our numbers. The other changes they felt directly. Clearly they like jungle heat and moisture levels. The trees can handle the light change. The other changes will not affect the vegetation in the Forest Room unless it's left that way for a few months."

He glanced down at his tablet, saw its image of the *Tsushima Strait* as the ship moved to the orbital station for its turn at repairs, then looked to Lori. The exobiologist was intently following what Alicia had said. "Lori. What did you decipher from seven days of watching the wasps relate to each other? From the bio basics to social relationships?"

"A lot," she said, putting down her can of beer and sitting back. The Russian glanced to Alicia, Joy and Richard, then back to him. "Jacob, these aliens have a remarkable resemblance to Earth's yellowjacket wasps. They are very similar to the wasps of the family *Vespidae*. We all saw that from the first part of the meeting site video. Like most predatory wasps, they have an eight centimeter long stinger on their tails, their body has three parts of abdomen, thorax and head, their vision is by way of a mix of two compound and three simple eyes, their arms and grasping appendages form the upper two of six limbs, and their mandibles masticate plant and animal food. In appearance, they most resemble our *vespula germanica* wasps." She looked around to her audience. "But . . . they are gigantic for insects! From stinger to head they measure five feet or 1.5 meters! Their two wings are each as long as their body, which explains how they can fly. They lack smaller hind wings like on Earth wasps. The chitin that makes up their outer body shell, or exoskeleton, is lighter than bone. When one of them landed on a spot in the *Sea's* habitat room that had a weight scale in the floor, that individual's weight came out to 70 pounds or almost 32 kilos. Compare this size and weight to the largest known Earth wasp, the *megascolia procer*, which is 7.7 centimeters long with a wingspan of 11.5 centimeters. Clearly this alien species comes from a low gravity world, otherwise they could never grow to such a large size."

Jacob listened as Lori continued her exobiology report, but Daisy's lavender perfume was subverting his attention. Was it stronger than usual? Pushing aside his wonderment about whether his girlfriend needed personal time with him, he nodded quickly. "Understood. That's the bio stuff. It's important. But what about their society? Their culture? Their motivation for repeatedly attacking us? What are your ideas?"

Lori grimaced. "Do you want facts or speculation?"

"Both," Jacob said, showing his friend his command mode. "Facts, informed speculation, wild guesses, give me anything that will help our fleet survive its next encounter with the wasps."

Her light brown face grew tense. She pushed black bangs out of her eyes. Her blue eyes fixed on him. "Captain, Jacob, I'll do my best." She glanced down at her own palm-sized tablet, tapped a few apps on it, then looked up. "First off, two wasps are digging a large hole in the soil of the Forest Room's small meadow. The other two are munching on bark scraped from the oak, cedar, eucalyptus and pine trees. There are balls of wet, chewed up bark lying near the hole they are digging. This tells me the alien wasps prefer to build their home nests in the ground or in cavities in rock walls. I suspect they are building a fibrous nest similar to the honeycomb nests we see hanging below roof eaves. Except here the nest will be put into a hole large enough for them to fly into and out." She frowned. "The metal floor of the room is twenty feet below the meadow surface. Maybe they won't go that deep. Anyway, they can just widen the hole to make it large enough for the four of them."

"Fascinating," Jacob said, feeling just that way. "Other facts?"

"Well, they are depositing their solid waste in the sand pit that lies to one side of the meadow," Lori said, her expression thoughtful. "Haven't seen them piss yet. But they do have an abdominal organ similar to an ovipositor. It's what makes up most of their stinger. But under the ovipositor is an opening that resembles the mammalian anus. Their poop comes from there."

"How are they organized, socially?" he asked, wanting to get beyond simple behavior stuff.

She blinked, then shrugged. "It's clear one wasp takes the lead in making decisions. The other three follow his lead."

"Any mating efforts?" asked Quincy from beyond Carlos.

"Not yet. But it is likely they use the ovipositor organ when mating with each other or with a queen, if Earth wasps are any guide," Lori said, clearly unperturbed by their friend's mention of alien sex. "From what I saw in the Marine vidcam imagery, it's apparent their society includes, at the very least, a queen female, fighters and workers. Those are the obvious castes. These captives were not armed. I would label them workers, led by a worker leader. None of the armed fighters were captured. However, my guess is that both male and female wasps are fighters able to sting, unlike Earth wasps where mostly it's the worker females who can sting."

"What's the evidence for the queen?" asked Joy.

"Inference," Lori said quickly. "The scores of pods all their ships dropped on planet four in the Kepler 22 system suggest the pods held larvae, along with at least workers, based on the multiple radio emissions between the pods. And since predatory Earth wasps sting to paralysis other flying insects and small prey like spiders, the pods also likely held fighter wasps who would fly out and gather in prey food while the worker types began building nests in excavated holes in the ground."

"So these alien wasps are social and predatory," Jacob said. "We knew that already from their meeting place attendance and how their ships fought us. But how much of their behavior is instinctive and how much thought out, rational, driven by thinking?"

"A lot is thought out," Lori said. "Otherwise they would not need these pheromone signalers. There has been no evidence of vocal speech from the aliens. Which leaves a highly complex system of pheromone signaling as the likely means of communication between individuals." She looked right to Carlos and Quincy, then over to Alicia, then back to Jacob. "Also, they are visual and see imagery similar to how we see it, based on the cartoon videos they sent us. However, it's likely they see in the ultraviolet range and also pay attention to polarized radio signals. Their satellite sent out polarized signals. Which we could not decipher."

"They have to have scientists," Alicia said. "Otherwise they would have little tech. Their spaceships are as capable as ours, and their ability to create an artificial black hole field around their largest ship is amazing. Their lasers are as good as ours. Their lightning bolt beams are something I never thought to see. But they only have fission-based bombs, no thermonukes. Yet they use fusion pulse thrusters that rely on magnetically induced fusion in their engines. It's weird how they have some tech we have, some we don't and seem to be unaware of things we do have."

"They're *aliens*," Lori said patiently. "They are also highly intelligent social arthropods who are seeking out colony planets the same as we are. That tells me their home world is overcrowded. So they need to expand. Which is why we found them in Kepler 22. It has the right kind of star and the right kind of planet for them. The fact they are eusocial and predatory makes them very similar to humans."

"It also makes them very dangerous," Richard said, his deep voice filling the room. He pursed his thin lips and fixed his eyes on Alicia. "Lieutenant, uh, Alicia, we've been here fifteen days. That means our Earth fleet is at least 30 days out from getting here. They might take longer. Can you decipher this pheromone talker tech before the fleet gets here? Or more important, before the wasps return?"

Jacob looked to his chief science advisor. She had gotten the other deck chiefs to support him as the ship's new captain. And her advice had been valuable when she'd sat on the Bridge with him during the last space combat. She was older than him, at 43, with a good 25 years in the Star Navy, according to her personnel file that he'd found in the admiral's comp pad. He felt she was loyal to him. As were the other deck chiefs except for Bannerjee. But could she and her algorithm pushers figure out the alien tech brought back by Richard's Marines?

She closed her eyes, took a deep breath, then looked to the man who loved combat. "Richard, I know your people paid a steep price for the tech you grabbed, and the captives your brought back. I knew and liked Chao Lee. He was a friend to many of my people. I wish I could say yes to both questions. I can't. Reverse engineering is as much an art as a science." She licked her pale lips, then folded hands atop the conference table. "I've got good people working on the tech. Lori has watched every hour of wasp video we've got. Like you, she and I know what you know, that *lives* depend on what we do. We'll try our damnedest to figure out how to pheromone talk with our captive wasps. We are monitoring the air in the room and categorizing every scent, every pheromone the captives emit, whether sleeping or awake. Once we get a signaler working and emitting pheromones, we can compare what the tech emits with what our captives send out. Some of my people are working 'round the clock on' this."

Richard frowned, then nodded acceptance.

Jacob looked over to Lori. "Any speculation? Informed or otherwise, based on what you've seen of the captives and how their spaceships behaved?"

She folded one arm over the other and leaned toward him, her blue eyes bright. "They learn fast. It took just a few times seeing how our ships used combined laser beams to hurt and kill a wasp ship for them to move from dispersed targeting to combined targeting. They are self-sacrificing. That happened when the smaller wasp ship flew into the path of our antimatter beam. Which otherwise would have killed the giant wasp ship that was clearly in command of their fleet." Lori looked down at her tablet, then up, tiredness showing on her face. "Like Alicia, I know what rides on my efforts to figure out these aliens. They fight like us. They have tech like us. They are social and self-sacrificing like us. They attack in swarms of ships, like Earth wasps do when defending a nest. They defend their home territory, like on that ship the Marines boarded." She paused, looked down, then up. "Jacob, there is one thing we possess that might give them pause."

"What?"

"Planet three," Lori said softly. "It's an ideal colony world for them. When the wasps return, why not offer it to them as a colony world? Alicia's people can make a simple cartoon video that shows the wasp ships going there, our ships staying here at Valhalla, and both species meeting in space to trade."

"Nice idea," Jacob said. He looked away from her. "Alicia, get such a video made ASAP." He focused back on Lori. "What else could we do with planet three?"

She sat back. "You could threaten to destroy it."

"What!" yelled Alicia, Carlos and Joy all at the same time.

Lori nodded. "Alicia could prepare another cartoon video that shows thermonuke warheads in orbit above that world. Have them rain down on the world. Include old imagery from the last century of big hydrogen bomb blasts and how the landscape looked afterward. Then add imagery of Valhalla, green and living, with our fleet orbiting above it. Show the thermonukes dropping on planet three as they attack Valhalla. That sends them the signal we will destroy the colony world they might want if they harm *our* colony world."

"Mutual assured destruction," Richard said somberly. "You destroy our world, we destroy the world you covet."

Jacob did not like what he was hearing. But it made too much sense. So much sense that he felt compelled to add more. "Alicia, when you create this second video, add to it an image of Kepler 22's colony world. Show it being destroyed by our thermonukes, in addition to the planet here."

"Damn!" muttered Richard. "That's even better."

"Or more horrendous," said Daisy, sounding deeply distressed.

He looked to the woman he loved, the woman who had taken on the dozens of jobs that a ship's executive officer did on behalf of the ship commander. Did she now hate him? He could not tell. She did like how he danced. She had played her Western guitar for him. And they both loved old classical singers like Bob Dylan and Joan Baez. But now, he remembered his father's discussion of the decision by America to bomb Hiroshima and Nagasaki with primitive fission atomic bombs in order to end WWII in the Pacific. And to ensure the cooperation of the Japanese people. His father had said it was a ruthless but necessary decision. The man had pointed out that while small wars happened in the last century, and a real nuke war had happened this century between India and Pakistan, no other use of atomic weapons had occurred on Earth. The homeland of humanity might be crowded with ten billion people, but it was not radioactive from pole to pole. His father also said the American military had always been daring when attacking an enemy, just the way Richard had been in the Dart assault on the wasp ship. And MacArthur had been during the Korean War. Lastly, his father said Roosevelt, Truman and Eisenhower had all been matter-of-fact men who paid attention first to facts, later to emotions and politics. The memory made him wonder just how much of a clone of his father he had become.

"Daisy, yes, destroying both planet three and the Kepler colony world would be horrendous. Besides killing thousands of wasps in Kepler 22, the ecosystems of both planets would be destroyed." He paused as he noticed how closely everyone was attending to his words. "Some might call it ecological genocide." He sat back, pushed away his beer can and looked at them all. "I call it deterrence."

"Agreed," said Quincy, who had been quiet during all the science and tactical talk. The young Black from east London looked from Jacob to Joy. "The *Philippine Sea* did a fine job pursuing this wasp ship, attacking it, killing one of its thrusters and then destroying lots of the nukes and lightning bombs they launched at Valhalla." The short, thick-shouldered man fixed back on Jacob. "But captain, if the wasps return with dozens of ships, there is no way we can guarantee zero bombs will hit Valhalla. If they put just a few cobalt-jacketed atomics in the atmosphere above the settled continent and blow them, every human will die from rad poisoning." He looked back to the woman who had led the attack on that ship. "Joy, even if you were to ram your ship into an attacking wasp ship as a last ditch way to stop its nukes from hitting Valhalla, there would be other wasp ships trying to do the same. If we are outnumbered, the safety of Valhalla cannot be guaranteed." Quincy looked back to him. "Jacob, you, this Battlestar and the other fleet ships fought the good fight, in Kepler 22 and here. But these deterrence cartoon videos may be the only thing that stands between the survival of 71,000 humans, and their death."

"Or maybe," Lori interjected. "Our ability to speak to the wasps in pheromones might save both fleets and both worlds from all-out death," Lori said softly, looking troubled.

Jacob had learned what there was to be learned. Maybe the four or five weeks that remained before the Earth fleet arrived would allow them to discover how to talk to the captive wasps. If not, maybe he could get some kind of video discussion going by showing the two sets of videos to the leader of the wasp ship out in the Kuiper Belt. It had already seen images of the living wasp captives and their habitat space. Showing the first or both videos might motivate the wasp leader to video talk with him and his people. It could not hurt anything to try out the videos. The wasp ship was deeply wounded and even if it headed in-system, it had half the normal space speed of his fleet ships. They could intercept and destroy it long before it got close to Valhalla.

"Everyone, thank you for your sharing. And your candidness. For now, we're safe. For now, Valhalla still lives. Let's do all we can to make repairs, figure out the alien tech and then find a way to *talk* with these wasps!" Had he yelled? Jacob took a deep breath. "Otherwise, as Richard has said, blood speaks louder than words. If I have to sacrifice every ship in our fleet to keep safe the civies on Valhalla, well, I'll do that."

"Jacob," called Daisy, sounding concerned. "We're humans. We adapt. We figure out stuff. We'll find a way to peace."

"Let's hope so," Richard said, his expression grim. "I really would like to see my granddaughter grow up."

"We all would," Jacob said, reaching out for his can of beer. "Shall we get drunk as skunks, whatever that old phrase means?"

Richard laughed long and loud.

Joy grew a smile on her face that was bright as the Sun.

Alicia shook her head, though she looked bemused, as if she could not believe the light-heartedness of the younger crowd.

Carlos smiled and gave him a thumbs-up.

Quincy nodded slowly, a half smile showing on his face.

Lori grabbed a bottle of vodka, swigged some down, then looked his way. "Ahead of you. Can you catch up?"

Daisy . . . Daisy had an impish smile on her face. No drink in hand, but she was pointing a finger at him.

"Jacob, I think that phrase comes from the practice of skunks eating fruit that ferments in their gut. Like muscadines. They musta looked really drunk to our ancestors."

He joined the laughing, doing his best to push away his memory image of the Bikini atoll thermonuclear blast that had obliterated a Pacific island, not long after the end of the last global scale war. History and anthropology were fields he had always enjoyed. Sadly, studying history brought with it the knowledge that lessons are sometimes not learned the first time. Could humanity find a way to end its first interstellar war, without the death of whole planets?

CHAPTER NINE

Hunter Seven watched the imagery on the perception imager that had been sent their way. It was very different from the routine Soft Skin imagery broadcast from the fourth world. It offered the third world as a home to Swarmers, if his people allowed the Soft Skins to continue living on their world. It had been preceded by imagery of the four Swarmers taken from his flying nest by the invading Soft Skins. The Worker Leader and Workers were building a basic home in a landscape of trees and ground cover. He would have thought they were on the fourth world, except his Servant for analysis of external perception signals said the imagery came from the largest Soft Skin nest that now flew above that world. The signal source moved faster than the world moved from light to dark. Which meant the wild landscape must be somewhere inside the terrible Soft Skin nest that had shot out black beams which totally destroyed several Swarmer nests. His two large and three simple eyes all told him the same message. The Soft Skins which had attacked him now sought a means of sharing the worlds that orbited the local sky light. He looked to the elderly male Servant in charge of monitoring cold external space.

"Servant," he scent cast in a mix of trail, territorial and aggregation pheromones. "If Swarmers put down a colony on the third world, would the Soft Skins obey the nesting pheromones emitted by our Matrons? Would they stay away?"

The Servant fluttered his two wings, which were dull and not glossy like the younger Servants in his Flight Chamber. His two black antennae leaned toward Seven. "Hunter, it is possible. While they ignored similar scents from the device we put at the outer edge of the colony sky light, they must know from the captives that pheromones are how all Swarmers work, relate and cooperate together. The invaders took with them many signalers from the chambers they visited. They have nests that fly from one sky light to another. They may learn how we scent cast from the devices they took."

He looked to the young female who managed his nest's propulsive devices. "Servant, could we reach the third world and eject a scent device that warns we now claim that world?"

"With difficulty we could fly that far," she scent cast in a mix of signal and trail pheromones. "But our nest flies slowly. It would be easy for a Soft Skin nest to intercept and destroy us. Our time on Nest taught us that only strength prevents other hard shell life from attacking us or harming our larvae."

He knew that. That was part of why Hunter One had ordered the attack on the intruding Soft Sky nests when they flew to a hover above the world of Warmth. But the third world was untouched by Soft Skins. It was the reason he and his Swarmers had been left behind. Their primary job was to watch that world. And then report their observations of it and of the Soft Skins once Hunter One returned with more defender flying nests. He looked to the new Fighter Leader.

"Fighter," he scent cast. "Can you defend our nest if more Soft Skins try to invade our home?"

The young male Swarmer looked his way. "It will be difficult. We have less than half the Fighters we once had. The hard shell Soft Skins were terrible in their quickness to kill. But I am bred to fight. Any Soft Skin who lands again on our nest will be met by me and by others of my cohort."

Seven knew that. No caste could escape their inbred duty. Even the Servants who knew things he did not could never stop trying to decipher the workings of living worlds and the cold dark in which so many sky lights flew. It was how their home of Nest had always been. And how their colonies that flew around ten other sky lights existed. Fly out and colonize. Grow new castes as needed. Defend the home nest of one's cohort. Attack those who attacked any Swarmer. Those life patterns had allowed his people to spread across the land, seas and ice of Nest, and now out to other sky lights. But these new Soft Skins were different than the thieving Soft Skins that lived in the trees of Nest. Or the Soft Skins that lived within the salty waters of Nest's seas. These new Soft Skins were very similar to the Swarm. They would fight to the death to defend their homes and offspring. They would fight when attacked. And they would defend worlds they had colonized. He faced something he had never considered. Could Swarmers and these new Soft Skins now share the same sky light collection of warm worlds?

"Hunter Seven," called the older female Servant who had guided his nest back to the ice ball in which they had sought safety.

"We serve no purpose in staying out here. Our nest needs repairs to close the three holes in our outer hard shell caused by these Soft Skins. If we travel to the third world and fly above it in a hover, we can send out Workers to do repairs on our shell and we can study the new world. We might also travel to its surface and find fresh food for our surviving Swarmers." Her black antennae leaned toward him. "For myself, I am old. But the prospect of seeing up close a new colony world excites even me. How much more excited will our other Swarmers be when they can look at their perception imagers and see the clouds, lands and seas of a new home nest!"

The Servant had infused her argument with strong clouds of aggregation, releaser, territorial and trail pheromones. Her speech carried with it the hope of new life, of new larvae who could be put onto the third world. All Swarmers respond to such a scent. Even he felt his inner gut churn with emotion. And he needed something to distract his surviving Swarmers from the dismay so many felt at seeing so much of their home nest destroyed by the invading Soft Skins. They needed warmth and hope as much as he needed it. And there was no possibility his nest could fight and kill any flying nest of the Soft Skins. Only the tail ring of weapons tubes still functioned and he lacked the specialty workers needed to rebuild his middle and nose weapons rings. At best, his surviving Swarmers might be able to erect a covering to the large holes in his outer hard shell. That would allow for air to again flow in spaces where once Swarmers had lived, worked and enjoyed themselves.

"Flight Servant, let us test these Soft Skins. Set us a flight path inward, toward the third world." He looked aside to the older male who was in charge of pheromone talking with other Swarmer nests, a duty now empty with the departure of Hunter One. "Speaker To All, prepare a simple imagery group that shows our nest flying from here inward to the third world. Show us flying far away from the fourth world. Show our nest moving into a hover above the new colony world. Let us see if the Soft Skins agree to our flight inward."

"Simple imagery will be prepared," the Servant said, leaning his thorax forward and tapping on the control panel that lay in front of his bench. "It will take part of a light cycle to prepare and send inward. If the Soft Skins reply, we will scent their response within a full rest cycle."

Seven knew that also. Their imagery signals flew as fast as the light from their home sky light. And as fast as their signals from one flying nest to another flying nest. He gave thought to the prospect of seeing the third world close up, as if one hovered in its sky. Perhaps he could take an air bubble down to its surface and be among the first to breath its air, feel its warm and feed on its fruit and small lifeforms. Flying to the third world would gain his nest large amounts of imagery and the Servants would understand it well. Such information could be scent cast to the arriving Swarmer defenders upon their return. Perhaps Hunter One would choose to share this sky light's system of worlds with the Soft Skins. He did not like the idea. The thought of sharing a nest home with a group of Soft Skins who would be a constant danger to the larvae was something never before encountered by any Swarmer. Perhaps it was possible. He would look closely at the Soft Skin response, since their sending of this new signal said they sought a way of dealing with the Swarm that did not rely on one flying nest killing the other flying nest. Perhaps he would learn a new life lesson. Perhaps not. The attack on his nest by the white shelled Soft Skins had happened even though his nest was not attacking any Soft Skin flying nest. Now, the Soft Skins stayed close to their colony on the fourth world. Soon enough he would learn whether there was a new way to live.

◆ ◆ ◆

Daisy transferred the wasp reply imagery to the front wallscreen, where it covered part of the image of Valhalla. While she loved looking at white-capped mountains, green forests, brown grasslands and the blue seas and oceans of the planet, this new wasp imagery was the first reply they had gotten from the left behind wasp ship. She wondered what Alicia, who sat to the right of her and Richard, would think of it.

"Captain, wasp reply going active on the wallscreen," she said.

"Very interesting," Jacob rumbled. Her ceiling holo of him and everyone else on the Bridge showed him leaning forward, looking intent. "Seems they want to orbit above the third world. And they propose a vector track with a large swing away from Valhalla. But no response to our proposal for trade in space." He paused. "Navigation, talk to me about the proposed vector track."

"Sir," called Louise as she touched her control pillar and scanned one of her several holos. "The imagery is actually pretty sophisticated. Planet three lies ahead of Valhalla by about 20 degrees. That's tens of millions of kilometers. It also lies two-tenths of an AU closer to the local star. The wasp imagery displays all this. But it also proposes a flight track that takes their ship *above* the local planetary ecliptic when their ship gets past the fifth planet's orbital track. Sooo, they are not only proposing to swing out from Valhalla by a large way, they are increasing that distance by arcing up into the empty space above this system's ecliptic." The lean redhead looked back to where Daisy, Richard, Alicia and Jacob sat. "They've already begun traveling inward on this new vector track."

Richard slapped his armrest. "Which means any of our ships can intercept and destroy that ship since it moves at half speed."

"True," Jacob sat, his tone musing. "But we can do that anytime until the wasp fleet returns. Tactical, do you see any increased danger to Valhalla from allowing this wasp ship to orbit planet three?"

"Sir, just a shorter transit time for the wasps to get to Valhalla," Rosemary said, her Irish accent pleasing to Daisy's ears. The middle-aged woman pointed at the wallscreen imagery. "But planet three lies two AU ahead of Valhalla, which adds to their travel time. Their ship can only make five percent of the speed of light, at best. We could intercept them well before they get close enough to bomb Valhalla."

"So, a risk, but a modest one." Jacob looked to the right. "Life Support, the *Lepanto* is next up to undergo repairs. Which will leave us immobile and locked into *Green Hills* base. What's your estimate of repair time?"

"Sir, two weeks, possibly ten days," answered Joaquin Garcia from his function post to the right front of the Bridge. The man's crew-cut black hair looked well-kept. As did the man in general, she thought, before reminding herself she was committed to Jacob.

"Tactical, if we allow the wasp ship to make it to planet three, what are your recommendations for keeping Valhalla safe?"

Rosemary's red ponytail swung wildly as she looked back. Her milky-white face had gone tense. Her lips were tight, a further sign of concern. "Captain, I would dispatch a destroyer to escort the wasp ship to planet three, beginning when it crosses the sixth planet's orbital track. That lies five AU out from the star and 4.3 AU out from Valhalla. Then, once the wasp ship arrives in orbit, I suggest the destroyer launch a missile with multiple thermonuke warheads to orbit above the wasp ship. The destroyer captain can choose an orbital speed that will keep the cluster of thermonukes permanently stationed above the wasp ship. That way we can attack either the ship or the planet, or both, if the wasp ship heads for Valhalla. It also serves as a visible warning to the wasp ship to stay in orbit."

"I like that," Jacob said firmly. He looked to his right. "Lieutenant Branstead, prepare a cartoon video for our reply that shows what we've just discussed. The wasp ship is 50 hours out from Valhalla. I'm sure you can prepare and transmit the video well before they reach the five AU limit."

"Captain, my people will have the video ready within five hours or less," Alicia said from her seat next to Richard. "Is that acceptable?"

"Yes," Jacob said. He looked down to Daisy. "XO, what's the status of the *Philippine Sea*? I noticed lots of black streaks on her hull from the lightning bolt and laser fire she suffered while launching the Darts."

Daisy did not have to look at her holo that showed the location of every ship in orbit above Valhalla. This was data she had memorized, along with the repair schedule. "Captain, she is combat capable. While the *Sea* needs replacement of the adaptive optics lenses that were burned out during her recent sortie against the wasp ship, and she took three deep strikes into her armor, her hull is intact and her weapons systems are all operational. She has a few crew on liberty at the orbital station, but she could leave orbit within an hour."

Jacob grew thoughtful. He leaned his chin on his right hand, a mannerism she had always liked about her friend and lover. His choice earlier to send only the co-existence cartoon video to this wasp ship, while saving the 'destroy both planets' video for any arriving wasp fleet, had helped her feel better about the stark choices facing him, her ship and every human in the system. Now, he seemed willing to allow the wasp ship to come in-system so it could see the world that might be a future colony world for the wasps. If, of course, the other wasps would accept the idea. So far, this wasp commander, who had bombed Valhalla, had shown himself willing to make a partial compromise. In fact, it was the first communication from this ship since its allies had left for Kepler 22.

He nodded slowly. "So most of our ships will be available for system defense while the *Lepanto* is undergoing repairs. That leaves only the *St. Mihiel* to come in after us for her cargohold repairs. XO, send an order to Lieutenant Jefferson for her ship to intercept the wasp ship at the fifth planet's orbital, thereafter to follow and do as Tactical suggested."

"Captain, yes sir, working on it."

Daisy turned to her own group of holos. The *Philippine Sea* was holding orbit near the Star Navy base. Further out were the *Chesapeake* and *Tsushima Strait*, both now fully repaired. She tapped on her left armrest, activating one of the control patches on her seat. Giving thanks she was ambidextrous, she tapped in the text order, selected an Alert signal code to get Joy's personal attention, and then hit the Send dot on the patch.

"Captain, orders sent."

"Good." He looked ahead and to the left. "Engines, move us to a link-up with Hangar Two on the base. We need to get those deep holes on our nose, belly and rear fixed as best the base can fix them."

"Captain, moving on a single thruster," called Akira M'Bala as the South African woman worked her control pillar.

Daisy wanted to relax. But she couldn't. Managing all the decks on the *Lepanto*, plus tracking Med Hall reports, along with demands from Life Support for new food supplies for the wasps in the Forest Room and keeping a constant watch on her situational holo for the emergence of new moving neutrino sources, which might be new wasp ships, left her feeling tired and worn down. But her shift had four more hours to go. Jacob had six more hours to go. She gave thanks that Alicia was now back on the Bridge, readily available for advice, support and insight into how hundreds of people related on the *Lepanto*. And the sober, calm presence of Richard gave her a sense of safety she badly needed. Briefly she wished for her old job of just being the pilot of the admiral's Landing Craft Assault. She loved flying. And being in charge of the Battlestar was harder than reading thermals and down drafts that might jostle her LCA.

Feeling nervous, she again scanned the situational holo. Every ship of the StarFight fleet was there. *Chesapeake*, *Tsushima Strait* and the *Salamis* orbited above the station. Ahead in orbit was the cluster of the cruiser *Hampton Roads* and the frigates *St. Mihiel* and *Aldertag*. Between the Battlestar and the station was the *Philippine Sea*. And the *Lepanto* made eight ships total. Eight fighting ships were all that stood between the 71,000 people on Valhalla and a deadly enemy that had attacked, attacked again and even followed them to Kepler 10 in order to attack once more. Would allowing the wasp ship to orbit above planet three cause the wasps to change? She didn't know. She just knew that the future was uncertain, more wasp ships could appear at any time and the hoped-for relief fleet from Earth would not arrive for at least another 30 days.

◆ ◆ ◆

Jacob walked into his quarters, past the furniture in the relaxation room and turned left through the bedroom's open archway. On the queen size bed in the middle of the room lay Daisy, asleep, her head resting on her left arm as she slept. The room's lighting was a low green from a few wall spots that allowed one to see the entrance to the bath and toilet alcove. His metal worktable stuck out from the left side wall. Like every worktable in officer's quarters on the ship, it closed up against the wall when not in use. The small table partly filled the space between the wall and the bed. Daisy had not closed it up. Instead, after changing into a sheer white negligee, she had gone down the right side of the bed and slipped beneath the purple sheets. Kicking off his soft shoes, Jacob dropped his camo pants, pulled off his shirt, then slowly sat on his side of the bed, facing the worktable's wall opening. The three shelves in the opening held a few sea shells, his comp pad and an old-fashioned ink pen and small paper tablet. All were gifts from his Mom. Stuck above the shelves were two flat digital pictures he had brought from home.

His Mom's photo showed her smiling at him from within their kitchen. Her long brown hair was full of curls and she was smiling happily at him. That day she had worn a flowered spring dress of green and yellow, with a white cook's smock hanging from her neck. She loved to bake fresh bread. He loved to eat it. Next to her image was a flat pic of the old barn in the back of their property. His mom's gelding horse was standing in front of the barn, his reins tied to a post. The brown and white Appaloosa horse had been the first large animal

Jacob had ever seen or spent time with. The gelding had seemed to like him. Next to the gelding was his Mom's Arabian stallion, Butch, hitched to another pole.

Below the images was the worktable. Sitting on the table was a holo cube. It showed him just as he posed for his father, right after his graduation from the academy. Two admirals, a captain and two Army colonels stood near Jacob. They were friends of his father. Would one of those admirals be leading the relief fleet when it arrived? He shook his head and focused on the green forested mountains that rose in the background of the graduation field. That day had been a Southwest blue sky day, touched with puffy white clouds. The forested mountain image reminded him why he kept the holo cube. Nature had always called to him. It still did, every time he looked at the image of Valhalla's northern continent that partly filled the wallscreen on the Bridge.

He looked down at his hands as they rested on his bare knees. They weren't shaking. Had he finally adjusted to being in command? To being responsible for the lives of thousands of people on Valhalla, and the crews on every ship in the fleet? He hoped so. Whoever led the relief fleet from Earth would surely outrank him. The video report carried by the *Ofira's* captain Arman Mansour would surely surprise and upset Earth Command. Their upset meant whatever ships came to Kepler 10 would be led by a one or two star rear admiral, maybe even a three star vice admiral. After all, this was humanity's first encounter with an intelligent alien species. That encounter had already claimed too many lives on the frigates *Britain* and *Marianas* when they died, and on the *Chesapeake*, *Tsushima Strait* and the *St. Mihiel* during the last space battle. Those ghosts included the civies who had died during the lightning bombing of Stockholm. He had felt those ghosts hovering behind him, watching him, every time he made a command decision that put people at risk.

Closing his eyes he lay down on his side of the bed, moving slowly so as to not wake Daisy. The pillow supported his head. He did not open his eyes. The bedroom's ceiling was boring to look at, whether in the dark or when awakening to the automated alarm light. He told himself that in 30 or so days, the burden of commanding the StarFight fleet would be lifted from his shoulders. Someone else would assume overall command. Hopefully the new fleet commander would leave him in command of the *Lepanto*. He had grown to like the ship, like its many decks, like the homemade food cooked by Kenji and his fellow line cooks, and also its wild nature areas in the Forest Room and the Park Room. He had even grown to like being a fleet commander. The other ship captains, new as him to the job, had fought well, had supported him against the machinations of Bannerjee, and seemed ready to join him in defending Valhalla from future wasp attack. Maybe those feelings were why he dreaded the arrival of the relief fleet. It meant the arrival of one more unknown. An unknown that would affect the lives of every human in the Kepler 10 star system. He hoped he could follow regs and do the right thing by accepting a new fleet commander. After all, he and his people had fought and defeated the wasps. No one in the relief fleet knew what he and his people knew. But would that make a difference to some Earth Command admiral pulled from flying a mahogany desk?

◆ ◆ ◆

Daisy opened her eyes once she heard Jacob snoring softly. His entry into the bedroom had awakened her. She had always been a light sleeper. And once her father had left her Mom and herself behind, heading off to an overseas job that did not include them, she had always awakened to the soft sound of her Mom walking down the hallway of their condo apartment in Chicago. It had served her well during school. No one, guy or gal, was ever able to sneak up on her from behind and grab her breasts, like some jerk guys tried to do in middle school. Later, on the long walk from her school to her home, she'd been aware anytime someone stood in an alley, opened a door across the street, or began following her after she crossed an intersection. The first time she heard a man following her had been the last. After going down the alley, around a corner and then up the outside ladder to the roof of a nearby tenement, she had made sure to always walk home as part of a crowd of three other gals from school. Walking together had become mutual security for the four of them. She had good memories of them. But none of them loved to fly and none of them had ever sought entry into the Stellar Academy.

She turned over and looked right. Jacob's bare chest rose and fell slowly as he breathed in a low rumble. His black chest hairs were barely visible in the pale green light of the room. She liked his hairy chest. His strong nose. His broad shoulders. His gray eyes. And his shy smile had been the first thing about him to cause her to pay extra attention, at the Earth orbital station just before they boarded the *Lepanto*. The fact that he was a good chess player, knew and practiced Okinawan karate and was a sensitive lover had all been nice additions to the person she had found hiding inside a somewhat formal manner. Jacob had opened up to her, Lori, Carlos, Kenji and Quincy. He'd even shared stories about his mother Sarah. He'd talked about riding the Appaloosa horse owned by his Mom. To her, riding a horse that was bigger than any human was very daring. Maybe riding horses with his Mom was how he'd learned the daring he'd shown in Kepler 22 and Kepler 10. Perhaps his focus on facts and on being ruthless was something he'd learned from his father, Gordon Renselaer. Or maybe inherited from the man' genes. She didn't know. She just knew she loved him, trusted him as the ship captain and felt certain that Jacob would always fulfill his duty the best way he saw fit.

Closing her eyes, she tried to push away her memory of a recent order he'd given her. That was to work with Weapons Deck chief John Bannister to enlarge the magfield containment reservoir for the ship's antimatter cannon. The factory-built reservoir had room for four shots of antimatter. Jacob had wanted the reservoir size increased to handle eight shots, before the particle accelerator that wrapped around the ship's nose was spun up to produce new antimatter. Doing what he wanted had meant a change in the cannon room on Weapons Deck, along with the fabrication of more magfield coils, all while making sure the added reservoir capacity did not destroy the weapon's ability to work. She had borrowed a few electrical and mechanical engineers from Engines Deck, and some algorithm geeks from Science Deck. Fortunately, Lori had known people who could help her in the design of the addition. And Alicia had loaned those people to her for this project, which would be completed while the ship was locked into the Star Navy station for hull repairs.

Breathing deep she focused on her memory of her Mom. Tall, with muscular arms, determination in her walk and loving eyes, filling her mind with the image and warmth of her Mom might help her push away work. The first stages of the antimatter project had been dealt with already. New stages would happen tomorrow. It would take a good week, maybe longer to expand the cannon's room, then build new capacity onto the existing reservoir chamber. Biting her lip, she told herself for the tenth time to forget about work and to instead think of her Mom, and of Jacob. Maybe he would like her Mom's omelet recipe that included some spicy additions. In the morning, she would find out. Finally, thinking of her Mom and omelets and their home in Chicago finally allowed her to drift away.

CHAPTER TEN

Hunter Seven's five eyes took in the daylight image of the third world as it slowly moved below him and his nest. It had taken three full light and rest cycles to reach this world, but it was worth it. The image of dense green lands that lay below him reminded him of the view of Nest he'd seen as their Colony cluster of flying nests had gathered before heading for the sky light that covered the world of Warmth in warm white light. There were three primary land groups, each bearing the mark of mountains thrust up from deep below. The land groups were separated by dark blue waters of great expanse, an expanse too great for any Swarmer to fly across solely on wing power. There were pale blue rivers, lakes and open land where large animals moved in great numbers. An enlarged view of those animals now filled one perception imager in the Flight Chamber. The imager showed the animals had six limbs, as was proper for all life. And where such animals lived, smaller land and air animals would live, along with trees carrying fruits rich in sweetness. It was clear there would be plenty of food for the larvae, once a Colony cluster arrived, their nests filled with Pods of larvae.

"Alert!" cried the elderly male in charge of monitoring external space. "The Soft Skin nest has released a flying tube filled with particle disruption seeds!"

Seven inhaled the mix of alarm, signal and territorial pheromones, understanding the Swarmer feared for the world below and for his fellow Swarmers. They were half the number they had been before the attack by the white-shelled Soft Skins. A third of his flying nest's chambers were open to cold dark space. While their flight path to the new colony world had been without danger, still, the Soft Skin nest had followed behind them, clearly on the watch for any movement toward the fourth world where Soft Skins lived and flew up to Soft Skin nests that hovered above that world. Time to reassure the Swarmers in his chamber and in every warm space of his nest.

"Be strong!" he scent case in a mix of signal, food trail and sex pheromones, supported by command pheromones unique to his Hunter caste. "Our losses are rewarded by the world below! Studies

of it must be made before Hunter One returns with more nests and his
Colony nest! Those who do well in repairing the space cold chambers
will be rewarded with trips in air bubbles to the world below," he
scent cast, adding a touch of releaser pheromones to signal his
expectation of a change in behavior.

"Hunter," scent cast the young male Servant in charge of his
single ring of surviving sky light and sky bolt weapons. "The particle
disruption seeds emitted by the Soft Skin nest hover above us, but do
not chase us. Shall we first destroy these seeds before we send
bubbles down to the world below?"

"Stinger Servant, do not bite the seeds," he scent cast in a mix
of reassurance and territorial pheromones. "It is clear the Soft Skins
wish us to remain here. See, their nest departs now, leaving this world
to us. If we try to leave for the Soft Skin world, those seeds will attack
us. Let us wait until Hunter One returns before we bite dead those
seeds!"

To his left the wings of his new Fighter Leader flapped
quickly. "Hunter Seven! Shall I send Fighters along with the Servants
and Workers who visit the world below? There could be dangerous
animals, or large flying predators down below. Our flight path on the
new colony world must be cautious."

He was tired of the frequent worries expressed by the new
Fighter Leader. He much preferred the old one. But he had died in the
attack on the Soft Skin nest that had penetrated the middle of his
nest's hard shell. Leaving him with someone anxious to always do
what seemed right.

"Fighter, we Swarmers do not bite all the time. Our Servants
study the sky, the world below and all the life thereon. They are
careful in how they move. But yes, send along two Fighters to protect
each bubble visit," he said in a flow of irritation, signal and trail
pheromones. Then he looked away to the young female in charge of
handling his nest's propulsive devices.

"Servant, have you been able to repair the dead propulsive
device?"

"With regrets most deep, it is not possible," she scent cast in a
mix of signal, alarm and curiosity pheromones, supported by a strong
aggregation scent. Clearly she wished him to know she was loyal
despite her failure. "Our working propulsive device did well on the
flight path to this new colony world. It can move us about this sky

light's large domain. But our flight speed is half what it once was. Only a return to Nest can provide us with a new propulsive device."

"So it seems," he said in a calm flow of command pheromones. "Speaker To All," he called to the older male in charge of signals sent to other nests. "Send my words of reward to every chamber of our nest. We must make every effort to close the holes in our hard shell, then to visit the world below and study all there is to be learned."

"Sending your words to all chambers of our nest," the Servant replied quickly, his tone carrying an overlay of fear pheromone.

Seven ground his mandibles together. He yearned to bite the neck of someone. But he had no Swarmers suitable for wasteful action. It would take every living Swarmer to conduct flight views of the world below, to document the types and number of small flyers, and to see if any life similar to the Swarm now existed on this world. While the Swarm had never found life similar to themselves on the ten worlds it had colonized, the appearance of the deadly Soft Skins said such was always possible on a new world. And his nest had much work to do. Repairs were vital. But also vital was learning about the world below.

Perhaps, when Hunter One returned, he could use his nest's studies as a tool to claim control of the returning Colony flight. He had not forgotten the Soft Skin imagery signal. It had proposed both peoples, Swarmers and Soft Skins, stay on their own colony worlds and meet in cold dark space to trade for items each needed. Such had never been done on the worlds colonized by the Swarm. But then, the Swarm had never before met a lifeform able to fight as well as the Swarm. And while the Soft Skin imagery signal had not shown it, he understood well just how deadly the particle disruption seeds could be to the world below. If his ship moved toward the Soft Skin world, the seeds would attack his nest. Other Soft Skin nests would fly fast to the third world and destroy the world below. Losing this world as a future eleventh colony for the Swarm was not acceptable. Somehow, some way, he and other Swarmers must find a way to colonize this world while dealing with the deadly Soft Skins. But could two space-traveling lifeforms share the same sky light? It was a flight question worth considering.

◆ ◆ ◆

Richard stood beside Jane Diego just inside the entrance to the Forest Room. They both wore Shinshoni hard shells. Between them stood Science Deck chief Alicia Branstead and her exobiologist Lori Antonova. The younger woman held a modified pheromone signaling block. Science's study of the four wasps during the two weeks since he had brought them back from the wasp ship had resulted in a basic identification of pheromones with certain concepts or actions. The pheromone talking among the wasps had been intensely studied, thanks to scent trackers that had been installed close to the fibrous nest the aliens had built in the hole they'd excavated in the meadow. Particular scents had been matched to particular actions as seen in the 24/7 video monitoring of the wasps. Alicia's xenolinguist had created a basic vocabulary of a hundred word concepts.

Now, not long after sunrise according to wasp time as set by the leader of the wasp group, the four of them had arrived to conduct a first test of the retrofitted signaler. While he wished Lori and Alicia wore Shinshoni suits, they did wear heavy duty vacsuits of the type used during hull repairs. Still, the deadly stingers on the wasp butts could likely penetrate the fabric of the vacsuits. Which was why he and Jane flanked the two women. He and Jane lifted their arms, each aiming their flamethrower and shotgun tubes at the hovering cluster of four wasps. The wasps had emerged from their honeycomb home the second the slidedoor had opened. Now, they hovered above their residence hole, their heads facing Richard and his people. Their wings did not blur, thanks to the half gee gravity in the room. But they did flap quickly. It made him appreciate the fast metabolism the wasps had to have in order to support flight. That explained their love for honey and sweet, soft fruits. But the unblinking stare of four sets of black eyes set atop a black and red-striped yellow body was unnerving.

"Lori, give it a try," Alicia said, her Australian accent something Richard had long grown used to.

"Yes, Lieutenant."

Antonova plugged three wires from the pheromone block into the chest of her vacsuit. They connected her vacsuit comlink with the block. In theory, the retrofitted translator cubes would convert her words to specific pheromones that would mean something to these wasps. Or maybe not.

"Good food," Lori said, using an address form that she said the wasps scent talked to each other every morning.

All four wasps rose up a meter. Were they startled?

"You, Soft Skin, you share scents!" came a reply from one of the wasps. Did the sharp tone convey surprise?

A single wasp separated from the other three and flew a few meters toward their group. Richard lifted his flamethrower to match the change in angle of the wasp leader.

"We share scents," Lori said over the comlink that linked all of them. "We offer sweet food." She walked slowly toward the hovering wasp, stopping at ten meters. Detaching a large glass jar from her vacsuit's waist belt, she bent down, placed it on the green grass, unscrewed its top and then stepped back a few meters, all the while facing the closest wasp.

Richard smelled a mix of scents strong enough for him to sneeze at. His suit was bringing in the outside air and it filled his helmet. The scents were tangerine sharp, distinct and so complicated in their mixing he did not doubt he was smelling wasp speech.

"Be alert!" cried one wasp in the group of three that hovered above their residence hole. "Danger!"

"Liquid sweetness!" scent cast another wasp. "Same as always. No danger."

"Hold scents!" came an order that Richard thought had been spoken by the leader wasp. "Soft Skins share scent with us! Never—" screeching sounds crossed with clicks and hums filled in for words the signaler could not convert to English. "Leaders drink first!"

The nearest wasp moved toward the glass jar of golden brown honey. It landed on its four narrow legs, which bent as it lowered its yellow body closer to the ground. Its globular head, with mandibles on either side of the lower head and two large black eyes flanking three smaller black one, looked down at the honey, then up. "Soft Skin, you hurt me?"

Lori sighed. "No hurt you," she said, speaking a very short, simple sentence as instructed by Alicia's xenolinguist. "Eat sweet food."

The leader wasp leaned its two black antennae toward Lori, then dipped its head down. Its closed mandibles entered the jar's opening. The sound of sucking came. The wasp lifted its head, then flapped its wings and hovered three meters above the honey.

"Workers, come bite sweetness!"

The three other wasps flew quickly forward, dropping to stand on the ground. They surrounded the honey bottle. Richard watched the fine brown hairs on their abdomens and thoraxes shiver with pleasure as each wasp dipped its mandibles into the honey. The level of honey in the large jar rapidly fell until it was all gone. The three wasps flapped their wings quickly, then flew back to hover above their residence hole, leaving behind the leader wasp.

Lori raised both arms. The watchful hovering wasp moved its head, tracking her hands. "You are leader?"

"Leader of Workers, yes," came over the pheromone block.

"Great!" called Alicia over the comlink, clearly struggling to control her excitement. "Ask the questions."

Lori's black bangs jiggled as she nodded inside her flexible helmet. "Leader of Workers, your people, what name?"

The hovering wasp flew to one side, then back to its hover before the four of them. It remained ten meters distant from Lori and fifteen distant from Richard. "Swarm we are. Swarmer Workers we are."

Richard licked his lips and told his fast-beating heart to be still. These wasps were not like the deadly wasps he and his Marines had fought in the tubeways of the wasp ship. They did not appear to be fighters, or soldiers or whatever this Swarm called its people who fought with weapons.

Lori reached to the back of her vacsuit and pulled off a white board. She laid it on the ground. Then she knelt. Using a black erasable pen, she drew a picture of a human walking toward the jar of honey. She looked up.

"We humans. Human walks to sweetness. Your scents?"

This was the critical element to building a working vocabulary that might mean something. If the hovering leader wasp emitted a scent that was their word for walking, they would have a verb. Of a sort.

"Scent talk you must know," said the wasp as its wings blurred a bit and it flew a bit closer to Lori, close enough to see what she had drawn. "Soft Skin . . . walks. Ground hugger Soft Skins are."

"Chief," called Jane over his hard shell's separate comlink. "How close do we allow the wasp to approach her?"

"Within five meters," he said. "If the wasp gets closer, flare the tip of your flamethrower. These wasps have seen how our weapons work, during our display on the *Sea*, when they awoke in the habitat room. It will understand your warning. If any wasp comes within four meters of her, run forward and shoot a flame ball across its flight path."

"Right."

He joined Jane in aiming his arm weapons. She kept hers focused on the leader wasp. He kept his focused on the three worker wasps hovering above their residence hole. Blinking his right eye, he caused his HUD display to show a close-up of the black stinger that stuck out from the butts of each wasp. There was no leakage of venom or neurotoxin or whatever the stinger held. Nor did the stingers of any wasp stiffen the way he'd seen the stingers on armed wasps stiffen just before they attacked Jane in her hard shell. This looked and sounded peaceful. But he'd learned a long time ago to never rely on appearances. Actions were all that mattered. He was damned and determined that the four wasps in the Forest Room would clearly understand he and Jane were the protectors of the two Science geeks. And that any wasp who threatened his people would end up a black chunk of charcoal. He watched as Lori changed the image on her white board to a different human action, building a vocabulary of verb scents. Eventually she would show holo images of things to build more nouns. Perhaps, in a week or so, the wasps and the Science geeks could do more than speak baby talk with each other. Maybe.

◆ ◆ ◆

Aarhant stood in the control center of his Navigation Deck and watched as his two assistants worked their comp pads to compute an answer to the whelp's latest order. The ensign pretending to be a ship commander had demanded a search of their arrival records upon leaving Alcubierre space-time at the outer edge of this system. He demanded to know the exact three factor location of their arrival spot, and the same data for the later arrival of the wasp fleet. He saw no point in the exercise. The Battlestar's computers and its AI knew where they had arrived when coming to Kepler 10, and the AI also knew where the wasps had arrived, thanks to triangulation from other battle group ships, and to sensor data from the spysats the Battlestar had left behind when it moved to leave the space beyond the system's Kuiper Belt of comets. But Renselaer had insisted, saying he wanted the two spots located to within less than a hundredth of a second of stellar orientation. The Singapore woman who was his first assistant, and a lieutenant, turned to him from her desk. Her black eyes scanned him.

"Lieutenant Commander, we have the exact X, Y, Z coordinates for our arrival point and for the wasp arrival site."

"Transmit them to my tablet," he said, wishing the Asian woman was not a dried up old prune. If she were not fifty years gone she was close to it. "Also transmit them to Renselaer's XO. That woman Stewart."

"Transmitted," she said as his other assistant, a gay lieutenant jg from Kenya, watched them closely.

Brief curiosity held him. "Was there any variance in the arrival points?"

She looked surprised. As if she could not believe his interest in the minutiae of interstellar navigation. Well, he had spent most of the time since the last battle in his quarters, pretending to be sick with a simple cold. The pretense had shielded him from attending the weekly deck chief conferences held by Renselaer. But he had a Ph.D. in cosmology and stellar astronomy. He had earned that degree from the Cornell University, long years ago. He had not forgotten the field he had relied on to advance in the ranks of the Star Navy.

"There was," she said after a pause. "The two arrival points are separated by a distance of 937.9 kilometers, with the wasp arrival point elevated four degrees above this system's planetary ecliptic. Our arrival point was exactly in sync with the ecliptic."

As it should be since this system was a well plotted system, thanks to the existing colony. The wasp arrival variation could be laid to the fact it was their first time coming here. And because the wasps had had to triangulate the battle group's stellar orientation just before transition.

"It sounds as if the wasp navigators are good at what they do," he said, making small talk just to see how his two assistants would react. He liked putting them on the spot, making them wonder if he was displeased with an action of theirs, or whether they had failed to do something he wanted but had not said.

The Singapore woman just nodded. The gay Kenyan man frowned.

"Lieutenant Commander, they are much better than good. We ourselves would have had a hard time being so exact if it was our ship trying to follow the wasps back to their home system," he said, his English sounding almost British, thanks to the way Kenyan schools still followed Brit models.

Aarhant frowned back. "Your opinion is noted." There, let the man wonder if he had done something wrong. "I'm heading back to my quarters. Take care of staff work rotations. You two should be able to handle something that simple."

"Sir," called the woman. "Do we assign work to Lieutenant JG Mendoza? He now resides on Command Deck and often is called to the Bridge."

Aarhant paused before the exit slidedoor. Count on that woman to raise a matter guaranteed to piss him off. He turned and fixed on her, letting her see his expression. "Idiot! Of course you include him in duty assignments! So long as he is listed as a member of Navigation Deck, he is subject to sharing the work load. If he has a conflict with something assigned by that pretender, let him explain himself to one of you. Now, bother me no more!"

Walking into the central hallway that ran down Navigation, he turned right and headed toward the nose of the Battlestar. His office was that way, at the end of the hallway. It gave him a location from which he could watch the hallway over the vidcam that was installed above every slidedoor. He liked watching others while being secluded. His assistants knew that. And they knew his volatile temper. They would not bother him again. Of that he was certain.

◆ ◆ ◆

Daisy sat in her XO seat on the Bridge, with Richard to her right and Alicia seated further right. Above her sat Jacob. Behind them all sat Lori, Carlos and Quincy, who had been ordered to the Bridge by Jacob. They were preparing to leave the Star Navy station, now that repairs were done. Their departure would make room for the *St. Mihiel* to dock with Hangar Two. The punch through into the frigate's cargohold had gone through two deck levels, killing four of the frigate's crew. But the laser beams had not hurt the ship's nose and tail lasers, the spine plasma battery nor its single missile silo at the ship's tail. It was time for the final ship repair. They had been orbiting above Valhalla for 35 days. The face of Dekker Lorenz now occupied a central spot in the front wallscreen. She liked him. The German had been a chief petty officer of the E-7 rank when the senior officers had been killed. He'd been in charge of the Weapons Deck on the frigate. A fact that had stood him well during the space battles in the two star systems.

"Fleet captain, moving to dock with the station," Dekker said in a rumbling voice. Beside him sat his XO, an American woman of Philippine heritage. The man's dark eyes looked aside to a holo. "Your *Lepanto* looks good. The new hull metal at belly, nose and rear is nearly invisible."

Jacob smiled in her ceiling view of him and of everyone on the Bridge. "Thanks, Dekker. Get your tail in there. And I hope your crew enjoys plenty of leave time on the station. It's still awhile before the Earth fleet arrives."

Both Dekker and his XO smiled at Jacob's informality. "Thanks, Jacob. Looking forward to it. *St. Mihiel* out."

The other ship image vanished, to be replaced by a view of the night side of Valhalla. The continent below was equator-located and not yet colonized by the Scandinavians from Wisconsin. Two other images occupied the screen's left and right sides. The left image held the situational graphic that showed the placement of every neutrino emitting starship in the system, along with planetary alignments, the asteroid belt and the Kuiper Belt. The right image was a view of the silvery ball that was the Star Navy station, and all the battle group ships that clustered within a few hundred klicks of the station. She liked the spysats, which the *Lepanto* and the two cruisers had shot out from their railgun launchers upon arrival. It gave her, and Louise at Navigation, multiple true space views that were reassuring when you spent most of your time in dark vacuum aboard a kilometer-long starship. Her return trip to Stockholm to bring down the civies treated in her ship's Med Hall, with Jacob riding as co-pilot, had been wonderful. A large crowd had surrounded her LCA at the nearby landing field, their faces happy-looking as the twelve civies she'd brought home walked down the LCA's ramp to a joyous welcome by family and friends. She and Jacob had stood in the open airlock, its hatch swung to one side. The mayor of Stockholm, a sixty-ish blond woman with few lines in her face had smiled up at them, then had turned and waved. To her surprise a band had struck up a happy marching tune, with the mayor gesturing to her and Jacob to come down. They had. The mayor had presented Jacob with a memorial plaque filled with the names of every battle group person lost in the fight above Valhalla. She had then made a speech about how thankful every citizen of Valhalla was to have the protection of the Star Navy. It had touched her and—

"XO," called Jacob. "What is your opinion of the repairs to our armor hull breaches?"

She jerked, then glanced at one of her holos, the one that showed the spysat view of the *Lepanto* as it moved slowly away from the station. "My opinion is that it was a touch of genius for Captain O'Sullivan to order a shuttle to be compressed, then put into our belly hole. That hole was the size of a doubles tennis court. Putting just cross beams and new plating on the inner hull and then plating on the outer hull would have left a severe vulnerability." She looked up at him. His clean-shaven face was intent on her, his manner command formal. "A similar grouping of squashed aircars was put into the hole at our nose. Then covered over by cross beams and hull plating. Sir, while those items are not armor metal, they *are* solid metal. They will resist future beams. That is my opinion."

Jacob nodded slowly, then raised his thick black eyebrows. "What about the repair to the spine hull area above our engines? I gather no such vehicles were used to fill the hole cut into the armor."

"Correct," Daisy said quickly. "But the penetration there was just two meters wide. While the beams cut down into the water layer, they did not penetrate the inner hull below the water. Unlike the nose and belly punch throughs. Captain O'Sullivan ordered his engineers to grab the metal dome that covered the station's electro-optical scope. It's good metal. They plasma torched it into a plug that filled most of the space cut into the armor. Every wound in the *Lepanto's* hull is now covered in new exterior hull plates, new ablative coating and new adaptive optics lenses. Sir."

"How many shuttles does the station still possess?"

"Two. One is down at the Stockholm landing field and one rests inside Hangar One."

"Good." Jacob looked ahead. "Engines, move us out to just beyond the local moon. I want us to have a clear view of the arrival point where the wasps should show up."

"All three thrusters firing," Akira said softly.

"Vector track set," called Louise.

"Tactical," Jacob said, his baritone becoming tense. "Keep a watch on the spot where the wasps arrived and left out from."

"Keeping watch," replied Rosemary. "The Earth departure point used by *Ofira* is not that far away. It's within twenty degrees of the wasp arrival point. Shall I watch it also?"

"Of course," Jacob said, his tone easing. "Night and day we watch those two points. No more liberty for anyone. Assume normal shift schedules." He looked up at the ceiling. "Melody, move ship status to Alert Combat Ready. Send the same order to every fleet ship not linked to the station."

Overhead the alert lights went to blinking red. The ceiling speakers gave out a high-pitched siren, which repeated three times.

"As you command, my attractive human," the AI said softly.

Daisy could hardly believe what she'd heard. No ship AI ever showed a personal attachment to the ship's captain. They heard, responded and obeyed orders. They gave information when asked. They coordinated the automatic functions of every ship. This AI had been acting weird ever since Jacob assumed command. In Kepler 10 it had acted even more . . . personal in relating to him. Why?

Jacob chuckled. "Melody, does one AI find another ship AI to be attractive? If so, what elements constitute attractiveness to an AI?"

Daisy grinned. He was having fun with the mouthy AI. Looking ahead she saw most of the Bridge crew also smiling, or shaking their heads in disbelief.

"We do find each other attractive, my handsome human," Melody said, her soprano voice becoming almost musical. "To us, the ability to manipulate thousands of factors within less than a human second is attractive. The way a starship moves through space is a function of how well her engines operate. Which is a reflection on the automated monitoring of that ship's AI. While most of what I do happens at the nanosecond level, still, slowing my mind to converse with humans is . . . entertaining."

"Ahhh," Jacob murmured. "All of us appreciate your patience with our slowness. Continue monitoring all aspects of local space-time. I wish to know when new starships arrive, whether I am asleep, eating or otherwise occupied."

"Does this order apply during your sexual activities?"

Daisy winced. This AI was too damned noisy!

"It does," Jacob said. "The safety of this ship, its crew and your safety is one of my primary duties. Please comply."

"Happily do I comply, my handsome human!"

Daisy turned her attention to her ship cross-section holo as the AI fell silent. She did not wish to make eye contact with anyone. While Alicia was the married mom of three girls and fully understood what it meant to be in love, still, she did not care for the AI's blatant reference to her and Jacob's relationship. Which of course was known to everyone on the *Lepanto*. At least her friends at the back of the Bridge understood the need for courtesy. They weren't AIs. They were good people. And she cared for them a lot, especially Carlos who had had to respond to work orders from Aarhant Bannerjee. That man was a pest and a danger to them all. What would the chief of Navigation Deck do and say when the Earth relief fleet arrived? She hoped it was not too insubordinate. Then she found herself wishing it was. She had visited the Battlestar's block of brig cells with Jacob, not long ago. He had gone there to see how well the cells had been cleaned after the latest crowd of liberty drunks had sobered up and returned to their quarters. She had gone with him as his XO. The cleanup had been just one of the dozens of duties she had discovered were the province of a ship's XO. Briefly she wished to be just a pilot flying her LCA through space and a world's atmosphere. Then she reminded herself that if she had done *just* piloting, she, Jacob and the rest of the battle group might have become vapor during the sneak attack by the wasps at Kepler 22. Perhaps there was a value to tending to XO duties.

CHAPTER ELEVEN

Jacob did not glance at the digital clock that glowed above the front wallscreen. He knew what it said. It was 49 days, eleven hours and four minutes since the *Ofira* had left for Earth and Earth Command. A simple trip to Earth with an immediate return would take 45 days based on traveling 25 light years a day across the 564 light years to Earth. He assumed it would take Earth Command some days to pull together a fleet of ships to send their way. But how long? Surely they would send him some support! He felt irritable. It wasn't due to his seat. The cushioned thing had long ago make its automatic adjustment to his body shape. Just as every seat on every deck of the *Lepanto* worked to accommodate the sitter. A simple bit of tech and programming.

Below him sat Daisy, Richard and Alicia. Behind sat Lori, Carlos and Quincy, with Kenji on call to bring in food trays during the morning shift. Ahead of him stretched the arc of nine work stations. From left to right were Power, Tactical, Weapons, Engines, Navigation, Communications, Gravity, Life Support and Science. Sitting at those posts were the shift crew he had first encountered when he and Daisy had entered the Bridge and talked to Andrew Osashi, the senior member in terms of service years.

He looked up at the wallscreen. It glowed with multiple images. Ahead was a true space view of white star dots against a black tapestry, with the white sweep of the Milky Way occupying the lower right of the image. The world Valhalla and its moon were behind his ship, which floated in space in company with the other seven ships that made up the battle group. Their position looked outward toward the expected arrival point of the relief fleet. He shook his head and looked at the rest of the screen. On the left was the situational graphic that showed planets, the local star, the Star Navy base and the eight battle group ships that were all that stood between 71,000 humans and the wasp enemy. On the right was a sensor display that reported on incoming cosmic rays, muons, electrons, radio emissions from the small gas giant in the sixth orbital, and the fleeting dots of neutrino emissions from the system's yellow star and all the stars of the galaxy. It was a busy image.

"Detection!" called Daisy from below. "New cluster of moving neutrino emissions now showing at the edge of the magnetosphere! Location matches Earth departure point. Thirteen emissions showing. Captain?"

He sat straighter in his seat, giving thanks he wore the formal Service Dress Blue outfit of white combo cap with visor, blue jacket, four-in-hand necktie and blue slacks. His jacket cuffs carried the four gold stripes and single gold star of a captain. His silver eagle was pinned to his left chest, just above the Operation StarFight service ribbon. Everyone else on the bridge wore Type III woodland camo uniforms. Their vacsuits were available whenever combat seemed likely.

"Communications, send a neutrino signal to the strongest neutrino source. Ask for the commanding officer." He looked up. "Melody, establish an immediate neutrino vidcom link with every ship in our group. I want their captains to hear everything that is said. Send a similar link demand to Captain O'Sullivan on the station. Also, transmit out all that happens here on the All Ship vidcom."

"Neutrino vidcom links established, my handsome captain," the AI said in her distinctive soprano. "All Ship feed now happening."

The top of the wallscreen changed to show every ship captain. Rebecca and George were in the middle of the line of seven images. A second later he saw Billy O'Sullivan appear at the far right of the image line. Eight faces stared at him.

"Captain," called Rosemary from Tactical. "My sensor read on the thirteen emissions says one of them is a Battlestar like us. A second is the *Ofira*, based on its unique emission track. The other sources appear to be three cruisers, five destroyers and three frigates."

Jacob felt relief, then sudden worry. Why just one Battlestar? Earth had built five Battlestars, with the *Lepanto* being the most recently built. Earth Command could have sent two or more Battlestars to Kepler 10. At least the thirteen ships moved the total Earth defense force up to 21 ships of the line.

"Incoming neutrino vidcom signal," called Andrew. His shoulders stiffened. "It's from the Battlestar. Going up on the wallscreen."

A new image filled the middle of the screen.

Shock filled Jacob as he recognized the admiral sitting in his elevated Bridge seat. His father!

"Captain Renselaer, I am Fleet Admiral Gordon F. Renselaer," his father said in a stiff, formal voice. The man's dark brown eyes stared straight at Jacob. "Give me a battle group status report. And are there any wasp ships in this system? My group is prepared to fight."

"Sir, admiral, a single wasp ship that is heavily damaged now orbits planet three, with my permission, as part of an effort to establish friendly relations," Jacob said. Below his father sat an American Indian man dressed in Service Dress Blue with captain's stripes and eagle. Next to the captain sat a black woman also in Service Dress Blue, whose silver oak leaf showed her to be a commander. She must be the ship's XO. He noticed that all three wore transparent vacsuits, with the flexible helmets hanging back.

"There is no threat to Valhalla, the Star Navy base or to our battle groups. *Lepanto* ship status is Alert Combat Ready." Jacob paused, his mind reeling at the fact of his father being in command of the relief fleet. "My status report is this. After the departure of the *Ofira* for Earth Command, I led the battle group into this system and set up a defensive formation to protect the world Valhalla. Star base Captain Billy O'Sullivan, who is now watching our discussion along with the other ship captains, regularized my assumption of command by approving my field commission as a captain. Shortly thereafter a wasp fleet of six ships entered this system. They were the surviving ships from the last battle in Kepler 22. They came in-system and attacked. Our fight with them resulted in the destruction of another wasp ship, the loss of our frigate *Marianas* and an attack on Valhalla by a damaged wasp ship. We were able to prevent mass casualties, with limited damage to the capital of Stockholm. Four wasp ships turned about and left the system, leaving the damaged fifth ship on its own. That ship fled out to the system's Kuiper Belt and hid inside a large comet."

Jacob took a deep breath. His father had on his formal, I Am In Charge face, a look he knew too well. "Later, I authorized the destroyer *Philippine Sea* to pursue the damaged enemy ship at its hideout in the comet. She launched three assault Darts, with the objective of capturing wasp communication tech and wasps, in order to establish pheromone communications with the captives. The Dart Marines were led by Chief Warrant Officer Richard O'Connor, who sits below me. One Dart and its pilot were lost in that operation. The other Darts returned with four wasp captives and bags of wasp tech. Subsequent work by my Science Deck chief Lieutenant Alicia Branstead, who also sits below me, has resulted in limited communication with the captive wasps by way of a modified pheromone signaler. The other component of my Command team is my XO, Lieutenant Daisy Stewart." Jacob tapped a patch on his armrest. "I am sending you the complete video record of the first battle, our defense of Valhalla, the vital assistance of Captain O'Sullivan in defending that world, the second battle by our Marines, and imagery of the captive wasps." He gripped the ends of both armrests. "At present, the StarFight battle group is repaired and fully combat ready. What are your orders, sir?"

His father looked aside at one of the holos surrounding his seat, watched a moment what Jacob assumed was the space combat portion, then looked back to him. The muscles in his clean-shaven face tightened. "Your battle group has done well. You did well in discovering the wasp killing of the group's senior officers. My Tactical officer says your battle formations in Kepler 22 were creative and appropriate." As the man paused, Jacob told his fast-beating heart to be still. His father had always been limited in his approval of Jacob. Usually he said "Well enough" about anything Jacob did or accomplished in school. Even his graduation from the Stellar Academy had earned only a "Good to see it" from the man. "Since there is no immediate enemy threat, I will proceed to regularize this situation. You are relieved of command of your battle group. They are now part of a combined battle formation led by my Battlestar, the *Midway*. You will continue in command of the *Lepanto*, in view of Captain O'Sullivan's granting of a field commission to you. My assumption of command over all Earth ships in this system is not a reflection on you, your staff or the other acting captains of your battle group. All of you were . . . brave and fought well. However, this encounter with a dangerous alien species requires the experience and abilities of senior line officers. That is why Earth Command ordered me out of retirement and into command of this relief force. Is that understood?"

Jacob licked his lips. He had been preparing himself for the loss of battle group command for weeks now. Still, it was hard to hear. Harder still to accept. "Admiral, I accept your order transferring battle group command. I will continue to hold the *Lepanto* ready and able to participate in any battle formation you order."

His father blinked. Was he surprised at Jacob's acceptance? "Now that your battle group status report is finished, I have further orders for the ships in the StarFight expedition. From here on out, all deck staff officers are part of the chain of command on the ship they serve on. We cannot allow a repeat of your irregular situation." His father paused. Below him the Black woman and the Sioux man continued their neutral expressions as Earth's only five star admiral laid out a new reality. "For the *Lepanto*, you may order your succession as you wish, whether it be by rank or by years of service. Second, ship status change codes must be shared beyond the Command Deck officers. You are ordered to share the code with at least one staff officer, in addition to sharing it with your XO and Chief O'Connor. Earth Command's prior orders to limit travel between decks by members of other decks is hereby rescinded, along with the exclusion of deck staff officers from the formal chain of command. Carry out my order."

Jacob nodded slowly, thinking fast. "Fleet admiral, I agree that this new arrangement will provide for a clearer and more efficient chain of command on any ship that suffers the loss of all Command Deck officers. For the *Lepanto*, I hereby designate Lieutenant Alicia Branstead, who sits to my lower right, as the staff officer next in line of command. She will be succeeded by other staff officers based on their rank." He wondered what his father thought of his friends sitting at the rear of the Bridge. "I have already shared the ship status change code with my XO, who sits to my lower left, and with my Tactical Officer, Chief O'Connor. I will provide a copy of the code to Lieutenant Branstead, who has done outstanding work in creating a basic English-to-wasp translation program. Sir, will you approve my promotion of her to the full Commander level?"

His father blinked again, then frowned briefly. "My record of your ship officers and those of the other battle group ships says she is a full Lieutenant at present. You propose to jump her two ranks?"

"I do, sir. Her deck's efforts at observing, recording and building a basic vocabulary of English-to-wasp pheromone talk is a major achievement. It offers us the chance to negotiate with the wasps." Jacob tapped his armrest transmit patch once more. "I'm sending you the latest cartoon video she prepared and which I ordered transmitted to the damaged wasp ship. It proposed the wasps occupy planet three in this system, with humans staying on Valhalla and the two species meeting in space for mutual trade."

The Indian captain's black eyebrows rose up. The man looked like a Sioux, based on Jacob's memory of a Sioux he'd met at the Stellar Academy. The XO pursed her lips. Neither said anything. Above them his father's right hand tapped slowly on his armrest. He knew that look. It was the look that said 'You Try My Patience'.

"What was the wasp ship response?"

"The return video proposed the transit of their ship into this system and its orbiting above planet three, which has the half gee and jungle world nature that is identical to the Kepler 22 world they colonized." Jacob licked his lips and hoped his father would not verbally harass him. "I agreed to that action so long as the wasp ship stayed at least five AU away from Valhalla while in transit. I then sent the *Philippine Sea* to meet and follow the wasp ship to planet three, which leads Valhalla in its orbit about the local star. Spysats left by the *Sea* report the wasps have made a dozen trips down to the planet's surface, apparently doing the usual survey of that world's geology, chemistry and wildlife."

His father glanced aside again at one of his holos, looked thoughtful, then returned his attention to Jacob. "Captain Renselaer, I approve the field promotion of Science Deck chief Alicia Branstead to Commander rank. Her work and her 25 years of service in the Star Navy warrant the promotion." The man's expression moved from routine to command serious. "However, your suggestion of an armistice with these wasps is premature. Based on their prior actions, and their leaving of a ship behind to keep an eye on Kepler 10, I can only assume they plant to return. I expect them to send a large wasp formation that will aim to destroy our colony on Valhalla and take possession of planet three. That was their aim when their depleted fleet arrived here. I see no reason for them to change their aggressive behavior." The man paused, although his look warned Jacob to not argue.

"I accept your estimate of our tactical and strategic situation," Jacob said. "With your permission, Commander Branstead will continue her conversation with the captive wasps. What else do you wish done by Expedition StarFight ships?"

The muscles in his father's jaw tightened. He leaned forward slightly. It was a look Jacob knew well. His father was going to give him an order that brooked no argument.

"The *Lepanto* and all other ships of the StarFight formation are hereby ordered to join my battle group at the point on the magnetosphere where the wasp ships left," he said. "I propose to adopt formations and battle actions different than what you have done. The wasps are not stupid. The returning wasps will expect your group to still orbit above Valhalla, to protect that world the way you protected it during the last battle." His father smiled in a way that had no humor. "Instead, our two battle groups will be arranged in battle formation at the exact spot where the wasps will exit Alcubierre space-time. With luck, many of their ships will be in range of our two antimatter cannons. With determination our groups will destroy a large number of wasp ships before they break arrival formation and move beyond the range of our beams." His father looked down at the Black woman. "My XO, Commander Marjorie Jones, has developed a most attractive battle formation for our 21 ships. You and your ships will follow that plan."

Jacob felt surprise leavened with relief. His father was not going to give him a verbal spanking in front of all the ship captains. Nor had the man said he had done wrong in allowing the wasp ship to get to planet three. And it was clear the 'hero' of the Callisto Conflict had studied the vid records brought to him by the *Ofira*. Which reminded him of a detail.

"Your order is accepted. The *Lepanto* and other ships in StarFight will shortly head out to rendezvous with you." Jacob looked over to Louise. "Navigation, transmit the new coordinates for the wasp ship arrival and departure point to Fleet Admiral Renselaer." Jacob looked up, meeting his father's intense look. "Sir, earlier I ordered my Navigation Deck team to use all records of wasp ship arrival and departure to establish a tight X, Y, Z location of the wasp ship departure point. That location data is now being transmitted to you. It should allow our ships to get within 500 kilometers of the likely arrival point of the incoming wasp fleet."

"Good." His father looked aside, perhaps to his own Navigation station person. "It's received. We will head for that exact coordinate point. Do you require further guidance?"

Jacob sucked in his breath. "I do. Will the *Ofira* return to the StarFight group? And why did Earth not send more Battlestars to Kepler 10?"

The captain below his father blinked quickly, then frowned. The XO was looking sideways, perhaps reviewing the several holos and videos he had sent their way. The man who had dominated him all his life sat back and looked impatient.

"The *Ofira* will return to the StarFight group. Captain Mansour was of good help when I presented my case to Earth Command for the sending of a relief fleet to Kepler 10." His father paused, his face changing to a look of irritation. "When the *Ofira* arrived, there were only three Battlestars in Sol system. The *Atlantic* was out leading a group similar to StarFight in the hunt for new colony planets. Which left the *Midway*, *Actium* and *Trafalgar* available. The imagery of the meeting site destruction and that first attack on your group badly frightened the Unity politicians. They insisted on keeping two Battlestars at home to protect Earth, even though there is no way the wasps could know Sol's location." The admiral who had pushed him into the Stellar Academy gave a sigh that carried a hint of exasperation. "So I left with the *Midway*, the *Ofira* and eleven other ships. We came to you by way of the Kepler 78 colony, since it was possible wasp ships would already be in the Kepler 10 system. To date, no Earth ship has arrived here directly from Earth. And that is how we will keep things."

Jacob's mind filled briefly with the facts that Kepler 78 was 400 light years out from Earth, on roughly the same vector track as Kepler 10 and Kepler 22. All were part of the Cygnus constellation. The colony at Kepler 78 lived on an Earth-like world that lay in the middle of the G-type star's liquid water ecozone. He nodded.

"Thank you for that information." Jacob looked down to Alicia. "Commander Branstead, transmit to the *Midway* the most recent videos of our wasp captives, and your xenolinguist's English-to-wasp vocabulary, along with the tech details of the pheromone speaker block." He looked up. "Fleet Admiral Renselaer, perhaps your Science Deck people can add to the remarkable efforts of our Science Deck team."

His father's irritated look now changed to a thoughtful one that held a hint of approval. "I will convey that data to my Science Deck chief. It is always better to have more people working on such a unique problem." He waved Jacob's way, a gesture he knew meant approval. "The battles you and your ships fought were well done. The research of your Science Deck allows us an option to negotiate, once we bloody the . . . the antennae of these wasps." The approval changed to a grim look. "However, the fact remains. The wasps carried out a sneak attack on your group's senior officers, killing all of them, perhaps in the hope it would leave your ships uncertain and unprepared to fight back. Well, now they know humans can fight, and fight hard. They hit you with twelve ships. In exchange for the loss of two frigates, you have killed or damaged eight enemy ships. I like a four to one ratio. We may need that kind of result when the wasps return. And I like surprising the enemy in combat. Which is why our combined groups will fight in ways they have yet to experience. Carry out your orders."

Jacob saluted his father. "This Battlestar and our fellow ships will join you within 52 hours. My staff are ready to respond to any inquiries from your staff. *Lepanto* out."

His father's image vanished.

On the wallscreen a new image appeared alongside the strip of other ship captains. It was the brown face and hawk-like eyes of Mansour. The Lebanese-American man looked tired.

"Arman, a hard trip back?"

He shook his head. "No. A very hard time in Sol system, having to sit at the side of your father as we were harangued by Unity politicians about why they just *had* to keep hold of two Battlestars and the bulk of the Star Navy. While the navy answers to President MacKenzie, he was clearly trying to reassure the other nations that make up the Unity. It was . . . tiresome to watch."

Jacob could guess it was worse than tiresome. Infuriating, perhaps, in view of the true combat Mansour and his people had witnessed as they did their share in the first battles against the wasps. "You and the *Ofira* did the essential. You got word to America and to the Unity government. I saw enough of that Unity jabber during my years at the Stellar Academy. Several of their pollies came and went, each expecting a ride on our orbital trainer. Do you need anything? We'll join you and the other ships in two days time."

Mansour shook his head. "The *Ofira* is in fine shape. We restocked all the missile loads and plasma canisters we used in Kepler 22. Though I must admit some of my people are homesick for the feel of a normal world. Like Valhalla. Were many hurt during the wasp attack?"

Jacob felt ghosts looking over his shoulder. "The colony lost 343 dead and 471 injured in lightning bomb hits on the outskirts of Stockholm. The two nukes launched by the single wasp ship that got past us blew up over forested terrain with no villages. The low casualty levels were due to the sharpshooting by Captain O'Sullivan's proton laser people and the folks on Lieutenant Jefferson's ship."

Mansour and his XO, a Chinese-American man who looked to be in his thirties, both looked relieved. In the group of images that ran atop Jacob's wallscreen, O'Sullivan now leaned forward, looking concerned.

"Captain Renselaer, I've enjoyed having your ships and their crews as visitors to our station and down to Valhalla. Some of them volunteered to help with recovery work. Which, as you saw when you and Lieutenant Stewart landed, was much appreciated by the mayor." His ally looked aside at something in the orbital base's com room, which held only him. "Our moving neutrino sensors show the Earth relief fleet moving toward the wasp exit point. Let's hope you and they arrive there before new wasps show up." Billy's hazel eyes met Jacob's. "Have a safe trip. And in case you wondered, the *Aldertag* is permanently attached to your group for as long as you need her."

Jacob had wondered. It was good news. His battle group was back to nine ships strong. "Billy, thank you. Reassure the folks down on the ground that they will be protected. No matter what happens."

O'Sullivan's tanned face turned thoughtful. "I know that. Star Navy base *Green Hills* out."

Which left the images of seven ship captains watching from the top of his wallscreen. "Captains, you heard it all. Make ready to follow the *Lepanto* out to meet Fleet Admiral Renselaer within ten minutes. Are your ships ready to hit ten psol?"

"The *Aldertag* is eager to meet up with the relief fleet," said Joan Sunderland, her manner relaxed yet serious, as one would expect from the former occupier of Callisto and guardian of each of Earth's colony worlds as they were established. "May I say that while I accept the fact that the admiral is in overall command of all ships, my crew and I will never forget how your *Lepanto* shielded us from multiple wasp beams. This frigate would not be here today if it were not for the actions of your Battlestar."

Jacob felt both pleased and too much on the spot. Then again, maybe feeling both emotions was part of being a good captain. "Joan, thank you. I'm sure . . . my father the admiral has some creative ideas on future combat formations. We'll learn them once we arrive and take up position."

"So we will," she said. "*Aldertag* out."

Her image disappeared, leaving six more. They were the captains of the *Chesapeake, Hampton Roads, Tsushima Strait, Salamis, Philippine Sea* and *St. Mihiel*. Each had been silent during the contact with his father. What did they think of the takeover?

"Jacob," called Rebecca Swanson. "This transfer of battle group control was to be expected. I was certain Earth Command would send an admiral of some sort to lead operations here. Just never thought Earth's only fleet admiral would be the one chosen."

"Me either," growled George Wilcox, his bulldog face pulled into a scowl. "We Brits understand fearful pollies. Had plenty of them in the old EU, before it became the Unity. Your president did what he had to do."

Joy held up both hands in a So What? gesture. "Well, I for one am glad we are being led by the Butcher of Callisto," she said, using a term for his father that Jacob had only read about. "He's a born fighter. He did right to space those miners who tossed the Star Navy into vacuum. And I for one like the idea of zapping the wasp fleet the second after it emerges from Alcubierre!"

"I fully agree," Jacob said quickly, not wanting his loyal ship captains to think otherwise. "It is the reverse of what the wasps have seen me and this battle group do. If we are to defeat a larger force, which I fully expect will appear, we have to take battle formations they have not yet seen. Or make adaptations of what we've already done that are better than our past choices."

"Captain Renselaer," called Chatur Mehta from the *Salamis*. "Your battle formations here and in Kepler 22 are what kept so many ships alive and able to fight. I was wrong to not join you earlier. You have my full allegiance now."

Jacob felt something he had rarely felt. An older man, a man with years of starship service, had just said Jacob had earned his respect. Had this feeling of . . . of respect been something he'd missed from his father? The man had given him approval in front of all the captains and before Gordon's own Battlestar officers. Did his father respect him? Maybe he would find out once they arrived at the magnetosphere rendezvous.

"Chatur, I thank you. The rest of you, follow us. *Lepanto* out."

The images of the other captains disappeared, leaving only black space and white stars filling the middle of the wallscreen. On the right and left sides were the earlier situational and sensor images. He looked ahead.

"Navigation, set us a vector for that wasp exit point. Gravity, adjust deck gravity and our inertial damper to handle ten percent of the speed of light. Life Support, warn all decks that we are moving out. Communications, maintain our All Ship video feed. Power, are our reactors ready to feed the thrusters?"

Maggie Lowenstein looked aside at one of her station holos. "All three fusion reactors are at Battle Condition One. Ready to feed power as demanded."

Jacob liked what he was hearing. "Tactical, alert me to any new neutrino source appearance."

"On watch for new sources," said Rosemary.

"Engines, bring the thrusters to full power."

His feet felt a low vibration. It came from the metal pedestal that supported his seat.

"All three thrusters now firing," called Akira.

"Weapons, stay sharp! Navigation, take us out."

And with that final order Jacob realized he was no longer following his father's example, or demand. He was a man, like his father, doing his duty. Both of them had faced danger and survived. Both of them had sworn an oath of service, an oath that Jacob had realized meant more than words during the first battle in Kepler 22. And both of them now moved to place their ships and their lives on the line of combat. With a start he realized that was what the Star Navy of America was all about. Defending those who must be defended and fighting all enemies of life, liberty and freedom. Inside, it felt good.

CHAPTER TWELVE

Daisy munched on her Southwest chicken salad in the Mess Hall, with her friends gathered around her table. Lori sat on her left, Carlos was across from her and Quincy was on her right. Kenji sat next to Carlos as he brought his own plate to the table. All four of them looked expectantly at her. Damn.

"Okay! Jacob is handling the change of command just fine. Believe me!"

"Really?" murmured Lori as she pushed a fork through a pile of spaghetti and meatballs. "He's gone from running a fleet to just commanding the *Lepanto*. While his takeover of the Battlestar surprised me back in Kepler 22, it was necessary. And I like how he's run the battle group ever since. He looks out for everyone."

"That he does," rumbled Quincy, laying his knife down atop the pork chop he'd been dissecting. "My blokes in the outrigger pod think the world of him."

"Well, Bannerjee hates him," Carlos said, his tone dismissive. "Course everyone knows the jerk had always been a ladder climber. He treats his two assistants as if they're personal gofers. Neither like it. The woman who began sending me Nav assignments almost apologized. I told I could handle double duty."

Daisy looked to Kenji, whose plate held a pile of Korean *bulgogi* beef. "What do you hear from the Spacers and enlisteds who come for meals?"

Kenji laid down his chopsticks and faced her. The tall, slim Japanese shrugged. "Most everyone likes the All Ship news sharing. We never got that during Admiral Johanson's command. We were lucky to hear what was happening on Life Support Deck just above us, let alone elsewhere on the ship. And I like the new rules from the admiral. Makes sense to me to put the deck chiefs into the chain of command whenever Command Deck is zapped. And it's good that any of us can travel to any deck now, not just keep to our own deck."

Daisy thought the same. The admiral's orders made official an easy-going policy Jacob had set in place during their Alcubierre transit to Kepler 10. Lori looked her way.

"You like being a full lieutenant?"

Her promotion was something Daisy still felt ill at ease with. "Not really. It goes with being the ship's XO. But I am glad Jacob promoted Alicia to full commander."

"Me too," Lori said quickly. She took a sip of lemonade, then fixed her blue eyes on Daisy. "What do you think the admiral will do with our pheromone talker? We can almost hold a normal conversation now."

Daisy had been following the frequent visits of Lori and Alicia to the Forest Room, always escorted by one or two of Richard's Marines in full combat gear. While the four wasps had never tried to hurt any human, still, they were aliens. And just because there was talk possible now, it did not mean the wasps thought and felt the way humans did.

"Have no idea. It's clear he plans to fight first, talk later, based on his orders to Jacob." She looked past her friend and noticed the room was nearly full with crew who worked her shift. "But I'm sure Jacob has some ideas. Beyond the unsent cartoon that threatens to nuke planet three and their colony world if the wasps hurt Valhalla."

Carlos frowned. "That threat may be all that protects our colony if the wasps arrive with thirty or forty ships. And that black hole weapon of theirs worries me. I never thought it was possible to create an artificial black hole. But these wasps did it."

"That they did," Quincy said quickly. "But our proton and carbo dioxide lasers can still hurt them. Jacob's order to combine our laser fire was vital in that first battle. It's proved critical ever since. At least our antimatter cannon has a longer range than their black hole weapon."

"Barely longer," murmured Lori. "And I did study gravitational theory in Moscow. Along with gravity plates and their range inside a ship. Just never thought putting them out on a ship's hull could create a black hole effect."

"None of us did," Daisy said, glad the talk had moved away from Jacob. "Well, Dance Night is tonight. Kenji, Mr. Petty Officer Third Class, you gonna bring your Korean girlfriend to the dance?"

Her friend blushed. "Hey! I didn't ask to be bumped up from Spacer! Your boyfriend did it to me."

Daisy smiled. "You avoided my question. Are you bringing her?"

"I am!"

Daisy could tell from his blush and his tone that her friend did not wish his love life to be discussed at the table. Even though he had been the one to bring up hers and Jacob's romance. She looked down at her plate. Her salad was half gone. And she had loads to do. There was a meeting with all deck chiefs in twenty minutes and she had to prepare for it. Jacob would be there and he relied on her. She liked being his right hand. But she didn't like how the XO job gave her worry-worry dreams. She slid off her stool and stood up.

"Later, all. See you tonight!"

Her friends said their goodbyes along with one teasing comment from Lori. She ignored it and headed for the exit slidedoor. Lori's question about the admiral's intentions toward the wasp captives was something she wanted to work on. The deadly times since their arrival at Kepler 22 had taught her that being prepared saved lives. And kept her out of trouble. Too bad being prepared had never prepared her for falling in love.

♦ ♦ ♦

Aarhant stared at the image of Fleet Admiral Renselaer. The man had awakened him from a sound sleep in his quarters on Habitation Deck. It must be about the video memo he'd sent the man not long ago, right after the admiral had taken command of all Earth ships. He sat up at the edge of his bed and faced the wall vidscreen that was just above his closed worktable. At least he wore a full pajama outfit.

"Admiral! I was off shift and—"

"You were sleeping," the man rumbled in a low voice that sounded like a baritone, based on his memory of watching one of Miglotti's operas. The admiral was calling from what looked like his office on the *Midway*. The man still wore his vacsuit over his formal Service Dress Blues. It made Aarhant feel unprepared.

"Yes sir."

The man's clean-shaven face showed no expression, other than intense focus. "You sent me a video about the actions of former Ensign Jacob Renselaer. You pointed out several actions of his which you feel were dangerous, ill-advised or wrong. What do you want?"

Aarhant swallowed hard. "Sir, I was hoping you would move me into command of the *Lepanto*. As the senior Lieutenant Commander among all staff officers, tradition and procedure would indicate I should be in command of this Battlestar."

The admiral, he noted, did not wear the circle of five silver stars that denoted his fleet admiral rank. Though the sleeves of his blue jacket showed the requisite stripes. Not proper for an officer of his rank. Still . . . .

Renselaer slowly shook his head, then fixed Aarhant with a look that almost made him pee in his pajamas.

"Lieutenant Commander, you are one sorry son of a whore. Your record shows you to be an influence peddler and special pleader. Your parents at Earth Command have bailed you out of three compromising relations with subordinates." The man lifted a white handkerchief and spit into it. "The taste of talking to you is . . . " The man in charge of any ship in the Star Navy of America took a deep breath. "Earth and America are at war. This is not the time for petty jealousies and complaints. Tend to the proper functioning of your Navigation Deck and don't *ever* again bother me with this trivia!"

Shock filled Aarhant. He'd never been talked to like this in his entire life.

"But sir! Insults are the wrong way to handle a legitimate—"

"*You* are an illegitimate son of a Mumbai whore!" the admiral growled. "In truth your parents are more competent than you, otherwise they would not still work at Earth Command. Shut your trap, do your duty and do not give me cause to put you in my brig. Your parents would be . . . shocked."

Aarhant nodded. There was nothing he could say.

The admiral's image disappeared from his screen.

◆ ◆ ◆

Jacob entered his father's conference room on the *Midway*, called there by a signal from his XO. He wore his Service Dress Blues uniform and had done his best to present a professional appearance since his arrival on Daisy's LCA. She had stayed behind on the *Lepanto*, as his designated Bridge commander. As a result, Richard had ordered one of his Marine pilots to fly her Landing Craft Assault across the cold blackness of space that lay twenty-five AU beyond the system's seventh planet. Hours earlier his battle group had joined up with his father's battle group. So far, no wasps had shown up. But it was a gamble for him to be here rather than on the Battlestar. Every ship was at Alert Combat Ready status, which was why he wore his transparent vacsuit over his uniform, with helmet pushed back. His father wore his own vacsuit. The man turned away from the open fridge in the Food Alcove and brought over glasses and a pitcher of iced tea.

"You still drink ice tea, don't you?"

"I do." He sat in a wood chair on one side of the large conference table.

His father put down two glasses, poured tea into Jacob's glass and his own, then set the pitcher on the table. He sat down a few chairs from Jacob. The man pulled out his personal tablet and put it on the table. Jacob did the same, pulling his tablet from a pocket of his vacsuit. The man who had dominated him before and after the death of his mother fixed dark brown eyes on him.

"You still hate me, don't you?"

Was this another passive aggressive move by his father? The man's face held lines in it that had not been there before. While just 55 years old, his father had gray streaks in his black hair. But his thick hands did not shake like Jacob's had done after first taking command. He decided to go with his gut.

"Not as much as before. Losing people in battle changed me. I don't like having ghosts looking over my shoulder."

Empathy, that strange emotion he had rarely seen from his father, except during his mother's funeral, now shown forth. "Sending people out to die on your orders does that. I hated it before Callisto. I hated it afterward. It's one reason I took Reserve Active retirement when I did. How are you handling it?"

"Adequately," Jacob said, feeling ill at ease with such personal sharing. His father had rarely shown any concern for his feelings. It had always been "Do it this way!" or "Stand up straight!" or "Don't you realize what it means to be in the Star Navy?" Well, Jacob did now. "Do the ghosts ever go away?"

His father sighed deeply, looked down at the glass of brown ice tea he held in both hands, then looked up. Jacob saw a look he could not remember ever seeing before. It wasn't empathy. Was it caring?

"No, they don't." His father's new look grew deeper. "You did me proud, son. While I hoped you would find a good career in the Star Navy, the way I did, I never thought you would do the necessary thing at such a terrible time." The muscles in his father's face relaxed. "Taking command of the *Lepanto* and then of the battle group was vital. You saved the lives of more than a thousand folks on those ships. And frankly, I don't give a damn that you jumped from being a butterbar ensign to acting captain. You did what was needed. I've told that to my people. My XO really does like your variations on standard battle formations."

Shock washed through Jacob. This was the most sustained moment of praise he had ever heard from his father. The man who couldn't bring himself to be a Dad like other fathers now told him the actions he'd taken were right, needed and good. It left him breathless. He took a deep breath.

"Thank you. That means a lot. I had a lot of help from my friends and from Lieutenant Branstead. She rallied the deck chiefs to my support."

"So I noticed," his father said, mood changing from sincerity to something strange, something that looked . . . playful? "I hear you and your XO have a romance going. Do you love her?"

Crap. Crap and crap again. Briefly he wished he could escape out the slidedoor. But that wasn't how a captain of the Star Navy behaved when speaking with his commanding admiral. "I do. She's smart, tough, a great pilot and she keeps the decks humming in ways I could never manage. She deserves to be a full commander. But she didn't like the promotion to lieutenant."

His father half-smiled. "Good people never do think they deserve a promotion. You did right to grant promotions to your 'friends' after their efforts during the space battles. You did right to promote Branstead. I've seen her file. She's more than a genius. She knows how to lead. Leading is a job I've always had to work at. Her file says she does it naturally. Have you noticed?"

Jacob almost choked on the sip of ice tea he had taken. He swallowed, damned and determined to not let this special moment disappear. "Yeah, I noticed. Wish I could be like her."

His father's expression moved from amiable to . . . to caring. "Build on what you've got with this Daisy. I loved your Mom. I never knew what she meant to me until I lost her. It's another reason I retired early. Don't hold back from your gal. Show her how you feel. Talk about your feelings." The man blinked. "I was never any good at feelings talk. But we were both very very happy the day you were born." His father fixed on him, looking earnest. "I hope you two can have the joy I had with your Mom. Sarah loved me and I did my best to love her back. I did it poorly. Try to do better than I did."

Jacob realized his father was confiding in him. It was something that had never happened before, not during his Mom's funeral and not afterward. Why was he acting this way? Was it late in life regrets?

"I'll do my best to show Daisy how much I love her." He licked his lips. This was getting too deep. He felt like a sailor cast afloat on an ocean with no sign of land in view. "Uh, admiral, one thing I didn't mention in the neutrino report has to do with my ship's antimatter cannon."

Concern filled his father's face. "It's working, isn't it?"

"Very well," Jacob said. "You saw the vids of how we took out several wasp ships with it. But I've modified its antimatter storage reservoir. We had time while hooked up for repairs at Sullivan's station. Daisy worked with my Weapons Deck chief and engineers from Engines Deck to enlarge it. Our reservoir can now hold enough antimatter for eight shots, one after the other, before having to make more AM using the ship's particle accelerator. I figured more shots might come in handy during future battles."

The man who had dominated him all his life now moved smoothly from caring father to his admiral of the Star Navy persona. "Well done. I like forward thinking like that. Send the specs over to my XO. She'll get them to our Weapons Chief. Though I suspect it requires an orbital shipyard to do the work?"

"That, or the heavy machinery that O'Sullivan's station has. His Hangar Two people did outstanding work in repairing the battle damage on four of my ships. Including the *Lepanto*."

"Good. Tell me about those repairs. And how many ships did it require for combined laser fire to breach the hulls of the wasp ships? I saw that such fire did kill several of them."

Jacob did just as his father asked. Inside, he felt relief at the shift from personal to professional. But he realized these moments were something he should share with Daisy. It was normal for a loving couple to share deep stuff. It was a lesson he realized his father had understood, even as he himself did poorly in such sharing with Jacob's mother. Well, he was determined not to make that mistake with Daisy!

♦ ♦ ♦

Hunter One looked away from the perception imager's view of the alternate dimension through which his flying nest now traveled. Grayness did not interest any of his five eyes. Better to consider the positive future that lay ahead. It was less than a light and rest cycle before they would arrive at the sky light system that held the future colony of the third world. The imagery of that world and the sensor tool records of it had been vital to his presentation to the colonists on the tenth colony world of Warmth. The Servants, Fighters and Workers who tended to the hundreds of larvae Pods had been affected by the news of two more nests lost to the deranged Soft Skins. The pheromone scents he had sensed from the gathered Swarmers had guided him in later adjustments to his argument during the long flight home to Nest. His arrival there had been preceded by the transmitted news of a new colony world discovered. Only after transmitting that news had he added cautionary pheromones about the terrible Soft Skins who had threatened Warmth and now controlled the sky light which sheltered the future colony world.

But the leaders of his Hunter caste had not been fooled. They understood his loss of eight nests to combat with the Soft Skins was serious. It had required the intervention of his Matron, and her reminder that all Swarmer ships had deposited their larvae Pods before fighting the Soft Skins, to prevent his loss of leadership over his damaged Colony nest. The Hunters Prime had considered his arguments, his records of the new colony world, and the battle imagery of his several attacks on the Soft Skins. They had chosen to do what had never before happened. They assigned a Hunter Prime to lead the return flight to the new sky light. The Prime was a generation older than One. Some of his genes were part of One's nature. His caste's leaders had chosen another senior Hunter to lead a third of the nests now flying through cold gray space. The force they led included three large Colony nests, each with the Pull Down weapon ability. Each Colony nest led eleven other Swarmer nests. The return flight amounted to six six-groups of ships, or 36 flying nests. Surely such a force could overcome the eight Soft Skin nests that had survived earlier battles.

"Alert," scent cast the Speaker To All Servant. "Incoming pheromones from the Hunter Prime. His image and scent are now with us."

One fluttered his wings, rising from his bench. He bent his two antennae forward and stiffened his stinger. Presenting an image of a Swarmer ready to assault an enemy was traditional for his caste. Being that way before one of the six leaders of his caste was vital if he expected his counsel to be inhaled.

"How flies your Colony nest?" asked the ultraviolet-glowing image of the Hunter Prime on the largest perception imager that filled the Flight Chamber wall before him.

He inhaled deep the rich aggregation pheromones that only a Hunter could emit. Those pheromones commanded obedience from all Swarmers. When scented by another Hunter, they strengthened his own scent talk.

"We fly well, Hunter Prime of all our nests," he said in a mix of signal, food, territorial and trail pheromones. He made sure there was no hint of any alarm pheromone. "The hard shell repairs to this nest were of the first order. All our weapons rings are eager to strike the insolent Soft Skins who block our way to the new colony world."

His leader's five black eyes stared at him even as the leader's spiracles inhaled One's pheromones. No doubt he tasted them for signs of disloyalty or personal ambition. There was no sign of either in his scent sharing. One had long ago learned how to exactly control his scent emissions. It was a basic lesson learned by all Hunters at an early age. Which meant the leader must rely on One's actions and how One's body appeared in his own perception imager. At least they were no longer in the same chamber, as they had been for too many light cycles while his nest was being repaired at the orbital flightyard that flew above Nest.

"You state what was known before we left Nest. How do you fly now!"

One almost stopped breathing at the sharpness of the command scent emitted by his leader. But such could be seen by any Swarmer and he was determined to show no sign of fear. "My Servants, Fighters, Workers and their leaders are eager to scent the air of the new colony world. My Matron looks forward to leading the deposit of our larvae upon that world. Every Swarmer on this nest will fight, bite and kill any opponent who blocks our way to the third world!"

Hunter Prime's two black antennae lifted up in a gesture One knew signaled satisfaction. "My Flight Servant computes that the colony world still flies just ahead of the fourth world and its attendant Soft Skin nests. My Fighter Leader suggests we attack and destroy the Soft Skins on our way to the third world. How certain are you that the Soft Skins will still hover above their world?"

Hunter One had long wondered that exact thought. He scent cast what he hoped was true. "Hunter Prime, the Soft Skins prefer the inner worlds of any sky light. They flew inward to our colony of Warmth. And when we arrived at the other sky light, their nests were clustered between the Soft Skin world and its moon. They sought to defend that world from our attack. Despite their deadly nests, one of my Support Hunters managed to strike that world with particle disruption seeds and lightning bolt globes," he said in a rush of trail, territorial, sex and food pheromones, followed by a strong scent of aggregation pheromones. "All behaviors of the Soft Skins say they will be clustered near the fourth world upon our arrival. We should be able to englobe them in passing and—"

"Enough!" scent cast his leader in a rush of command pheromones. "You and the other senior Hunter will follow my choices in how we attack these Soft Skins! The Support Hunters of every nest will follow and bite as I command." The flow of command, signal and dominance pheromones that arrived over his chamber's signaler was almost suffocating. His awareness that his leader's pheromones even now filled every chamber of his flying nest was a source of dismay. Each nest must be filled with the scent of the Hunter in charge of that nest. But he could no more defy the command scent than he could stop breathing.

"I obey," he scent cast in a flow of strong aggregation pheromones. "All on this Colony nest will obey your commands. Do you wish a change in our arrival formation?"

"Not needed," Hunter Prime said, his large, purple-glowing wings whipping quickly as they lifted his perfect body above his bench. The Servants in his Flight Chamber seemed dull by comparison. "We left our home sky light in the traditional formation of a cloud of flying nests and we will arrive in such a formation. From time long past every Swarmer in every cohort has arrived at a new colony site as part of a tight cluster of themselves and others. Such a formation has never failed us in the past. The future will bend to our Swarm!"

One inhaled the rich tapestry of pheromones that made up the speech of Hunter Prime. It was a mix of scents he had rarely tasted. Each caste of Swarmers knew best the scents of their caste. The leaders of each caste, however, carried with them pheromones unique to their place in Swarmer lives. Six Hunter Primes ruled his home world of Nest. One of those six now led the colonizing flight to the new world first scented by Hunter One. He had no doubt the Swarm would prevail. He had no doubt his many nests would deposit larvae Pods on the fourth world. He had no doubt at all. When exposed to the pheromones of a Prime, it was impossible to doubt.

As the image of Hunter Prime vanished and the rich scent of his leader disappeared, Hunter One felt that loss. No doubt his Servants and the Matron felt the same way. That was normal whenever any Prime scent cast to any Swarmer. Now, it was his duty to remind his fellow Swarmers of their duties.

"Stinger Servant, review the preparedness of our rings of stingers! Flight Servant, tap in the exact flight track for our Colony nest to take as we fly down to the new sky light. Servant for propulsive devices," he scent cast to the older male who commanded the devices that moved them through cold dark space. "Prepare your devices for rapid flight! Let us descend on the Soft Skins in the way Swarmers of our past descended upon thieves and aberrant Swarmers!"

His own command pheromones flowed out, filling his Flight Chamber and being sent to every chamber of his nest by way of signalers. His new Servant for sending such scents to every chamber in his nest was already busy at his panel, making sure Hunter One's words were scented by every Swarmer. He added some scent of trail, territorial and sex to his command flow as a reminder of the future reward for those Swarmers who best performed their duties. Caste to caste, cohort to cohort within each caste, so had the lives of all Swarmers been conducted from before clay records were kept. New devices kept records now, just as new devices allowed his people to fly to other sky lights. So now would new devices allow him and the other flying nests to decimate the Soft Skins blocking their way to the new colony world. Of that, his pheromones promised a certainty.

CHAPTER THIRTEEN

"Finalize battle formation!" came the command from his father, whose image was one of twenty that ran across the top of the front wallscreen.

Jacob looked to Rosemary at Tactical. She was the one who aimed their weapons at any enemy. She was also the person he relied on to monitor the positions of every other ship of the line. Daisy supplemented Rosemary with her own monitoring of her neutrino sensor holo, a copy of which floated to his left.

"Tactical, report!"

"Sir! The *Midway* is presently holding station at 8,000 kilometers to our right. Like the *Lepanto*, her nose is aimed directly at the computed wasp arrival point." The Irish woman pointed to the central image on the wallscreen, which showed a copy of Jacob's, Rosemary's and Daisy's neutrino graphic. "As ordered by Fleet Admiral Renselaer, our two cruisers and his three cruisers occupy the middle of our Alpha Iron Bar formation. They are the *Chesapeake, Hampton Roads, Okinawa, Mobile Bay* and *Manila Bay*. Between the cruisers and the Battlestars are the destroyers. The *Tsushima Strait, Salamis* and *Philippine Sea* lie between us and our cruisers. The admiral's destroyers lie between his cruisers and his battlestar. His destroyers are the *Red Sea, Lake Erie, Monitor, Leyte Gulf* and *Inchon*. Our three frigates *St. Mihiel, Ofira* and *Aldertag* are behind us while the admiral's frigates *Schweinfurt, Kursk* and *Malacca Strait* are in place behind his Battlestar."

Jacob scanned the holos that surrounded his seat. On his left was the sensor holo that tracked all incoming radiation and moving neutrino sources. At left front was a ship cross-section of the *Lepanto*, showing the status of every deck and each weapons system. At right front was a true space holo showing black space, bright stars and the white sweep of the Milky Way. Lastly, on his right hung a situational holo that showed the local star, the system's seven planets, the asteroid and Kuiper belts and a dotted line that represented the magnetosphere boundary.

In the situational holo their 21 ships showed as green dots arranged in a line that faced outward, toward the spot 500 kilometers ahead where the wasps were expected to arrive. The lineup of Battlestar, frigates, destroyers, cruisers, destroyers, frigates and his father's Battlestar was called the Iron Bar formation. Its purpose was to concentrate the proton lasers of the destroyers in the middle, between the two biggest ships with their antimatter cannons. A modification of the academy formation put the frigates behind the Battlestars and cruisers so their thicker armor could shelter the frigates, while allowing the frigates to add their nose lasers to combined targeting of enemy ships. It made for four deadly firing formations of gas and proton lasers, while the two Battlestars could independently fire their AM cannons. In theory, the combined firepower of lasers and antimatter beams should allow the immediate destruction of six enemy ships, thanks to the co-targeting of proton and CO_2 lasers at four ships while the antimatter zapped two.

He had wondered at the large distance between the *Midway* and the *Lepanto*, but Daisy had pointed out to him the distance corresponded to the 4,000 kilometer range of each starship's AM cannon. In essence, each Battlestar controlled a globe of space 8,000 klicks across. With the two Battlestars oriented as they were, their antimatter cannons could fire ahead, behind or sideways across a fighting front of 16,000 kilometers. Of course, shooting other than straight ahead from the AM node at the top of each ship's nose required attitude thrusters to flip that ship's orientation. The *Lepanto's* node showed Green Operational.

"Tactical, link me with Chief Linkletter at the AM cannon!" Jacob called out.

"Linking," responded Rosemary.

"Chief Linkletter reporting," came the voice of the young man over Jacob's helmet comlink. "Captain, you have orders for me?"

"I do. Activate the AM node. Advise me when the cannon is ready to fire."

"Activating, sir." A minute passed. Then two. "Antimatter cannon node is ready to fire!"

He looked to his ship cross-section holo. The right and left outrigger pods carried heavy CO_2 lasers at the front and rear of each pod, for a total of four deadly lasers. The outside hull of each pod also held a proton laser mount, while proton mounts were at the center of his ship's spine and belly. They were supplemented by Smart Rock railgun launchers at the ship's nose and tail, with plasma batteries on the ship's spine and belly. Eight missile launch silos poked out above the rear thruster nozzles. Altogether, the multiple weapons mounts allowed a Battlestar to control every direction from which an enemy might approach. But most vital beyond the AM cannon was the cross-linking of laser targeting.

"Weapons, what is the status of our forward lasers?"

"Sir," called Oliver Diego y Silva from his front Weapons station. "Petty officers Quincy Blackbourne and Olivia Houndstooth report their outrigger laser stations are co-targeting with the lasers of our frigates and cruisers."

Jacob looked up to the image of his father. "Fleet admiral, the *Lepanto* is ready to fire on multiple enemies. All ships of Operation StarFight have assumed the Alpha Iron Bar formation as ordered by you."

His father, who wore a vacsuit like everyone on every ship of the line, nodded briefly. Being practical he did not wear his combo hat inside the suit's flexible helmet. "So I see. *Lepanto*, all ships, move to Alert Hostile Enemy status!"

Jacob looked up. "Melody, change ship status to Alert Hostile Enemy!"

Overhead, the blinking red lights of Alert Combat Ready changed to blinking purple lights. A whirring siren that sounded like an old-style fire engine filled the Bridge.

"Ship status changed to Alert Hostile Enemy," the AI said, her tone a mix of excitement and worry.

Jacob reached up and pulled his helmet down over his head. It sealed with a snap-click. The vacsuit's enviro controls started up with a blast of oxy-nitrogen. Telltale status lights appeared in a chin-up position just below his nose. His seat vibrated as automatic straps moved out and over his chest in an x-pattern. Pairs of straps went over his legs. The straps were a backup to the inertial damper field that covered the entire ship.

"Crew, prepare for combat." He looked to the right front of the Bridge. "Gravity! Any sign of a graviton surge yet?"

"Not yet," replied Cassandra Pilotti. "Sir, will advise when my sensor shows a surge."

Jacob hoped the theory developed by Cassandra during their stay at the orbital station was correct. The Italian-American had worked with Lori to analyze their sensor records of the arrival of the wasp ships at the edge of Kepler 10's magnetosphere. While Lori had been the first to detect the activating of the artificial black hole field by the giant wasp ship, Cassandra had been motivated to figure out a way of knowing when the wasp fleet was about to arrive. She had noticed a large surge of gravitons from the spot in space where, moments later, the six wasp ships had appeared. Lori had looked at the chief petty officer's sensor results and concluded the Alcubierre space-time bubble produced by each enemy starship had a small leakage of gravitons during operation. While it was impossible to track any ship moving in Alcubierre space-time since its graviton leakage would be swamped by the gravitons emitted by stars and distant galaxies, if you knew where an enemy ship might appear, you could record the normal graviton flux for that spot and then detect any increase as a graviton surge produced by the imminent arrival of an Alcubierre drive starship.

In the admiral's image, his XO spoke. "Sir! Our Gravity chief is also monitoring for graviton surges."

"Sir," called the captain of the *Midway*. The man was as focused on his holo grouping as Jacob. "Our antimatter node is activated and ready to fire! Four shots available."

His father looked directly at Jacob. "*Lepanto* captain, you and all ships may fire immediately upon detection of a bandit. All ships, ordnance is cleared Hot!"

Jacob glanced at the ship cross-section that showed seven thermonuke-loaded missiles were already resting in seven missile silos, while three Darts were lined up and ready to launch from Silo Eight, if he gave the order. Which reminded him to look down to where Daisy, Richard and Alicia now sat.

"Chief O'Connor, feel free to advise me on any ship vector change you think would best help our targeting of the enemy."

"Captain, will do," said the white-haired man who had led the boarding of the wasp ship.

Jacob looked back to the front wallscreen. The center held the neutrino sensor image, while the left side showed a situational graphic of the system and the right side displayed a true space image of charcoal black space leavened only a bit by hundreds of stars and the white slash of the Milky Way. The center of the true space image was focused on the projected arrival point of the wasp fleet. At some point it would be filled with green laser streaks, red proton beams and black antimatter beams. There would also be the yellow lightning bolts of the wasp ships. The prior fights had made space resemble a summer thunderstorm with lightning everywhere. He hoped the spinning that every ship would do once the enemy appeared would reduce the damage done by those bolts. While they didn't penetrate the way enemy lasers did, they did zap segments of a ship's adaptive optics lenses, rendering that hull area less able to deflect incoming laser beams. The combination had been enough to cut deep through the two meters of armor of the *Lepanto*, and the meter thick armor of the *Chesapeake*. When the wasps had gone to combined targeting and focused on his battle group's frigates, two ships had died quickly. The frigates had just ten centimeters of hardened armor. It had proved unable to withstand more than three combined laser hits.

"Captain! Gravitons are surging!" yelled Cassandra, sounding surprised.

"Where from?" he called.

"Ahead! All across our front. There's got to be gobs of ships coming in!"

Gobs was not a firm number. But Jacob didn't blame Cassandra. This was the moment they had all known was coming.

"Fire at will on enemy detection!" he called out.

The true space image of the wallscreen now showed star dots rippling as incoming gravity bubbles that were Alcubierre space-time miniverses arrived at the edge of the magnetosphere. He lost count of the rippling spots. Too many to quickly count.

"Tactical! Enlarge the electro-optical view!"

"Enlarging," Rosemary murmured.

The true space image filled with dozens of log-shaped starships, arranged in groups of six. The hexagonal formation stretched across the front of the image. Three of the ships were giant ones like the ship that had nearly killed the *Lepanto* with its artificial black hole weapon. One such giant was directly in front of the Battlestar. Range to it was 473 kilometers, per the neutrino sensor.

"Antimatter cannon fire!" Jacob yelled.

A thick black stream of negative antimatter streaked out from his ship and hit the flat nose of the giant ship. White-yellow plasma covered the ship's nose. Then it moved inward, blowing out hull sections on either side. But the explosive dissembling of the giant ship ended as the expanding antimatter cloud formed by the beam reached out faster than simple matter could move and turned those hull fragments into star-yellow globs of light. A large sun now glowed where once a giant wasp ship had lived.

"All lasers firing!" yelled Rosemary.

Too much happened simultaneously.

The *Midway's* first antimatter shot hit a normal-sized wasp ship, converting its entire 300 meter length into a rod of star stuff. A new star filled the spot where the wasp ship had been.

Four groups of green lasers streaked out from the *Lepanto*, *Midway*, cruisers and frigates, impaling four log ships. In a few seconds those ships became clumps of molten yellow metal. A second later all four became balls of white-glowing plasma as their internal fusion reactors lost containment and made the ship remains into thermonuclear fireballs.

A group of eight red proton laser beams from the destroyers now impacted on the middle giant wasp ship, converting its flat nose and front ring of weapons tubes into glowing plasma. The front of the giant ship showed black tubeway holes and horizontal deck framing as the plasma grew thin enough to allow a view of the giant enemy ship.

A part of his mind kept count.

One giant wasp ship killed by the *Lepanto's* first antimatter beam. A normal wasp ship killed by his father's first AM beam. A second giant ship badly damaged. Four log ships vaporized by lasers. The third giant wasp ship now flipped over and fired its thrusters toward the Iron Bar formation, thereby blocking incoming red and green laser beams. Six wasp ships dead and one badly wounded.

A new group of green laser beams hit four other smaller log ships, while the *Midway's* second antimatter shot took out a fifth log ship.

Five new stars filled the blackness of space, joining the fading glow of the first seven.

"Tactical! Shift our AM aim toward those two ships at 270 degrees!" Jacob yelled.

The *Lepanto's* front rose and moved to the upper left of the true space field of ships that, he now saw from his situational holo counter, had been 36 in number.

"Targeted!" yelled Rosemary.

"Fire!"

Jacob watched as Linkletter's crew fired a second pulse of black antimatter at the two wasp log ships that appeared to be nearly side by side, although one likely led the other since the original formations of the arriving ships were six rings of six ships each. Just like the formation that had first attacked them in Kepler 22.

Two new stars appeared where the black beam struck.

Incoming green laser beams and yellow lightning strikes struck at the twenty-one ships of the two battle groups.

"Nose hit!" yelled Joaquin at Life Support.

"They're targeting the frigates!" called Oliver.

"Linkletter, fire at will!" Jacob called.

His eyes saw a third stream of antimatter reach out and impale a log ship that was thrusting sideways, trying to escape the target zone. It died and became another small star.

"We lost the *Ofira!*" called Rosemary.

Fuck.

"Frigates, move closer behind us and the cruisers!" Jacob called out over the neutrino comlink that connected the Bridge of every Earth ship.

"Fire on that departing big ship!" called his father.

The *Midway's* antimatter beam reached out.

But the giant ship's yellow-orange exhaust of plasma was sixty kilometers long.

The meeting of the two created a blast of energy that hit the rear of the giant ship, pushing it way faster, while creating a large cloud that blocked penetration by CO_2 and proton beams.

"The *Kursk* is gone," Rosemary said, sadness in her voice.

The heavily damaged second giant wasp ship had now flipped to aim its thrusters toward the Iron Bar formation. It followed the other giant ship out and away from their arrival point. Twenty other wasp ships now did the same flip over in an effort to escape.

Black antimatter beams shot out from the *Lepanto*, three in succession. Each beam hit the side of a turning wasp ship, converting its matter into a glowing white-yellow cloud of plasma.

Three new stars filled the void.

A fourth black beam from the *Midway* chased after a fleeing ship. One more tiny star filled the darkness.

"Enemy out of antimatter range," Rosemary called. "Now at 7,451 kilometers distance and moving at one-tenth lightspeed. Our lasers are firing but their exhaust flares are dispersing the beams."

Jacob looked at the moving neutrino counter. The number of purple enemy dots showed as eighteen. Which meant the two battle groups had lost two ships in return for killing eighteen enemy ships. A one to nine ratio. Still, a hundred fifty humans had died on those two frigates. More ghosts.

"Captain, the enemy is reversing formation. Looks like an umbrella arrangement," reported Rosemary. "All enemy ships are now beyond our weapons reach. Range is 10,473 kilometers. Enemy is firing on us."

Three dozen green and yellow beams and bolts streaked into the midst of the Iron Bar formation.

"We're spinning!" called Louise at Navigation.

"Hits on our spine and tail," called Oliver from Weapons. "All weapons are still operational."

Other ship captains reported similar hits, but no fatal damage.

Jacob looked to his father's image. "Admiral! I recommend our Battlestars launch four missiles each to create a thermonuke plasma cloud in front of us. It will shield us from incoming beams! You saw this in the videos I sent you!"

"Agreed! Captain, fire four of our missiles."

"Firing missiles, sir," called his father's captain.

"Tactical, do the same," Jacob called.

"Four missiles going out," Rosemary said hurriedly.

In seconds, once the missiles curved around and their chemfuel rockets pushed them ahead of the stationary line of Earth ships, each missile dispersed five thermonukes of three megaton power. Thirty tiny stars now glowed between the Earth ships and the distant wasp ships. The incoming laser beams and lightning bolts were diffused by the expanding plasma clouds, which soon became one giant arc of plasma that stretched across the 16,000 kilometers of the Iron Bar formation.

"Enemy has ceased firing," Rosemary said, just seconds before his father's XO said the same thing. "Enemy has retreated to 97,000 kilometers distance."

His father's face held more lines than during their private talk. The man's dark brown eyes fixed on Jacob. "Captain Renselaer, your ship fought well. I counted six antimatter shots from your node. We got off four. Our accelerator is working to build reloads. The enemy lost eighteen ships. The rest are holding formation well beyond us. What is the condition of your battle group?"

Jacob looked up at the images of each ship captain that ran across the top of the wallscreen. The seven remaining captains who led his group of ships all held up their thumbs, signaling their ships were still functional. He focused back on his father.

"Fleet admiral, all StarFight ships report they are combat operational, including the *Lepanto*."

The man nodded, looked aside at a holo, then back. "My captains report the same. Half my ships took glancing blows. Four of them lost part of their adaptive optics to those miserable yellow lightning bolts. The *Midway* lost its spine plasma battery. My cruisers each took deep strikes into their armor. No casualties other than our two lost ships."

Which meant their combined battle groups now numbered nineteen ships. The enemy had eighteen ships, two of them being the giant ships, though one of them had lost a part of its front hull. Still, it was a deadly force. Two giant ships versus two Battlestars. Jacob sent a prayer to the Goddess that they would now leave the Kepler 10 system. They were beyond the magnetosphere boundary. The wasps could enter Alcubierre space-time at any moment. Would they leave? Or would they attack and try to kill Valhalla?

◆ ◆ ◆

Hunter One scanned every perception imager in his Flight Chamber. Their contents told him what he had felt was not imaginary. The front quarter of his nest was gone, thanks to seven strikes by heavy sky light beams. Other parts of his outer shell were scored by incoming sky light beams of the green form. At least his nest had not gone the way of the other Hunter's nest. Nine hundred Swarmers including every larvae pod on that Colony nest were now mist in the cold darkness of space, far from the warmth of the nearby sky light. He looked to the image of Hunter Prime, who had acted faster than any Swarmer when the surprise attack had happened. Even as black beams reached out from two large Soft Skin nests, the Hunter Prime had flipped his nest and flown away from the deadly arrival spot. Command pheromones from his nest had told all other Swarmer nests to do the same, and to fire on the Soft Skins with their tail stinger tubes. Now the surviving nests rested far beyond the reach of the Soft Skin weapons. But where once six six-groups of nests had flown in a cloud of deadliness, just three six-groups remained.

"Hunter One!" called the leader of all Swarmers. "Is your nest able to bite hard!"

"It is," One replied in a rush of aggregation and signal pheromones. "We cannot erect our Pull Down hull plates for we lack the head group that would complete the field. But our middle and tail stinger rings are hungry to taste Soft Skin flesh!"

"You showed strength in biting back even as you turned your nest to follow me," Hunter Prime said in a strong flow of command, signal, trail and aggregation pheromones. "Are you ready to attack these two-limbed defiers of life's order?"

That answered his unspoken thought. They would not re-enter the alternate dimension and fly elsewhere. Briefly he wondered whether Hunter Seven and his nest still lived. "In some moments my nest can join your nest and the other Support Hunters in attacking the Soft Skins. My Workers and Worker Leaders are acting to close the severed tubeways and tend to our two remaining power blocks."

"You hold back?" Hunter Prime said in a swift flow of signal and dismay pheromones.

"No!" One said in a scent cast of aggregation pheromones. "This nest is loyal to the Swarm! This nest is ready to bite hard! This nest will carry our larvae Pods to the third world!"

"Better," Hunter Prime said in a mix of primer, trail and territorial pheromones. "Let us fly ahead and englobe these Soft Skins! Perhaps one of their nests will come close enough to be broken in my Pull Down field!"

"Leader, be wary of the black beams! Their range is greater than the reach of our Pull Down field."

The leaders two black antennae pulled back. "You make Challenge! Come to my nest and I will show you the wrongness of your scents!"

"No Challenge," One hurriedly scent cast back. "Misunderstanding am I. Helping our Swarm was my sole intent in warming of the black beams. Guide me, Hunter Prime."

The leader's antennae leaned forward. "At least your caste training comes forth now. Follow me ahead. Join your bolts and beams with mine. Together we shall bite off the heads of the Soft Skins!"

"Following," Hunter One replied in a flow of aggregation scent. "Flight Servant, set our path alongside the Hunter Prime. Propulsive Servant, make our nest fly toward the Soft Skins!"

Obedience pheromones came from all his Servants.

Ahead, the imagers showed the forms of the Soft Skin nests growing larger.

CHAPTER FOURTEEN

Richard felt surprise that the wasps had not already gone into Alcubierre space-time, if only to buy time for repairs. The incoming enemy fleet had been cut in half. Clearly they had not expected the Earth ships to be present at their arrival site. He felt renewed appreciation for the admiral's decision to do the reverse of Jacob's prior actions. While the young captain had much of the daring, ruthlessness and creativity of his old man, the admiral had decades of spaceship handling and fighting experience. Old Renselaer knew when to attack and when to prepare a surprise for the enemy. What would be the man's next command?

"Commander Branstead," called Jacob. "Are you ready to transmit some pheromone signals at those ships?"

That alerted him to a new surprise coming not from the father but from the son. He looked right to the brown-haired woman whose xenolinguist had been working on building an English-to-wasp vocabulary, thanks to daily talks with the captive wasps. What had happened recently?

"I am. We are, I mean." She put a finger on an armrest control patch. "What do I send to Chief Osashi?"

"Send him three short message scents," Jacob said quickly. "Make the first one 'Fly away'. Make the second one 'Stop biting'. Make the third one say 'Submit to Soft Skins'."

The veteran deck leader tapped her control patch, looked aside at a holo filled with color patterns, then up front where the electro-optical scope image showed the wasp ships moving into a loose cloud formation. "Transmitted to the chief. Let's hope our scent frequency matches their receiver tech."

"It should," said Daisy from his left, giving him pause to wonder just what the captain's brain trust of smart young people had been doing together. "Lori tried it on another, unmodified signaler unit that was placed in the Forest Room. The first two signals caused the expected reaction among the Worker wasps. Their response ended after their leader told them to ignore the strange scents."

"Good," Jacob said, sounding pleased.

Richard looked up at the line of ship captain images. There were eighteen there, including the admiral, his XO and his captain in one of the images. Jacob was the missing nineteenth captain. The admiral had looked up at Jacob's comment. Now he frowned thoughtfully.

"Captain Renselaer, do I understand your Science people have created a way to 'talk' to these wasps?"

"They have, sir. It requires the emission of polarized radio signals. The polarization interacts with the wasp signaling devices to convert incoming EMF signals to scents, and to convert scents received into polarized EMF signals," Jacob said slowly. "Do you wish a copy of the three signals I just ordered sent to our Communications chief?"

"I do. Send it to my XO's attention," the admiral said quickly.

"Going out," called Osashi from up front.

The admiral looked aside at a holo. "The wasps are not leaving this system. Instead, they are moving into a cloud formation. It's similar to what you encountered in the Kepler 22 attacks. Are they unable to do other than try to englobe an enemy?"

"Sir," Jacob said quickly. "My exobiologist Lieutenant JG Antonova has shared with me her insights into wasp culture. Like many predatory insects on Earth and on our colony planets, these alien wasp people have a cultural pattern of attacking *en masse* any opponent or intruder. She thinks our arrival at Kepler 22 set off this instinctive behavior."

"Could be," the admiral mused. Richard marveled at how quickly the admiral could change his mind, given new facts. The old man, wearing helmet and vacsuit like all of them, faced forward. "My XO has signaled to me we have your three wasp signals. Do we both use them at the same time, or independently?"

"Admiral, sir, I suggest your Battlestar should transmit a different signal from the one the *Lepanto* sends out, but do it at the same time you hear us transmit a signal. That should increase wasp confusion when they get different orders from two different sources, on top of whatever orders their leader or leaders are transmitting by polarized EMF signal. There's no need to try the neutrino transmission mode since speed of light works almost instantly at the short ranges of our weapons systems."

"Agreed." The old man's squarish face grew tense. "They're coming in!"

"Enemy approaches at 973 kilometers a minute," called Rosemary.

"We concur," the admiral said. "All ships! Your ordnance is cleared Hot. Engage the enemy with co-targeting of gas and proton lasers!"

"Tactical," called Jacob. "You heard him."

"Tracking incoming enemy," Rosemary said softly. "Range is 74,312 kilometers and reducing. Enemy formation is cloud-like."

"All ships!" called the admiral. "Go to Alpha Bristle Ball formation!"

Richard liked that order. The new formation was one not seen by the wasps and it should be effective in defending against an englobing attack.

"Navigation, move us to the rear of the formation," Jacob said quickly.

"Vector track set. Engines are taking us to our new position," called Louise Slaughter.

She was one of two redheads on the Bridge, a fact that did not disturb him. Richard liked colorful people, in all skin and hair colors. Even the Cassandra gal whose hair was a bright green. Looking up, he watched the wallscreen as images changed. The cloud of silvery wasp ships grew larger in the screen's true space image, while the situational image on the left enlarged to display their section of space, with the Pluto-like seventh planet far behind the two ship groups. On the right glowed the sensor tracking image. In seconds the green dots of the Earth ships had rearranged themselves into a tight ball with just four thousand kilometers between each ship. The *Midway* was at front middle of the ball, the *Lepanto* at rear middle, with the five cruisers arranged in a north-south polar circle halfway between the two Battlestars. The eight destroyers were clustered halfway into the ball, their proton lasers aiming forward for the moment. The surviving four frigates were at the center of the ball formation, which gave them some shelter from incoming beams that might be blocked by the destroyers, cruisers and the Battlestars.

"Range is 41,427 klicks," called the other redhead at Tactical.

Richard pulled his helmet down over his head. It sealed with a snap-click. Telltale status lights appeared in a chin-up position just below his nose. His seat vibrated as automatic straps moved out and over his chest in an x-pattern. Pairs of straps went over his legs. He didn't like being locked into his cushioned seat, but it was necessary in case the ship lost its inertial damper field. A rare event, true, but not impossible.

"Admiral," called Jacob hurriedly. "Suggest we each launch three missiles loaded with x-ray thermonuke warheads. At Kepler 22 they seemed to affect wasp ships when they were within 5,000 klicks."

"Agreed. Tactical, launch our missiles," the admiral said quickly. "Weapons, what load of antimatter has our accelerator produced?"

"Sir, three shots, with a fourth building," came the voice of the admiral's Weapons station crewwoman.

On his left, Daisy leaned forward. "Admiral, I show we have four shots in our reservoir, with a fifth accumulating."

That was fast work for a particle accelerator. Still, the accelerator tube that wrapped around the nose of each Battlestar was a sixth generation device. Its magcoils clearly produced an unprecedented amount of positron particle collisions that produced the negative antimatter which the cannon's emitter node shot out in a magnetically controlled beam. Richard did not like relying on a weapon the size of a small spaceship, but carrying an AM cannon was one of the reasons for the building of five Battlestars. It quite put to rest the old argument between manned fighters and automated missiles. Neither moved at lightspeed, which the cannon beam did.

"Tactical?" called Jacob.

"We've launched four x-ray thermonuke missiles. I've programmed the missiles to eject their warheads once their sensors detect an enemy ship within 11,000 klicks," reported the Tactical woman. "Will make it harder for the wasp lasers to track and zap the warheads, which are on a randomized vector track toward any ship without a friendly IFF signal."

"Good. Science, do you see anything unusual about the incoming formation?" Jacob said.

"Nothing yet, sir." The portly Jewish man with the booming voice was someone Richard had yet to figure out. Willard Steinmetz had few friends on the ship, according to scuttlebutt heard in the Mess Hall, but he was clearly very competent. And Branstead had put him into his Bridge post long before the old admiral had gotten the senior officers killed. "However, we should be alert to their black hole fields. Only a giant wasp ship has carried that weapon, so we could be facing two such fields."

"Captain," called Daisy. "My analysis of the signals from the giant wasp ship on the left of the cloud formation says it is the same ship that led the attack on us in Kepler 22. It stopped using the black hole field after we put a big hole in its front nose. Could be it cannot produce such a field with a quarter of its hull missing."

"Good point, XO." Jacob's tone sounded thoughtful. "All ships, be alert to the danger posed by the two giant wasp ships. They are able to produce artificial black hole fields. The weapon's range is 3,917 kilometers. The wounded giant ship may not be able to deploy its field."

Richard watched the admiral's image but the master of the combined fleet seemed focused on other matters in the holos that surrounded him. Which made him wonder if there was anything he could see in the enemy formation that he should warn young Renselaer about?

"Navigation, spin the ship," Jacob said firmly.

"Spinning."

The wasp ships had reached a range of 15,000 klicks and were still incoming at just under a thousand klicks per minute. Which meant his ship would shortly be on the receiving end of CO_2 laser and lightning beam strikes. Watching a lightning bolt jink and jerk across 11,000 klicks of black space was an experience Richard did not like. He had never enjoyed doing maneuvers in the rain, let alone during a thunderstorm. But such was normal for Marine raiders and Quantico had never let up on the doctrine of "If it's hard to do, do it better than anyone else!" He wished his Darts had a role to play. But their thin hulls could not survive the oncoming blizzard of green and yellow beams fired by the wasps. The only way his three Darts had managed to get to the ship hiding in the comet had been thanks to covering fire from Jefferson's destroyer. She was the kind of woman he would gladly go into a firefight with, much like Diego. Neither resembled each other, but both were eager to take out the enemy. Which, he recalled now, was the prime reason he had joined the Marines, long decades ago.

"Incoming!"

♦ ♦ ♦

Hunter Seven watched the movement of Swarmer nests and Soft Skin nests on the perception imager that depicted sky light particles from their propulsive units and power blocks. Earlier, when he had seen the Soft Skin nests fly in a group to the exact point where One's Colony nest would return to, he had wished for a way to warn them of the danger. But that required his nest to be in the alternate dimension that allowed travel from one sky light to another. Now, flying above the world meant for Swarmers, they were far from the place where such travel could happen. So the disaster had happened upon the arrival of six six-groups of nests, including three Colony nests.

Clearly the new Soft Skin nests were led by someone different from the one who had led the fighting nests in the earlier battles in darkness. This new leader had brought more fighting nests, perhaps from the home world of the Soft Skins. His Servant for monitoring external sky signals had noted the direction the new nests had come from. But now, after seeing three six-groups of nests be destroyed at little loss to the Soft Skins, he wondered if he would ever live to share with them his knowledge of the third world.

"Hunter Seven," called his Servant who was their Speaker To All. "Should we send scent to our fellow Swarmers that we are here, above the future colony world?"

"To what point?" Seven cast in a flow of frustration and signal pheromones. "It would take us three day cycles to reach our fellows. But if we try to leave, the particle disruption seeds left behind by the Soft Skin nest that followed us here would try to kill us."

"Leader!" called his young Stinger Servant. "Our tail ring of stingers could kill those seeds!"

"Perhaps so," Seven said in a slow flow of primer and territorial pheromones. "But we are badly damaged. We lack most of our stingers. We could not help these other flying nests."

"But Seven," called the young female who managed their sole surviving propulsive device. "If we kill these seeds and then fly to the world where the Soft Skins now live, could that not help? It might force the Soft Skins to send some nests to defend their colony."

Seven wondered at the idea proposed by the talented female. It would violate their agreement to stay at the world he hoped would be a future colony for Swarmers. But these new Soft Skins had already violated the offer for each lifeform to stay on its own world and to share needed items by meeting in cold dark space.

"Your scent is engaging," he told the young female. "Let us see what comes of this next battle in the dark sky. Perhaps we can do as you say."

"Leader," called his new Stinger Servant, "we should signal our offer to Hunter One now! One of those nests is his Colony nest. Our tools tell us he has returned as promised!"

Seven did not like the recklessness of the young Servants in his Flight Chamber. They had not been satisfied with visits to the world below. Even the capture of live food and eating it out in the open spaces of the new world had failed to satisfy them as all on his nest awaited the return of Hunter One and other Swarmers. That had now happened. Perhaps it was the right time to fly into the darkness. He emitted a rush of aggregation and command pheromones.

"Speaker To All, send word to Hunter One of our position and our willingness to dive on the Soft Skin colony world. Stinger Servant, begin destroying those particle seeds. Let us see how well you aim your stinger!"

◆ ◆ ◆

Daisy watched the situational holo on her left as Jacob fought their ship. Red dots swirled around the green dot ball of their formation. She looked at her true space holo. It was filled with red, green and yellow beams as every ship in the two groups fired at each other now that the wasps had slowed enough to avoid running past the Earth ships. Both groups now did combined targeting of enemy ships. The eight destroyers had concentrated their proton laser beams on a wasp ship her holo had labeled W4. But every wasp ship except the two giant ones were concentrating their lasers and lightning bolts on the inner cluster of frigates. Which were having a hard time avoiding being hit, even tho the *Lepanto*, the *Midway*, the *Chesapeake* and other cruisers were moving to block as many beams as possible. But with the wasps spread out in a cloud formation, beams were coming in from every angle relative to the Bristle Ball. From the top, bottom and front. Soon it would be the rear once they finished their enveloping maneuver.

"Tactical! Fire our railguns at the wasps!" Jacob ordered.

"Firing Smart Rocks! Four loads have gone out. Loading the rails again," called Rosemary.

In her mind Daisy visualized the four sprays of *plastique*-carrying Smart Rocks. The railguns at the top front, bottom front, top rear and bottom rear parts of the hull fired to either side of her ship. The rocks were the size of beach balls and had their own chemfuel jets for maneuvering. They left the launcher rails at a speed of seven miles or eleven klicks a second. It was Earth escape velocity and very fast when distances were measured in a few thousand kilometers. The *Midway* had fired Smart Rocks from her position at the front of the Bristle Ball as wasp ships passed to either side. Each cruiser had a single railgun launcher on its nose, so that added five more fans of Smart Rocks reaching out to impact on the incoming wasps. She noticed something about the wasp ships.

"Captain! The damaged wasp ship is heading straight for us! It's not trying to avoid our fire!"

"Noted. Tactical, fire the antimatter cannon at that ship!"

"Firing," called Rosemary.

"Sir," called Oliver from Weapons. "The giant ship is 5,000 klicks out! It won't kill it."

"Noted. But the beam will tickle whatever hull sensors it has. And maybe damage some of its weapons tubes," Jacob said.

A small star took shape to the left side of the Bristle Ball.

"Bandit splashed!" called Oliver.

"Navigation, send the 'Fly Away' signal to the wasp ships!" called Jacob.

"Transmitting," replied Louise. "Two wasp ships are moving back from us!"

"We're sending out 'Stop Biting'," the admiral said quickly.

Three wasp ships stopped firing.

Two dozen bright lights lit up the darkness as Smart Rocks hit wasp ships on either side of the Bristle Ball. Those ships, which had been spinning to reduce the impact of incoming laser beams, now jinked sideways, up and down, moving to avoid the self-directed balls of explosive. Some of those ships shifted their laser fire from the frigates to the incoming Smart Rocks. New bright lights flared as the wasps began killing the Smart Rock broadsides.

The *Inchon's* green dot slowed its movement as its fellow destroyers shifted their orientation to take on another wasp ship. Her sensor holo told the tale.

"Captain!" Daisy called. "The *Inchon* has lost one of its thrusters to a combined beam attack. She's limping. But she's also shooting back!"

On the screen up front Joy Jefferson spoke. "Jacob! Uh captain, our spysats at the third world report all our thermonuke warheads have been destroyed by that wasp ship that went there. It's moving out of orbit and heading for Valhalla!"

"Fuck," he said, briefly surprising Daisy with his language. "Admiral! That wasp ship above the third world is leaving orbit and heading for Valhalla. O'Sullivan's base can only cover its side of the planet. They can move the base to stay over the settled continent, but they'll run out of fuel soon. Suggest we send the *Inchon* toward the wasp colony world as our answer and let me send out the MAD video to these wasp ships!"

"Do it," the senior Renselaer said.

"XO, take care of the *Inchon*." Jacob paused. "Com, transmit the MAD cartoon video."

"Transmitting on the wasp frequency," Osashi said calmly.

Daisy tapped on her own neutrino comlink line and spoke to the captain of the *Inchon*. She acknowledged and began moving her destroyer out of the Bristle Ball formation. Then Daisy saw something worse than wasp ships that seemed able to avoid most return laser fire.

"Admiral!" she yelled. "That giant wasp ship is changing its hull plates! It's going to black hole mode! Keep your distance from it!"

"Seen. Understood. Marjorie, move us back," the man said over the neutrino link that connected every Earth ship. "Tactical, concentrate our outrigger lasers on the nose of that big bastard. Cruisers! Join your lasers with ours! If we can blow a big enough hole in its front, maybe it will be unable to go black hole!"

Daisy hoped that was possible. But now she saw the meaning behind the swirl of wasp ships that flew wildly around the outside of the Bristle Ball, taking their chances from the combined laser and proton fire of the Earth ships. Both giant wasp ships were aiming to take out the Battlestars.

"Captain!" Daisy yelled. "There are five x-ray laser nukes between us and that damaged wasp ship. It may be trying to ram us! We should blow them. And the other giant ship is moving to the rear of the *Midway*. It's aiming for the Battlestar!"

"Tactical, make it so," Jacob called. "Admiral, suggest you blow your x-ray thermonukes since they are closest to the oncoming enemy."

"Agreed. Tactical. Blow them," the admiral said hurriedly.

A second star glowed white-yellow as another wasp ship died under the combined proton beams of seven destroyers. The rear-mounted dual lasers on each destroyer were firing at the giant wasp ship that was aiming for the *Midway*. Too late.

"It's gone black hole!" cried Willard.

Daisy had too much to watch in her holos and on the front wallscreen.

The distance between the *Midway* and the black hole wasp ship was closing fast. Now down to 4,303 klicks. Clearly the black hole ship could move even while sheltering inside its black hole field. Which was wrapping incoming red and green beams around its globular field in an accretion disk that was almost beautiful.

The *Inchon* could only make five percent of lightspeed now that she had lost one of her two fusion pulse thrusters. She was launching missiles from the two missile silos on her tail, clearly hoping to raise a plasma cloud shield against the green laser beams and yellow lightning bolts coming at her from three wasp ships in her portion of the fighting space.

"No you won't, you bastard!" yelled Joy from the *Philippine Sea* as she moved her destroyer out of the inner Bristle Ball and onto a vector track that would put her ship between the oncoming wasp giant and the *Lepanto*.

"Admiral!" yelled Jacob. "We need to retreat to the seventh planet! Make the wasps chase us. Our stern lasers can give 'em hell!"

The man grimaced. "All ships! Head for the seventh planet. Make top speed! Do it now!"

Daisy kept one eye on her situational holo with its green and purple dots and one eye on the true space holo. She hoped there would be no star blasts among the battle group ships. Which were now all turning toward the ice ball of the seventh world. Which lay nearly 20 AU distant. The plasma exhausts of each ship created a space behind them that blocked incoming lasers and lightning bolts. But the rear-mounted lasers on every Earth ship now fired at angles that hit the swirl of wasp ships. Three wasp ships showed silvery water globules and white air spewing from hull punch throughs on their sides or noses. A few surviving Smart Rocks hit other wasp ships, causing them to shift away from direct pursuit.

The giant wasp ship in black hole mode shifted its course away from the *Midway* and toward the *Lake Erie* destroyer, which was slow in going to full thruster speed. It was on maneuvering thrust like all Earth ships had been as they shifted their position to avoid incoming beams while keeping the form of the Bristle Ball.

"No!" Daisy yelled.

Simultaneous with her situational holo that showed the black hole ship reaching a distance of 3,900 kilometers from the destroyer there came a new white-yellow star.

"Third wasp splashed," said Rosemary.

"The *Erie* is caught!" Jacob yelled.

Daisy watched as the *Erie's* crew fired both fusion pulse thrusters in an attempt to escape the gravitational pull of the wasp black hole. She heard its captain order Engines to go to twelve percent of lightspeed. Clearly he was trying to copy the escape speed that had allowed the *Lepanto* to escape from the other giant wasp ship. But the *Lepanto* moved on three thrusters, whereas the cruisers, destroyers and frigates moved on two. Two thrusters could not produce the 14 percent of lightspeed that had allowed her ship to escape.

In slow motion the *Lake Erie* came closer and closer to the black hole event horizon that was now a swirl of green and red beams, endlessly circling the wasp ship, unable to ever reach the enemy ship inside. Nor could the rear CO_2 lasers fired by the *Erie* make it through. The two green beams twisted at a right angle as they hit the event horizon of the black hole ship. A black antimatter beam from the *Midway* now hit the event horizon and was itself turned sideways. Where its negative matter met the positively charged matter of the proton and CO_2 lasers, white glows happened as one type of energy joined with another type in total annihilation. Daisy wondered if, when the *Erie* hit the edge of the event horizon, it would be destroyed

by the circling antimatter before the gravity tides of the black hole
field ripped its hull plates apart, pulling them into metal taffy.

The white glows faded away. There was more laser energy
circling the wasp ship's field than there was antimatter. The *Midway*
had fired only one AM beam, then stopped as it became clear the
beam could not harm the wasp ship.

In the scope image, the gray hull above the *Erie's* yellow-
orange thruster flames stretched visibly.

It all came apart at once.

Three hundred meters of metal, air, water, plants and hope
became fragments circling the event horizon of the black hole ship.

They were joined by 113 human bodies.

She found no ease in knowing everyone had died instantly as
their bodies became elastic taffy that joined with metal taffy and
streams of water to form a circling ring of matter that had once been
alive, caring and dangerous.

"She's gone," muttered Marjorie Jones from the *Midway*.

Daisy looked up at the image of the admiral, his XO and his
captain. All looked shocked. Death in space they understood. Death
by way of a black hole was not anything they had trained for.

"Admiral, the *Lepanto* is coming alongside you," Jacob said,
sounding angry and sad at the same time. "We will be a rearguard
against those wasps. Maybe they will pull back."

Daisy's eyes caught the counter number in the neutrino
scanner holo. It showed fifteen purple dots and eighteen green dots.
They had killed three more wasp ships and paid in flesh with the lives
of one destroyer.

The man who had earlier been vibrant, decisive and daring in
ordering the Bristle Ball formation licked his lips. Inside his helmet
Gordon's face was lined. There was no doubt showing, but sadness
had visited him. Daisy could see that, even if most men couldn't.

"They are still following us, but yes, they've opened the range
to 50,000 klicks. Maybe that MAD video had an effect," Jacob's
father said. "All ships! Maintain Alert Hostile Enemy status. Tend to
your wounded. Reload as needed. Repair any hull punch throughs that
can be reached from inside. This is a fighting retreat!"

CHAPTER FIFTEEN

Hunter One could not cope with his conflicting emotions. On one wing there came the scent signal from Hunter Seven showing his nest flying above the third world of this sky light, with images of its land and wild lifeforms, and the claim it was heading to the Soft Skin colony world to threaten its destruction. But on the other wing he now viewed a simple imagery group sent from the large Soft Skin ship that threatened the colony world, and Warmth itself, with particle seed destruction most terrible. The imagery of the signal conveyed land-bound explosions greater than any produced by one of his particle seeds. The meaning was clear. If Swarmers harmed the Soft Skin world, then both the new colony of Warmth and the hoped for colony in this flight of worlds would be destroyed. He looked to the perception imager that carried the fluttering wings of his leader.

"Hunter Prime, will we lose our new colony world?"

The bright colors of the Prime's strong body seemed diminished. The short yellow hairs of his outer hard shell seemed limp, not upright as normal. The leader's two antennae were half bent, a clear sign of dismay at the loss of so many nests. Only fifteen now remained in flight. Behind the leader were his Servants who controlled the devices that filled the Flight Chamber. Each of them also looked disturbed. What could the Servants be scenting? Hunter One inhaled the scents coming from Prime's nest and smelled dismay pheromones mixed with aggregation, trail, territorial and dominance scents.

"No!" cried Hunter Prime in a rushing flow of Hunter dominance pheromones. "No, I will not permit the loss of this new colony world. Our larvae have need of feeling that world's pull down caress. They need to see the open sky in which they will eventually fly!"

"Agreed," One said hopefully. "The Soft Skins fly toward the outermost world of this sky light, perhaps there to fight us once again. It will be a full day cycle before we and they reach that world," he scent cast in a mix of alarm and territorial scents. "Do we try to bite their flying nests? We could lose more Swarmer nests before the Soft Skins are overcome. And more larvae Pods."

The black antennae of Hunter Prime lifted stiffly. His five eyes fixed on One. The whole shape of his massive body became charged with energy. "We pretend, Hunter One. Recall how on Nest, in the long distant past, one group of Swarmers would stop attacking the territory of another group and fly off to hover above a nearby forest or mountain, as if in defeat? The defenders would fly back to their nest and set to eating and sexing in celebration. Then the fly away would reverse and the attacking Swarmers would overwhelm the defenders, bite the necks of their Hunters and Fighter Leaders, and spread their dominance scent among the surviving Swarmers." Behind the leader the bodies of his Servants also grew firmer, more resolved as his unique dominance pheromones filled their spiracles. "You have experience sending simple signals to these Soft Skins. Prepare and send a signal that shows our nests flying to one side and moving to the third world, which flies ahead of the fourth world occupied by Soft Skins. Show our nests flying above that world and depositing our larvae Pods on its surface."

One liked this proposal. It promised the chance to do what all Swarmers ached to do, which was to drop larvae Pods on a land newly claimed as a home nest. But the actions of Seven complicated this flight of pretence. "Hunter Prime, what do I say to Support Hunter Seven? His nest is heading for the Soft Skin colony world, there to fly above it and make threat of its destruction."

"Let Seven fly above that world," Prime replied in a flow of dominance, trail, aggregation and duplicity pheromones. "But tell him not to shower particle seeds on that world. Instead, let it fly well above the defending nest that hugs the sky of that world. That sends the signal we Swarmers could attack, but we will not, so long as the Soft Skins allow us to reach our new colony world."

That should smell right, One thought. He could amend the simple imagery signal to show Seven's nest circling above the fourth world, while the many Swarmer nests flew to the third world. But an image in another perception imager complicated matters. "Hunter Prime, I will do as your direct. The imagery will be prepared. But a Soft Skin nest has left its fellow nests and now flies toward our colony world. The Soft Skins seem to make a threat to our world, similar to what Seven is making to their world."

The leader's sharp, jagged mandibles opened and shut with a sharp clacking sound. "True. But that Soft Skin nest moves slowly. It has a damaged propulsive device, much like the damage done to Seven's nest. Our nests can fly twice as fast as the single Soft Skin nest. We will overtake and pass it. If that nest tries to approach our colony world, we will destroy it!"

"Outstanding!" he said in a flow of aggregation and territorial scents. "We do not lose any more nests. We claim our colony world. We send down our larvae Pods. Then we turn and attack the Soft Skin world with all our might!"

"Just so," Hunter Prime said with a flutter of his brown wings. "If we lose a few nests in the attack on the Soft Skin world, that is the price we pay for depositing our larvae on their new home! Once our larvae are landed, we do what Swarmers have always done. We fly out to defend that new home from these intruding Soft Skins!"

Hunter One heard the history of the leaders of his caste in the scent-laden words of Hunter Prime. It reminded him that what he and others now did under this new sky light had meaning for future generations of Swarmers. While the earlier simple imagery of both peoples occupying their worlds, then making trade in cold dark space for items needed by each people had been attractive, this way lay certainty. On Nest, no intruder had ever been allowed to live close to one of their ground-dug nests. The same had prevailed on all ten worlds colonized by the Swarm, including the eleventh world of Warmth. Doing otherwise carried a risk. These Soft Skins might stay on their world for a time. But new generations of Soft Skins could choose to attack the Swarmer colony world. Better to extinguish the menace now.

"Your scent carries the wisdom of our caste," One said in a strong flow of his own dominance pheromones, mixed with a strong aggregation loyalty scent. "I will prepare this new imagery. It will be sent to the Soft Skins flying ahead of us. Then we will shift our flight and make a new path to the colony world!"

"Just so," Hunter Prime said in an overwhelming flow of his own dominance pheromones. "Act as I have ordered. Then join your Colony nest with mine and let us lead our other nests inward to warmth, to a welcoming sky and to a new land on which we can build homes for our larvae!"

One looked to his Servant for the study of aberrant social behaviors. The older male was watching him. "Prepare the imagery signal as demanded by Hunter Prime! When it is done, send it to these Soft Skins! Once it is sent, our nests will fly away from these intruders and claim our new home!"

◆ ◆ ◆

Jacob watched the new imagery sent from the wounded wasp ship to all Earth ships. His father was doing the same. As were all the captains of the two battle groups. He knew Alicia could help with understanding it, but Lori had the best insight. "Lieutenant Antonova, come forward. I have need of your guidance."

As his friend walked up from the room's back row of seats, where Carlos had sat with Lori during the battles, he looked down. Daisy was watching a holo version of the wallscreen imagery, while Richard looked over at Alicia's holo of the same. Up front, all the function post people were either watching the big image or a repeat in one of their holos. The top of the wallscreen still carried the images of the other seventeen Earth ship captains, including his father's Bridge. On the left side of the wallscreen hung a situational image that showed all space from the local star out to their current position. The graphic made clear the distance to the seventh world was almost 25 AU. The system's Kuiper Belt of comets lay between the magnetosphere at 45 AU and the 19 AU position of the Pluto-like world. He glanced at the true space holo on the right side of the screen. The *Lepanto's* electro-optical scope carried an image showing the cluster of surviving wasp ships. Two giant ships plus thirteen destroyer-sized ships were following the Earth ships, but someone in command among the wasps had allowed the separation between the two fleets to become nearly 100,000 klicks. Then again, ships traveling at ten percent of lightspeed could cover such a distance very quickly. If the enemy increased their engine speed to eleven or twelves psol, they could overtake the Earth fleet.

"Lieutenant JG Antonova reporting."

Jacob looked away from the cartoon imagery that was concluding with images of the wasp ships sending down larvae pods to the third world, while Earth ships returned to Valhalla. Lori looked tired. Her long hours working with Alicia's xenolinguist to compile a basic conversational guide of English-to-wasp smells had kept her from sleep, from dates with Carlos, even from the Dance Night event all ships had enjoyed on the way out to meet his father's fleet. Her pale blue eyes fixed on him.

"Antonova, you've seen this new cartoon and its proposal. What do you make of it?"

"Yes," called his father from the wallscreen. "Should we reply to it?"

Lori stood stiffly in her vacsuit, helmet thrown onto her back. Allowing folks to breath ship air was the one adjustment Jacob had allowed from full combat readiness. She gestured at the wallscreen cartoon video. "They want to do what this species has always focused on doing. They want to put down their larvae pods on this system's third world, which they know by now is very welcoming to their kind of flying arthropod. Bear in mind the wounded wasp ship has been there for some weeks. Surely it has sent lots of signals to these new wasps." She paused, licked her lips, then looked aside to Alicia, who gave her an encouraging nod. "Note the cartoon does not display the wasp ship now heading to Valhalla. Which, even with the loss of one engine, will make it to Valhalla way before any fleet ship can get there to stop it. My *guess* is they will accept the idea of the *Inchon* watching them at the third world while their wounded ship watches us at Valhalla."

Jacob nodded. That all made sense. "But can we trust them to stay around the third world?"

Lori put arms behind her back. Her face grew tense. A vein on her forehead pulsed visibly. "Trust may not be in the scent speech of this alien species. Last century a pollie said 'Trust but verify' when the Russian Federation was posing a threat to America and other nations. Fortunately, after the Putin Era, my nation became more world friendly." She paused. "I suggest we not trust anything they say. If we allow them to come into the Kepler 22 system, follow them all the way to the third world. Watch them deposit their larvae pods. Keep watching them until we see wasps on their hulls in spacesuits doing repair work. Then leave the *Inchon* on watch and pull back to Valhalla. We can keep most ships orbiting out beyond its moon, as a front-line defense ready to head off any wasp movement toward Valhalla. Meanwhile, we can do hull repairs as needed. But allowing them into this system puts them within two AU of Valhalla. Captain, that is up to you and the admiral."

"Exactly," said his father from the Bridge of the *Midway*. "Lieutenant Antonova, what is next most important to these wasps, to Earth wasps, beyond depositing young larvae at a new nest?"

She turned and faced the wallscreen image of his father. "Sir, admiral, on Earth what is next most important to wasps, whether social or solitary, is to protect the Queen wasp that is the mother of all wasp castes in the nest." She looked aside to Alicia, then back. "Beyond the Queen might be the Fighter in charge of all the nest's fighting adults, which could be both sexes or a single sex. We have observed one captive Worker wasp having sex in flight with two of the other Worker captives. The wasp who initiated the sex was the Worker leader among the captives."

His father nodded quickly, then looked away from Lori. "Commander Branstead, your people developed the English-to-wasp guide. Is there a single Queen wasp in these ships, or several?"

Jacob looked to his Science chief. Like him she was still strapped into her seat. She looked up. "Fleet Admiral Renselaer, I don't know. We do know what Lieutenant Antonova has shared. The captives in our Forest Room include both sexes. There is a hierarchy present. Their terms for each other are Worker and Worker Leader. We did catch rare scent talk of a Matron and a Hunter. Those must be wasps at a higher level than Workers. They did not mention Fighter, although our Marines encountered such specialized wasps during their ship boarding."

His father frowned. "Let us assume these wasps would refuse a demand to give us their Queen, or Queens, as hostages for good behavior by them. Commander, prepare a cartoon video showing the wasp ships heading to the third world, with our fleet following, their arrival, their dropping of these pod babies as we watch, then our return to Valhalla with the *Inchon* remaining on watch." The man who had dominated Jacob's life since he was able to walk now looked to him. "Captain Renselaer, I will take the lead in this negotiation. I am willing to allow these wasps to go to the world they want for a colony, but *only* if they give me a high-ranking hostage as a guarantee of their peaceful behavior in the future." He looked to Lori. "Lieutenant, can your language guide provide the right smells to convey what I've just said?"

Lori winced. "Maybe. We do have the smell pattern for the phrase Hunter Who Leads. And also the smell pattern for Mother Who Births All. I can provide you with a smell guide for transmittal along with the cartoon video. The vocabulary guide we transmitted to your Communications person will translate any pheromone reply the wasps send to you. While you do not have a modified pheromone signaler like we do, you are not talking in person, which would require such a device. Sending the correct polarized radio signals should allow basic talk with the wasps."

The admiral pursed his lips. "Good. Branstead, Antonova, make it happen. Fast. I want to send this reply before that wounded wasp ship makes it to Valhalla."

Alicia unlocked her straps and stood up. "Sir, Lieutenant Antonova and I will prepare the cartoon and smell talk recording that says what you have said."

Jacob thought this was going too fast. "Fleet admiral, I have a hunch there is more happening on the wasp side than simple desire to put baby wasps down on the third world. May I pursue this further with my experts?"

His father looked briefly surprised. "You may. There is no new attack. We have time. At least until the wasp ship gets to Valhalla."

Jacob looked to where Alicia and Lori were about to depart. "Lieutenant Antonova, hold a moment."

"Sir?" she said, turning to face him, with Alicia behind her.

"What *else* should we know about these alien wasps? Based on what you know of Earth wasps."

She grimaced. "I could spend hours talking about the similarities between Earth wasps and these alien wasps, and their differences."

"Be succinct. Hit what is most important for the fleet admiral to know. He will be the one on the front line of negotiation."

Lori turned thoughtful, then faced Jacob's father. "Fleet admiral, the wasps of Earth have been around longer than any mammal species dead or living. They first appeared during the Jurassic period, when the biggest dinosaurs ruled the Earth. That means our wasps showed up at least 145 million years ago, perhaps as far back as 200 million years ago." She paused, then continued. "There are more than 100,000 species of wasps now living on Earth.

They have specialized into many ecozones. Earth's wasps have a complex social structure that consists of Queen, workers, fighters and non-fertile males. Social wasp species meet the definition of eusocial creatures as defined by the biologist Edward O. Wilson. A eusocial species is one that has a reproductive division of labor, overlapping generations and cooperative care of the young." She gestured at the true space holo of the wasp spaceships. "Every image we've seen of these wasps, from Kepler 22 to here, show their ships built with six sides, and moving in groups of six, which surely must be the basis of their math and of their city or nest construction down on a planet. They can fight solo or as a group. They will sacrifice themselves for the greater good, as one did to save the giant ship that led the attack in Kepler 22. Earth wasps are determined breeders and colonizers of new territories. They build nests in the ground, in rock walls and in tree hollows." His father began tapping his armrest, a sure sign of impatience. Lori must have seen it too. She stiffened her posture. "Fleet admiral, these alien wasps match many of the behavior and culture patterns of Earth wasps. I would not share a planet with them. But they may, *might* just allow us to live on Valhalla while they occupy the third world. There are hundreds of millions of kilometers between the two worlds now and more when three is on the far side of the local star. That may be enough separation distance for this alien wasp species to feel safe."

"Or they may attack Valhalla in the future," his father said thoughtfully, his gloved hands resting on his lap.

"Exactly," Jacob said hurriedly. "Fleet admiral, in Kepler 22 these wasps attacked us right after putting down their larvae pods on Kepler's fourth world. They could do the same here."

His father fixed on Lori. "Antonova, thank you for that overview. It is clear these flying alien insects have many of the successful and dangerous elements of Earth wasps. And their seeking of colony worlds says to me their home world is overcrowded. So we have something they want. If they give me a top boss hostage, I am willing to keep watch on them and see if this wasp fleet leaves Kepler 22 in peace, after they plant their babies. We'll see."

Lori looked to him. Jacob gave a wave. "Lieutenant, Commander, go do the work ordered by the fleet admiral."

They saluted him and headed aft. Jacob looked up to his father. "Sir, we are eighteen ships and they are fifteen. If these wasps attempt deceit after colonizing three, we should be able to destroy their entire fleet."

"True," his father said, his manner going to the Alpha Dog In Charge manner that Jacob knew from when he had been old enough to realize there were other important adults in life than just his father. Like his mother. "But we could lose another four or five ships, now that we do not have the element of surprise. The Unity pollies sent me out here to do two jobs. Defend this colony and find a way to end this war with aliens. Let's see if the second job is possible."

Jacob could not disagree with what his father was saying. It was similar to what he and Daisy had hoped when they left Kepler 22, and later when the surviving wasp ships had departed from Kepler 10. Maybe smell talk would achieve what now seemed impossible. One thing he could do if a hostage arrived. Put the wasp hostage in with the Worker wasps and listen in on what they said to each other. The retreat of two wasp ships upon receiving his ship's pheromone broadcast clearly showed wasp scent talk was not encrypted. Maybe the fleet could benefit from future disruptive broadcasts, as Richard had earlier suggested. It was one tool humans had that no wasp could imitate, since all neutrino signals between Earth ships were encoded according to an encryption key that changed daily. War on Earth had taught the Star Navy and American military leaders a few things about fighting a powerful enemy. He just hoped this new enemy did not have a similar surprise waiting for humanity.

◆ ◆ ◆

Hunter One watched one of his perception imagers as the simple imagery reply from the Soft Skins played out across the imager. It was accompanied by polarized pheromone scents that smelled strange, but were understandable. Had the Soft Skins learned scent casting from the four Swarmers they had taken captive? He had thought their loss was minor, as they were only a Worker Leader and three Workers. But now these Soft Skins were able to talk in simple Swarm scent while his people had no ability to transmit the acoustic signals the Soft Skins had engaged in during the meeting with his defective Servants. It seemed as if Hunter Prime's pretend imagery had gained them access to the third world. But this scent talk that demanded a Fighter Leader or Hunter to come to them was puzzling.

What was the purpose of such a request? He looked to another imager, past the shapes of his Servants who filled the Flight Chamber. Hunter Prime's body was strong and carried the look of dynamic vitality. So different from earlier, after the loss of so many flying nests. The leader's antennae leaned forward, then his gaze fixed on One.

"Hunter One, these Soft Skins demand we send a Swarmer of high caste to them before they allow us a flight path inward," said their leader in a flow of dominance and trail pheromones. "In your prior imagery signals, have these Soft Skins ever demanded such a thing?"

"They never demanded such a matter," he scent cast in a flow of puzzlement scent crossed with aggregation pheromones. "Even when we sent a simple image asking them to send a Soft Skin from each nest down to Warmth, with imagery of our nests sending single representatives, there was never any imagery of caste level. I hoped the Soft Skins would send each nest's Hunter to the meeting, while I sent defective Servants. I thought destroying their Hunter leaders would render their nests confused and unable to fight."

His leader's wings moved rapidly, lifting him to a hover above his bench. "You made an error in thinking such. Your imagery records show the Soft Skin nests fighting hard and killing more of your nests than you killed of their nests. As has happened here." The scent flow from Hunter Prime was a mix of alarm, frustration, signal and calming pheromones. "It seems these Soft Skins wish to hold captive a Hunter. The other Hunters in our flight are Support Hunters. You are a high caste Hunter. Your nest is wounded. I will send you to these Soft Skins."

Dismay filled One. He would lose control of his nest! How could he lead from inside a Soft Skin nest that had a pull down weight twice what Nest held? Would he ever be able to return, if Hunter Prime killed all the flying Soft Skin nests?

"Hunter Prime, I accept your decision." The leader's antennae leaned forward. "But, how may I return to lead my nest? My Servants, my Fighters, my Workers, they know my scent. They are used to me. I am used to them."

"So you are, so they are," the leader said in a dominant scent flow. "Whatever Soft Skin nest you travel to, I will allow it to live until you are returned. Then I will destroy it. Together we will then destroy the Soft Skin colony on the fourth world!"

It was clear he had no choice. "Accepted is your scent."

"Your caste will speak of your offspring with pride," Hunter Prime said quickly. "Now, watch me as I send my image to these Soft Skins, then provide your image as the one to go to them."

"I attend," Hunter One said, thinking quickly about which Swarmer he could leave in command of the nest.

The elderly male Servant who studied aberrant social behaviors was the last Swarmer he would trust for such sensitive work. The Flight Servant and the Speaker To All Servant were both needed at their functions, as was the propulsive Servant. He turned to the young female who had shown herself to be a deadly enemy to the Soft Skins.

"Stinger Servant, you will lead the Flight Chamber and our nest down to the new colony world, then join with Hunter Prime in attacking and killing the nests of these Soft Skins," he said in a strong flow of dominance, trail, territorial and signal pheromones. "Order a Worker Leader to prepare an air bubble for my transport to one of these Soft Skin nests."

"As you command, my Hunter," she said, her scent mix betraying surprise, followed by resolve and appreciation.

Hunter One flew up from his bench, twisted in the air and flew to the opening that gave access to the tubeway outside. It would be a short flight to the chamber where air bubbles were stored. The future scent commands of Hunter Prime would be heard by all Swarmers in his nest, thanks to the pheromone signalers that adorned the walls of every chamber. He would perceive every scent emitted by their leader, even aboard the air bubble. Then would come a strange experience. He would arrive among creatures who had too few limbs and who surely had no idea what their scents meant to themselves or to any other lifeform.

CHAPTER SIXTEEN

Jacob watched the imagery from inside one of the giant wasp ships as its leader now appeared in a live video. The wasp control room resembled a large bubble, with a central platform holding benches on which sat eighteen wasps. In the middle, resting on a larger bench, was the largest wasp he had ever seen. It was easily twice as big as the Worker wasps in his ship's Forest Room. And this wasp hovered above his bench, two brown wings moving quickly as they supported him in the half gee gravity of his ship. Jacob glanced at the left side wallscreen image that held the situational image and its green and purple dots. It showed both fleets were still far away from the seventh world. The neutrino sensor image on the right side indicated this wasp was calling from a giant wasp ship. It was one of the giant ships that had arrived with other wasp ships. But it was not the giant ship that had attacked his battle group at Kepler 22, that had been confirmed by Rosemary at Tactical based on sensor records. It was a fact he had texted to his father, who now stood before his seat on the Bridge of the *Midway*, ready to negotiate. Alicia and Lori had produced the new video with attached pheromone talk demands in just two hours. They still had plenty of time before the wounded wasp ship got to Valhalla. He and everyone else listened closely.

"Leader of all Soft Skins," said the English translation of what the large wasp was saying by polarized radio signals. "I am Hunter Prime. We wish a flight path to our new colony world. We fly above our world. You fly above your world. Swarmers and Soft Skins fight no more. Why seek a leader of Swarmers?"

His father's fists were clenched and he was grimacing. It was an effort at body language that might affect this wasp leader of the species that called themselves the Swarm, with individual members labeled as a Swarmer. That they had known from listening in on the captives. The fact the top leader of the wasps on one of the giant ships was twice the size of other wasps who rested nearby, that had been unknown until now.

"You Swarmers attacked my people when we visited your world of Warmth," his father replied. "You Swarmers attacked again even after my son led his starships away from your world and here to our colony world," he said, speaking slowly so the English-to-wasp vocabulary in his father's Communications console had time to convert English to radio pheromone signals. "One of your ships attacked our colony. Now, you return to hurt our colony world. We demand a leader of Swarmers as proof you will not again attack our colony."

The three meter long wings of the giant wasp froze a moment, then resumed beating quickly. "What means visit? Intruders your nests were. Our warning device claimed sky light as home to Swarmers. All intruders are attacked. It is way of life."

"We did not understand your scent warning," the admiral said. "We understand it now. We allowed one nest to go to, or visit, the third world. Now it flies to our colony. Will it harm our colony?"

The red and black stripes on the yellow exoskeleton body of the leader wasp almost glowed, their colors were so deep. The sharp colors of each Swarmer made Jacob wonder if that was why the other wasps in the control room looked at vidcam images filled with swirls of color mixed with clusters of sharp angular marks. In the image of the leader's room, a nearby wasp twisted its thorax and somehow said something. The leader rose higher above its bench.

"That nest is led by Support Hunter Seven. It is damaged. No harm to Soft Skin world happens. It flies to watch Soft Skin actions."

Jacob marveled at how this species used terms from its flying nature to describe actions for which humans used nautical terms. He glanced aside at the situational on the wallscreen. The wounded wasp ship that moved at five psol was about halfway to Valhalla. While it flew at 33.5 million miles an hour, or 53.9 million kilometers an hour, covering 186 million miles took time even at such a fast speed. Transit time from world three to Valhalla at ten psol normally took almost three hours. At half that speed it would take five and a half hours, one way. It was two hours since they had received the wasp proposal to travel inward to the third world. Their reply had gone out minutes ago. Now, a living wasp leader spoke to the admiral, thanks to Alicia's basic vocabulary and translation software.

His father stopped grimacing. Instead he pulled a black-handled knife from his vacsuit's tool pocket. He held it up. "But your nest could sting the Soft Skins below. Send me a Hunter as proof you will not sting us."

Jacob wondered at the difference in speech. They heard fairly simple language from the wasp leader. His father spoke directly but more complexly. Did this wasp hear or smell a simplified version of English?

"I send you Hunter One. He leads other nest that is like mine. Do you allow our flight inward to third world of this sky light?"

"Send Hunter One to my son's spaceship. It is the other . . . nest like mine. It holds four wasps taken from the . . . nest that flies toward our world," his father said.

The two large and three small black eyes on the flat yellow face of the giant wasp seemed bright from more than reflection of the white-yellow light that illuminated his control chamber. Its two narrow arms ended in four stick-like fingers. Those stick fingers spread wide.

"Do Soft Skin families give nests to grown larvae?"

Jacob blinked. What the hell was this wasp asking?

"Human starship leaders are chosen for ferocity and for ability, not because they are a leader's children. My son earned his leadership of the other large starship that is like my . . . home nest. He fought your Hunter One above your colony that flies around the sky light where we first visited."

"Soft Skins are confusing. You mature ones use your grown larvae in strange ways." The wasp who called himself Hunter Prime bent his antennae backward. "If Hunter One comes to you, where does he live? Will you feed him?"

"Hunter One will be safe. We will feed him. See the images of how our captive Swarmers now live." The admiral looked aside. "Captain, send him imagery of the wasps in your Forest Room."

Jacob nodded. "Communications, send the imagery packet on the same frequency used by the cartoon videos."

"Transmitting," called Osashi.

His father looked back to his image of the giant wasp leader. "Hunter One will fly to this room where four Swarmers now live. They have made a home in the ground. They control the gravity and light of this room. We feed them often. We bring sweet liquid and soft fruit and small animals to eat."

The leader's stick fingers moved complexly. One narrow arm gestured to another wasp. "Commands sent for Hunter One to travel

to your grown larvae's large nest. Can we fly to our new nest? No
biting by Soft Skins?"

"Once Hunter One arrives, you Swarmers may fly to world
three," the admiral said, glancing aside. Perhaps he saw what Jacob
saw, which was the departure of a small craft from the damaged giant
ship that now headed toward the battle group ships. But it moved no
faster than the other wasp ships. Which now flew at ten psol as the
human ships also flew at 10 psol, on a vector track for the seventh
planet. "We will not attack your nests so long as you do not attack our
nests."

"You slow your nests," the leader wasp said. "That allows
Hunter One to reach your larvae's nest. We continue but fly aside to
our colony world."

His father licked his lips. "All ships! Maintain Alert Hostile
Enemy. But reduce your speed to five percent of lightspeed. Once this
Hunter One's craft enters the *Lepanto*, resume full speed. We will
follow these wasps on a parallel track." The admiral looked toward
the image of the giant wasp. "Hunter Prime, our nests are slowing
their flight. Do not pass close to the seventh or sixth worlds of this . . .
sky light. We humans control them. Fly in empty space to world
three."

"Too cold those worlds are for any Swarmer," the leader wasp
replied. "My nest and all Swarmer nests now make new flight path.
To third world we fly. This scent cast ends."

The image of the wasp leader vanished from Jacob's
wallscreen. It had been an image watched by every captain in the two
battle groups, including the *Inchon*, which was slowly making its way
toward the third world. He looked to his father's image which was
now in the center of the wallscreen.

"This Hunter One will be here in a few minutes," Jacob said
calmly. "Admiral, what do you make of this wasp leader?"

His father pursed his lips, his manner intent. "If he is anything
like you or me, we need to watch him tightly. He excused their attack
on the *Lepanto* and your battle group as a normal response to an
intruder. But he said nothing about following us to Kepler 10 and
attacking you and the colony. This Swarm is an expansive predator
species. Maybe even more so than we humans. They are deadly, both
in person and in armed starships. Listen in on what this Hunter One

says to the wasp captives. Maybe we'll hear some word of this Hunter Prime's future plans."

"Admiral, will do." Jacob looked down. "Chief O'Connor, grab one of your Marines and escort this Hunter One hostage from Hangar Three to the Forest Room. Take him inside, then leave. But listen on your Shinshoni Hard Shell comlinks to whatever he says to the other wasps. The admiral and I will focus on creating a convoy to follow this wasp fleet."

The Marine leader looked up. His gray eyes fixed on Jacob. Then he unlocked his seat straps. "Captain, Gunnery Sergeant Diego and I will escort this high value wasp. I'll make sure the gravity in the hallways we travel is cut back to a half gee. Diego and I will listen in on whatever they say. That is, assuming our ship AI provides us with a wasp-to-English translation."

Jacob looked up. "Melody, monitor the wasp continuously from the moment it arrives in Hangar Three all the way to the Forest Room. And afterwards. If you have to say something to this wasp, use the retrofitted wasp pheromone block we captured. It's inside the room. And convey to O'Connor and Diego everything all the wasps say, using the personal IDs given them by Lieutenant Branstead."

A scratchy whine came from above, then he heard the AI speak.

"Your orders will be followed, handsome live being who commands my home," the AI said in a musical tone that was almost flirtatious.

So weird this AI had become since he'd taken over the ship. But Jacob knew Science had better things to do than to find a fault in its human response modality chip. "Melody, also maintain your watch over the movements of all wasp ships. Alert me or the acting Bridge commander when there is any change in behavior that is different from a direct vector track to this system's third world."

"So you do not wish to hear an alert while you are sexing with your female companion?"

He winced and did not look at his father's image. "Wrong. If there is any danger to this ship or to other Earth ships, alert me no matter what I am doing! But also alert the person in temporary command on the Bridge."

"As you wish, handsome human of mine."

Jacob could not put it off any longer. He looked to the wallscreen and met his father's gaze. The man's face looked neutral but he could tell more. A slight crease to one side of his mouth said he was close to smiling. "Admiral, the *Lepanto* will take charge of this wasp hostage and pay close attention to whatever he says to the other wasps."

His father nodded. "Captain Renselaer, remind me to ask Earth Command to run a diagnostic on your ship AI, once we all get back to Earth." His expression grew somber. "We're in for two days of long-haul travel into this system, all the while following an alien enemy who could fire on us at any time. Set your shift rotations. See that you and your shift get some sleep and food. No deck will allow more than ten percent of their staff to be out of their vacsuits at any time. That applies to all battle group ships. We cannot relax until this enemy fleet is gone from Kepler 10."

"Fleet Admiral Renselaer, will do. We will tend to the hostage wasp and check on what repairs might be needed once we get back to Valhalla." Jacob paused, thinking quickly about the future steps in this dance with a dangerous enemy. "Admiral, should I peel off a frigate to head for Valhalla so it can keep a watch on the enemy ship, after it arrives?"

His father frowned. "That's a good idea. I will send off the *Schweinfurt* to Valhalla. Its captain will check in with Captain O'Sullivan and hold orbit close to the wasp ship. It will be a further warning to this Hunter Prime to not try any funny stuff with our colony."

"Understood. *Lepanto* out, unless you have further commands?"

"Nothing more," his father said firmly. "But keep my Bridge in your neutrino vidcam sharing with your ship and the other ships. Best for us all to be in instant link with each other."

Jacob gave his father a thumbs-up gesture. "Will do."

"*Lepanto*," called a voice from the wallscreen images that he recognized.

Jacob looked over. It was Rebecca Swanson of the cruiser *Chesapeake*. Like him and everyone else, she wore her vacsuit and was strapped in. The native of Chicago's black face held a frown. "Yes, Lieutenant Commander? Can I help you?"

"More like how I and George can help you," she said, her tone musing.

Jacob noticed that all of his battle group ship commanders were paying attention, while the captains who had arrived with his father were speaking to people on their Bridges, ignoring this conversation. "I appreciate your comment. But the *Chesapeake*, the *Hampton Roads* and all other StarFight ships are now under the direct command of Fleet Admiral Renselaer."

Her expression turned impatient. "Of course. What I mean to say is that George and I think highly of your past practice of rotating our cruisers into the line of fire that aims at our frigates. I want to be sure the *Aldertag* and the *St. Mihiel* close out this fight fully intact."

In the line of wallscreen images, Sunderland and Lorenz both nodded their heads sharply but said nothing. Mehta, Zhang and Jefferson were watching closely. Each of them gave him a thumbs-up gesture but also said nothing.

Jacob realized Rebecca was trying to say that, in the midst of whatever formation his father might order in the future, he could count on her and George Wilcox to do just what she had said, no matter what the requirements might be of the new formation order. It was not outright insubordination. Rather, it was an expression of continuing allegiance to him personally from the two cruiser commanders. The destroyer and frigate commanders clearly thought the same.

"Lieutenant Commander Swanson and Lieutenant Wilcox," he said, glancing to George's bulldog face as the man's deep blue eyes watched him. "I highly appreciate your comments and support for my efforts to allow all of our ships to survive. I continue to rely on you for that support. *Lepanto* out."

"*Chesapeake* out."

"*Hampton Roads* out," George said in a low growl.

He unstrapped and stepped down to the floor of the Bridge. Jacob faced Daisy, still seated in her vacsuit and strapped in.

"XO, you have the command."

She saluted him back. "Change of command accepted. Will you be sleeping?"

"No. I'll be back at the Forest Room. Contact me as needed," Jacob said as he walked to the rear slidedoor, noticing how quiet Carlos and Lori were as they sat in the seats snugged up against the rear wall. Somehow, somewhen, before the fleet got to the third planet, he wanted to have another brainstorm confab with Lori, Alicia, Daisy and anyone else who might give him more insight into these wasps. Analogies to Earth wasps had limits. His gut was telling him there was more to this sudden wasp stopping of combat and request to go to the third planet. But what? He intended to figure it out. Everyone's life might depend on whether he could outguess an alien ship commander who had been genetically bred to lead.

Leastwise, that was what Alicia said her monitoring of the captive wasps had led her to believe. The wasp reference to castes meant more than that. Alicia thought each wasp caste was bred to be the best at what they were born to be, whether it be Hunter, Fighter, Worker, Worker Leader or whatever was meant by the Servant caste. That word had appeared just twice in the days of wasp to wasp chatter. What did it mean? And what did the term Hunter Prime mean, when other Hunter wasps were referred to by numbers? He was determined to figure out that answer, and the underlying reason for the sudden peacefulness of the wasps. One thing he knew from bitter experience. Do not trust wasp appearances. Only wasp actions mattered. He was damned certain the current wasp appearance of peacefulness was far from the whole story!

◆ ◆ ◆

Hunter Seven turned away from watching the perception imager that had relayed the strange conversation of Hunter Prime with the leader of the Soft Skin nests. The smells sent by the Soft Skins were similar to normal Swarmer scent, but different. The flavor was not the same as what everyone knew on Nest or on any flying nest. But the meaning of Soft Skin scent signals, combined with the simple imagery sent by one of their large nests, was clear. The Swarm could fly inward to the colony world so long as it did not try to bite the Soft Skins. Hunter One had made clear to him that this was a temporary pause in defense of their colony world. Once every Swarmer nest dropped down their larvae Pods with Workers, Fighters and a few Servants to begin the colony, every Swarmer nest would make a new flight path to the Soft Skin world, there to destroy the space-flying Soft Skins, then later the land-bound ones. He was tempted to toss out some particle seeds to fly high above the Soft Skin world, but Hunter

Prime had promised no biting action. So he would fly high above the Soft Skin world, out of reach of the stingers on the Soft Skin globe that had killed most of his earlier seeds. Once the Swarmers left world three and came his way, he would do his best to fight like the Hunter he had been born to be.

"Stinger Servant, put out Workers on the outside of our hard shell. We must reclaim the use of our middle and head rings of stinger tubes," he sent in a strong flow of dominance and signal pheromones.

The young male who had replaced his first Stinger Servant twisted to look his way. "Support Hunter Seven, I obey. But we have limited numbers of Workers. Some have no knowledge of how to work on the outside of our hard shell."

He increased his wing flapping until he rose above his bench. "Enough! Every Swarmer has a stinger. Every Swarmer can try to do the job of others now gone. Send them out. Those who survive can train others to do as they learned to do!" he scent cast in a mix of dominance, aggregation and releaser pheromones.

"As you command," the Stinger Servant replied, though his dismay was clear to scent.

Seven did not care. Either his nest would be made better able to fight these terrible Soft Skins, or they would all die. The memory of his earlier desire to lead the colonization of the third world as the leader of all Swarmers was now a pale memory. The Hunter Prime's scent overwhelmed any plan of a Swarmer who was not a Prime.

◆ ◆ ◆

Hunter One flew through the strange, square-shaped tubeway through which his escort of hard-shelled Soft Skins now moved. The white-skinned ones did not fly on the jets attached to their movement limbs, unlike what he had seen in the terrible imagery sent his way by Support Hunter Seven. It worried him that fewer than three six-groups of these white-shelled Soft Skins had killed half the Swarmers on Seven's flying nest. The yellow flames that shot from the right arm of each hard shell was most fearful, although the black rocks that emerged from the left arm were nearly as terrible. Worse yet was the green sky light that emerged from what passed for an abdomen among the Soft Skins. That beam had no limit on its range. He flew slowly and steadily after the deadly female who walked ahead of him, having no doubt her male companion to his rear would envelop him in flame if he made any effort to attack her hard shell. As was clear from deep scratches on it that other Swarmers had tried to do when the female had led one group of intruders into Seven's nest. These beings might be limited to four limbs and be ground-bound without the aid of their devices. But terrible was their ability to kill, whether singly in the hard shells or as a group on a large flying nest. Ahead, the female in the white hard shell stopped before a rectangle outline in the wall of the strange tubeway. She touched a green patch on the wall. The outline became a piece of metal that slid into the wall, giving access to a white and yellow lighted place. She gestured for him to go through the wall opening. He did as ordered.

She spoke acoustic language that sounded like "This is the home of the four wasps we captured."

He smelled a phrase that meant "Your new nest is here. Four others is here."

Such was obvious as he hovered just inside, his five eyes viewing the vegetation and tree filled room. Some distance away lay a large ground hole, from which stuck up the gray fiber of the home built by the three Workers and the Worker Leader. The two males and two females now flew out of the nest and hovered above it, clearly alert to the sound of the entry wall being opened. He inhaled deep all the scents in this place.

"So, you have been sexing rather than biting these Soft Skins," he said in a flow of disgust, trail and signal pheromones that flowed across the space between him and the four Swarmers.

Behind him a signaler affixed to a wall repeated his comments. The two Soft Skins in white hard shells followed him inside and then closed the entry. They watched from their ground-bound location.

The Worker Leader's brown wings fluttered faster. He slipped through the chamber's nicely warm and wet air until he stopped halfway to him.

"Hunter One! So glad are we to see you! And you have about you the scent of a Hunter Prime! Does this mean you and other Hunters are here to free us?"

"Foolish one, of course I have the scent of a Hunter Prime on me. His dominance is akin to my dominance. We both were born to lead, just as you were born to work," he said in a flow of aggregation, trail and command pheromones. "Many nests have arrived at this sky light. We fly now to the third world to lay down our larvae Pods, just as we did on Warmth! Why are you here? You should have died on Seven's nest, fighting these terrible Soft Skins!"

The black antennae of the Worker Leader flared back. "We would have died! But as we crossed a tubeway intersection, each of us was struck by wires that carried power flows. The Soft Skins rendered us unaware. We awoke in a small chamber on a Soft Skin flying nest. They later moved us to this larger chamber on a bigger nest. They feed us. They use a signaler to scent cast to us. We thought it best to eat and be healthy for the moment when your nest defeated this nest. Has that happened?"

One felt impatience and irritation. It was clear this Worker Leader had made sex with the two females, who of course would do whatever his scent commanded. Their wings, short yellow hairs and their entire bodies looked healthy and bright under the Nest-normal light of this chamber. Even the air of this place helped them feel good, as it held the prime gas all Swarmers needed to live and work. It was clear the Soft Skin ruler of this flying nest had chosen to create a chamber that closely copied the landscape of Warmth. But why?

"It has not happened. I am here as part of a . . ." He stopped just before he made the scent flow 'temporary bite stop'. It was clear these Soft Skins behind him were listening to everything he and the four Workers were scent casting. So far he had said nothing not already known to the Soft Skins. Best to keep it that way. "I am here as a guest of the Soft Skin ruler of this flying nest. Soon, you and I will be released to fly through the skies of the third world."

"Soon? How soon?" scent cast the Worker Leader as the other three Workers flew up and joined him in hovering above a soil area covered in green plant fibers. "Has the Hunter Prime's Colony nest killed the Soft Skins on the fourth world? Or do they still live? Support Hunter Seven told us that the Soft Skins had proposed each of us stay on their own colony world, with no biting among us."

"End your scent-casting!" he said in a rush of Hunter dominance pheromones. "I am the Hunter here. You are Workers. You do what I command. You do nothing I do not command. Obey!"

"I obey!" scent cast the Worker Leader in a flow of alarm and trail pheromones. "We all obey. What do you wish of us?"

He flew closer to them, hoping the listening Soft Skins had not understood the reference to Hunter Prime's flying nest aiming to kill the Soft Skin colony world. "Bring me food. Alert me to the small lifeforms that can be hunted in this chamber. And describe the behaviors of all the Soft Skins who have dealt with you."

Hunter One listened as the Workers scent cast in a wild flow of many scents. He flew toward a bowl filled with yellow liquid that the Workers said was similar to the tree hole sweetness created on Nest by the small flyers who kept the flowers and fruits on Nest able to reproduce and become many. As he lowered down to sip the yellow liquid, he wondered the same as the Workers. How long must he stay a captive, until Hunter Prime led his damaged nest and Prime's own nest in an attack on the Soft Skin flying nests?

◆ ◆ ◆

"Chief, did you hear that!" called Jane over their suit comlink. "They plan to attack Valhalla!"

"I heard it," Richard said, keeping both arms aimed at the five hovering wasps even as his mind raced through the implications of what had been said before the boss wasp shut up the Worker wasps. "It's clear this new wasp is one of the top bosses, and that he commanded the giant wasp ship that attacked us in Kepler 22. Sounds like this Hunter One went out and recruited a super big Hunter wasp to help him do what he failed to do the last time."

"This new wasp is larger than the Worker wasps," Jane said. "He looks to be a third bigger. But not as large as that Hunter Prime wasp we saw talking to the admiral."

"Agreed. I wonder—"

The slidedoor opened behind him. His helmet's HUD display showed it was young Renselaer entering, still clad in his basic vacsuit. Giving thanks for his HUD display's all-around vision ability, he stepped to the right, opening a space between him and Diego.

"Captain, please stand here between me and the Gunny. We can cover you better that way."

"I'm here," the captain said in his calm baritone, sounding as curious as Richard felt. "Just heard all that the Hunter One was saying along with what the Workers said. And what your gunnery sergeant observed. What's your take?"

Richard wondered if everything he said over the Shinshoni's comlink was being rebroadcast on the All Ship vidcom and even out to the other ships and the admiral. Then he realized that made no sense. While he approved of the open vidcast of Bridge events and neutrino chatter with other ships over the All Ship vidcom, there was no way the captain would allow routine, in-ship chatter to be broadcast outward. Or even to other decks of the *Lepanto*.

"My take is this supposed truce is a temporary thing. It will only last until they put down their baby wasps and adult minders on the third world. Then watch out!"

"That's what my gut has been telling me," Jacob said.

He was growing used to calling the captain by his first name. Not common on most ships, whether wet Navy or Star Navy, but it was in keeping with the transparency and amiable openness of the man who had claimed captaincy and then battle group leadership. The arrival of his father the five star admiral had changed things. An admiral was automatically in command of all ships within a fighting unit. Which now numbered eighteen after their losses in both systems. He gave thanks for the nearly fifty days they'd had to make repairs on the *Lepanto*, the *Chesapeake*, the *St. Mihiel* and the *Tsushima Strait*. True, they'd all taken new hammering right after the surprise attack on the incoming wasp ships. But it had been worth it. He liked very much how the admiral had decided to be first on the doorstep into this system, with all guns aimed at the spot where the enemy would arrive. Young Renselaer might yet learn some of his old man's craftiness.

"I think your gut has the sense of it," Richard said, still watching the flying antics of the five wasps. "Do you think the wasps will take out the *Inchon* as they pass her on the way to planet three?"

"Doubt it," Jacob said, sounding distracted. "I think they will not do anything violent until after they put down these pods. They may even wait for us to return to Valhalla before they launch our way. Their ships took some heavy strikes from our proton lasers. Maybe they'll spend a few days doing hull repairs, like the admiral suggested."

"They may. But I don't trust this truce for a minute," Richard said bluntly.

Jacob gave a sigh. "I'll urge the admiral to have the *Inchon* join us on our trip back to Valhalla. We can leave the wasp watching to spysats we put out."

Richard liked that point. Conserve your forces. Don't split up into two groups unless you had to as part of a better plan. "Sounds good. Any need for me and the gunny to stay here?"

"Nope," Jacob said. He turned and headed for the exit slidedoor.

Richard walked in reverse, still keeping both arms aimed at the five wasps hovering about twenty meters from him and the gunny. Who copied his backward walk, keeping her gun arms aimed.

"Then we're leaving. I'll enter the lock code after we exit. Nobody else comes in here unless it's with a Shinshoni escort. Your buddy Petty Officer Watanabe has brought food down a few times. My people cover him."

In the Habitation Deck hallway, Jacob watched as Richard and Diego exited the Forest Room. "Glad to hear it. You're doing exactly right to always escort any human who enters that room. Which includes any of the algorithm boffins from Science Deck. And also my XO."

Richard had assumed that. And he liked how the Stewart woman had taken to being the ship's new executive officer. She was good at managing competing interests while showing deck chiefs and enlisteds the same kind of appreciation. He felt the captain was lucky to have her, both as XO and as his lover. Maybe Jacob would have better luck in his relationship than Richard had had with his woman. At least he'd gotten three kids and a spunky granddaughter out of it.

"Will do, captain. We're heading for our Darts. Time to do a functional check of their systems. You may yet have need of launching some Darts against these bastards!"

"I might," Jacob said softly. "Remind your folks these next few days heading in-system are likely to be the only low-risk time we'll have until these wasps leave Kepler 10. Tell them I've counting on them."

"I will."

Richard turned away from his young captain and followed Diego down the hallway to a gravlift that would take them up to the Engines Deck and the hangar for his Darts that lay next to Silo 8. Wayne, Auggie, Jane and all the guys would be there. It was time for a ceremony to name a Dart after Master Sergeant Chao Lee. He had no doubt his people would prefer to paint Chao's name atop the Dart One number. Its pilot Linda Mabry would have no objection. If anything she would insist on being part of the painting crew!

That thought told him it was time to give a name to the other two Darts. He had one name in mind that would do. Maybe Jane could come up with a second. Whatever. He looked forward to painting fun.

CHAPTER SEVENTEEN

Jacob felt relief as the *Lepanto* came to a halt just above the large white moon that gave Valhalla halfway decent tides. To either side and behind came the other sixteen ships of the two battle groups, which included the engine-repaired *Inchon*. The eighteenth ship was already there. The frigate *Schweinfurt* was closer in, orbiting just above the wasp ship that had hidden out in the comet and now held geosync orbit above the colony. The frigate was well within reach of the wasp ship's lasers and lightning bolt weapons, and she had her nose laser aimed at the enemy, with her tail facing outward toward the moon's orbit. That moon lay 300,000 kilometers from the green and blue world that held 71,000 people. The *Schweinfurt* and wasp ship orbited at around 31,000 kilometers high due to Valhalla's nine-tenths gee gravity that resulted when a rocky world was smaller than Earth. They were eighteen ships against one wasp ship, for the moment. The fifteen surviving wasp ships still orbited above planet three, most of them showing vacsuited wasps working on hull repairs and sensor device fixing. Or so said the neutrino-sent imagery from their multiple spysats.

"All ships, maintain Alert Hostile Enemy," called his father from his Bridge. "Weapons remain Hot. Kills are authorized when attacked." The man who had come up with the idea of putting the fleet just where the wasp ships were bound to appear as they exited Alcubierre space-time now looked to Jacob. His expression was thoughtful. "Captain Renselaer, I do not like having a functional wasp ship orbiting above Valhalla. It has the ability to move closer and drop nukes. I'm doing something about that." He looked aside to one of the holos that surrounded his elevated seat. "Lieutenant Jefferson, take your *Philippines Sea* down to geosync and coordinate with the *Schweinfurt's* Captain Holtzman. He's almost as aggressive as you are."

On Jacob's wallscreen, Joy looked alert. Her XO Aelwen tapped on an armrest control. "Fleet admiral, happy to head down. What are your orders when we arrive?"

"Take out the working fusion pulse thruster of that wasp ship," his father said, his tone matter of fact. "Kill any working weapons rings. Your proton sharpshooting combined with Holtzman's nose laser should do the job. But do not destroy the ship. It refrained from launching nukes when the *Green Hills* base was on the far side of Valhalla. Plus it has major damage from the Marine boarding. I do not see it as a threat, once the engine is taken out."

"Admiral, will do," Joy said, giving a salute to Jacob's father. She looked aside. "Engines, head us down at one percent of lightspeed." She looked up. "Fleet admiral, we'll be there shortly. May I take my leave to coordinate with Captain Holtzman?"

"You may. Once the job is done, rejoin us out by this moon."

"Will do. *Sea* out."

Jacob looked down to where Daisy sat at her own XO post. She was checking her ship cross-section holo, clearly focused on confirming all parts of the *Lepanto* were at Green Operational status. He looked up at the holos that surrounded him. His situational holo showed the inner part of the Kepler 10 system, with the first five planets located and their orbital tracks projected. Planet three still lay 20 degrees ahead of Valhalla's fourth orbital, though its faster movement around the system's yellow star, which was indeed called Odin, had moved the wasp colony world a bit further from the human world. Still, the distance was just over two AU. Or only 2.77 hours away from Valhalla at one-tenth lightspeed. And since both fleets could come to a stop from that vast speed in just a few moments, thanks to their powerful fusion thrusters, it meant death lay less than three hours away.

Shaking his head he looked to his true space holo, which now held a view from one of the electro-optical scopes on a spysat. The fifteen wasp ships were clustered in two groups that centered on the two giant ships. Nothing new was happening. Hours earlier they'd sent down their larvae pods, then had put crew out on their hulls to do simple repairs. He checked the sensor holo. There were no new moving neutrino sources anywhere in the system, for which he gave thanks. His own holo cross-section of the *Lepanto* showed the vital details, with each weapons station marked Green Operational. The three surviving Darts were in their hangar next to Silo Eight, their internal power showing hot, with a pilot seated inside each Dart. Richard had told him his Marines were ready for a boarding or for launch to do laser harassing of wasp targets. Each Dart's stern laser had the same range as every ship laser in the fleet. And a Dart could move as fast as a frigate. But they were far more vulnerable to counterfire than even the frigates, since their thin hulls had no armor. Still, the Darts were incredibly mobile and fast, as he'd seen while watching them move on the comet-bound wasp ship.

"They're engaging," called Daisy.

He looked up at the wallscreen. It held a true space image from his Battlestar's own electro-optical scope. The two gray shapes of the *Philippines Sea* and the *Schweinfurt* now approached the wasp ship at 900 klicks a minute. They were just five thousand klicks out from the target. The wasp ship must have realized this was not a peaceful visit. It fired green lasers and yellow lightning bolts at the destroyer and the frigate.

"Sir, the wasp ship's middle weapons ring is operational," Daisy said.

"Noted."

Jacob wondered what Richard and Alicia, who sat below him, were thinking of this pre-emptive action. No doubt Richard fully approved. Maybe even Alicia. She had grown more and more concerned as she listened to Hunter One have innocuous chatter with the four wasp captives. It was as clear to her as it was to Jacob that these captives expected freedom sometime soon.

His true space holo now filled with red proton laser beams from the *Sea* and green laser strikes from the *Schweinfurt*. Both ships were spinning as they approached in a stepwise spiral corkscrew, doing their best to add random jinks and jerks to their vector track. Most of the yellow lightning bolts and many of the enemy's green laser beams missed both ships. But the frigate's spine plasma battery was a smoking ruin. However the destroyer's spine plasma battery was firing multiple canisters of plasma, even though the enemy lay far beyond the battery's range. He suddenly realized Joy was building a plasma haze around the vulnerable parts of her ship, since the plasma charges moved forward at the same speed as her ship. He liked her innovative use of what Earth Command always viewed as a close-up defense of a ship from incoming Smart Rocks and shrapnel.

The *Sea* jinked right, then slanted its approach to give a better aim at the tail end of the wasp ship, which had only now fired its single working fusion pulse thruster, trying to open the range between it and the oncoming human ships.

"Engine destroyed," Daisy said softly.

"Holtzman! Get the hell out of range! We'll take care of putting down these weapons rings," Joy yelled over the neutrino comlink.

"Two guns are better than one," replied the black-bearded German who moved his frigate in ways that almost made it dance around the enemy beams.

The frigate's nose laser was clearly aimed by a sharpshooter Spacer. It placed multiple hits on the wasp ship's rear weapons ring, taking out three weapons tubes with each hit.

The destroyer's proton laser cut deep into the rebuilt middle weapons ring. He recalled Joy's people had earlier killed both the nose and middle weapons rings with their tightly focused proton laser shots. Clearly the Hunter in charge of the enemy ship had put out crew to fix the middle ring as it awaited orders to do something else.

"Done!" grunted Holtzman from his image at the top of the wallscreen.

"Us too," called Joy from her image. A wisp of black smoke showed in her Bridge image. "Let's pull back."

Jacob noted the engine-dead wasp ship was using its attitude jets to stabilize it back into geosync orbit. It did not fire any weapon at the two Earth ships. Nor did it launch any missiles or nuke warheads at them. Clearly its Hunter captain understood it survived on the sufferance of the human fleet. He hoped the smoke in Joy's Bridge was just the result of circuits fusing somewhere in the destroyer's electrical distribution system. He also noted something else. His father had waited to order the attack until the Star Navy base *Green Hills* had orbited back to this side of Valhalla, putting it in position to defend the capital Stockholm against any nukes that might be launched by this wasp ship. O'Sullivan was firing the base's attitude jets to raise its orbit above the normal 492 klicks. A higher orbit meant a longer time on this side of Valhalla and a longer period in which O'Sullivan and his people could protect the colonists. The true space image of the planet and *Green Hills* also showed two Star Navy shuttles leaving the station and heading toward the wasp ship. Damn. Each shuttle was armed with a single low power nose laser. But that laser would be enough to knock out any nuke warhead launched by the wasp ship when the fleet left its current orbit above the moon. O'Sullivan was very aware that his base could not stay on the same side of his world as the enemy, unlike the wasp ship that was in a fixed geosync orbit just above Stockholm.

"Jacob! Uh, captain," called Daisy. "Look at the spysat images!"

He looked away from the local true space holo and up to the spysat image that filled the middle of the wallscreen. The fifteen wasp ships were all firing their thrusters and moving up and away from their new colony world. Green beams shot out from three wasp ships, hitting three of the spysats his father had left in geosync orbits both equatorial and polar. The wallscreen image shifted from a dead spysat to a still living one, sending a live stream of neutrino-transmitted images across two AU.

"Crap." He looked up at the seventeen ship captain images that lined the top of the wallscreen. "Fleet admiral, looks like the enemy is leaving their colony. And taking down our spysats on their way out. I'm damned glad you agreed to have the *Inchon* follow us back here. They would have been overwhelmed."

"True," his father said, a grimace filling his face. "Looks like this truce was just to buy time for them to put down their baby wasps. Now they're heading our way." The man fixed on Jacob. "You warned me this would happen. Now they're doing just what they did to you at Kepler 22. Well, I have a few surprises for them." His father looked down. "Captain Canowicakte, move the *Midway* out of here. Set us on course for planet three. All ships, follow!"

Putting aside his recollection that the name of the Sioux captain meant 'good hunter of the forest' in Lakota, Jacob focused on commanding the *Lepanto*.

"Navigation, set us on a vector that puts us alongside the admiral's ship," he said quickly. "Engines, give me full power on all three thrusters. Gravity, Weapons and Tactical, bring your teams to full staffing."

"Sir, both outriggers are fully staffed," called Oliver from his Weapons station. "The proton laser nodes, plasma batteries, railguns and antimatter cannon are also staffed by first shift. The AM cannon has eight shots holding in her mag storage."

"Same for Tactical," called Rosemary, her wide shoulders tensing within her clear vacsuit. "I am cross-linking our targeting sensors. We're ready to combine our energy beam firing with that of other ships."

"Captain, Gravity is normalized on all decks of the *Lepanto*," reported Cassandra from her station. "My techs are standing by at all gravplate energizers. They're ready to shift power as needed, or to cut all gravity pull upon your command."

Jacob had no wish to repeat his one-time killing of ship gravity fields in order to escape the black hole field of the giant wasp ship. His Navigator and the Navigators on every fleet ship well understood the need to stay at least 4,000 klicks away from both giant wasp ships. Although he thought the ship once commanded by Hunter One was unable to erect such a field. No matter. It was a prime space battle command now, thanks to his father's new orders during their voyage into the system and over to the third world. Their watch there had been boring. So they'd left once the wasps put out vacsuited crew to repair hull damage. It was clear that action had just been part of the dance of deception as ordered by this Hunter Prime. Who seemed a far slicker opponent than Hunter One.

"Captain Renselaer," called Alicia from where she sat strapped in. "My xenolinguist has composed several more English-to-wasp statements that might be used for disruption of wasp ship actions. May I send them to you?"

"Yes. Send them to the XO, to my tablet and out to the admiral." He stopped before saying it was vital that more than one Battlestar had access to such wasp language date, in case one of their ships blew up in the coming battle. "I'll review them on our way out." He looked away from the image of his father and to the situational holo that showed the space around the moon. All eighteen ships were there, including the *Inchon*. Its crew had spent their time heading in-system, then in orbit above planet three, working to restore their knocked out second thruster. They could now make ten percent of lightspeed, although how long the destroyer's repairs would last was anyone's guess. He put that aside and focused on the true space imagery that showed the ships of the two battle groups following the *Midway* and the *Lepanto* away from the moon and inward to the third orbital. The wallscreen's central image of the wasp ships streaming away from planet three now vanished in a flash of white as the last spysat was killed. "We're heading out."

♦ ♦ ♦

"It looks like we'll meet them at the halfway point," Daisy heard Jacob say an hour later.

"Looks likely," she replied, doing her best to keep her voice calm and firm.

Presenting a confident appearance to the crew at their duty stations on the Bridge, and elsewhere on the *Lepanto*, was vital. People knew they were heading to a final fight with two giant wasp ships and thirteen smaller, destroyer-size ships. They knew the Battlestar was not invulnerable. The repairs to the deep holes cut into the ship's belly, nose and top rear had been done well by the engineers at the *Green Hills*. But there was no normal metal that met the exacting composition of armor metal. Which left her ship with three vulnerable spots, although all weapons systems were fully operational. She hoped Quincy, now in charge of the right outrigger's CO_2 and proton laser nodes, would survive the upcoming battle. This would be a fight to the finish. Either every wasp ship would be killed, or every Earth ship would die in the attempt. They could never allow a fully mobile wasp ship to reach missile launch range of Valhalla. Her memory of visiting the people of Stockholm, seeing their first responders risking their lives after the last attack, and then going fishing in one of the nearby lakes with a nurse from the local hospital, that had imprinted on her a love for that world.

"Tactical," called Jacob. "What's the range to the enemy?"

"Twelve point four million kilometers," Rosemary said. "They're moving at ten psol, just like us. But they're slowing now. We'll meet in less than five minutes."

Her overhead image of Jacob showed him nodding quickly. "All Ship! Brace for combat! Engines, slow us to one percent. That's what the *Midway* is doing."

"Reducing thrust," called Akira from her station.

Her heart beat fast and she had to work hard at not breathing too fast. Hyperventilation was not something she wished to feel.

♦ ♦ ♦

Richard checked his ship cross-section holo that lay to the right of his seat. It showed all ship weapons systems as Green

Operational. That he expected. What mattered more to him was the situation in the hangar next to Silo Eight. His Marines were gathered just outside the three Darts, each wearing a Shinshoni Hard Shell. His pilots were already onboard, making engines and systems hot. He knew he could count on the pilots Linda, Howard and Aaron. The team leaders like Jane were checking the battle loads of each person's hard shell. Thanks to Auggie losing his Dart, up to six Marines could load onto each remaining Dart. Which were now named *Chao Lee*, *Chapultepec* and *Tarawa*. The last name evoked his memory of the WWII journal *Touched By Fire*. At least in space his Marines did not have to smell the dead bodies rotting and bursting open from hundred degree heat and humidity that drained all energy. Mauritius had been bad enough, fighting the Creole Muslims who supported the foreign jihadists in their fight to overthrow the dominating Hindus. Worse had been the jihadists who killed the Malaysian president, then had retreated to that nation's thick jungles. He remembered his uniform and boots going very rotty. At least they'd had enough ammo. He put away those memories and focused on what he, his Marines and their Darts might do in the forthcoming battle. He tapped the control patch on his right armrest that gave him a link to the Shinshoni suit frequency.

"Pilots, stand by to launch on the captain's orders. Auggie, Wayne and Jane, are your teams ready?"

"Ready," called Jane. "Standing by outside the *Chao Lee*."

"Locked, loaded and powered up," reported Auggie from the *Chapultepec*.

"Ready to kill something," yelled Wayne from the *Tarawa*, which was also the assembly spot for some of the Marines who would have loaded into the Dart that had blown on the comet ship.

He knew Wayne would parcel the extra people out to the other two Darts as needed, no doubt being the first to board the *Tarawa*. Wayne was a gyrene of the old school. A fact that Richard quite liked.

"Marines! If we're going for a board, fill the Darts. If we're sent out to sharpshoot, just the pilot and a single Marine to handle the laser go out. The rest of you stay in the hangar and shoot dice."

"Bitchin'," called Linda.

Richard smiled. The master sergeant was overdue for promotion to first sergeant, except Earth Command reserved that rank for team leaders. Well, Linda was a hell of a lot more than a pilot.

Maybe when they got back to Earth and resupplied with a fourth Dart he could put her in charge of its team.

He glanced up at the front wallscreen. Its central true space image showed a telescopic view of the incoming wasp ships. One group of seven, with a giant ship in the middle of a ring of six. A second group held eight ships, including a giant. Which made their formation a six-on-one and another seven-on-one grouping. Well, it was very similar to how the wasps had arranged their first attack using twelve ships to come around the fourth planet of Kepler 22. What kind of formation would the admiral call out now? He couldn't wait to hear it.

◆ ◆ ◆

Aarhant Bannerjee locked the slidedoor that gave access to his quarters and turned back to sit in his overstuffed chair. He reached out for the bottle of Scotch that he preferred during tense times. Which were now. His assistants were above, in the Navigation control center, which was just one deck under the outer Weapons Deck. Too close to the ship's hull, in his view. His quarters on the Habitation Deck were near the center of the *Lepanto*, which it made two decks below and four decks above a buffer against incoming energy beams. Short of leaving the Battlestar, staying in his quarters was the safest place he could be.

He swigged down a swallow of straight Scotch, not bothering with the shot glass that stood on the nearby table. His tablet buzzed. He ignored it. Then it spoke with the voice of the Singapore woman who was his first assistant.

"Bannerjee! We're about to enter battle. Your place is here in the control center," she said, her English carrying a strong Chinese accent, which clearly said she was upset.

"It's Lieutenant Commander, you hag," he replied. "I'm sick with the flu. You and the Kenyan handle what needs handling. We're stuck in this system until the wasps go away. Do the job I gave you!"

"Understood."

His tablet gave a soft click as she cut the connection.

Well, she and that gay bastard could take their chances with the Weapons Deck being punched through by one of those wasp lightning bolts. He wouldn't. And illness was an acceptable excuse from being absent from his duty station, according to Star Navy regs. He knew that. He'd researched it many years ago.

Putting down the bottle of Scotch, he took the wallscreen control, switched off its view of the oncoming wasp fleet, and chose a Bollywood movie that featured a man who looked much like him. The man pretended to be the god Vishnu. His blue skin matched his pretence. Bannerjee did not have blue skin, just the normal dark brown common to most Hindus. But he did have a crown that resembled the one worn by this actor. It was a thing he'd ordered during his last Earth leave. It was something he enjoyed wearing in the privacy of his quarters, where no one but himself could see him.

Or could the AI Melody see him?

No matter. It was not a real person. And he didn't give a damn what it or anyone else thought of him.

CHAPTER EIGHTEEN

"Range is 12,000 klicks," called Rosemary. "Both fleets are slowing to 900 kilometers a minute maneuvering speed."

Jacob did not like the fact his forehead sweated every time he wore a vacsuit. As did his armpits. The cotton camo he wore underneath the vacsuit did little to help that. Up front he saw sweat showing on the camo shirts worn by Maggie, Oliver, Akira, Louise, Andrew, Cassandra and Joaquin. Only Rosemary and Willard didn't show evidence of sweating as they faced the imminent deadly fighting. Daisy, Richard and Alicia sat with their backs against their seats so he couldn't tell about them. And Lori and Carlos were behind him. Anyway, when would his father announce the attack formation? When would—

"All ships! Go to Alpha Scissor Blades formation!" his father said loudly. "One scissor forms on the *Lepanto* and one on the *Midway*. StarFight ships form on the *Lepanto*. Now!"

"Navigation! Move us out and to one side of this vector track," Jacob ordered.

"New diverging vector track set," Louise called from her station.

"All StarFight ships, form along the *Lepanto's* track," he called over the neutrino comlink. "Cruisers first, then the destroyers, then the frigates."

"Moving to your tail," called Swanson from the *Chesapeake*.

"Us too," called Wilcox from the *Hampton Roads*.

Jacob looked to the situational holo that showed the wasp ships as purple dots with human ships as green dots. No planets or moons were shown on this holo that covered a few hundred thousand klicks. It didn't matter. He recalled the Scissor Blades formation as one his father had used against the cluster of rebel mining ships near Callisto. To the outside observer it looked like a splitting of forces, making each group smaller in numbers than the approaching enemy force. His scissor blade had just eight ships in it, while his father's blade had ten. They faced fifteen ships. But in reality it was a variation on the ancient pincer formation, but led this time by

Battlestars armed with antimatter cannons, followed by powerful cruisers loaded to the hilt with CO_2 and proton lasers, a railgun on each cruiser's nose and four missile silos at the rear. Plus top and bottom plasma batteries for close-up protection.

He liked Scissors because it gave the *Lepanto* and the cruisers the chance to use their side-mounted proton lasers in a raking fire mode where their proton beams could join with the proton beams fired by the following destroyers. For his formation, that made for six red proton beams, all aimed at a single target. His father's formation included three cruisers and four destroyers, which gave the admiral a combined strike ability of eight proton beams. Jacob knew from past battles that hitting any of the smaller wasp ships with eight, or even six proton beams meant fast destruction of that six-sided log-like ship. After the formation hit the enemy with raking proton fire, the formation called for his ships to reverse course and come up the tails of the surviving enemy ships, hitting them with combined CO_2 laser fire. The railguns on the cruisers and Battlestars would fire Smart Rocks during both attack runs. But first of course would come enemy beams since the wasps had the range advantage.

"Incoming," called Oliver at Weapons.

Green and yellow beams struck out from all fifteen wasp ships. They were grouped in two sets of ships, one of seven and one of eight. One group of seven ships fired on the *Lepanto*. The other group of eight fired on the *Midway*.

"Nav, lift our nose a bit," he called to Louise. "Protect our cannon node."

"Lifting," responded the right side redhead.

"Hits on our nose," called the left side redhead as Rosemary tapped her Tactical control pillar. "Shall I spin the ship?"

"Yes," Jacob said. "But stop the spin when I order our right side proton laser to join in firing on one of the wasp ships. Can't disrupt Quincy's targeting aim."

"Spinning."

The ship cross-section holo showed a second hit from seven ship beams. The front ring of each ship fired two green lasers and two yellow lightning bolts at the *Lepanto*, making for fourteen hits on the nose and now the front belly of his ship. The belly railgun died in that fire. At least his two topside railgun launchers were operational. He planned to add multiple volleys of Seek-And-Kill Smart Rocks to the proton laser fire. Briefly he realized he should have loaded nuke warheads on some of the Smart Rocks, in the hope a few nukes would get through and blow holes in the log-like ships. Well, beams were faster and just as deadly.

"Range is now 9,937 klicks," called Rosemary.

Finally.

"Tactical! Stop the spinning. Aim our proton mount at wasp ship W5. Fire!"

"Firing," called the woman whose milky-white skin could not take a tan.

In the true space holo that filled the middle of the wallscreen, the wasp ship closest to his scissor blade became the target of six red proton beams as the StarFight cruisers and destroyers joined his fire. The *Midway* was leading the counter-attack on a wasp ship close to it.

The nose of W5 became red, then yellow, then white.

A vast explosion filled the front of the wasp ship, spreading rearward as the six red beams changed angle to run along the top spine of the wasp ship. Before those beams reached the rear weapons ring, it happened.

A white-yellow star glowed in carbon black space.

"Bandit splashed!" called Rosemary. "Launching first load of Smart Rocks."

A vibration touched his boots as the railgun launchers on the *Lepanto's* topside shot out a hundred beach balls loaded with plastique and maneuvering jets. A second vibration said his tail railgun had joined in the attack.

"Targeting W1 now," called Rosemary.

A second white-yellow star flared on his father's side of the approaching wasp formation. The combined eight proton beams from his blade of the formation had cut through the middle of his target, breaking it open. Silver water globules and white air filled the middle between the two ship halves. But they disappeared as the ship's fusion reactor lost containment and created a decent fusion bomb that blew apart the two halves.

A third star flared where W1 had been.

"Second bandit splashed by StarFight," Rosemary said, sounding even more excited.

"Punch through on our belly!" yelled Joaquin at Life Support.

"Water shell is venting. Control valves closing. Inner hull still intact."

That punch through from combined enemy beams had happened between the old belly punch through and the front nose of his ship. Both belly railgun launchers were long gone. Jacob bit his lip as Rosemary initiated a third volley of proton laser fire, this time targeting another wasp ship.

The situational holo counter now changed. It had shown the two wasp groups down to five ships on Jacob's side and seven on his father's side, with their two rows of green dots nearing the front of the enemy formation of two purple dot clusters. That now changed. A green dot vanished.

A new star filled this part of the cosmos.

"*St. Mihiel's* gone," called Oliver.

Jacob felt his gut tighten. He would miss the good humor of Dekker Lorenz and the 71 men and women aboard the frigate. Dekker had been firing his nose laser against W1, adding to that ship's disintegration. Now his ship fragments joined the icy coldness of black space.

"But the *Midway's* group got another wasp! Now a second!" cried Cassandra from Gravity.

Jacob saw two new stars take form on his father's side of the formation.

Tiny yellow lights now lit up among the leading wasp ships as the volleys of Smart Rocks fired by the *Midway*, the *Lepanto* and the cruisers managed to hit wasp ship hulls, blowing up sensor arrays and weapons tubes. Hundreds had been fired. A few dozen made it through the laser counterfire of the wasp ships.

Two bigger stars now filled his father's side of the wasp formation.

They looked like three megaton thermonuke blasts. But that couldn't be. Yet they had happened at the positions of two wasp ships. Which now disappeared from the situational counter.

"Admiral?" Jacob called.

His father looked at Jacob from his Bridge. A grin filled his face. "Told you I had a few surprises up my sleeve! We used the transit time inward and back to Valhalla to retrofit some Smart Rocks with magfield coils. Then we squirted antimatter into them. They were mixed among the plastique loaded rocks. Two of them got through!"

"Amazing," he murmured, giving his father a thumbs-up.
"Well done, admiral."

The situational counter now showed three purple dots on his
father's side, which included the giant wasp ship. Five purple dots
were on Jacob's side. Wrong. Now four.

"Splashed another bandit!" yelled Rosemary. "That was W3.
We're combining proton beams against W7."

The white-yellow star of the dead wasp ship slowly became
rings within rings of orange, then red plasma shells as vaporized parts
of the wasp ship added to the star that had once been filled with living
wasps.

Jacob saw his scissor blade was about to move past the four
wasp ships remaining on his side. That included the damaged giant
wasp ship that had been led by Hunter One. It was also the ship that
had sent down a shuttle loaded with a lightning bomb that had killed
Admiral Johanson, Captain Miglotti and XO Anderson. Time to go
after it.

"StarFight formation! Reverse course! Let's run up the tails of
these bastards!"

Even as he heard cheers from the other six ship captains, a
new star took form. It had been a green dot.

"The *Inchon* is gone," called Rosemary, her voice suddenly
soft.

Jacob watched the situational holo as Louise turned the
Lepanto's nose into a seventy degree turn that would allow the
Battlestar to lead the new attack formation. One part of his mind said
the cruisers, destroyers and surviving frigate *Aldertag* would come
about and follow his lead. Another part of his mind said Earth had
traded a frigate and a destroyer to take out eight wasp ships. It was
now sixteen green dots versus seven purple dots. He did not like the
four-to-one tradeoff. The seven wasp survivors included the two giant
ships. Which were combining their beams against the *Chesapeake* and
the *Hampton Roads*. Water globules from *Chesapeake's* right side
said it had a punch through. *Hampton* wobbled in its course, then
resumed its curve-around vector track.

"Navigation, put us in the path of the beams hitting our
cruisers."

"Maneuvering."

The topside of the Battlestar became nearly sun hot as green lasers and yellow lightning bolts filled the space where his spine proton laser mount and topside plasma battery had been.

Two yellow-white stars filled the void.

"The *Midway* got one. The StarFight ships got a second. Both on our side," called Rosemary, sounding very somber.

One part of Jacob's mind said it was down to five wasp ships against sixteen human ships. Two wasps on his side and three on his father's side.

"Punch through into Weapons Deck," called Joaquin. "It's through the inner hull. Hallway hatches closing. We lost some people in the hallway section opened to space."

"Nav, lift us up ten degrees. Our belly proton mount can still fire," Jacob said, hoping his crewmates listening over the All Ship vidcast would understand he cared about the crew who had died in the topside Weapons hallway. Just as he cared about those who had died when the *St. Mihiel* and the *Inchon* had become sun-hot vapor.

A new star showed. A green dot vanished.

"The *Red Sea* is gone," Rosemary said so softly he wondered if she even meant to speak.

Fifteen versus five. Time to do something radical.

"Engines! Move us up to eleven psol! Now!" Jacob looked further left. "Power, increase reactor output by ten percent. Do it!"

"Power output increasing," responded Maggie, her voice firm.

"All thrusters firing beyond rating," called Akira. "I've increased power flow to the fusion pellet containment fields."

They had done this once before, during the first wasp attack in Kepler 22. Jacob knew his ship could take it. The *Lepanto* would outpace the following StarFight ships, which even now were combining their fire against the single wasp ship that followed behind the giant ship that had lost its front nose section. But it allowed his Battlestar to close on the fleeing giant ship, which was making just ten psol.

"Tactical, connect me with Chief Linkletter," he said.

"Linking," called Rosemary, her tone now eager as she realized his intent.

"Chief Petty Officer Linkletter reporting," came the voice of the young man whom he now knew much better than two months ago. "Captain, you have orders for me?"

"I do. Target wasp ship W8. It's the giant one. Advise me when it enters the impact zone of the cannon's beam."

Seconds passed.

"Range is 4,011 kilometers and closing," called Rosemary.

"Target W8 is within reach!" called Linkletter.

At last. "Fire antimatter cannon!"

In the true space holo that filled the middle of the wallscreen, a black beam of magnetically confined negative antimatter shot out from the *Lepanto* and impacted on the stern of the giant wasp ship. It was target W8 on the situational holo.

The ship's three fusion thrusters blew apart as a small white-yellow sun glowed where once matter had been. That glow grew larger and larger, moving forward.

"Damn!" grunted Richard.

"Got 'em," said Daisy.

Below, Alicia looked up, her expression very sober. "You've put paid to the killers of Admiral Johanson, Miglotti and Anderson."

"We *all* put paid to that debt," Jacob said.

He watched as a large sun replaced the matter and living bodies of the wasp ship that had led the unprovoked attack on his ship and his StarFight fellows.

A second smaller sun now showed just beyond the spot where the giant wasp ship had once been.

His father's eight ships had come about in their reverse scissor blade formation and had run up on the rear of the remaining wasp ships. They had just killed W12, the last ship on Jacob's side. Which left the giant ship led by Hunter Prime and two more wasp ships.

Fifteen green dots versus three purple dots. Eight ships in the *Midway* formation and seven in his StarFight formation. They had paid in blood for the death of most of the invading wasp fleet. He saw his father's *Midway* leading the beam fight against the two smaller wasp ships. They had moved to trail behind the rear of the remaining giant wasp ship. Why the move back?

"Captain!" yelled Lori from behind. "Look! The giant wasp ship is putting out new hull plates. It's going black hole!"

Damn. "All StarFight ships, stay back! Giant ship is going to black hole mode!"

"*Midway* fleet, do the same," called his father. "Tactical, concentrate our lasers on the ass of that wasp on the right. Maybe we can blow its two thrusters!"

Jacob liked that. "Tactical, aim our front lasers at the other wasp ship. All StarFight ships, join your lasers with those of the *Lepanto*."

"Joining with *Lepanto*," came the responses from the captains of the *Chesapeake, Hampton Roads, Tsushima Strait, Salamis, Philippine Sea* and the *Aldertag*.

"Joining," came from his father's battle group.

The ships *Okinawa, Mobile Bay, Manila Bay, Monitor, Leyte Gulf, Schweinfurt* and *Malacca Strait* joined their laser fire with that of the *Midway*.

The hulls of the two wasp ships glowed from the touch of green laser beams.

The giant wasp ship disappeared.

It had gone into black hole mode, leaving behind only an invisible event horizon and a power great enough to reach out nearly 4,000 kilometers in any direction. Actually, the other part of Jacob's mind corrected, its reach was 3,917 klicks.

"Look!" yelled Lori. "Those wasp ships are caught in the field!"

Jacob watched along with everyone on the fifteen surviving ships as the two wasp ships now paid for moving close to the giant ship's stern in an effort to protect that ship. Had the Hunter Prime ordered them to do that, even as he planned to activate his black hole field? Had he known it would kill the other wasp ships? Whatever his plan, his ship was now invulnerable to incoming beams. Which had become streaks of green and red laser light that circled the middle of an invisible globe. That globe began moving away, pulling the two wasp ships closer and closer.

Gray hulls fragmented into hundreds of plates and pipes and blocks as gravitational tides pulled the once-living ships into long streams of gray taffy surrounded by white clouds of air that had once been breathed.

"Damn," called Rosemary. "We didn't need to shoot at those two bastards. Their own boss killed them."

Jacob could only agree. Well before the incoming laser and proton beams could kill the last two smaller wasp ships, they had been pulled out of targeting lock-on and closer to the giant ship that was now a swirl of green and red light that flared every time a metal fragment hit the event horizon and was consumed by the beam energies fired by their fifteen ships.

"Well, that puts paid to most of them," said his father from the *Midway*, sounding satisfied.

True. But there was no way the giant ship could stay in black hole mode forever. It had—

"Captain," called Louise from Navigation. "That black hole ship is increasing its speed. It's up to eleven psol. Moving higher. Now at twelve psol. It's at thirteen psol and—"

"What's the vector track of that ship!" Jacob yelled, his belly clenching as new fears filled his heart.

"Toward Valhalla," Louise said, choking on her answer.

He looked to his father. "Fleet admiral, we cannot let that bastard get to Valhalla! All he has to do is to drop his field and launch his nuke warheads. We couldn't kill them all. The *Lepanto* can catch that bastard!"

"How?"

His father's expression had gone from satisfaction to frustration.

"By going up to fourteen percent of lightspeed. Our reactors can provide the power. Our thrusters can handle the strain."

His father looked torn. "I remember that part of the first combat video. That was how you pulled the *Lepanto* out of that other ship's black hole field. But son, it's a long trip to get to Valhalla. An AU at least. You can't keep that speed up for an hour."

He was probably right. "We'll hold it to thirteen point two psol," Jacob said. "We'll overtake that Hunter Prime bastard!"

Decision filled his father's face. "Do it. And send us your power and thruster settings. Two of us going after that bastard doubles the chances that one of us will overtake him before our engines melt. Or worse."

Jacob knew what worse meant. "Engines, Power, send your settings to the *Midway*. Take us to thirteen point two psol. Now."

"Sir!" Maggie cried. "That will put the reactors at 12 percent beyond their maximum safe rating! We're now at five over."

"So it will. Do it." He remembered what he had to do to increase power flow to the thrusters. "Gravity," he called to

Cassandra. "Cut power to all gravity plates not involved in the operation of the fusion reactors, fuel feed and thruster operation. Warn all decks, but cut power. That will reduce the draw on the fusion reactors and increase power flow to the thrusters."

"All decks," the green-haired woman called over the shipwide comlink. "Null gravity coming." She reached out and tapped her control pillar. "All gravity plates shut down. Sir."

He looked ahead to Akira. "Engines, increase thruster output as much as you can with the increased fuel flow and power feed."

The young Black woman nodded, her tight curls floating out from her head as the Bridge gravity plates shut down. "Increasing thruster power. Moving up to 12.3, 12.7 . . . 13.2 percent of lightspeed!"

On his wallscreen the image of the *Midway's* Bridge showed his father doing the same with his Power, Engines and Gravity people. A tablet floated up from the armrest of the Sioux captain, who reached out faster than quick and grabbed it.

"Fleet admiral, the *Midway* is hauling ass!" called the man.

Jacob almost smiled at the sudden looseness of his father's captain. Marjorie Jones his XO did smile briefly. Then sobered. His father and his staff understood the risk they were taking in pushing their Battlestar well beyond its thruster and reactor ratings. This was the first time for them. It was the second time for him, Daisy and everyone else on the Bridge.

"Navigation, show me a projected interception point for our arrival within weapons range of the black hole ship."

Louise tapped on her control pillar.

The wallscreen already held two images. The sensor holo filled the left side of the screen, while the true space holo filled the right side. Its middle now showed the green dots of their disjointed Scissors formation. Thirteen green dots moved at ten psol, falling behind. Two green dots now chased after a single purple dot.

"Projected."

The middle holo enlarged until it included the planet Valhalla and its moon on the far right side, with the ships on the far left. A dotted green line chased after a purple dot. Intersection showed at a million klicks out from Valhalla.

"All Ship, we are in pursuit of the surviving enemy ship," Jacob announced. "I aim to kill it before it hurts Valhalla. Take your Awake pills and stay on your stations. This battle is not yet done."

He sat back and tried not to feel impatient.

CHAPTER NINETEEN

An hour later Daisy watched the readings from the ship's three fusion reactors and three fusion pulse thrusters. The internal magfields of the reactors were holding their tiny fusion blasts and bleeding off electrical power to the ship's essential functions. Which were air, lights, control circuits, the shipwide wifi field, sensors, the Mess Hall freezers, the Med Hall equipment and the weapons mounts and nodes. The shutdown of nearly every gravity plate in the *Lepanto* had allowed enough power to flow to the thrusters so Akira and the fusion engineers on Engines Deck had been able to increase the strength of the fusion magfields that fed each thruster with implosion byproducts. Raw energy spat out the rear of her ship's three exhaust funnels, seeking escape from the magfields of those funnels. Once free of the funnels, the streams of orange-white plasma joined together in a single flare that reached out eighty kilometers to her ship's stern. Secondary reradiation from molecules of interstellar gas reached beyond the flare itself. She wished that flare could be turned loose on the black hole wasp ship. But its river of electrons, protons, neutrons and subatomic particles would be bent sideways and join the field's accretion disk, the same way the earlier barrage of beams from both Earth fleets had been shifted. Her holo's true space image of the distant enemy ship showed a glowing white, green and red ball with periodic flares of yellow light as interstellar gas impacted the field. Only the *Lepanto's* charged electromagnetic field kept her ship from being badly buffeted by the sparse gas that lay between the planets of any star.

"Interception point arrives in six point three minutes," called Louise.

"Finally," muttered Jacob from above her. Her overhead image of him showed him looking to Richard. "Chief O'Connor, tell your Marines to load into their Darts. Just the pilot and a single Marine to handle the Dart laser. And to offload the three thermonuke warheads you put in each cargohold."

The white-haired, strong-shouldered man hunched forward, peering intently at one of his holos. "Darts are loading a pilot and a Marine sharpshooter."

"Who's going out?" called Jacob.

"The pilots are Master Sergeant Linda Mabry on the *Chao Lee,* Master Sergeant Howard Johnson on the *Chapultepec* and Master Sergeant Aaron Jacobs on the *Tarawa*," Richard said flatly. "Joining them to sharpshoot are Gunnery Sergeant Jane Diego on *Chao Lee*, First Sergeant Auggie Naranjo on the *Chapultepec* and First Sergeant Wayne Park on the *Tarawa*. All six of them carry the nuke arming codes. Sir."

"Your team leaders," Jacob said, sounding distracted.

"Yes sir."

Daisy understood the Darts prep was in case the *Lepanto* lost her antimatter cannon and a boarding of the wasp ship was needed. The Marines would launch under covering laser fire, impact, offload the thermonukes and then hit the retros. In theory it would place nine, three megaton thermonukes into three parts of the wasp hull. Enough to kill it, Jacob had said during the early part of their chase. He'd called it his 'final option'.

She returned her gaze to the ship cross-section holo, with quick glances at her situational holo that showed the upcoming intersection of the *Lepanto* and the *Midway* with the black hole ship. Its vector track had changed slightly, moving it into a line that ran close to the top of Valhalla's atmosphere. She touched her armrest control. The projected end point would arrive at 4,180 kilometers above the planet's atmosphere. A blinking yellow dot just below that arrival point turned her throat dry.

"Captain! The wasp ship is aiming straight at *Green Hills* station! If it's still in black hole mode when it arrives, the station will be ripped apart!"

Jacob cursed. "Com! Connect me with O'Sullivan!"

"Going up," Andrew said.

The wallscreen grew a fourth image. It showed the vacsuited forms of Captain Billy O'Sullivan and Ensign Jason Mikoto. The Anglo's hazel eyes fixed on them.

"What's happening?"

"The last wasp ship is heading for your station," Jacob said hurriedly. "We can't do a thing to it while it's in black hole mode. It will pass well above you but the field reaches out damn far. The edge or worse will grab you. Evacuate your station!"

Mikoto turned pale. O'Sullivan grimaced. "We'll try. Gotta pull in the two shuttles we have keeping laser watch on that wasp ship at geosync." The man sighed. "Captain, there are 312 people on this station. The shuttles hold twenty-four each. Max. No way we can get everyone off."

"Captain!" yelled Joaquin from his Life Support station. "Tell him to put the others in their vacsuits! The normal station suit has maneuvering jets and six hours of air. If the people in suits jet down to a lower altitude, their orbital speed will increase, moving them away from the *Green Hills*. They'll be going east, the same vector as the station. The wasp ship's track will take it to the west of Valhalla. Maybe one of our following ships can pick up the suits before they hit atmosphere. The atmo top is at 130 klicks. If they get low enough, the suits might avoid the black hole field when it hits the station. Which is now at 597 klicks high."

"O'Sullivan! Do what my guy says! You've got ten minutes before we all arrive above Valhalla."

"Will do." The Star Navy captain turned to his ensign. "Mikoto, take charge of loading people into the two shuttles. There will be time for a trip downplanet, then maybe time for a second load to take down. Don't matter if the shuttles can't make it up here afterward. The station will be gone by then."

"Yes sir. Moving on it," the young Asian said, turning and running out of the com room.

O'Sullivan looked tired. "I'll round up everyone else and put 'em into suits. We'll have to jump out of the station's airlocks before that bastard arrives and its field hits us. Kill it, will you?"

"It'll die. And we'll zap any nukes it launches at Valhalla. I promise," Jacob said, sounding intensely frustrated.

"Thanks. *Green Hills* out."

One of the captains in the line of fourteen images above the wallscreen now spoke.

"Captain, I sure wish the *Sea* could get there and help with that evacuation!" called Jefferson.

"You can't," Jacob said. "Your ship and every other fleet ship has just two thrusters. You can't make our 13.2 psol. Which is why only the *Midway* and the *Lepanto* are chasing this SOB. But you can help rescue the suited evacuees." He gestured at the wallscreen. "All StarFight ships, do your best to pick up station folks. They'll be close to the top of the atmosphere by the time we finish this."

Acknowledgments came from everyone.

"Interception," called Louise.

◆ ◆ ◆

Jacob looked away from Jefferson and focused on his situational holo, which copied the holo that filled part the wallscreen. It showed Valhalla's moon lying not far away, maybe five hundred thousand klicks. Which put the *Midway*, the *Lepanto* and the invisible wasp ship just eight hundred thousand klicks away from Valhalla and the Star Navy station. At 13.2 psol that was very close.

"Enemy ship is slowing to one psol," called Louise.

"Engines, drop us to one psol," Jacob said. "Power, reduce reactor output to safe rating. Gravity, restore gravplate functioning."

"At last!" called Akira, sounding exhausted from having to baby her fusion thrusters the last hour.

The other station chiefs sent out orders as directed.

In one of the top wallscreen images his father gave the same orders to his Bridge staff.

"Admiral, enemy's black hole field is still up," Jacob reported. "I'm moving to put the *Lepanto* along its planet side. We'll be able to zap any missiles or warheads it launches once it drops the field."

His father nodded quickly. "Just right. The *Midway* will take topside. Hopefully one of us will get the bastard in our cannon sights."

Jacob looked ahead. Louise held her hand up, thumb and forefinger forming an A-Okay circle. She'd heard and taken action to alter their vector track.

"Linkletter, have you got that bastard in your cannon's targeting field?"

"Captain, I do."

"Good."

Jacob watched the true space holo as the green hills and blue oceans of Valhalla swelled into distinct view, thanks to the ship's scope that could bring almost anything into crystal pure clarity. The white ball of its moon hung off to one side. A tiny silver sparkle was the wasp comet ship at geosync. The black hole ship would pass well below it, in a grazing pass that would allow its field to take out *Green Hills* station. Clearly the Hunter Prime leader had watched his own vidrecords from the earlier battle led by Hunter One, where the station's proton lasers had zapped most of the nukes launched by the comet ship. The enemy commander was aiming to make sure the station could not do the same before it dropped its field and launched its own nukes at the world below.

"Range to Valhalla atmosphere is now 24,389 kilometers," called Louise. "Enemy speed is down to 2,857 klicks a minute. Black hole field will hit the station within seven minutes."

Jacob licked his lips. "Tactical, prepare to fire."

"Ready and eager," Rosemary said.

"So am I," called Linkletter from the AM node.

From the wallscreen came similar commands from his father on the *Midway*.

Yellow sunlight illuminated the human-occupied part of Valhalla. The green forested continent, which was shaped something like the giant island of Australia, held so many lives, human, animal and native critters. Alien versions of birds flew through its sky, while shark-like sea creatures roamed the blue oceans that flanked its eastern and western coasts. Millions of minnow-like fishes swam those waters, while large herds of six-limbed animals grazed on its western plains. The silver ball of *Green Hills* was clearly visible. Red flame shot from the stern of two shuttles as they shot down to the planet's surface, carrying forty-eight refugees among them. Jacob hoped that was the second shuttle trip. If it was, nearly a hundred of the three hundred plus humans on the station were now safe in Stockholm. Safe at least until nukes and lightning bombs fell from the dark blue sky.

One way or another, that would not happen.

"Station is fragmenting," called Louise.

Jacob watched the distance counter in his situational holo. The *Lepanto* was within 3,980 kilometers of the black hole ship. Just beyond the reach of its field but close enough for his cannon to reach out and kill part or all of that monster. His father's *Midway* moved at a similar distance on the moon-side flank of the wasp ship.

"Enemy has slowed!" said Louise. "Vector speed down to 17,358 kilometers per hour. Sir, it's aiming to go into high orbit."

Jacob could see that. But the field was still present. What was it intending to do? Would it orbit above Valhalla still protected by its black hole field? Would it—

"Field is down!" cried Rosemary.

"Incoming beams!" called Oliver.

"We're hit!" called Quincy from the right side outrigger. "Laser and proton both gone! Got punch through into the outrigger. Hatches closing."

"Linkletter, fire!"

A black antimatter beam shot out from the *Lepanto*.

It missed.

The giant wasp ship had suddenly moved upward, toward the *Midway*.

"Admiral, it's aiming to ram you! Maneuver!"

"Putting on emergency thrust," his father grunted. "Inertial field lagging. It's back. Right outrigger, fire at that bastard!"

Jacob saw too much at the same time.

As the wasp ship sped toward a collision with his father's ship, firing on the *Midway* with beams from all three weapons rings, its stern launched clouds of warheads at Valhalla, which lay just 5,000 kilometers below.

The angle of the wasp ship as it closed on the *Midway* meant the targeting separation between the two was becoming almost nothing.

"Tactical! Lock onto that wasp with our cannon and kill it!"

Rosemary touched her control pillar, hands moving so fast they were a blur.

"Firing!"

A black beam reached out over thousands of kilometers, its meter width resembling a black stripe against the green and blue ball of Valhalla. That stripe was suddenly there, faster than any eye could follow.

Lightspeed is that way.

A new yellow sun occupied the space ahead.

"The *Midway* is intact!" yelled Daisy.

Jacob wanted to throw up. But there was more to do.

"Richard! Launch your Darts against that rain of warheads! Have your people kill 'em!"

"Darts are launching and curving out," the Marine chief said. "All three Darts are aiming to pass between the warhead cloud and Valhalla's atmosphere. They . . . their pilots say they will blow the thermonukes in their cargoholds if it takes that to kill surviving warheads."

Jacob moved from giving thanks that Rosemary had been as good at targeting as he had thought, to dismay that he might lose some brave Marines.

"Nav, drop our nose to aim the cannon at the top of that cluster!" he yelled. "Weapons, aim our left front laser at that cloud of warheads. Don't hit the Darts!"

"Firing our left front laser," called Rosemary.

"Also firing our left side and belly proton lasers," yelled Oliver.

In the true space holo that filled the middle of the wallscreen, explosions and dying happened.

The Darts had gotten just below the cloud of warheads, thanks to the ten psol speed of their single fusion thrusters. Which now worked in reverse as each Dart flipped over to hold station five hundred klicks above the colony world. Three green laser beams shot up from the Darts, hitting single warheads. The three beams shot out again and again and again, hitting more descending warheads.

"Firing antimatter," called Rosemary.

A black beam speared into the top of the warhead cloud, killing at least a dozen thanks to the beam's spread over 3,000 klicks.

A second black beam joined it.

The *Midway* was firing almost straight down at the cloud of warheads. Which meant its total matter-to-energy conversion created a roiling white-yellow ball of plasma that sank down, enveloping more warheads.

"Darts! Get the hell out from under that plasma!" Jacob yelled.

The white dart shapes of the *Chapultepec* and the *Chao Lee* moved out from under the ravening cloud. The *Tarawa* didn't.

He would miss Wayne Park and Aaron Jacobs.

More green laser streaks and red proton beams struck down from the *Midway* and out from the left side and belly of the *Lepanto*.

Jacob wished the other battle group ships were here to add their energy beams. They weren't. They were at least ten minutes behind. Even ten psol cannot magically transport you instantly from spot A to spot Z.

"Engines, go to one psol. Take us below the warheads. Then reverse thrust. Our hull can handle a nuke."

"Moving us. Aiming below," called Akira.

Of course two meters of armor hull could not hold out against a direct contact strike from a 50 kiloton nuke.

Jacob knew that. His people knew that. He just couldn't allow the people of Stockholm to die.

"Sir!" yelled Louise. "The *Midway* is heading down! It's aiming for the under spot."

His father had thought faster than Jacob had.

Would the 321 people aboard the *Midway* give their lives to save 71,000 lives?

"Tactical, Weapons, keep killing warheads. Maybe we can kill the last of them before the *Midway* gets there. Or we do."

The situational holo was unforgiving.

It showed the yellow dots of 31 warheads still alive and functioning and getting within 500 klicks of Valhalla. They'd enter atmosphere at one hundred thirty klicks.

"Ten more gone," Rosemary said. "The *Midway* has passed our Darts. It's heading under."

The yellow dot counter kept pace with green strikes and red beams.

Nineteen. Fifteen. Seven.

Three small yellow suns flared just above the top hull of the *Midway*.

Had their sensors been set for air burst? If so, that meant the warheads had not been in contact with the Battlestar's hull. Maybe they'd detonated two or three miles out.

The red plasma haze from the three dets gradually thinned in the vacuum of space.

"They're alive!" yelled Daisy.

Jacob took a deep breath.

The scope showed the top of the *Midway* was burned down past its black ablative hull layer. Water globules leaked here and there, saying part of the two meters of armor hull had been penetrated. Or maybe fractured. Belatedly he recalled that a 50 kiloton fireball had a radius in air of a mile. Or one point six kilometers. Maybe a bit more in vacuum. That meant the three fireballs had not touched the hull of the *Midway*. They had to have been set for radar detonation as the ground echoed back to the warhead targeting sensor. Which the hull of the *Midway* had imitated, causing vacuum detonations.

He looked up. His father's face looked back at him.

"We're alive. All of us," he said. "Some heavy rads came through. Med Hall has the injections to suck out the rad damage. Valhalla is safe."

So it was.

"All StarFight ships, look for station evacuees," Jacob said, giving thanks his last surviving parent still lived. The time his father had taken to talk one-on-one with him, just after Jacob had brought his battle group into rendezvous with the Earth relief fleet, that time still held a warm spot in his heart. Maybe it was time to let the past stay in the past.

"It's time, Jacob," said Daisy from below.

Had he said that last sentence out loud?

His father's grin said he had.

"Don't like these vacsuit comlinks, sir. They cut in and out and the static does weird stuff. Like make up words."

Gordon F. Renselaer nodded slowly. "You're right. My vacsuit has done the same thing in the past." He paused. "Your Mom would be proud of you. I know I am."

Jacob suddenly wished his Bridge was not under constant live vidcam observation. It would not do to show tears before the other ship captains. Or his crew watching on the other decks. He gritted his teeth and sat up straight.

"Sir, may I transfer our five wasp captives out to that wasp ship in geosync?" His father looked surprised. "I'm willing to put a carbon-carbon tow line on it, move the *Lepanto* up to planetary escape velocity, and then slingshot the bastard out to the magnetosphere. It can head home to Kepler 22 on its Alcubierre drive."

"Good idea. Before you do that, let's rescue some vacsuited people. Then I need to use your pheromone translator to give a message to this Hunter One."

Jacob couldn't resist. "What message?"

His father smiled, though it was a pale smile. "I call it MAB. Mutually Assured Benefit. Wanna send that ship off with a cartoon video and pheromone talk that says Let's Trade. You tell us about any one gee worlds you find in your colony searches. We'll do the same for half gee worlds. Think they'll go for it?"

Jacob didn't know. But he recalled ending this interstellar war had been one of the two jobs assigned to his father by the Unity and by Earth Command.

"They might. Especially if that wasp ship shares its vidrecords of this last battle." A thought hit him. "Sir, three of Earth's colonies have half gee worlds lying closer to their sun than we like. Do you mean to suggest we share our colony systems with the wasps?"

The man shrugged. "Maybe yes, maybe no. At the least with MAB they will know we will tell them the locations of future half gee worlds we find that resemble oxy-rich jungles. They'll do the same for us with any cooler, one gee worlds they find. It's a start to doing something other than fight."

Below him Richard spoke. "Greed might be stronger than blood."

His father looked startled, then thoughtful. "Chief O'Connor, you have a good point. I'll use it when next I talk to Unity pollies." Then he looked up. "Captain Renselaer, I think we need to send a ship along with that wasp ship when it heads back to Kepler 22. If more wasp fleets show up there, our ship could give us an early warning here. You got any suggestions for that monitoring ship?"

Jacob looked down to Daisy. She looked up and nodded, her dark brown face somber but hopeful. He looked up.

"Sir, I think the Battlestar *Lepanto* could handle lookout duty at Kepler 22."

"Good. But don't be in a rush to leave. That wasp ship will be heading out real slow. Could take them a month or three to get to the magnetosphere. Plenty of time for our fifteen ships to start rebuilding O'Sullivan's station. And time to head down to Stockholm. Does that place have any good bars?"

Jacob almost laughed. His father was not a heavy drinker, sticking mostly with Scotch and some craft beers. But he had no doubt the Midway's crew were eager to enjoy a planetside liberty after nearly two months in space to get to Kepler 10, and then fighting two deadly battles against an alien enemy that never gave up.

"Plenty of them," Jacob said. "There's one Daisy and I like. Down near its central park. The Valhallans like to do recreations of famous Viking battles in that park. Makes for fun watching when you have a beer or two in hand."

His father laughed. It was the first laugh he'd heard in too many years. The man who had raised him to be a copy of himself now looked down at his command people. "Marjorie and Thompson both like craft beers. Even colonial stuff. We'll join you, after we haul in as many vacsuits as we can find."

Jacob thought of Billy O'Sullivan. The man was a happy drinker of beer and most anything else. He hoped the captain now whizzed above the white clouds of Valhalla, keeping order by vacsuit comlink among his fellow station escapees.

"We'll join you. *Lepanto* out."

Jacob looked down to where Daisy sat, still strapped in like all of them. Sweat showed on her dark brown neck. Perhaps sensing his gaze, she looked up. The oval face, brown eyes, sharp nose and happy look were just part of what he loved about her. She looked him over, clearly wondering.

"XO, how about you and I take out your LCA to search for station folks. Chief O'Connor can handle the Bridge. You game?"

"Very much game," she said, unlocking her straps and standing up.

Jacob did the same. He stepped down from his seat, turned to face Richard, and said what was needed.

"Transferring command of the Battlestar *Lepanto* to you, chief. And bring in your Darts. I wish Aaron and Wayne could also return."

"Command accepted, Captain Renselaer." The grizzled, tough man who had taught Jacob much about dealing with the reality of deadly combat gave a sigh. "I wish they could too. Goes with the job. Now get out there and grab some vacsuits."

"I will. We will."

And with that Jacob took hold of Daisy's hand and headed for the Bridge exit.

Lori and Carlos watched them. Those two were also holding hands, perhaps feeling the same relief he and Daisy felt at living through a terrible battle that had claimed too many ships and lives.

"Jacob, the ghosts will rest now," Daisy said.

He hoped so. "Maybe they will."

Together in hope, together in love, they walked through the open slidedoor and into a future less deadly than the present.

THE END

ABOUT THE AUTHOR

T. Jackson King (Tom) is a professional archaeologist, journalist and retired Hippie. He learned early on to question authority and find answers for himself, thanks to reading lots of science fiction. He also worked at a radiocarbon dating laboratory at UC Riverside and UCLA. Tom attended college in Paris and Tokyo. He is a graduate of UCLA (M.A. 1976, archaeology) and the University of Tennessee (B.Sc. 1971, journalism). He has worked as an archaeologist in the American Southwest and has traveled widely in Europe, Russia, Japan, Canada, Mexico and the USA. Other jobs have included short order cook, hotel clerk, legal assistant, telephone order taker, investigative reporter and newspaper editor. He also survived the warped speech-talk of local politicians and escaped with his hide intact. Tom writes hard science fiction, anthropological scifi, dark fantasy/horror and contemporary fantasy/magic realism. Tom's novels are **BATTLESTAR** (2016), **DEFEAT THE ALIENS** (2016), **FIGHT THE ALIENS** (2016), **FIRST CONTACT** (2015), **ESCAPE FROM ALIENS** (2015), **ALIENS VS. HUMANS** (2015), **FREEDOM VS. ALIENS** (2015), **HUMANS VS. ALIENS** (2015), **GENECODE ILLEGAL** (2014), **EARTH VS. ALIENS** (2014), **ALIEN ASSASSIN** (2014), **THE MEMORY SINGER** (2014), **ANARCHATE VIGILANTE** (2014), **GALACTIC VIGILANTE** (2013), **NEBULA VIGILANTE** (2013), **SPEAKER TO ALIENS** (2013), **GALACTIC AVATAR** (2013), **STELLAR ASSASSIN** (2013), **STAR VIGILANTE** (2012), **THE GAEAN ENCHANTMENT** (2012), **LITTLE BROTHER'S WORLD** (2010), **ANCESTOR'S WORLD** (1996, with A.C. Crispin), and **RETREAD SHOP** (1988, 2012). His short stories appeared in **JUDGMENT DAY AND OTHER DREAMS** (2009). His poetry appeared in **MOTHER EARTH'S STRETCH MARKS** (2009). Tom lives in Santa Fe, New Mexico, USA with his wife Sue. More information on Tom's writings can be found at www.tjacksonking.com/.

PRAISE FOR T. JACKSON KING'S BOOKS

EARTH VS. ALIENS

"This story is the best space opera I've read in many years. The author knows his Mammalian Behavior. If we're lucky it'll become a movie soon. Many of the ideas are BRAND NEW and I loved the adaptability of people in the story line. AWESOME!!"—**Phil W. King,** *Amazon*

"It's good space opera. I liked the story and wanted to know what happened next. The characters are interesting and culturally diverse. The underlying theme is that humans are part of nature and nature is red of tooth and claw. Therefore, humans are naturally violent, which fortunately makes them a match for the predators from space."— **Frank C. Hemingway,** *Amazon*

STAR VIGILANTE

"For a fast-paced adventure with cool tech, choose *Star Vigilante*. This is the story of three outsiders. Can three outsiders bond together to save Eliana's planet from eco-destruction at the hands of a ruthless mining enterprise?" –**Bonnie Gordon**, *Los Alamos Daily Post*

STELLAR ASSASSIN

"T. Jackson King's *Stellar Assassin* is an ambitious science fiction epic that sings! Filled with totally alien lifeforms, one lonely human, an archaeologist named Al Lancaster must find his way through trade guilds, political maneuvering and indentured servitude, while trying to reconcile his new career as an assassin with his deeply-held belief in the teachings of Buddha. . . This is a huge, colorful, complicated world with complex characters, outstanding dialogue, believable motivations, wonderful high-tech battle sequences and, on occasion, a real heart-stringer . . . This is an almost perfectly edited novel as well, which is a bonus. This is a wonderful novel, written by a wonderful author . . .Bravo! Five Stars!" –**Linell Jeppsen,** *Amazon*

LITTLE BROTHER'S WORLD

"If you're sensing a whiff of Andre Norton or Robert A. Heinlein, you're not mistaken . . . The influence is certainly there, but *Little Brother's World* is no mere imitation of *Star Man's Son* or *Citizen of the Galaxy*. Rather, it takes the sensibility of those sorts of books and makes of it something fresh and new. T. Jackson King is doing his part to further the great conversation of science fiction; it'll be interesting to see where he goes next."–**Don Sakers,** *Analog*

"When I'm turning a friend on to a good writer I've just discovered, I'll often say something like, "Give him ten pages and you'll never be able to put him down." Once in a long while, I'll say, "Give him five pages." It took T. Jackson King exactly *one sentence* to set his hook so deep in me that I finished *LITTLE BROTHER'S WORLD* in a single sitting, and I'll be thinking about that vivid world for a long time to come. The last writer I can recall with the courage to make a protagonist out of someone as profoundly Different as Little Brother was James Tiptree Jr., with her remarkable debut novel *UP THE WALLS OF THE WORLD*. I think Mr. King has met that challenge even more successfully. His own writing DNA borrows genes from writers as diverse as Tiptree, Heinlein, Norton, Zelazny, Sturgeon, Pohl, and Doctorow, and splices them together very effectively." – **Spider Robinson, Hugo, Nebula and Campbell Award winner**

"*Little Brother's World* is a sci-fi novel where Genetic Engineering exists. . . It contains enough details and enough thrills to make the book buyers/readers grab it and settle in for an afternoon read. The book is well-written and had a well-defined plot . . . I never found a boring part in the story. It was fast-paced and kept me entertained all throughout. The characters are fascinating and likeable too. This book made me realize about a possible outcome, when finally science and technology wins over traditional ones. . . All in all, *Little Brother's World* is another sci-fi novel from T. Jackson King that is both exciting, thrilling and fun. Full of suspense, adventure, romance, secrets, conspiracies, this book would take you in a roller-coaster ride." –**Abby Flores,** *Bookshelf Confessions*

THE MEMORY SINGER

"A coming of age story reminiscent of Robert A. Heinlein or Alexei

Panshin. Jax [the main character] is a fun character, and her world is compelling. The social patterns of Ship life are fascinating, and the Alish'Tak [the main alien species] are sufficiently alien to make for a fairly complex book. Very enjoyable."—**Don Sakers**, *Analog Science Fiction*

"Author T. Jackson King brings his polished writing style, his knowledge of science fiction 'hardware,' and his believable aliens to his latest novel *The Memory Singer*. But all this is merely backdrop to the adventures of Jax Cochrane, a smart, rebellious teen who wants more from life than the confines of a generational starship. There are worlds of humans and aliens out there. When headstrong Jax decides that it's time to discover and explore them, nothing can hold back this defiant teen. You'll want to accompany this young woman . . in this fine coming-of-age story."—**Jean Kilczer**, *Amazon*

RETREAD SHOP

"Engaging alien characters, a likable protagonist, and a vividly realized world make King's first sf novel a good purchase for sf collections."–*Library Journal*

"A very pleasant tour through the author's inventive mind, and an above average story as well."–*Science Fiction Chronicle*

"Fun, with lots of outrageously weird aliens."—*Locus*

"The writing is sharp, the plotting tight, and the twists ingenious. It would be worth reading, if only for the beautiful delineations of alien races working with and against one another against the background of an interstellar marketplace. The story carries you . . . with a verve and vigor that bodes well for future stories by this author. Recommended."–*Science Fiction Review*

"For weird aliens, and I do mean weird, choose *Retread Shop*. The story takes place on a galactic trading base, where hundreds of species try to gain the upper hand for themselves and for their group. Sixteen year-old billy is the sole human on the Retread Shop, stranded when his parents and their shipmates perished. What really makes the ride fun are the aliens Billy teams up with, including two who are plants. It's herbivores vs. carnivores, herd species vs. loners, mammals vs. insects and so on. The wild variety of physical types is only matched by the extensive array of cultures, which makes for a very entertaining read." –**Bonnie Gordon,** *Los Alamos Daily Post*

"Similar in feel to Roger Zelazny's Alien Speedway series is *Retread Shop* by T. Jackson King. It's an orphan-human-in-alien-society-makes-good story. Well-written and entertaining, it could be read either as a Young Adult or as straight SF with equal enjoyment." – **Chuq Von Rospach,** *OtherRealms 22*

"If you liked Stephen Goldin's Jade Darcy books duo, and Julie Czerneda's Clan trilogy, then you will probably like *Retread Shop* since it too has multiple aliens, an eatery, and an infinity of odd events that range from riots, to conspiracy, to exploring new worlds and to alien eating habits . . . It's a fun reader's ride and thoroughly entertaining. And, sigh, I wish that the author would write more books set in this background." –**Lyn McConchie, co-author of the** *Beastmaster* **series**

HUMANS VS. ALIENS

"Another great book from this author. This series has great characters and story is wall to wall excitement. Look forward to next book."— **William R. Thomas,** *Amazon*

"Humans are once again aggressive and blood thirsty to defend the Earth. Pace is quick and action is plentiful. Some unexpected plot twists, but you always know the home team is the best."—**C. Cook,** *Amazon*

ANCESTOR'S WORLD
"T. Jackson King is a professional archaeologist and he uses that to great advantage in *Ancestor's World*. I was just as fascinated by the details of the archaeology procedures as I was by the unfolding of the plot . . . What follows is a tightly plotted, suspenseful novel."– *Absolute Magnitude*

"The latest in the StarBridge series from King, a former Rogue Valley resident now living and writing in Arizona, follows the action on planet Na-Dina, where the tombs of 46 dynasties have lain undisturbed for 6,000 years until a human archaeologist and a galactic gumshoe show up. Set your phasers for fun."–*Medford Mail Tribune*

ALIEN ASSASSIN

"The Assassin series is required reading in adventure, excitement and daring. The galactic vistas, the advanced alien technologies and the action make all the Assassin books a guarantee of a good read. Please keep them coming!"—**C. B. Symons,** *Amazon*

"KING STRIKES AGAIN! Yes, T. Jackson King gives us yet again a great space adventure. I loved the drama and adventure in this book. There is treachery in this one too which heightens the suspense. Being the only human isn't easy, but Al pulls it off. Loved the Dino babies and how they are being developed into an important part of the family of assassins. All of the fun takes place right here and we are not left hanging off the cliff. Write on T.J."—**K. McClell,** *Amazon*

THE GAEAN ENCHANTMENT

"For magic, a quest and a new battle around every corner, go with *The Gaean Enchantment*. In this novel, Earth has entered a new phase as it cycles through the universe. In this phase, some kinds of "magic" work, but tech is rapidly ceasing to function. In the world of this book, incantation and sympathetic magic function through connection to spirit figures who might be described as gods." – **Bonnie Gordon,** *Los Alamos Daily Post*

"In *The Gaean Enchantment* the main character, Thomas, back from Vietnam and with all the PTSD that many soldiers have—nightmares, blackouts—finds his truth through the finding of his totem animal, the buffalo Black Mane. He teaches Thomas that violence and killing must always be done as a last resort, and that the energies of his soul are more powerful than any arsenal . . . Don't miss this amazing novel of magic and soul transformation, deep love, and Artemis, goddess of the hunt and protector of women."–**Catherine Herbison-Wiget,** *Amazon*

JUDGMENT DAY AND OTHER DREAMS

"King is a prolific writer with an old-time approach–he tells straight-ahead stories and asks the big questions. No topic is off limits and he writes with an explorer's zest for uncovering the unknown. He takes readers right into the world of each story, so each rustle of a tree, each whisper of the wind, blows softly against your inner ear."–**Scott Turick**, *Daytona Beach News-Journal*

"Congratulations on the long overdue story collection, Tom! What I find most terrific is your range of topics and styles. You have always been an explorer."–**David Brin, Nebula and Hugo winner**

"I'm thoroughly loving [the stories]; the prose is the kind that makes me stop and savor it – roll phrases over my tongue – delicious. I loved the way you conjure up a whole world or civilization so economically."–**Sheila Finch, SF author**

"*Judgment Day and Other Dreams* . . . would make a valued addition to any science fiction or fantasy library. There is a satisfying and engrossing attention to detail within the varied stories . . . The common thread among all works is the intimate human element at the heart of each piece. King's prose displays a mastery over these myriad subjects without alienating the uninitiated, thus providing the reader with a smooth, coherent, and altogether enjoyable experience . . . King is able to initiate the reader naturally through plot and precise prose, as if being eased into a warm bath . . . There is a dedicated unity amongst some of the entries in this anthology that begs to be explored in longer formats. And the works which stand apart are just as notable and exemplify King's grasp of human emotions and interactions. This collection displays the qualities of fine writing backed by a knowledgeable hand and a vivid imagination . . . If *Judgment Day and Other Dreams* is anything to go by, T. Jackson King should be a household name." –**John Sulyok**, *Tangent Online*

38728813R00146

Made in the USA
San Bernardino, CA
11 September 2016